YEAR'S BEST FANTASY
2

Edited by David G. Hartwell

**Edited by David G. Hartwell
and Kathryn Cramer**

YEAR'S BEST FANTASY

⌁2⌁

EDITED BY DAVID G. HARTWELL
AND KATHRYN CRAMER

An Imprint of HarperCollins*Publishers*

This is a work of fiction. Names, characters, places, and incidents are products of the author's imagination or are used fictitiously and are not to be construed as real. Any resemblance to actual events, locales, organizations, or persons, living or dead, is entirely coincidental.

EOS
An Imprint of HarperCollins*Publishers*
10 East 53rd Street
New York, New York 10022-5299

Copyright © 2002 by David G. Hartwell and Kathryn Cramer
ISBN: 0-7394-2844-6

To Pauline Cramer

Contents

Introduction

Welcome to the second volume of the *Year's Best Fantasy*, representing the best of 2001. Like last year's volume, this book should give you a convenient reference to what's going on now, to who is writing some of the best fantasy fiction published, and should provide a collection of excellent stories for your reading pleasure. Our general principle for selection: This book is full fantasy—every story in it is clearly that and not something else. We (Kathryn Cramer and David G. Hartwell) edit the *Year's Best Science Fiction* in paperback from Eos as a companion volume to this one—look for it if you enjoy short science fiction, too.

In this book, and this anthology series, we will use the broadest definition of fantasy (to include wonder stories, adventure fantasy, supernatural fantasy, satirical and humorous fantasy). We believe that the best-written fantasy can stand up in the long run by any useful literary standard in comparison to fiction published out of category or genre; and furthermore, that out of respect for the genre at its best we ought to stand by genre fantasy and promote it in this book. Also, we believe that writers publishing their work specifically as fantasy are up to this task, so we set out to find these stories, and we looked for them in the genre anthologies, magazines, and small press pamphlets. Some fine fantasy writers will still be missing. A fair number of the best fantasy writers these days write only novels, or if they do write short fiction, do so only every few years, and sometimes it is not their best work.

In 2001, books by the big names were selling better than ever, sliding through the publishing and distribution process perhaps even easier than before. Hardcover editions contribute substantially to the support of every fantasy and science fiction publishing line. The trade paperback is now well-established as the safety net of a number of publishers and writers.

The year ended with the Christmas of Harry Potter and Tolkien movies (and of new Robert Jordan and Terry Goodkind blockbuster fantasy novels), which we hope has given a push to fantasy sales in general during difficult times.

The small presses were again a vigorous presence this year. We have a strong short fiction field today because the small presses and semiprofessional magazines and anthologies are printing and circulating a majority of the high quality short stories published in fantasy, science fiction, and horror. The U.S. is the only English language country that still has any professional, large-circulation magazines, though Canada, Australia, and the UK have several excellent magazines. The semiprozines of our field mirror the "little magazines" of the mainstream in function, holding to professional editorial standards and publishing the next generation of writers, along with some of the present masters. What a change that is in the U.S., though it has been gradually emerging for more than a decade.

The best original anthologies of the year in our opinion were *Starlight 3,* edited by Patrick Nielsen Hayden (Tor) and *Red Shift* edited by Al Sarrantonio (Roc). Of those, the particular excellences of *Starlight* were mostly in the realm of fantasy, and the especial pleasures of *Red Shift* were mostly in SF. Also of interest is *Fantasmas: Supernatural Stories by Mexican American Writers,* edited by Rob Johnson, from Bilingual Press of Tempe Arizona, a volume of reinterpretations of folktales in contemporary settings.

We write in January 2002, but the anxious outlines of the publishing future are becoming clear for the coming year. Fantasy and science fiction publishing as we have always known it is concentrated in nine mass market and hardcover publishing lines (Ace, Bantam, Baen, DAW, Del Rey, Eos, Roc, Tor, and Warner), and those lines are hard-pressed to continue distributing the number of new titles they have been able to in the past. Mass market distributors in general are pressing all publishers to reduce the number of titles and just publish "big books."

The last sf and fantasy magazines that are widely distributed (*Analog, Asimov's, F&SF, Realms of Fantasy*) are being charged more by the same distributors for distribution because they are not as high-circulation as *The New Yorker* or *Playboy* (who are also under pressure). So the in-field magazines are hard-pressed but are only a special case of the widespread difficulties facing all magazines.

In 2001, electronic text failed to live up to the advance publicity (both Random House and Warner closed their etext operations by the end of 2001). Print-on-demand became a very small success. *The Wall Street Journal,* in a recent article surveying 2500 titles, quoted the figure of 88 copies as the average sale of a print-on-demand title. Of the several high-paying online short fiction markets announced last year that helped to cushion the loss of print media markets for short fiction, one survives.

It was another good year to be reading the magazines, both pro and semiprofessional. It was a strong year for novellas, and there were more than a hundred shorter stories in consideration, from which we made our final selection. So we repeat, for readers new to this series, the usual disclaimer: This selection of stories represents the best that was published during the year 2001.

We try to represent the varieties of tones and voices and attitudes that keep the genre vigorous and responsive to the changing realities out of which it emerges. This is a book about what's going on now in fantasy. The stories that follow show, and the story notes point out, the strengths of the evolving genre in the year 2001.

David G. Hartwell & Kathryn Cramer
Pleasantville, NY

YEAR'S BEST FANTASY
2

The Finder

Ursula K. Le Guin

Ursula K. Le Guin [www.ursulakleguin.com] is one of the finest living SF and fantasy writers. She also writes poetry, mainstream fiction, children's books, literary essays, and has recently published Steering the Craft, *a good book on how to write narrative fiction and nonfiction, and co-edited* The Norton Book of Science Fiction, *an influential anthology. She has published seventeen novels and eight short story collections to date. She is one of the leading feminists in SF, and in recent years a supporter of the James Tiptree, Jr. Awards, named in honor of Le Guin's peer and friend Alice Bradley Sheldon's SF pseudonym. Le Guin's work is widely read outside the SF field and she is taken seriously as a contemporary writer. In recent years she has published a number of distinguished short stories, and in 2000 not only did she continue to do that, but published her first SF novel in more than ten years,* The Telling. *Recent publications include two books of Earthsea—*Tales from Earthsea *and a novel,* The Other Wind *(both 2001)—and a collection of science fiction,* The Birthday of the World *(2002).*

"The Finder," which appeared in Le Guin's collection, Tales from Earthsea, *is, as Michael Swanwick put it in a review of the book, "a novella that could easily have been stretched out to novel length had the author not had bigger fish to fry." It goes back to a time in Earthsea before the beginning of her earlier novels.*

~ I. In the Dark Time

This is the first page of the *Book of the Dark*, written some six hundred years ago in Berila, on Enlad:

After Elfarran and Morred perished and the Isle of Soléa sank beneath the sea, the Council of the Wise governed for the child Serriadh until he took the throne. His reign was bright but brief. The kings who followed him in Enlad were seven, and their realm increased in peace and wealth. Then the dragons came to raid among the western lands, and wizards went out in vain against them. King Akambar moved the court from Berila in Enlad to the City of Havnor, whence he sent out his fleet against invaders from the Kargad Lands and drove them back into the East. But still they sent raiding ships even as far as the Inmost Sea. Of the fourteen Kings of Havnor the last was Maharion, who made peace both with the dragons and the Kargs, but at great cost. And after the Ring of the Runes was broken, and Erreth-Akbe died with the great dragon, and Maharion the Brave was killed by treachery, it seemed that no good thing happened in the Archipelago.

Many claimed Maharion's throne, but none could keep it, and the quarrels of the claimants divided all loyalties. No commonwealth was left and no justice, only the will of the wealthy. Men of noble houses, merchants, and pirates, any who could hire soldiers and wizards called himself a lord, claiming lands and cities as his property. The warlords made those they con-

quered slaves, and those they hired were in truth slaves, having
only their masters to safeguard them from rival warlords seizing
the lands, and sea-pirates raiding the ports, and bands and
hordes of lawless, miserable men dispossessed of their living,
driven by hunger to raid and rob.

The *Book of the Dark*, written late in the time it tells of, is a compi-
lation of self-contradictory histories, partial biographies, and garbled
legends. But it's the best of the records that survived the dark years.
Wanting praise, not history, the warlords burned the books in which the
poor and powerless might learn what power is.

But when the lore-books of a wizard came into a warlord's hands he
was likely to treat them with caution, locking them away to keep them
harmless or giving them to a wizard in his hire to do with as he wished.
In the margins of the spells and word lists and in the endpapers of these
books of lore a wizard or his prentice might record a plague, a famine, a
raid, a change of masters, along with the spells worked in such events
and their success or unsuccess. Such random records reveal a clear
moment here and there, though all between those moments is darkness.
They are like glimpses of a lighted ship far out at sea, in darkness, in the
rain.

And there are songs, old lays and ballads from small islands and
from the quiet uplands of Havnor, that tell the story of those years.

Havnor Great Port is the city at the heart of the world, white-
towered above its bay; on the tallest tower the sword of Erreth-Akbe
catches the first and last of daylight. Through that city passes all the
trade and commerce and learning and craft of Earthsea, a wealth not
hoarded. There the King sits, having returned after the healing of the
Ring, in sign of healing. And in that city, in these latter days, men and
women of the islands speak with dragons, in sign of change.

But Havnor is also the Great Isle, a broad, rich land; and in the villages inland from the port, the farmlands of the slopes of Mount Onn,
nothing ever changes much. There a song worth singing is likely to be
sung again. There old men at the tavern talk of Morred as if they had
known him when they too were young and heroes. There girls walking
out to fetch the cows home tell stories of the women of the Hand, who
are forgotten everywhere else in the world, even on Roke, but remembered among those silent, sunlit roads and fields and in the kitchens by
the hearths where housewives work and talk.

In the time of the kings, mages gathered in the court of Enlad and
later in the court of Havnor to counsel the king and take counsel
together, using their arts to pursue goals they agreed were good. But in

the dark years, wizards sold their skills to the highest bidder, pitting their powers one against the other in duels and combats of sorcery, careless of the evils they did, or worse than careless. Plagues and famines, the failure of springs of water, summers with no rain and years with no summer, the birth of sickly and monstrous young to sheep and cattle, the birth of sickly and monstrous children to the people of the isles—all these things were charged to the practices of wizards and witches, and all too often rightly so.

So it became dangerous to practice sorcery, except under the protection of a strong warlord; and even then, if a wizard met up with one whose powers were greater than his own, he might be destroyed. And if a wizard let down his guard among the common folk, they too might destroy him if they could, seeing him as the source of the worst evils they suffered, a malign being. In those years, in the minds of most people, all magic was black.

It was then that village sorcery, and above all women's witchery, came into the ill repute that has clung to it since. Witches paid dearly for practicing the arts they thought of as their own. The care of pregnant beasts and women, birthing, teaching the songs and rites, the fertility and order of field and garden, the building and care of the house and its furniture, the mining of ores and metals—these great things had always been in the charge of women. A rich lore of spells and charms to ensure the good outcome of such undertakings was shared among the witches. But when things went wrong at the birth, or in the field, that would be the witches' fault. And things went wrong more often than right, with the wizards warring, using poisons and curses recklessly to gain immediate advantage without thought for what followed after. They brought drought and storm, blights and fires and sicknesses across the land, and the village witch was punished for them. She didn't know why her charm of healing caused the wound to gangrene, why the child she brought into the world was imbecile, why her blessing seemed to burn the seed in the furrows and blight the apple on the tree. But for these ills, somebody had to be to blame: and the witch or sorcerer was there, right there in the village or the town, not off in the warlord's castle or fort, not protected by armed men and spells of defense. Sorcerers and witches were drowned in the poisoned wells, burned in the withered fields, buried alive to make the dead earth rich again.

So the practice of their lore and the teaching of it had become perilous. Those who undertook it were often those already outcast, crippled, deranged, without family, old—women and men who had little to lose. The wise man and wise woman, trusted and held in reverence, gave way to the stock figures of the shuffling, impotent village sorcerer with his trickeries, the hag-witch with her potions used in aid of lust, jealousy, and malice. And a child's gift for magic became a thing to dread and hide.

This is a tale of those times. Some of it is taken from the *Book of the Dark*, and some comes from Havnor, from the upland farms of Onn and the woodlands of Faliern. A story may be pieced together from such scraps and fragments, and though it will be an airy quilt, half made of hearsay and half of guesswork, yet it may be true enough. It's a tale of the Founding of Roke, and if the Masters of Roke say it didn't happen so, let them tell us how it happened otherwise. For a cloud hangs over the time when Roke first became the Isle of the Wise, and it may be that the wise men put it there.

⌒ *II. Otter*

There was an otter in our brook
That every mortal semblance took,
Could any spell of magic make,
And speak the tongues of man and drake.
  So runs the water away, away,
  So runs the water away.

Otter was the son of a boatwright who worked in the shipyards of Havnor Great Port. His mother gave him his country name; she was a farm woman from Endlane village, around northwest of Mount Onn. She had come to the city seeking work, as many came. Decent folk in a decent trade in troubled times, the boatwright and his family were anxious not to come to notice lest they come to grief. And so, when it became clear that the boy had a gift of magery, his father tried to beat it out of him.

"You might as well beat a cloud for raining," said Otter's mother.

"Take care you don't beat evil into him," said his aunt.

"Take care he doesn't turn your belt on you with a spell!" said his uncle.

But the boy played no tricks against his father. He took his beatings in silence and learned to hide his gift.

It didn't seem to him to amount to much. It was such an easy matter to him to make a silvery light shine in a dark room, or find a lost pin by thinking about it, or true up a warped joint by running his hands over the wood and talking to it, that he couldn't see why they made a fuss over such things. But his father raged at him for his "shortcuts," even struck him once on the mouth when he was talking to the work, and insisted that he do his carpentry with tools, in silence.

His mother tried to explain. "It's as if you'd found some great jewel," she said, "and what's one of us to do with a diamond but hide it? Anybody rich enough to buy it from you is strong enough to kill you for it. Keep it hid. And keep away from great people and their crafty men!"

"Crafty men" is what they called wizards in those days.

One of the gifts of power is to know power. Wizard knows wizard, unless the concealment is very skillful. And the boy had no skills at all except in boat-building, of which he was a promising scholar by the age of twelve. About that time the midwife who had helped his mother at his birth came by and said to his parents, "Let Otter come to me in the evenings after work. He should learn the songs and be prepared for his naming day."

That was all right, for she had done the same for Otter's elder sister, and so his parents sent him to her in the evenings. But she taught Otter more than the song of the Creation. She knew his gift. She and some men and women like her, people of no fame and some of questionable reputation, had all in some degree that gift; and they shared, in secret, what lore and craft they had. "A gift untaught is a ship unguided," they said to Otter, and they taught him all they knew. It wasn't much, but there were some beginnings of the great arts in it; and though he felt uneasy at deceiving his parents, he couldn't resist this knowledge, and the kindness and praise of his poor teachers. "It will do you no harm if you never use it for harm," they told him, and that was easy for him to promise them.

At the stream Serrenen, where it runs within the north wall of the city, the midwife gave Otter his true name, by which he is remembered in islands far from Havnor.

Among these people was an old man whom they called, among themselves, the Changer. He showed Otter a few spells of illusion; and when the boy was fifteen or so, the old man took him out into the fields by Serrenen to show him the one spell of true change he knew. "First let's see you turn that bush into the seeming of a tree," he said, and promptly Otter did so. Illusion came so easy to the boy that the old man took alarm. Otter had to beg and wheedle him for any further teaching and finally to promise him, swearing on his own true and secret name, that if he learned the Changer's great spell he would never use it but to save a life, his own or another's.

Then the old man taught it to him. But it wasn't much use, Otter thought, since he had to hide it.

What he learned working with his father and uncle in the shipyard he could use, at least; and he was becoming a good craftsman, even his father would admit that.

Losen, a sea-pirate who called himself King of the Inmost Sea, was then the chief warlord in the city and all the east and south of Havnor. Exacting tribute from that rich domain, he spent it to increase his soldiery and the fleets he sent out to take slaves and plunder from other lands. As Otter's uncle said, he kept the shipwrights busy. They were grateful to have work in a time when men seeking work found only beggary, and rats ran in the courts of Maharion. They did an honest job, Otter's father said, and what the work was used for was none of their concern.

But the other learning he had been given had made Otter touchy in these matters, delicate of conscience. The big galley they were building now would be rowed to war by Losen's slaves and would bring back slaves as cargo. It galled him to think of the good ship in that vicious usage. "Why can't we build fishing boats, the way we used to?" he asked, and his father said, "Because the fishermen can't pay us."

"Can't pay us as well as Losen does. But we could live," Otter argued.

"You think I can turn the King's order down? You want to see me sent to row with the slaves in the galley we're building? Use your head, boy!"

So Otter worked along with them with a clear head and an angry heart. They were in a trap. What's the use of a gift of power, he thought, if not to get out of a trap?

His conscience as a craftsman would not let him fault the carpentry of the ship in any way; but his conscience as a wizard told him he could put a hex on her, a curse woven right into her beams and hull. Surely that was using the secret art to a good end? For harm, yes, but only to harm the harmful. He did not talk to his teachers about it. If he was doing wrong, it was none of their fault and they would know nothing about it. He thought about it for a long time, working out how to do it, making the spell very carefully. It was the reversal of a finding charm: a losing charm, he called it to himself. The ship would float, and handle well, and steer, but she would never steer quite true.

It was the best he could do in protest against the misuse of good work and a good ship. He was pleased with himself. When the ship was launched (and all seemed well with her, for her fault would not show up until she was out on the open sea) he could not keep from his teachers what he had done, the little circle of old men and midwives, the young hunchback who could speak with the dead, the blind girl who knew the names of things. He told them his trick, and the blind girl laughed, but the old people said, "Look out. Take care. Keep hidden."

In Losen's service was a man who called himself Hound, because, as he said, he had a nose for witchery. His employment was to sniff Losen's food and drink and garments and women, anything that might be used by enemy wizards against him; and also to inspect his warships. A ship is a fragile thing in a dangerous element, vulnerable to spells and hexes. As soon as Hound came aboard the new galley he scented something. "Well, well," he said, "who's this?" He walked to the helm and put his hand on it. "This is clever," he said. "But who is it? A newcomer, I think." He sniffed appreciatively. "Very clever," he said.

They came to the house in Boatwright Street after dark. They kicked the door in, and Hound, standing among the armed and armored men, said, "Him. Let the others be." And to Otter he said, "Don't move," in a low, amicable voice. He sensed great power in the young man, enough that he was a little afraid of him. But Otter's distress was too great and his training too slight for him to think of using magic to free himself or stop the men's brutality. He flung himself at them and fought them like an animal till they knocked him on the head. They broke Otter's father's jaw and beat his aunt and mother senseless to teach them not to bring up crafty men. Then they carried Otter away.

Not a door opened in the narrow street. Nobody looked out to see what the noise was. Not till long after the men were gone did some neighbors creep out to comfort Otter's people as best they could. "Oh, it's a curse, a curse, this wizardry!" they said.

Hound told his master that they had the hexer in a safe place, and Losen said, "Who was he working for?"

"He worked in your shipyard, your highness." Losen liked to be called by kingly titles.

"Who hired him to hex the ship, fool?"

"It seems it was his own idea, your majesty."

"Why? What was he going to get out of it?"

Hound shrugged. He didn't choose to tell Losen that people hated him disinterestedly.

"He's crafty, you say. Can you use him?"

"I can try, your highness."

"Tame him or bury him," said Losen, and turned to more important matters.

Otter's humble teachers had taught him pride. They had trained into him a deep contempt for wizards who worked for such men as Losen, letting fear or greed pervert magic to evil ends. Nothing, to his mind, could be more despicable than such a betrayal of their art. So it troubled him that he couldn't despise Hound.

He had been stowed in a storeroom of one of the old palaces that Losen had appropriated. It had no window, its door was cross-grained oak barred with iron, and spells had been laid on that door that would have kept a far more experienced wizard captive. There were men of great skill and power in Losen's pay.

Hound did not consider himself to be one of them. "All I have is a nose," he said. He came daily to see that Otter was recovering from his concussion and dislocated shoulder, and to talk with him. He was, as far as Otter could see, well-meaning and honest. "If you won't work for us they'll kill you," he said. "Losen can't have fellows like you on the loose. You'd better hire on while he'll take you."

"I can't."

Otter stated it as an unfortunate fact, not as a moral assertion. Hound looked at him with appreciation. Living with the pirate king, he was sick of boasts and threats, of boasters and threateners.

"What are you strongest in?"

Otter was reluctant to answer. He had to like Hound, but didn't have to trust him. "Shape-changing," he mumbled at last.

"Shape-taking?"

"No. Just tricks. Turn a leaf to a gold piece. Seemingly."

In those days they had no fixed names for the various kinds and arts of magic, nor were the connections among those arts clear. There was— as the wise men of Roke would say later—no science in what they knew. But Hound knew pretty surely that his prisoner was concealing his talents.

"Can't change your own form, even seemingly?"

Otter shrugged.

It was hard for him to lie. He thought he was awkward at it because he had no practice. Hound knew better. He knew that magic itself resists untruth. Conjuring, sleight of hand, and false commerce with the dead are counterfeits of magic, glass to the diamond, brass to the gold. They are fraud, and lies flourish in that soil. But the art of magic, though it may be used for false ends, deals with what is real, and the words it works with are the true words. So true wizards find it hard to lie about their art. In their heart they know that their lie, spoken, may change the world.

Hound was sorry for him. "You know, if it was Gelluk questioning you, he'd have everything you know out of you just with a word or two, and your wits with it. I've seen what old Whiteface leaves behind when he asks questions. Listen, can you work with the wind at all?"

Otter hesitated and said, "Yes."

"D'you have a bag?"

Weatherworkers used to carry a leather sack in which they said they kept the winds, untying it to let a fair wind loose or to capture a contrary one. Maybe it was only for show, but every weatherworker had a bag, a great long sack or a little pouch.

"At home," Otter said. It wasn't a lie. He did have a pouch at home. He kept his fine-work tools and his bubble level in it. And he wasn't altogether lying about the wind. Several times he had managed to bring a bit of magewind into the sail of a boat, though he had no idea how to combat or control a storm, as a ship's weatherworker must do. But he thought he'd rather drown in a gale than be murdered in this hole.

"But you wouldn't be willing to use that skill in the King's service?"

"There is no king in Earthsea," the young man said, stern and righteous.

"In my master's service, then," Hound amended, patient.

"No," Otter said, and hesitated. He felt he owed this man an explanation. "See, it's not so much won't as can't. I thought of making plugs in the planking of that galley, near the keel—you know what I mean by plugs? They'd work out as the timbers work when she gets in a heavy sea." Hound nodded. "But I couldn't do it. I'm a shipbuilder. I can't build a ship to sink. With the men aboard her. My hands wouldn't do it. So I did what I could. I made her go her own way. Not his way."

Hound smiled. "They haven't undone what you did yet, either," he said. "Old Whiteface was crawling all over her yesterday, growling and muttering. Ordered the helm replaced." He meant Losen's chief mage, a pale man from the North named Gelluk, who was much feared in Havnor.

"That won't do it."

"Could you undo the spell you put on her?"

A flicker of complacency showed in Otter's tired, battered young face. "No," he said. "I don't think anybody can."

"Too bad. You might have used that to bargain with."

Otter said nothing.

"A nose, now, is a useful thing, a salable thing," Hound went on. "Not that I'm looking for competition. But a finder can always find work, as they say . . . You ever been in a mine?"

The guesswork of a wizard is close to knowledge, though he may not know what it is he knows. The first sign of Otter's gift, when he was two or three years old, was his ability to go straight to anything lost, a dropped nail, a mislaid tool, as soon as he understood the word for it. And as a boy one of his dearest pleasures had been to go alone out into the countryside and wander along the lanes or over the hills, feeling through the soles of his bare feet and throughout his body the veins of water underground, the lodes and knots of ore, the lay and interfolding of the kinds of rock and earth. It was as if he walked in a great building, seeing its passages and rooms, the descents to airy caverns, the glimmer of branched silver in the walls; and as he went on, it was as if his body became the body of earth, and he knew its arteries and organs and muscles as his own. This power had been a delight to him as a boy. He had never sought any use for it. It had been his secret.

He did not answer Hound's question.

"What's below us?" Hound pointed to the floor, paved with rough slate flags.

Otter was silent a while. Then he said in a low voice, "Clay, and gravel, and under that the rock that bears garnets. All under this part of the city is that rock. I don't know the names."

"You can learn 'em."

"I know how to build boats, how to sail boats."

"You'll do better away from the ships, all the fighting and raiding. The King's working the old mines at Samory, round the mountain. There you'd be out of his way. Work for him you must, if you want to stay alive. I'll see that you're sent there. If you'll go."

After a little silence Otter said, "Thanks." And he looked up at Hound, one brief, questioning, judging glance.

Hound had taken him, had stood and seen his people beaten senseless, had not stopped the beating. Yet he spoke as a friend. Why? said Otter's look. Hound answered it.

"Crafty men need to stick together," he said. "Men who have no art at all, nothing but wealth—they pit us one against the other, for their gain not ours. We sell 'em our power. Why do we? If we went our own way together, we'd do better, maybe."

Hound meant well in sending the young man to Samory, but he did not understand the quality of Otter's will. Nor did Otter himself. He was too used to obeying others to see that in fact he had always followed his own bent, and too young to believe that anything he did could kill him.

He planned, as soon as they took him out of his cell, to use the old Changer's spell of self-transformation and so escape. Surely his life was in danger, and it would be all right to use the spell? Only he couldn't decide what to turn himself into—a bird, or a wisp of smoke, what would be safest? But while he was thinking about it, Losen's men, used to wizard's tricks, drugged his food and he ceased to think of anything at all. They dumped him into a mule-cart like a sack of oats. When he showed signs of reviving during the journey, one of them bashed him on the head, remarking that he wanted to make sure he got his rest.

When he came to himself, sick and weak from the poison and with an aching skull, he was in a room with brick walls and bricked-up windows. The door had no bars and no visible lock. But when he tried to get to his feet he felt bonds of sorcery holding his body and mind, resilient, clinging, tightening as he moved. He could stand, but could not take a step toward the door. He could not even reach his hand out. It was a horrible sensation, as if his muscles were not his own. He sat down again and tried to hold still. The spellbonds around his chest kept him from breathing deeply, and his mind felt stifled too, as if his thoughts were crowded into a space too small for them.

After a long time the door opened and several men came in. He could do nothing against them as they gagged him and bound his arms behind him. "Now you won't weave charms nor speak spells, young 'un," said a broad, strong man with a furrowed face, "but you can nod your head well enough, right? They sent you here as a dowser. If you're a good dowser you'll feed well and sleep easy. Cinnabar, that's what you're to nod for. The King's wizard says it's still here somewhere about these old mines. And he wants it. So it's best for us that we find it. Now I'll walk you out. It's like I'm the water finder and you're my wand, see? You lead on. And if you want to go this way or that way you dip your head, so. And when you know there's ore underfoot, you stamp on the place, so. Now that's the bargain, right? And if you play fair I will."

He waited for Otter to nod, but Otter stood motionless. "Sulk away," the man said. "If you don't like this work, there's always the roaster."

The man, whom the others called Licky, led him out into a hot, bright morning that dazzled his eyes. Leaving his cell he had felt the spellbonds loosen and fall away, but there were other spells woven about other buildings of the place, especially around a tall stone tower, filling the air with sticky lines of resistance and repulsion. If he tried to push forward into them his face and belly stung with jabs of agony, so that he looked at his body in horror for the wound; but there was no wound. Gagged and bound, without his voice and hands to work magic, he could do nothing against these spells. Licky had tied one end of a braided leather cord around his neck and held the other end, following him. He let Otter walk into a couple of the spells, and after that Otter avoided them. Where they were was plain enough: the dusty pathways bent to miss them.

Leashed like a dog, he walked along, sullen and shivering with sickness and rage. He stared around him, seeing the stone tower, stacks of wood by its wide doorway, rusty wheels and machines by a pit, great heaps of gravel and clay. Turning his sore head made him dizzy.

"If you're a dowser, better dowse," said Licky, coming up alongside him and looking sidelong into his face. "And if you're not, you'd better dowse all the same. That way you'll stay above ground longer."

A man came out of the stone tower. He passed them, walking hurriedly with a queer shambling gait, staring straight ahead. His chin shone and his chest was wet with spittle leaking from his lips.

"That's the roaster tower," said Licky. "Where they cook the cinnabar to get the metal from it. Roasters die in a year or two. Where to, dowser?"

After a bit Otter nodded left, away from the gray stone tower. They walked on toward a long, treeless valley, past grass-grown dumps and tailings.

"All under here's worked out long since," Licky said. And Otter had begun to be aware of the strange country under his feet: empty shafts and rooms of dark air in the dark earth, a vertical labyrinth, the deepest pits filled with unmoving water. "Never was much silver, and the watermetal's long gone. Listen, young'un, do you even know what cinnabar is?"

Otter shook his head.

"I'll show you some. That's what Gelluk's after. The ore of watermetal. Watermetal eats all the other metals, even gold, see. So he calls it the King. If you find him his King, he'll treat you well. He's often here. Come on, I'll show you. Dog can't track till he's had the scent."

Licky took him down into the mines to show him the gangues, the kinds of earth the ore was likely to occur in. A few miners were working at the end of a long level.

Because they were smaller than men and could move more easily in narrow places, or because they were at home with the earth, or most likely because it was the custom, women had always worked the mines of Earthsea. These miners were free women, not slaves like the workers in the roaster tower. Gelluk had made him foreman over the miners, Licky said, but he did no work in the mine; the miners forbade it, earnestly believing it was the worst of bad luck for a man to pick up a shovel or shore a timber. "Suits me," Licky said.

A shock-haired, bright-eyed woman with a candle bound to her forehead set down her pick to show Otter a little cinnabar in a bucket, brownish red clots and crumbs. Shadows leaped across the earth face at which the miners worked. Old timbers creaked, dirt sifted down. Though the air ran cool through the darkness, the drifts and levels were so low and narrow the miners had to stoop and squeeze their way. In places the ceilings had collapsed. Ladders were shaky. The mine was a terrifying place; yet Otter felt a sense of shelter in it. He was half sorry to go back up into the burning day.

Licky did not take him into the roaster tower, but back to the barracks. From a locked room he brought out a small, soft, thick, leather bag that weighed heavy in his hands. He opened it to show Otter the little pool of dusty brilliance lying in it. When he closed the bag the metal moved in it, bulging, pressing, like an animal trying to get free.

"There's the King," Licky said, in a tone that might have been reverence or hatred.

Though not a sorcerer, Licky was a much more formidable man than Hound. Yet like Hound he was brutal not cruel. He demanded obedience, but nothing else. Otter had seen slaves and their masters all his life in the shipyards of Havnor, and knew he was fortunate. At least in daylight, when Licky was his master.

He could eat only in the cell, where they took his gag off. Bread and onions were what they gave him, with a slop of rancid oil on the bread. Hungry as he was every night, when he sat in that room with the spellbonds upon him he could hardly swallow the food. It tasted of metal, of ash. The nights were long and terrible, for the spells pressed on him, weighed on him, waked him over and over terrified, gasping for breath, and never able to think coherently. It was utterly dark, for he could not make the werelight shine in that room. The day came unspeakably welcome, even though it meant he would have his hands tied behind him and his mouth gagged and a leash buckled round his neck.

Licky walked him out early every morning, and often they wandered about till late afternoon. Licky was silent and patient. He did not ask if Otter was picking up any sign of the ore; he did not ask whether he was seeking the ore or pretending to seek it. Otter himself could not have answered the question. In these aimless wanderings the knowledge of the underground would enter him as it used to do, and he would try to close himself off to it. "I will not work in the service of evil!" he told himself. Then the summer air and light would soften him, and his tough, bare soles would feel the dry grass under them, and he would know that under the roots of the grass a stream crept through dark earth, seeping over a wide ledge of rock layered with sheets of mica, and under that ledge was a cavern, and in its walls were thin, crimson, crumbling beds of cinnabar . . . He made no sign. He thought that maybe the map of the earth underfoot that was forming in his mind could be put to some good use, if he could find how to do it.

But after ten days or so, Licky said, "Master Gelluk's coming here. If there's no ore for him, he'll likely find another dowser."

Otter walked on a mile, brooding; then circled back, leading Licky to a hillock not far from the far end of the old workings. There he nodded downward and stamped his foot.

Back in the cell room, when Licky had unleashed him and untied his gag, he said, "There's some ore there. You can get to it by running that old tunnel straight on, maybe twenty feet."

"A good bit of it?"

Otter shrugged.

"Just enough to keep going on, eh?"

Otter said nothing.

"Suits me," said Licky.

Two days later, when they had reopened the old shaft and begun digging toward the ore, the wizard arrived. Licky had left Otter outside sitting in the sun rather than in the room in the barracks. Otter was grateful to him. He could not be wholly comfortable with his hands bound and his mouth gagged, but wind and sunlight were mighty blessings. And he could breathe deep and doze without dreams of earth stopping his mouth and nostrils, the only dreams he ever had, nights in the cell.

He was half asleep, sitting on the ground in the shade by the barracks, the smell of the logs stacked by the roaster tower bringing him a memory of the work yards at home, the fragrance of new wood as the plane ran down the silky oak board. Some noise or movement roused him. He looked up and saw the wizard standing before him, looming above him.

Gelluk wore fantastic clothes, as many of his kind did in those days. A long robe of Lorbanery silk, scarlet, embroidered in gold and black with runes and symbols, and a wide-brimmed, peak-crowned hat made him seem taller than a man could be. Otter did not need to see his clothes to know him. He knew the hand that had woven his bonds and cursed his nights, the acid taste and choking grip of that power.

"I think I've found my little finder," said Gelluk. His voice was deep and soft, like the notes of a viol. "Sleeping in the sunshine, like one whose work has been well done. So you've sent them digging for the Red Mother, have you? Did you know the Red Mother before you came here?

Are you a courtier of the King? Here, now, there's no need for ropes and knots." Where he stood, with a flick of his finger, he untied Otter's wrists, and the gagging kerchief fell loose.

"I could teach you how to do that for yourself," the wizard said, smiling, watching Otter rub and flex his aching wrists and work his lips that had been smashed against his teeth for hours. "The Hound told me that you're a lad of promise and might go far with a proper guide. If you'd like to visit the Court of the King, I can take you there. But maybe you don't know the King I'm talking of?"

Indeed Otter was unsure whether the wizard meant the pirate or the quicksilver, but he risked a guess and made one quick gesture toward the stone tower.

The wizard's eyes narrowed and his smile broadened.

"Do you know his name?"

"The watermetal," Otter said.

"So the vulgar call it, or quicksilver, or the water of weight. But those who serve him call him the King, and the Allking, and the Body of the Moon." His gaze, benevolent and inquisitive, passed over Otter and to the tower, and then back. His face was large and long, whiter than any face Otter had seen, with bluish eyes. Gray and black hairs curled here and there on his chin and cheeks. His calm, open smile showed small teeth, several of them missing. "Those who have learned to see truly can see him as he is, the lord of all substances. The root of power lies in him. Do you know what we call him in the secrecy of his palace?"

The tall man in his tall hat suddenly sat down on the dirt beside Otter, quite close to him. His breath smelled earthy. His light eyes gazed directly into Otter's eyes. "Would you like to know? You can know anything you like. I need have no secrets from you. Nor you from me," and he laughed, not threateningly, but with pleasure. He gazed at Otter again, his large, white face smooth and thoughtful. "Powers you have, yes, all kinds of little traits and tricks. A clever lad. But not too clever; that's good. Not too clever to learn, like some . . . I'll teach you, if you like. Do you like learning? Do you like knowledge? Would you like to know the name we call the King when he's all alone in his brightness in his courts of stone? His name is Turres. Do you know that name? It's a word in the language of the Allking. His own name in his own language. In our base tongue we would say Semen." He smiled again and patted Otter's hand. "For he is the seed and fructifier. The seed and source of might and right. You'll see. You'll see. Come along! Come along! Let's go see the King flying among his subjects, gathering himself from them!" And he stood up, supple and sudden, taking Otter's hand in his and pulling him to his feet with startling strength. He was laughing with excitement.

Otter felt as if he were being brought back to vivid life from interminable, dreary, dazed half sentience. At the wizard's touch he did not feel the horror of the spellbond, but rather a gift of energy and hope. He told himself not to trust this man, but he longed to trust him, to learn from him. Gelluk was powerful, masterful, strange, yet he had set him free. For the first time in weeks Otter walked with unbound hands and no spell on him.

"This way, this way," Gelluk murmured. "No harm will come to you." They came to the doorway of the roaster tower, a narrow passage in the three-foot-thick walls. He took Otter's arm, for the young man hesitated.

Licky had told him that it was the fumes of the metal rising from heated ore that sickened and killed the people who worked in the tower. Otter had never entered it nor seen Licky enter it. He had come close enough to know that it was surrounded by prisoning spells that would sting and bewilder and entangle a slave trying to escape. Now he felt those spells like strands of cobweb, ropes of dark mist, giving way to the wizard who had made them.

"Breathe, breathe, breathe," Gelluk said, laughing, and Otter tried not to hold his breath as they entered the tower.

The roasting pit took up the center of a huge domed chamber. Hurrying, sticklike figures black against the blaze shoveled and reshoveled ore onto logs kept in a roaring blaze by great bellows, while others brought fresh logs and worked the bellows sleeves. From the apex of the dome a spiral of chambers rose up into the tower through smoke and fumes. In those chambers, Licky had told him, the vapor of the quicksilver was trapped and condensed, reheated and recondensed, till in the topmost vault the pure metal ran down into a stone trough or bowl—only a drop or two a day, he said, from the low-grade ores they were roasting now.

"Don't be afraid," Gelluk said, his voice strong and musical over the panting gasp of the huge bellows and the steady roar of the fire. "Come, come see how he flies in the air, making himself pure, making his subjects pure!" He drew Otter to the edge of the roasting pit. His eyes shone in the flare and dazzle of the flames. "Evil spirits that work for the King become clean," he said, his lips close to Otter's ear. "As they slaver, the dross and stains flow out of them. Illness and impurities fester and run free from their sores. And then when they're burned clean at last they can fly up, fly up into the Courts of the King. Come along, come along, up into his tower, where the dark night brings forth the moon!"

After him Otter climbed the winding stairs, broad at first but growing tight and narrow, passing vapor chambers with red-hot ovens whose vents led up to refining rooms where the soot from the burned ore was scraped down by naked slaves and shoveled into ovens to be burned again. They came to the topmost room. Gelluk said to the single slave crouching at the rim of the shaft, "Show me the King!"

The slave, short and thin, hairless, with running sores on his hands and arms, uncapped a stone cup by the rim of the condensing shaft. Gelluk peered in, eager as a child. "So tiny," he murmured. "So young. The tiny Prince, the baby Lord, Lord Turres. Seed of the world! Soul-jewel!"

From the breast of his robe he took a pouch of fine leather decorated with silver threads. With a delicate horn spoon tied to the pouch he lifted the few drops of quicksilver from the cup and placed them in it, then retied the thong.

The slave stood by, motionless. All the people who worked in the heat and fumes of the roaster tower were naked or wore only breech-clout and moccasins. Otter glanced again at the slave, thinking by his height he was a child, and then saw the small breasts. It was a woman. She was bald. Her joints were swollen knobs in her bone-thin limbs. She looked up once at Otter, moving her eyes only. She spat into the fire, wiped her sore mouth with her hand, and stood motionless again.

"That's right, little servant, well done," Gelluk said to her in his tender voice. "Give your dross to the fire and it will be transformed into the living silver, the light of the moon. Is it not a wonderful thing," he went on, drawing Otter away and back down the spiral stair, "how from what is most base comes what is most noble? That is a great principle of the art! From the vile Red Mother is born the Allking. From the spittle of a dying slave is made the silver Seed of Power."

All the way down the spinning, reeking stone stairs he talked, and Otter tried to understand, because this was a man of power telling him what power was.

But when they came out into the daylight again his head kept on spinning in the dark, and after a few steps he doubled over and vomited on the ground.

Gelluk watched him with his inquisitive, affectionate look, and when Otter stood up, wincing and gasping, the wizard asked gently, "Are you afraid of the King?"

Otter nodded.

"If you share his power he won't harm you. To fear a power, to fight a power, is very dangerous. To love power and to share it is the royal way. Look. Watch what I do." Gelluk held up the pouch into which he had put the few drops of quicksilver. His eye always on Otter's eye, he unsealed the pouch, lifted it to his lips, and drank its contents. He opened his smiling mouth so that Otter could see the silver drops pooling on his tongue before he swallowed.

"Now the King is in my body, the noble guest of my house. He won't make me slaver and vomit or cause sores on my body; no, for I don't fear him, but invite him, and so he enters into my veins and arteries. No harm comes to me. My blood runs silver. I see things unknown to other men. I share the secrets of the King. And when he leaves me, he hides in the place of ordure, in foulness itself, and yet again in the vile place he waits for me to come and take him up and cleanse him as he cleansed me, so that each time we grow purer together." The wizard took Otter's arm and walked along with him. He said, smiling and confidential, "I am one who shits moonlight. You will not know another such. And more than that, more than that, the King enters into my seed. He is my semen. I am Turres and he is me . . ."

In the confusion of Otter's mind, he was only dimly aware that they were going now toward the entrance of the mine. They went underground. The passages of the mine were a dark maze like the wizard's words. Otter stumbled on, trying to understand. He saw the slave in the tower, the woman who had looked at him. He saw her eyes.

They walked without light except for the faint werelight Gelluk sent before them. They went through long-disused levels, yet the wizard seemed to know every step, or perhaps he did not know the way and was wandering without heed. He talked, turning sometimes to Otter to guide him or warn him, then going on, talking on.

They came to where the miners were extending the old tunnel. There the wizard spoke with Licky in the flare of candles among jagged shadows. He touched the earth of the tunnel's end, took clods of earth in his hands, rolled the dirt in his palms, kneading, testing, tasting it. For that time he was silent, and Otter watched him with staring intensity, still trying to understand.

Licky came back to the barracks with them. Gelluk bade Otter goodnight in his soft voice. Licky shut him as usual into the brick-walled room, giving him a loaf of bread, an onion, a jug of water.

Otter crouched as always in the uneasy oppression of the spellbond. He drank thirstily. The sharp earthy taste of the onion was good, and he ate it all.

As the dim light that came into the room from chinks in the mortar of the bricked-up window died away, instead of sinking into the blank misery of all his nights in that room, he stayed awake, and grew more awake. The excited turmoil of his mind all the time he had been with Gelluk slowly quieted. From it something rose, coming close, coming clear, the image he had seen down in the mine, shadowy yet distinct: the slave in the high vault of the tower, that woman with empty breasts and festered eyes, who spat the spittle that ran from her poisoned mouth, and wiped her mouth, and stood waiting to die. She had looked at him.

He saw her now more clearly than he had seen her in the tower. He saw her more clearly than he had ever seen anyone. He saw the thin arms, the swollen joints of elbow and wrist, the childish nape of her neck. It was as if she was with him in the room. It was as if she was in him, as if she was him. She looked at him. He saw her look at him. He saw himself through her eyes.

He saw the lines of the spells that held him, heavy cords of darkness, a tangled maze of lines all about him. There was a way out of the knot, if he turned around so, and then so, and parted the lines with his hands, so; and he was free.

He could not see the woman anymore. He was alone in the room, standing free.

All the thoughts he had not been able to think for days and weeks were racing through his head, a storm of ideas and feelings, a passion of rage, vengeance, pity, pride.

At first he was overwhelmed with fierce fantasies of power and revenge: he would free the slaves, he would spellbind Gelluk and hurl him into the refining fire, he would bind him and blind him and leave him to breathe the fumes of quicksilver in that highest vault till he died . . . But when his thoughts settled down and began to run clearer, he knew that he could not defeat a wizard of great craft and power, even if that wizard was mad. If he had any hope it was to play on his madness, and lead the wizard to defeat himself.

He pondered. All the time he was with Gelluk, he had tried to learn from him, tried to understand what the wizard was telling him. Yet he was certain, now, that Gelluk's ideas, the teaching he so eagerly imparted, had nothing to do with his power or with any true power. Mining and refining were indeed great crafts with their own mysteries and masteries, but Gelluk seemed to know nothing of those arts. His talk of the Allking and the Red Mother was mere words. And not the right words. But how did Otter know that?

In all his flood of talk the only word Gelluk had spoken in the Old Tongue, the language of which wizards' spells were made, was the word *turres*. He had said it meant semen. Otter's own gift of magery had recognized that meaning as the true one. Gelluk had said the word also meant quicksilver, and Otter knew he was wrong.

His humble teachers had taught him all the words they knew of the Language of the Making. Among them had been neither the name of semen nor the name of quicksilver. But his lips parted, his tongue moved. *"Ayezur,"* he said.

His voice was the voice of the slave in the stone tower. It was she who knew the true name of quicksilver and spoke it through him.

Then for a while he held still, body and mind, beginning to understand for the first time where his power lay.

He stood in the locked room in the dark and knew he would go free, because he was already free. A storm of praise ran through him.

After a while, deliberately, he reentered the trap of spellbonds, went back to his old place, sat down on the pallet, and went on thinking. The prisoning spell was still there, yet it had no power over him now. He could walk into it and out of it as if it were mere lines painted on the floor. Gratitude for this freedom beat in him as steady as his heartbeat.

He thought what he must do, and how he must do it. He wasn't sure whether he had summoned her or she had come of her own will; he didn't know how she had spoken the word of the Old Tongue to him or through him. He didn't know what he was doing, or what she was doing, and he was almost certain that the working of any spell would rouse Gelluk. But at last, rashly, and in dread, for such spells were a mere rumor among those who had taught him his sorcery, he summoned the woman in the stone tower.

He brought her into his mind and saw her as he had seen her, there, in that room, and called out to her; and she came.

Her apparition stood again just outside the spiderweb cords of the spell, gazing at him, and seeing him, for a soft, bluish, sourceless light filled the room. Her sore, raw lips quivered but she did not speak.

He spoke, giving her his true name: "I am Medra."

"I am Anieb," she whispered.

"How can we get free?"

"His name."

"Even if I knew it . . . When I'm with him I can't speak."

"If I was with you, I could use it."

"I can't call you."

"But I can come," she said.

She looked round, and he looked up. Both knew that Gelluk had sensed something, had wakened. Otter felt the bonds close and tighten, and the old shadow fall.

"I will come, Medra," she said. She held out her thin hand in a fist, then opened it palm up as if offering him something. Then she was gone.

The light went with her. He was alone in the dark. The cold grip of the spells took him by the throat and choked him, bound his hands, pressed on his lungs. He crouched, gasping. He could not think; he could not remember. "Stay with me," he said, and did not know who he spoke to. He was frightened, and did not know what he was frightened of. The wizard, the power, the spell . . . It was all darkness. But in his body, not in his mind, burned a knowledge he could not name anymore, a certainty that was like a tiny lamp held in his hands in a maze of caverns underground. He kept his eyes on that seed of light.

Weary, evil dreams of suffocation came to him, but took no hold on him. He breathed deep. He slept at last. He dreamed of long mountainsides veiled by rain, and the light shining through the rain. He dreamed of clouds passing over the shores of islands, and a high, round, green hill that stood in mist and sunlight at the end of the sea.

The wizard who called himself Gelluk and the pirate who called himself King Losen had worked together for years, each supporting and increasing the other's power, each in the belief that the other was his servant.

Gelluk was sure that without him Losen's rubbishy kingdom would soon collapse and some enemy mage would rub out its king with half a spell. But he let Losen act the master. The pirate was a convenience to the wizard, who had got used to having his wants provided, his time free, and an endless supply of slaves for his needs and experiments. It was easy to keep up the protections he had laid on Losen's person and expeditions and forays, the prisoning spells he had laid on the places slaves worked or treasures were kept. Making those spells had been a different matter, a long hard work. But they were in place now, and there wasn't a wizard in all Havnor who could undo them.

Gelluk had never met a man he feared. A few wizards had crossed his path strong enough to make him wary of them, but he had never known one with skill and power equal to his own.

Of late, entering always deeper into the mysteries of a certain lorebook brought back from the Isle of Way by one of Losen's raiders, Gelluk had become indifferent to most of the arts he had learned or had discovered for himself. The book convinced him that all of them were only shadows or hints of a greater mastery. As one true element controlled all substances, one true knowledge contained all others. Approaching ever closer to that mastery, he understood that the crafts of wizards were as crude and false as Losen's title and rule. When he was one with the true element, he would be the one true king. Alone among men he would speak the words of making and unmaking. He would have dragons for his dogs.

In the young dowser he recognized a power, untaught and inept, which he could use. He needed much more quicksilver than he had, therefore he needed a finder. Finding was a base skill. Gelluk had never practiced it, but he could see that the young fellow had the gift. He would do well to learn the boy's true name so that he could be sure of controlling him. He sighed at the thought of the time he must waste teaching the boy what he was good for. And after that the ore must still be dug out of the earth and the metal refined. As always, Gelluk's mind leaped across obstacles and delays to the wonderful mysteries at the end of them.

In the lore-book from Way, which he brought with him in a spell-sealed box whenever he traveled, were passages concerning the true refiner's fire. Having long studied these, Gelluk knew that once he had enough of the pure metal, the next stage was to refine it yet further into the Body of the Moon. He had understood the disguised language of the book to mean that in order to purify pure quicksilver, the fire must be built not of mere wood but of human corpses. Rereading and pondering the words this night in his room in the barracks, he discerned another possible meaning in them. There was always another meaning in the words of this lore. Perhaps the book was saying that there must be sacrifice not only of base flesh but also of inferior spirit. The great fire in the tower should burn not dead bodies but living ones. Living and conscious. Purity from foulness: bliss from pain. It was all part of the great principle, perfectly clear once seen. He was sure he was right, had at last understood the technique. But he must not hurry, he must be patient, must make certain. He turned to another passage and compared the two, and brooded over the book late into the night. Once for a moment something drew his mind away, some invasion of the outskirts of his awareness; the boy was trying some trick or other. Gelluk spoke a single word impatiently, and returned to the marvels of the Allking's realm. He never noticed that his prisoner's dreams had escaped him.

Next day he had Licky send him the boy. He looked forward to seeing him, to being kind to him, teaching him, petting him a bit as he had done yesterday. He sat down with him in the sun. Gelluk was fond of children and animals. He liked all beautiful things. It was pleasant to have a young creature about. Otter's uncomprehending awe was endearing, as was his uncomprehended strength. Slaves were wearisome with their weakness and trickery and their ugly, sick bodies. Of course Otter was his slave, but the boy need not know it. They could be teacher and prentice. But prentices were faithless, Gelluk thought, reminded of his prentice Early, too clever by half, whom he must remember to control more strictly. Father and son, that's what he and Otter could be. He would have the boy call him Father. He recalled that he had intended to find out his true name. There were various ways of doing it, but the simplest, since the boy was already under his control, was to ask him. "What is your name?" he said, watching Otter intently.

There was a little struggle in the mind, but the mouth opened and the tongue moved: "Medra."

"Very good, very good, Medra," said the wizard. "You may call me Father."

"You must find the Red Mother," he said, the day after that. They were sitting side by side again outside the barracks. The autumn sun was warm. The wizard had taken off his conical hat, and his thick gray hair flowed loose about his face. "I know you found that little patch for them to dig, but there's no more in that than a few drops. It's scarcely worth burning for so little. If you are to help me, and if I am to teach you, you must try a little harder. I think you know how." He smiled at Otter. "Don't you?"

Otter nodded.

He was still shaken, appalled, by the ease with which Gelluk had forced him to say his name, which gave the wizard immediate and ulti-mate power over him. Now he had no hope of resisting Gelluk in any way. That night he had been in utter despair. But then Anieb had come into his mind: come of her own will, by her own means. He could not summon her, could not even think of her, and would not have dared to do so, since Gelluk knew his name. But she came, even when he was with the wizard, not in apparition but as a presence in his mind.

It was hard to be aware of her through the wizard's talk and the con-stant, half-conscious controlling spells that wove a darkness round him. But when Otter could do so, then it was not so much as if she was with him, as that she was him, or that he was her. He saw through her eyes. Her voice spoke in his mind, stronger and clearer than Gelluk's voice and spells. Through her eyes and mind he could see, and think. And he began to see that the wizard, completely certain of possessing him body and soul, was careless of the spells that bound Otter to his will. A bond is a connection. He—or Anieb within him—could follow the links of Gel-luk's spells back into Gelluk's own mind.

Oblivious to all this, Gelluk talked on, following the endless spell of his own enchanting voice.

"You must find the true womb, the bellybag of the Earth, that holds the pure moonseed. Did you know that the Moon is the Earth's father? Yes, yes; and he lay with her, as is the father's right. He quickened her base clay with the true seed. But she will not give birth to the King. She is strong in her fear and willful in her vileness. She holds him back and hides him deep, fearing to give birth to her master. That is why, to give him birth, she must be burned alive."

Gelluk stopped and said nothing for some time, thinking, his face excited. Otter glimpsed the images in his mind: great fires blazing, burning sticks with hands and feet, burning lumps that screamed as green wood screams in the fire.

"Yes," Gelluk said, his deep voice soft and dreamy, "she must be burned alive. And then, only then, he will spring forth, shining! Oh, it's time, and past time. We must deliver the King. We must find the great lode. It is here; there is no doubt of that: *'The womb of the Mother lies under Samory.'* "

Again he paused. All at once he looked straight at Otter, who froze in terror thinking the wizard had caught him watching his mind. Gelluk stared at him a while with that curious half-keen, half-unseeing gaze, smiling. "Little Medra!" he said, as if just discovering he was there. He patted Otter's shoulder. "I know you have the gift of finding what's hidden. Quite a great gift, were it suitably trained. Have no fear, my son. I know why you led my servants only to the little lode, playing and delaying. But now that I've come, you serve me, and have nothing to be afraid of. And there's no use trying to conceal anything from me, is there? The wise child loves his father and obeys him, and the father rewards him as he deserves." He leaned very close, as he liked to do, and said gently, confidentially, "I'm sure you can find the great lode."

"I know where it is," Anieb said.

Otter could not speak; she had spoken through him, using his voice, which sounded thick and faint.

Very few people ever spoke to Gelluk unless he compelled them to. The spells by which he silenced, weakened, and controlled all who approached him were so habitual to him that he gave them no thought. He was used to being listened to, not to listening. Serene in his strength and obsessed with his ideas, he had no thought beyond them. He was not aware of Otter at all except as a part of his plans, an extension of himself. "Yes, yes, you will," he said, and smiled again.

But Otter was intensely aware of Gelluk, both physically and as a presence of immense controlling power; and it seemed to him that Anieb's speaking had taken away that much of Gelluk's power over him, gaining him a place to stand, a foothold. Even with Gelluk so close to him, fearfully close, he managed to speak.

"I will take you there," he said, stiffly, laboriously.

Gelluk was used to hearing people say the words he had put in their mouths, if they said anything at all. These were words he wanted but had not expected to hear. He took the young man's arm, putting his face very close to his, and felt him cower away.

"How clever you are," he said. "Have you found better ore than that patch you found first? Worth the digging and the roasting?"

"It is the lode," the young man said.

The slow stiff words carried great weight.

"The great lode?" Gelluk looked straight at him, their faces not a hand's breadth apart. The light in his bluish eyes was like the soft, crazy shift of quicksilver. "The womb?"

"Only the Master can go there."

"What Master?"

"The Master of the House. The King."

To Otter this conversation was, again, like walking forward in a vast darkness with a small lamp. Anieb's understanding was that lamp. Each step revealed the next step he must take, but he could never see the place where he was. He did not know what was coming next, and did not understand what he saw. But he saw it, and went forward, word by word.

"How do you know of that House?"

"I saw it."

"Where? Near here?"

Otter nodded.

"Is it in the earth?"

Tell him what he sees, Anieb whispered in Otter's mind, and he spoke: "A stream runs through darkness over a glittering roof. Under the roof is the House of the King. The roof stands high above the floor, on high pillars. The floor is red. All the pillars are red. On them are shining runes."

Gelluk caught his breath. Presently he said, very softly, "Can you read the runes?"

"I cannot read them." Otter's voice was toneless. "I cannot go there. No one can enter there in the body but only the King. Only he can read what is written."

Gelluk's white face had gone whiter; his jaw trembled a little. He stood up, suddenly, as he always did. "Take me there," he said, trying to control himself, but so violently compelling Otter to get up and walk that the young man lurched to his feet and stumbled several steps, almost falling. Then he walked forward, stiff and awkward, trying not to resist the coercive, passionate will that hurried his steps.

Gelluk pressed close beside him, often taking his arm. "This way," he said several times. "Yes, yes! This is the way." Yet he was following

Otter. His touch and his spells pushed him, rushed him, but in the direction Otter chose to go.

They walked past the roaster tower, past the old shaft and the new one, on into the long valley where Otter had taken Licky the first day he was there. It was late autumn now. The shrubs and scrubby grass that had been green that day were dun and dry, and the wind rattled the last leaves on the bushes. To their left a little stream ran low among willow thickets. Mild sunlight and long shadows streaked the hillsides.

Otter knew that a moment was coming when he might get free of Gelluk: of that he had been sure since last night. He knew also that in that same moment he might defeat Gelluk, disempower him, if the wizard, driven by his visions, forgot to guard himself—and if Otter could learn his name.

The wizard's spells still bound their minds together. Otter pressed rashly forward into Gelluk's mind, seeking his true name. But he did not know where to look or how to look. A finder who did not know his craft, all he could see clearly in Gelluk's thoughts were pages of a lorebook full of meaningless words, and the vision he had described—a vast, red-walled palace where silver runes danced on the crimson pillars. But Otter could not read the book or the runes. He had never learned to read.

All this time he and Gelluk were going on farther from the tower, away from Anieb, whose presence sometimes weakened and faded. Otter dared not try to summon her.

Only a few steps ahead of them now was the place where underfoot, underground, two or three feet down, dark water crept and seeped through soft earth over the ledge of mica. Under that opened the hollow cavern and the lode of cinnabar.

Gelluk was almost wholly absorbed in his own vision, but since Otter's mind and his were connected, he saw something of what Otter saw. He stopped, gripping Otter's arm. His hand shook with eagerness.

Otter pointed at the low slope that rose before them. "The King's House is there," he said. Gelluk's attention turned entirely away from him then, fixed on the hillside and the vision he saw within it. Then Otter could call to Anieb. At once she came into his mind and being, and was there with him.

Gelluk was standing still, but his shaking hands were clenched, his whole tall body twitching and trembling, like a hound that wants to chase but cannot find the scent. He was at a loss. There was the hillside with its grass and bushes in the last of the sunlight, but there was no entrance. Grass growing out of gravelly dirt; the seamless earth.

Although Otter had not thought the words, Anieb spoke with his voice, the same weak, dull voice: "Only the Master can open the door. Only the King has the key."

"The key," Gelluk said.

Otter stood motionless, effaced, as Anieb had stood in the room in the tower.

"The key," Gelluk repeated, urgent.

"The key is the King's name."

That was a leap in the darkness. Which of them had said it?

Gelluk stood tense and trembling, still at a loss. "Turres," he said, after a time, almost in a whisper.

The wind blew in the dry grass.

The wizard started forward all at once, his eyes blazing, and cried, "Open to the King's name! I am Tinaral!" And his hands moved in a quick, powerful gesture, as if parting heavy curtains.

The hillside in front of him trembled, writhed, and opened. A gash in it deepened, widened. Water sprang up out of it and ran across the wizard's feet.

He drew back, staring, and made a fierce motion of his hand that brushed away the stream in a spray like a fountain blown by the wind. The gash in the earth grew deeper, revealing the ledge of mica. With a sharp rending crack the glittering stone split apart. Under it was darkness.

The wizard stepped forward. "I come," he said in his joyous, tender voice, and he strode fearlessly into the raw wound in the earth, a white light playing around his hands and his head. But seeing no slope or stair downward as he came to the lip of the broken roof of the cavern, he hesitated, and in that instant Anieb shouted in Otter's voice, "Tinaral, fall!"

Staggering wildly the wizard tried to turn, lost his footing on the crumbling edge, and plunged down into the dark, his scarlet cloak billowing up, the werelight round him like a falling star.

"Close!" Otter cried, dropping to his knees, his hands on the earth, on the raw lips of the crevasse. "Close, Mother! Be healed, be whole!" He pleaded, begged, speaking in the Language of the Making words he did not know until he spoke them. "Mother, be whole!" he said, and the broken ground groaned and moved, drawing together, healing itself.

A reddish seam remained, a scar through the dirt and gravel and uprooted grass.

The wind rattled the dry leaves on the scrub-oak bushes. The sun was behind the hill, and clouds were coming over in a low, gray mass.

Otter crouched there at the foot of the hillslope, alone.

The clouds darkened. Rain passed through the little valley, falling on the dirt and the grass. Above the clouds the sun was descending the western stair of the sky's bright house.

Otter sat up at last. He was wet, cold, bewildered. Why was he here?

He had lost something and had to find it. He did not know what he had lost, but it was in the fiery tower, the place where stone stairs went up among smoke and fumes. He had to go there. He got to his feet and shuffled, lame and unsteady, back down the valley.

He had no thought of hiding or protecting himself. Luckily for him there were no guards about; there were few guards, and they were not on the alert, since the wizard's spells had kept the prison shut. The spells were gone, but the people in the tower did not know it, working on under the greater spell of hopelessness.

Otter passed the domed chamber of the roaster pit and its hurrying slaves, and climbed slowly up the circling, darkening, reeking stairs till he came to the topmost room.

She was there, the sick woman who could heal him, the poor woman who held the treasure, the stranger who was himself.

He stood silent in the doorway. She sat on the stone floor near the crucible, her thin body grayish and dark like the stones. Her chin and breasts were shiny with the spittle that ran from her mouth. He thought of the spring of water that had run from the broken earth.

"Medra," she said. Her sore mouth could not speak clearly. He knelt down and took her hands, looking into her face.

"Anieb," he whispered, "come with me."

"I want to go home," she said.

He helped her stand. He made no spell to protect or hide them. His strength had been used up. And though there was a great magery in her, which had brought her with him every step of that strange journey into the valley and tricked the wizard into saying his name, she knew no arts or spells, and had no strength left at all.

Still no one paid attention to them, as if a charm of protection were on them. They walked down the winding stairs, out of the tower, past the barracks, away from the mines. They walked through thin woodlands toward the foothills that hid Mount Onn from the lowlands of Samory.

Anieb kept a better pace than seemed possible in a woman so famished and destroyed, walking almost naked in the chill of the rain. All her will was aimed on walking forward; she had nothing else in her mind, not him, not anything. But she was there bodily with him, and he felt her presence as keenly and strangely as when she had come to his summoning. The rain ran down her naked head and body. He made her stop to put on his shirt. He was ashamed of it, for it was filthy, he having worn it all these weeks. She let him pull it over her head and then walked right on. She could not go quickly, but she went steadily, her eyes fixed on the faint cart track they followed, till the night came early under the rain clouds, and they could not see where to set their feet.

"Make the light," she said. Her voice was a whimper, plaintive. "Can't you make the light?"

"I don't know," he said, but he tried to bring the werelight round them, and after a while the ground glimmered faintly before their feet.

"We should find shelter and rest," he said.

"I can't stop," she said, and started to walk again.

"You can't walk all night."

"If I lie down I won't get up. I want to see the Mountain."

Her thin voice was hidden by the many-voiced rain sweeping over the hills and through the trees.

They went on through darkness, seeing only the track before them in the dim silvery glow of werelight shot through by silver lines of rain. When she stumbled he caught her arm. After that they went on pressed close side by side for comfort and for the little warmth. They walked slower, and yet slower, but they walked on. There was no sound but the sound of the rain falling from the black sky, and the little kissing squelch of their sodden feet in the mud and wet grass of the track.

"Look," she said, halting. "Medra, look."

He had been walking almost asleep. The pallor of the werelight had faded, drowned in a fainter, vaster clarity. Sky and earth were all one gray, but before them and above them, very high, over a drift of cloud, the long ridge of the mountain glimmered red.

"There," Anieb said. She pointed at the mountain and smiled. She looked at her companion, then slowly down at the ground. She sank down kneeling. He knelt with her, tried to support her, but she slid down in his arms. He tried to keep her head at least from the mud of the track. Her limbs and face twitched, her teeth chattered. He held her close against him, trying to warm her.

"The women," she whispered, "the hand. Ask them. In the village. I did see the Mountain."

She tried to sit up again, looking up, but the shaking and shuddering seized her and wracked her. She began to gasp for breath. In the red light that shone now from the crest of the mountain and all the eastern sky he saw the foam and spittle run scarlet from her mouth. Sometimes she clutched at him, but she did not speak again. She fought her death, fought to breathe, while the red light faded and then darkened into gray as clouds swept again across the mountain and hid the rising sun. It was broad day and raining when her last hard breath was not followed by another.

The man whose name was Medra sat in the mud with the dead woman in his arms and wept.

A carter walking at his mule's head with a load of oakwood came upon them and took them both to Woodedge. He could not make the young man let go of the dead woman. Weak and shaky as he was, he would not set his burden down on the load, but clambered into the cart holding her, and held her all the miles to Woodedge. All he said was "She saved me," and the carter asked no questions.

"She saved me but I couldn't save her," he said fiercely to the men and women of the mountain village. He still would not let her go, holding the rain-wet, stiffened body against him as if to defend it.

Very slowly they made him understand that one of the women was Anieb's mother, and that he should give Anieb to her to hold. He did so at last, watching to see if she was gentle with his friend and would protect her. Then he followed another woman meekly enough. He put on dry clothing she gave him to put on, and ate a little food she gave him to eat, and lay down on the pallet she led him to, and sobbed in weariness, and slept.

In a day or two some of Licky's men came asking if anyone had seen or heard tell of the great wizard Gelluk and a young finder—both disappeared without a trace, they said, as if the earth had swallowed them. Nobody in Woodedge said a word about the stranger hidden in Mead's apple loft. They kept him safe. Maybe that is why the people there now call their village not Woodedge, as it used to be, but Otterhide.

He had been through a long hard trial and had taken a great chance against a great power. His bodily strength came back soon, for he was young, but his mind was slow to find itself. He had lost something, lost it forever, lost it as he found it.

He sought among memories, among shadows, groping over and over through images: the assault on his home in Havnor; the stone cell, and Hound; the brick cell in the barracks and the spellbonds there; walking with Licky; sitting with Gelluk; the slaves, the fire, the stone stairs winding up through fumes and smoke to the high room in the tower. He had to regain it all, to go through it all, searching. Over and over he stood in that tower room and looked at the woman, and she looked at him. Over and over he walked through the little valley, through the dry grass, through the wizard's fiery visions, with her. Over and over he saw the wizard fall, saw the earth close. He saw the red ridge of the mountain in the dawn. Anieb died while he held her, her ruined face against his arm. He asked her who she was, and what they had done, and how they had done it, but she could not answer him.

Her mother Ayo and her mother's sister Mead were wise women. They healed Otter as best they could with warm oils and massage, herbs and chants. They talked to him and listened when he talked. Neither of them had any doubt but that he was a man of great power. He denied this. "I could have done nothing without your daughter," he said.

"What did she do?" Ayo asked, softly.

He told her, as well as he could. "We were strangers. Yet she gave me her name," he said. "And I gave her mine." He spoke haltingly, with long pauses. "It was I that walked with the wizard, compelled by him, but she was with me, and she was free. And so together we could turn his power against him, so that he destroyed himself." He thought for a long time, and said, "She gave me her power."

"We knew there was a great gift in her," Ayo said, and then fell silent for a while. "We didn't know how to teach her. There are no teachers left on the mountain. King Losen's wizards destroy the sorcerers and witches. There's no one to turn to."

"Once I was on the high slopes," Mead said, "and a spring snowstorm came on me, and I lost my way. She came there. She came to me, not in the body, and guided me to the track. She was only twelve then."

"She walked with the dead, sometimes," Ayo said very low. "In the forest, down toward Faliern. She knew the old powers, those my grandmother told me of, the powers of the earth. They were strong there, she said."

"But she was only a girl like the others, too," Mead said, and hid her face. "A good girl," she whispered.

After a while Ayo said, "She went down to Firn with some of the young folk. To buy fleece from the shepherds there. A year ago last spring. That wizard they spoke of came there, casting spells. Taking slaves."

Then they were all silent.

Ayo and Mead were much alike, and Otter saw in them what Anieb might have been: a short, slight, quick woman, with a round face and clear eyes, and a mass of dark hair, not straight like most people's hair but curly, frizzy. Many people in the west of Havnor had hair like that.

But Anieb had been bald, like all the slaves in the roaster tower.

Her use-name had been Flag, the blue iris of the springs. Her mother and aunt called her Flag when they spoke of her.

"Whatever I am, whatever I can do, it's not enough," he said.

"It's never enough," Mead said. "And what can anyone do alone?"

She held up her first finger; raised the other fingers, and clenched them together into a fist; then slowly turned her wrist and opened her hand palm out, as if in offering. He had seen Anieb make that gesture. It was not a spell, he thought, watching intently, but a sign. Ayo was watching him.

"It is a secret," she said.

"Can I know the secret?" he asked after a while.

"You already know it. You gave it to Flag. She gave it to you. Trust."

"Trust," the young man said. "Yes. But against—Against them?—Gelluk's gone. Maybe Losen will fall now. Will it make any difference? Will the slaves go free? Will beggars eat? Will justice be done? I think there's an evil in us, in humankind. Trust denies it. Leaps across it. Leaps the chasm. But it's there. And everything we do finally serves evil, because that's what we are. Greed and cruelty. I look at the world, at the forests and the mountain here, the sky, and it's all right, as it should be. But we aren't. People aren't. We're wrong. We do wrong. No animal does wrong. How could they? But we can, and we do. And we never stop."

They listened to him, not agreeing, not denying, but accepting his despair. His words went into their listening silence, and rested there for days, and came back to him changed.

"We can't do anything without each other," he said. "But it's the greedy ones, the cruel ones who hold together and strengthen each other. And those who won't join them stand each alone." The image of Anieb as he had first seen her, a dying woman standing alone in the tower room, was always with him. "Real power goes to waste. Every wizard uses his arts against the others, serving the men of greed. What good can any art be used that way? It's wasted. It goes wrong, or it's thrown away. Like slaves' lives. Nobody can be free alone. Not even a mage. All of them working their magic in prison cells, to gain nothing. There's no way to use power for good."

Ayo closed her hand and opened it palm up, a fleeting sketch of a gesture, of a sign.

A man came up the mountain to Woodedge, a charcoal burner from Firn. "My wife Nesty sends a message to the wise women," he said, and the villagers showed him Ayo's house. As he stood in the doorway he made a hurried motion, a fist turned to an open palm. "Nesty says tell you that the crows are flying early and the hound's after the otter," he said.

Otter, sitting by the fire shelling walnuts, held still. Mead thanked the messenger and brought him in for a cup of water and a handful of shelled nuts. She and Ayo chatted with him about his wife. When he had gone she turned to Otter.

"The Hound serves Losen," he said. "I'll go today."

Mead looked at her sister. "Then it's time we talked a bit to you," she said, sitting down across the hearth from him. Ayo stood by the table, silent. A good fire burned in the hearth. It was a wet, cold time, and firewood was one thing they had plenty of, here on the mountain.

"There's people all over these parts, and maybe beyond, who think, as you said, that nobody can be wise alone. So these people try to hold to each other. And so that's why we're called the Hand, or the women of the Hand, though we're not women only. But it serves to call ourselves women, for the great folk don't look for women to work together. Or to have thoughts about such things as rule or misrule. Or to have any powers."

"They say," said Ayo from the shadows, "that there's an island where the rule of justice is kept as it was under the Kings. Morred's Isle, they call it. But it's not Enlad of the Kings, nor Éa. It's south, not north of Havnor, they say. There they say the women of the Hand have kept the old arts. And they teach them, not keeping them secret each to himself, as the wizards do."

"Maybe with such teaching you could teach the wizards a lesson," Mead said.

"Maybe you can find that island," said Ayo.

Otter looked from one to the other. Clearly they had told him their own greatest secret and their hope.

"Morred's Isle," he said.

"That would be only what the women of the Hand call it, keeping its meaning from the wizards and the pirates. To them no doubt it would bear some other name."

"It would be a terrible long way," said Mead.

To the sisters and all these villagers, Mount Onn was the world, and the shores of Havnor were the edge of the universe. Beyond that was only rumor and dream.

"You'll come to the sea, going south, they say," said Ayo.

"He knows that, sister," Mead told her. "Didn't he tell us he was a ship carpenter? But it's a terrible long way down to the sea, surely. With this wizard on your scent, how are you to go there?"

"By the grace of water, that carries no scent," Otter said, standing up. A litter of walnut shells fell from his lap, and he took the hearth broom and swept them into the ashes. "I'd better go."

"There's bread," Ayo said, and Mead hurried to pack hard bread and hard cheese and walnuts into a pouch made of a sheep's stomach. They were very poor people. They gave him what they had. So Anieb had done.

"My mother was born in Endlane, round by Faliern Forest," Otter said. "Do you know that town? She's called Rose, Rowan's daughter."

"The carters go down to Endlane, summers."

"If somebody could talk to her people there, they'd get word to her. Her brother, Littleash, used to come to the city every year or two."

They nodded.

"If she knew I was alive," he said.

Anieb's mother nodded. "She'll hear it."

"Go on now," said Mead.

"Go with the water," said Ayo.

He embraced them, and they him, and he left the house.

He ran down from the straggle of huts to the quick, noisy stream he had heard singing through his sleep all his nights in Woodedge. He prayed to it. "Take me and save me," he asked it. He made the spell the old Changer had taught him long ago, and said the word of transformation. Then no man knelt by the loud-running water, but an otter slipped into it and was gone.

⌒ *III. Tern*

> *There was a wise man on our hill*
> *Who found his way to work his will.*
> *He changed his shape, he changed his name,*
> *But ever the other will be the same.*
> *So runs the water away, away,*
> *So runs the water away.*

One winter afternoon on the shore of the Onneva River where it fingers out into the north bight of the Great Bay of Havnor, a man stood up on the muddy sand: a man poorly dressed and poorly shod, a thin brown man with dark eyes and hair so fine and thick it shed the rain. It was raining on the low beaches of the river mouth, the fine, cold, dismal drizzle of that gray winter. His clothes were soaked. He hunched his shoulders, turned about, and set off toward a wisp of chimney smoke he saw far down the shore. Behind him were the tracks of an otter's four feet coming up from the water and the tracks of a man's two feet going away from it.

Where he went then, the songs don't tell. They say only that he wan-

dered, "he wandered long from land to land." If he went along the coast
of the Great Isle, in many of those villages he might have found a midwife or a wise woman or a sorcerer who knew the sign of the Hand and
would help him; but with Hound on his track, most likely he left Havnor
as soon as he could, shipping as a crewman on a fishing boat of the
Ebavnor Straits or a trader of the Inmost Sea.

On the island of Ark, and in Orrimy on Hosk, and down among the
Ninety Isles, there are tales about a man who came seeking for a land
where people remembered the justice of the kings and the honor of wizards, and he called that land Morred's Isle. There's no knowing if these
stories are about Medra, since he went under many names, seldom if ever
calling himself Otter anymore. Gelluk's fall had not brought Losen
down. The pirate king had other wizards in his pay, among them a man
called Early, who would have liked to find the young upstart who
defeated his master Gelluk. And Early had a good chance of tracing him.
Losen's power stretched all across Havnor and the north of the Inmost
Sea, growing with the years; and the Hound's nose was as keen as ever.

Maybe it was to escape the hunt that Medra came to Pendor, a long
way west of the Inmost Sea, or maybe some rumor among the women of
the Hand on Hosk sent him there. Pendor was a rich island, then, before
the dragon Yevaud despoiled it. Wherever Medra had gone until then, he
had found the lands like Havnor or worse, sunk in warfare, raids, and
piracy, the fields full of weeds, the towns full of thieves. Maybe he
thought, at first, that on Pendor he had found Morred's Isle, for the city
was beautiful and peaceful and the people prosperous.

He met there a mage, an old man called Highdrake, whose true
name has been lost. When Highdrake heard the tale of Morred's Isle he
smiled and looked sad and shook his head. "Not here," he said. "Not
this. The Lords of Pendor are good men. They remember the kings. They
don't seek war or plunder. But they send their sons west dragon hunting.
In sport. As if the dragons of the West Reach were ducks or geese for the
killing! No good will come of that."

Highdrake took Medra as his student, gratefully. "I was taught my
art by a mage who gave me freely all he knew, but I never found anybody
to give that knowledge to, until you came," he told Medra. "The young
men come to me and they say, 'What good is it? Can you find gold?' they
say. 'Can you teach me how to make stones into diamonds? Can you give
me a sword that will kill a dragon? What's the use of talking about the
balance of things? There's no profit in it,' they say. No profit!" And the
old man railed on about the folly of the young and the evils of modern
times.

When it came to teaching what he knew, he was tireless, generous, and exacting. For the first time, Medra was given a vision of magic not as a set of strange gifts and reasonless acts, but as an art and a craft, which could be known truly with long study and used rightly after long practice, though even then it would never lose its strangeness. Highdrake's mastery of spells and sorcery was not much greater than his pupil's, but he had clear in his mind the idea of something very much greater, the wholeness of knowledge. And that made him a mage.

Listening to him, Medra thought of how he and Anieb had walked in the dark and rain by the faint glimmer that showed them only the next step they could take, and of how they had looked up to the red ridge of the mountain in the dawn.

"Every spell depends on every other spell," said Highdrake. "Every motion of a single leaf moves every leaf of every tree on every isle of Earthsea! There is a pattern. That's what you must look for and look to. Nothing goes right but as part of the pattern. Only in it is freedom."

Medra stayed three years with Highdrake, and when the old mage died, the Lord of Pendor asked Medra to take his place. Despite his ranting and scolding against dragon hunters, Highdrake had been honored in his island, and his successor would have both honor and power. Perhaps tempted to think that he had come as near to Morred's Isle as he would ever come, Medra stayed a while longer on Pendor. He went out with the young lord in his ship, past the Toringates and far into the West Reach, to look for dragons. There was a great longing in his heart to see a dragon. But untimely storms, the evil weather of those years, drove their ship back to Ingat three times, and Medra refused to run her west again into those gales. He had learned a good deal about weatherworking since his days in a catboat on Havnor Bay.

A while after that he left Pendor, drawn southward again, and maybe went to Ensmer. In one guise or another he came at last to Geath in the Ninety Isles.

There they fished for whales, as they still do. That was a trade he wanted no part of. Their ships stank and their town stank. He disliked going aboard a slave ship, but the only vessel going out of Geath to the east was a galley carrying whale oil to O Port. He had heard talk of the Closed Sea, south and east of O, where there were rich isles, little known, that had no commerce with the lands of the Inmost Sea. What he sought might be there. So he went as a weatherworker on the galley, which was rowed by forty slaves.

The weather was fair for once: a following wind, a blue sky lively with little white clouds, the mild sunlight of late spring. They made good way from Geath. Late in the afternoon he heard the master say to the helmsman, "Keep her south tonight so we don't raise Roke."

He had not heard of that island, and asked, "What's there?"

"Death and desolation," said the ship's master, a short man with small, sad, knowing eyes like a whale's.

"War?"

"Years back. Plague, black sorcery. The waters all round it are cursed."

"Worms," said the helmsman, the master's brother. "Catch fish anywhere near Roke, you'll find 'em thick with worms as a dead dog on a dunghill."

"Do people still live there?" Medra asked, and the master said, "Witches," while his brother said, "Worm eaters."

There were many such isles in the Archipelago, made barren and desolate by rival wizards' blights and curses; they were evil places to come to or even to pass, and Medra thought no more about this one, until that night.

Sleeping out on deck with the starlight on his face, he had a simple, vivid dream: it was daylight, clouds racing across a bright sky, and across the sea he saw the sunlit curve of a high green hill. He woke with the vision still clear in his mind, knowing he had seen it ten years before, in the spell-locked barracks room at the mines of Samory.

He sat up. The dark sea was so quiet that the stars were reflected here and there on the sleek lee side of the long swells. Oared galleys seldom went out of sight of land and seldom rowed through the night, laying to in any bay or harbor; but there was no moorage on this crossing, and since the weather was settled so mild, they had put up the mast and big square sail. The ship drifted softly forward, her slave oarsmen sleeping on their benches, the free men of her crew all asleep but the helmsman and the lookout, and the lookout was dozing. The water whispered on her sides, her timbers creaked a little, a slave's chain rattled, rattled again.

"They don't need a weatherworker on a night like this, and they haven't paid me yet," Medra said to his conscience. He had waked from his dream with the name Roke in his mind. Why had he never heard of the isle or seen it on a chart? It might be accursed and deserted as they said, but wouldn't it be set down on the charts?

"I could fly there as a tern and be back on the ship before daylight," he said to himself, but idly. He was bound for O Port. Ruined lands were all too common. No need to fly to seek them. He made himself comfortable in his coil of cable and watched the stars. Looking west, he saw the four bright stars of the Forge, low over the sea. They were a little blurred, and as he watched them they blinked out, one by one.

The faintest little sighing tremor ran over the slow, smooth swells.

"Master," Medra said, afoot, "wake up."

"What now?"

"A witchwind coming. Following. Get the sail down."

No wind stirred. The air was soft, the big sail hung slack. Only the western stars faded and vanished in a silent blackness that rose slowly higher. The master looked at that. "Witchwind, you say?" he asked, reluctant.

Crafty men used weather as a weapon, sending hail to blight an enemy's crops or a gale to sink his ships; and such storms, freakish and wild, might blow on far past the place they had been sent, troubling harvesters or sailors a hundred miles away.

"Get the sail down," Medra said, peremptory. The master yawned and cursed and began to shout commands. The crewmen got up slowly and slowly began to take the awkward sail in, and the oarmaster, after asking several questions of the master and Medra, began to roar at the slaves and stride among them rousing them right and left with his knotted rope. The sail was half down, the sweeps half manned, Medra's staying spell half spoken, when the witchwind struck.

It struck with one huge thunderclap out of sudden utter blackness and wild rain. The ship pitched like a horse rearing and then rolled so hard and far that the mast broke loose from its footing, though the stays held. The sail struck the water, filled, and pulled the galley right over, the great sweeps sliding in their oarlocks, the chained slaves struggling and shouting on their benches, barrels of oil breaking loose and thundering over one another—pulled her over and held her over, the deck vertical to the sea, till a huge storm wave struck and swamped her and she sank. All the shouting and screaming of men's voices was suddenly silent. There was no noise but the roar of the rain on the sea, lessening as the freak wind passed on eastward. Through it one white seabird beat its wings up from the black water and flew, frail and desperate, to the north.

Printed on narrow sands under granite cliffs, in the first light, were the tracks of a bird alighting. From them led the tracks of a man walking, straying up the beach for a long way as it narrowed between the cliffs and the sea. Then the tracks ceased.

Medra knew the danger of repeatedly taking any form but his own, but he was shaken and weakened by the shipwreck and the long night flight, and the gray beach led him only to the feet of sheer cliffs he could not climb. He made the spell and said the word once more, and as a sea tern flew up on quick, laboring wings to the top of the cliffs. Then, possessed by flight, he flew on over a shadowy sunrise land. Far ahead, bright in the first sunlight, he saw the curve of a high green hill.

To it he flew, and on it landed, and as he touched the earth he was a man again.

He stood there for a while, bewildered. It seemed to him that it was not by his own act or decision that he had taken his own form, but that in touching this ground, this hill, he had become himself. A magic greater than his own prevailed here.

He looked about, curious and wary. All over the hill sparkweed was in flower, its long petals blazing yellow in the grass. Children on Havnor knew that flower. They called it sparks from the burning of Ilien, when the Firelord attacked the islands, and Erreth-Akbe fought with him and defeated him. Tales and songs of the heroes rose up in Medra's memory as he stood there: Erreth-Akbe and the heroes before him, the Eagle Queen, Heru, Akambar who drove the Kargs into the east, and Serriadh the peacemaker, and Elfarran of Soléa, and Morred, the White Enchanter, the beloved king. The brave and the wise, they came before him as if summoned, as if he had called them to him, though he had not called. He saw them. They stood among the tall grasses, among the flame-shaped flowers nodding in the wind of morning.

Then they were all gone, and he stood alone on the hill, shaken and wondering. "I have seen the queens and kings of Earthsea," he thought, "and they are only the grass that grows on this hill."

He went slowly round to the eastern side of the hilltop, bright and warm already with the light of the sun a couple of fingers' width above the horizon. Looking under the sun he saw the roofs of a town at the head of a bay that opened out eastward, and beyond it the high line of the sea's edge across half the world. Turning west he saw fields and pastures and roads. To the north were long green hills. In a fold of land southward a grove of tall trees drew his gaze and held it. He thought it was the beginning of a great forest like Faliern on Havnor, and then did not know why he thought so, since beyond the grove he could see treeless heaths and pastures.

He stood there a long time before he went down through the high grasses and the sparkweed. At the foot of the hill he came into a lane. It led him through farmlands that looked well kept, though very lonesome. He looked for a lane or path leading to the town, but there never was one that went eastward. Not a soul was in the fields, some of which were newly plowed. No dog barked as he went by. Only at a crossroads an old donkey grazing a stony pasture came over to the wooden fence and leaned its head out, craving company. Medra stopped to stroke the gray-brown, bony face. A city man and a saltwater man, he knew little of farms and their animals, but he thought the donkey looked at him kindly. "Where am I, donkey?" he said to it. "How do I get to the town I saw?"

The donkey leaned its head hard against his hand so that he would go on scratching the place just above its eyes and below its ears. When he did so, it flicked its long right ear. So when he parted from the donkey he took the right hand of the crossroad, though it looked as if it would lead back to the hill; and soon enough he came among houses, and then onto a street that brought him down at last into the town at the head of the bay.

It was as strangely quiet as the farmlands. Not a voice, not a face. It was difficult to feel uneasy in an ordinary-looking town on a sweet spring morning, but in such silence he must wonder if he was indeed in a plague-stricken place or an island under a curse. He went on. Between a house and an old plum tree was a wash line, the clothes pinned on it flapping in the sunny breeze. A cat came round the corner of a garden, no abandoned starveling but a white-pawed, well-whiskered, prosperous cat. And at last, coming down the steep little street, which here was cobbled, he heard voices.

He stopped to listen, and heard nothing.

He went on to the foot of the street. It opened into a small market square. People were gathered there, not many of them. They were not buying or selling. There were no booths or stalls set up. They were waiting for him.

Ever since he had walked on the green hill above the town and had seen the bright shadows in the grass, his heart had been easy. He was expectant, full of a sense of great strangeness, but not frightened. He stood still and looked at the people who came to meet him.

Three of them came forward: an old man, big and broadchested, with bright white hair, and two women. Wizard knows wizard, and Medra knew they were women of power.

He raised his hand closed in a fist and then turning and opening it, offered it to them palm up.

"Ah," said one of the women, the taller of the two, and she laughed. But she did not answer the gesture.

"Tell us who you are," the white-haired man said, courteously enough, but without greeting or welcome. "Tell us how you came here."

"I was born in Havnor and trained as a shipwright and a sorcerer. I was on a ship bound from Geath to O Port. I was spared alone from drowning, last night, when a witchwind struck." He was silent then. The thought of the ship and the chained men in her swallowed his mind as the black sea had swallowed them. He gasped, as if coming up from drowning.

"How did you come here?"

"As . . . as a bird, a tern. Is this Roke Island?"

"You changed yourself?"

He nodded.

"Whom do you serve?" asked the shorter and younger of the women, speaking for the first time. She had a keen, hard face, with long black brows.

"I have no master."

"What was your errand in O Port?"

"In Havnor, years ago, I was in servitude. Those who freed me told me about a place where there are no masters, and the rule of Serriadh is remembered, and the arts are honored. I have been looking for that place, that island, seven years."

"Who told you about it?"

"Women of the Hand."

"Anyone can make a fist and show a palm," said the tall woman, pleasantly. "But not everyone can fly to Roke. Or swim, or sail, or come in any way at all. So we must ask what brought you here."

Medra did not answer at once. "Chance," he said at last, "favoring long desire. Not art. Not knowledge. I think I've come to the place I sought, but I don't know. I think you may be the people they told me of, but I don't know. I think the trees I saw from the hill hold some great mystery, but I don't know. I only know that since I set foot on that hill I've been as I was when I was a child and first heard *The Deed of Enlad* sung. I am lost among wonders."

The white-haired man looked at the two women. Other people had come forward, and there was some quiet talk among them.

"If you stayed here, what would you do?" the black-browed woman asked him.

"I can build boats, or mend them, and sail them. I can find, above and under ground. I can work weather, if you have any need of that. And I'll learn the art from any who will teach me."

"What do you want to learn?" asked the taller woman in her mild voice.

Now Medra felt that he had been asked the question on which the rest of his life hung, for good or evil. Again he stood silent a while. He started to speak, and didn't speak, and finally spoke. "I could not save one, not one, not the one who saved me," he said. "Nothing I know could have set her free. I know nothing. If you know how to be free, I beg you, teach me!"

"Free!" said the tall woman, and her voice cracked like a whip. Then she looked at her companions, and after a while she smiled a little. Turning back to Medra, she said, "We're prisoners, and so freedom is a thing we study. You came here through the walls of our prison. Seeking freedom, you say. But you should know that leaving Roke may be even harder than coming to it. Prison within prison, and some of it we have built ourselves." She looked at the others. "What do you say?" she asked them.

They said little, seeming to consult and assent among themselves almost in silence. At last the shorter woman looked with her fierce eyes at Medra. "Stay if you will," she said.

"I will."

"What will you have us call you?"

"Tern," he said; and so he was called.

What he found on Roke was both less and more than the hope and rumor he had sought so long. Roke Island was, they told him, the heart of Earthsea. The first land Segoy raised from the waters in the beginning of time was bright Éa of the northern sea, and the second was Roke. That green hill, Roke Knoll, was founded deeper than all the islands. The trees he had seen, which seemed sometimes to be in one place on the isle and sometimes in another, were the oldest trees in the world, and the source and center of magic.

"If the Grove were cut, all wizardry would fail. The roots of those trees are the roots of knowledge. The patterns the shadows of their leaves make in the sunlight write the words Segoy spoke in the Making."

So said Ember, his fierce, black-browed teacher.

All the teachers of the art magic on Roke were women. There were no men of power, few men at all, on the island.

Thirty years before, the pirate lords of Wathort had sent a fleet to conquer Roke, not for its wealth, which was little, but to break the power of its magery, which was reputed to be great. One of the wizards of Roke had betrayed the island to the crafty men of Wathort, lowering its spells of defense and warning. Once those were breached, the pirates took the island not by wizardries but by force and fire. Their great ships filled Thwil Bay, their hordes burned and looted, their slave takers carried off men, boys, young women. Little children and the old they slaughtered. They fired every house and field they came to. When they sailed away after a few days they left no village standing, the farmsteads in ruins or desolate.

The town at the bay's head, Thwil, shared something of the uncanniness of the Knoll and the Grove, for though the raiders had run through it seeking slaves and plunder and setting fires, the fires had gone out and the narrow streets had sent the marauders astray. Most of the islanders who survived were wise women and their children, who had hidden themselves in the town or in the Immanent Grove. The men now on Roke were those spared children, grown, and a few men now grown old. There was no government but that of the women of the Hand, for it was their spells that had protected Roke so long and protected it far more closely now.

They had little trust in men. A man had betrayed them. Men had attacked them. It was men's ambitions, they said, that had perverted all the arts to ends of gain. "We do not deal with their governments," said tall Veil in her mild voice.

And yet Ember said to Medra, "We were our own undoing."

Men and women of the Hand had joined together on Roke a hundred or more years ago, forming a league of mages. Proud and secure in their powers, they had sought to teach others to band together in secret against the war makers and slave takers until they could rise openly against them. Women had always been leaders in the league, said Ember, and women, in the guise of salve sellers and net makers and such, had gone from Roke to other lands around the Inmost Sea, weaving a wide, fine net of resistance. Even now there were strands and knots of that net left. Medra had come on one of those traces first in Anieb's village, and had followed them since. But they had not led him here. Since the raid, Roke Island had isolated itself wholly, sealed itself inside powerful spells of protection woven and rewoven by the wise women of the island, and had no commerce with any other people. "We can't save them," Ember said. "We couldn't save ourselves."

Veil, with her gentle voice and smile, was implacable. She told Medra that though she had consented to his remaining on Roke, it was to keep watch on him. "You broke through our defenses once," she said. "All that you say of yourself may be true, and may not. What can you tell me that would make me trust you?"

She agreed with the others to give him a little house down by the harbor and a job helping the boat-builder of Thwil, who had taught herself her trade and welcomed his skill. Veil put no difficulties in his path and always greeted him kindly. But she had said, "What can you tell me that would make me trust you?" and he had no answer for her.

Ember usually scowled when he greeted her. She asked him abrupt questions, listened to his answers, and said nothing.

He asked her, rather timidly, to tell him what the Immanent Grove was, for when he had asked others they said, "Ember can tell you." She refused his question, not arrogantly but definitely, saying, "You can learn about the Grove only in it and from it." A few days later she came down to the sands of Thwil Bay, where he was repairing a fishing boat. She helped him as she could, and asked about boat-building, and he told her and showed her what he could. It was a peaceful afternoon, but after it she went off in her abrupt way. He felt some awe of her; she was incalculable. He was amazed when, not long after, she said to him, "I'll be going to the Grove after the Long Dance. Come if you like."

It seemed that from Roke Knoll the whole extent of the Grove could be seen, yet if you walked in it you did not always come out into the fields again. You walked on under the trees. In the inner Grove they were all of one kind, which grew nowhere else, yet had no name in Hardic but "tree." In the Old Speech, Ember said, each of those trees had its own name. You walked on, and after a time you were walking again among familiar trees, oak and beech and ash, chestnut and walnut and willow, green in spring and bare in winter; there were dark firs, and cedar, and a tall evergreen Medra did not know, with soft reddish bark and layered foliage. You walked on, and the way through the trees was never twice the same. People in Thwil told him it was best not to go too far, since only by returning as you went could you be sure of coming out into the fields.

"How far does the forest go?" Medra asked, and Ember said, "As far as the mind goes."

The leaves of the trees spoke, she said, and the shadows could be read. "I am learning to read them," she said.

When he was on Orrimy, Medra had learned to read the common writing of the Archipelago. Later, Highdrake of Pendor had taught him some of the runes of power. That was known lore. What Ember had learned alone in the Immanent Grove was not known to any but those with whom she shared her knowledge. She lived all summer under the eaves of the Grove, having no more than a box to keep the mice and wood rats from her small store of food, a shelter of branches, and a cook fire near a stream that came out of the woods to join the little river running down to the bay.

Medra camped nearby. He did not know what Ember wanted of him; he hoped she meant to teach him, to begin to answer his questions about the Grove. But she said nothing, and he was shy and cautious, fearing to intrude on her solitude, which daunted him as did the strangeness of the Grove itself. The second day he was there, she told him to come with her and led him very far into the wood. They walked for hours in silence. In the summer midday the woods were silent. No bird sang. The leaves did not stir. The aisles of the trees were endlessly different and all the same. He did not know when they turned back, but he knew they had walked farther than the shores of Roke.

They came out again among the plowlands and pastures in the warm evening. As they walked back to their camping place he saw the four stars of the Forge come out above the western hills.

Ember parted from him with only a "Good night."

The next day she said, "I'm going to sit under the trees." Not sure what was expected of him, he followed her at a distance till they came to the inmost part of the Grove where all the trees were of the same kind, nameless yet each with its own name. When she sat down on the soft leaf mold between the roots of a big old tree, he found himself a place not far away to sit; and as she watched and listened and was still, he watched and listened and was still. So they did for several days. Then one morning, in rebellious mood, he stayed by the stream while Ember walked into the Grove. She did not look back.

Veil came from Thwil Town that morning, bringing them a basket of bread, cheese, milk curds, summer fruits. "What have you learned?" she asked Medra in her cool, gentle way, and he answered, "That I'm a fool."

"Why so, Tern?"

"A fool could sit under the trees forever and grow no wiser."

The tall woman smiled a little. "My sister has never taught a man before," she said. She glanced at him, and gazed away, over the summery fields. "She's never looked at a man before," she said.

Medra stood silent. His face felt hot. He looked down. "I thought," he said, and stopped.

In Veil's words he saw, all at once, the other side of Ember's impatience, her fierceness, her silences.

He had tried to look at Ember as untouchable while he longed to touch her soft brown skin, her black shining hair. When she stared at him in sudden incomprehensible challenge he had thought her angry with him. He feared to insult, to offend her. What did she fear? His desire? Her own?—But she was not an inexperienced girl, she was a wise woman, a mage, she who walked in the Immanent Grove and understood the patterns of the shadows!

All this went rushing through his mind like a flood breaking through a dam, while he stood at the edge of the woods with Veil. "I thought mages kept themselves apart," he said at last. "Highdrake said that to make love is to unmake power."

"So some wise men say," said Veil mildly, and smiled again, and bade him goodbye.

He spent the whole afternoon in confusion, angry. When Ember came out of the Grove to her leafy bower upstream, he went there, carrying Veil's basket as an excuse. "May I talk to you?" he said.

She nodded shortly, frowning her black brows.

He said nothing. She squatted down to find out what was in the basket. "Peaches!" she said, and smiled.

"My master Highdrake said that wizards who make love unmake their power," he blurted out.

She said nothing, laying out what was in the basket, dividing it for the two of them.

"Do you think that's true?" he asked.

She shrugged. "No," she said.

He stood tongue-tied. After a while she looked up at him. "No," she said in a soft, quiet voice, "I don't think it's true. I think all the true powers, all the old powers, at root are one."

He still stood there, and she said, "Look at the peaches! They're all ripe. We'll have to eat them right away."

"If I told you my name," he said, "my true name—"

"I'd tell you mine," she said. "If that . . . if that's how we should begin."

They began, however, with the peaches.

They were both shy. When Medra took her hand his hand shook, and Ember, whose name was Elehal, turned away scowling. Then she touched his hand very lightly. When he stroked the sleek black flow of her hair she seemed only to endure his touch, and he stopped. When he tried to embrace her she was stiff, rejecting him. Then she turned and, fierce, hasty, awkward, seized him in her arms. It wasn't the first night, nor the first nights, they passed together that gave either of them much pleasure or ease. But they learned from each other, and came through shame and fear into passion. Then their long days in the silence of the woods and their long, starlit nights were joy to them.

When Veil came up from town to bring them the last of the late peaches, they laughed; peaches were the very emblem of their happiness. They tried to make her stay and eat supper with them, but she wouldn't. "Stay here while you can," she said.

The summer ended too soon that year. Rain came early; snow fell in autumn even as far south as Roke. Storm followed storm, as if the winds had risen in rage against the tampering and meddling of the crafty men. Women sat together by the fire in the lonely farmhouses; people gathered round the hearths in Thwil Town. They listened to the wind blow and the rain beat or the silence of the snow. Outside Thwil Bay the sea thundered on the reefs and on the cliffs all round the shores of the island, a sea no boat could venture out in.

What they had they shared. In that it was indeed Morred's Isle. Nobody on Roke starved or went unhoused, though nobody had much more than they needed. Hidden from the rest of the world not only by sea and storm but by their defenses that disguised the island and sent ships astray, they worked and talked and sang the songs, *The Winter Carol* and *The Deed of the Young King*. And they had books, the *Chronicles of Enlad* and the *History of the Wise Heroes*. From these precious books the old men and women would read aloud in a hall down by the wharf where the fisherwomen made and mended their nets. There was a hearth there, and they would light the fire. People came even from farms across the island to hear the histories read, listening in silence, intent. "Our souls are hungry," Ember said.

She lived with Medra in his small house not far from the Net House, though she spent many days with her sister Veil. Ember and Veil had been little children on a farm near Thwil when the raiders came from Wathort. Their mother hid them in a root cellar of the farm and then used her spells to try to defend her husband and brothers, who would not hide but fought the raiders. They were butchered with their cattle. The house and barns were burned. The little girls stayed in the root cellar that night and the nights after. Neighbors who came at last to bury the rotting bodies found the two children, silent, starving, armed with a mattock and a broken plowshare, ready to defend the heaps of stones and earth they had piled over their dead.

Medra knew only a hint of this story from Ember. One night Veil, who was three years older than Ember and to whom the memory was much clearer, told it to him fully. Ember sat with them, listening in silence.

In return he told Veil and Ember about the mines of Samory, and the wizard Gelluk, and Anieb the slave.

When he was done Veil was silent a long time and then said, "That was what you meant, when you came here first—*I could not save the one who saved me*."

"And you asked me, *What can you tell me that could make me trust you?*"

"You have told me," Veil said.

Medra took her hand and put his forehead against it. Telling his story he had kept back tears. He could not do so now.

"She gave me freedom," he said. "And I still feel that all I do is done through her and for her. No, not for her. We can do nothing for the dead. But for . . ."

"For us," said Ember. "For us who live, in hiding, neither killed nor killing. The dead are dead. The great and mighty go their way unchecked. All the hope left in the world is in the people of no account."

"Must we hide forever?"

"Spoken like a man," said Veil with her gentle, wounded smile.

"Yes," said Ember. "We must hide, and forever if need be. Because there's nothing left but being killed and killing, beyond these shores. You say it, and I believe it."

"But you can't hide true power," Medra said. "Not for long. It dies in hiding, unshared."

"Magic won't die on Roke," said Veil. "*On Roke all spells are strong.* So said Ath himself. And you have walked under the trees . . . Our job must be to keep that strength. Hide it, yes. Hoard it, as a young dragon hoards up its fire. And share it. But only here. Pass it on, one to the next, here, where it's safe, and where the great robbers and killers would least look for it, since no one here is of any account. And one day the dragon will come into its strength. If it takes a thousand years . . ."

"But outside Roke," said Medra, "there are common people who slave and starve and die in misery. Must they do so for a thousand years with no hope?"

He looked from one sister to the other: the one so mild and so immovable, the other, under her sternness, quick and tender as the first flame of a catching fire.

"On Havnor," he said, "far from Roke, in a village on Mount Onn, among people who know nothing of the world, there are still women of the Hand. That net hasn't broken after so many years. How was it woven?"

"Craftily," said Ember.

"And cast wide!" He looked from one to the other again. "I wasn't well taught, in the City of Havnor," he said. "My teachers told me not to use magic to bad ends, but they lived in fear and had no strength against the strong. They gave me all they had to give, but it was little. It was by mere luck I didn't go wrong. And by Anieb's gift of strength to me. But for her I'd be Gelluk's servant now. Yet she herself was untaught, and so enslaved. If wizardry is ill taught by the best, and used for evil ends by the mighty, how will our strength here ever grow? What will the young dragon feed on?"

"This is the center," said Veil. "We must keep to the center. And wait."

"We must give what we have to give," said Medra. "If all but us are slaves, what's our freedom worth?"

"The true art prevails over the false. The pattern will hold," Ember said, frowning. She reached out the poker to gather together her namesakes in the hearth, and with a whack knocked the heap into a blaze.

"That I know. But our lives are short, and the pattern's very long. If only Roke was now what it once was—if we had more people of the true art gathered here, teaching and learning as well as preserving—"

"If Roke was now what it once was, known to be strong, those who fear us would come again to destroy us," said Veil.

"The solution lies in secrecy," said Medra. "But so does the problem."

"Our problem is with men," Veil said, "if you'll forgive me, dear brother. Men are of more account to other men than women and children are. We might have fifty witches here and they'll pay little heed. But if they knew we had five men of power, they'd seek to destroy us again."

"So though there were men among us we were the *women* of the Hand," said Ember.

"You still are," Medra said. "Anieb was one of you. She and you and all of us live in the same prison."

"What can we do?" said Veil.

"Learn our strength!" said Medra.

"A school," Ember said. "Where the wise might come to learn from one another, to study the pattern . . . The Grove would shelter us."

"The lords of war despise scholars and schoolmasters," said Medra.

"I think they fear them too," said Veil.

So they talked, that long winter, and others talked with them. Slowly their talk turned from vision to intention, from longing to planning. Veil was always cautious, warning of dangers. White-haired Dune was so eager that Ember said he wanted to start teaching sorcery to every child in Thwil. Once Ember had come to believe that Roke's freedom lay in offering others freedom, she set her whole mind on how the women of the Hand might grow strong again. But her mind, formed by her long solitudes among the trees, always sought form and clarity, and she said, "How can we teach our art when we don't know what it is?"

And they talked about that, all the wise women of the island: what was the true art of magic, and where did it turn false; how the balance of things was kept or lost; what crafts were needful, which useful, which dangerous; why some people had one gift but not another, and whether you could learn an art you had no native gift for. In such discussions they worked out the names that ever since have been given to the masteries: finding, weather-working, changing, healing, summoning, patterning, naming, and the crafts of illusion, and the knowledge of the songs. Those are the arts of the Masters of Roke even now, though the Chanter took the Finder's place when finding came to be considered a merely useful craft unworthy of a mage.

And it was in these discussions that the school on Roke began.

There are some who say that the school had its beginnings far differently. They say that Roke used to be ruled by a woman called the Dark Woman, who was in league with the Old Powers of the earth. They say she lived in a cave under Roke Knoll, never coming into the daylight, but weaving vast spells over land and sea that compelled men to her evil will, until the first Archmage came to Roke, unsealed and entered the cave, defeated the Dark Woman, and took her place.

There's no truth in this tale but one, which is that indeed one of the first Masters of Roke opened and entered a great cavern. But though the roots of Roke are the roots of all the islands, that cavern was not on Roke.

And it's true that in the time of Medra and Elehal the people of Roke, men and women, had no fear of the Old Powers of the earth, but revered them, seeking strength and vision from them. That changed with the years.

Spring came late again that year, cold and stormy. Medra set to boatbuilding. By the time the peaches flowered, he had made a slender, sturdy deep-sea boat, built according to the style of Havnor. He called her *Hopeful*. Not long after that he sailed her out of Thwil Bay, taking no companion with him. "Look for me at the end of summer," he said to Ember.

"I'll be in the Grove," she said. "And my heart with you, my dark otter, my white tern, my love, Medra."

"And mine with you, my ember of fire, my flowering tree, my love, Elehal."

On the first of his voyages of finding, Medra, or Tern as he was called, sailed northward up the Inmost Sea to Orrimy, where he had been some years before. There were people of the Hand there whom he trusted. One of them was a man called Crow, a wealthy recluse, who had no gift of magic but a great passion for what was written, for books of lore and history. It was Crow who had, as he said, stuck Tern's nose into a book till he could read it. "Illiterate wizards are the curse of Earthsea!" he cried. "Ignorant power is a bane!" Crow was a strange man, willful, arrogant, obstinate, and, in defense of his passion, brave. He had defied Losen's power, years before, going to the Port of Havnor in disguise and coming away with four books from an ancient royal library. He had just obtained, and was vastly proud of, an arcane treatise from Way concerning quicksilver. "Got that from under Losen's nose too," he said to Tern. "Come have a look at it! It belonged to a famous wizard."

"Tinaral," said Tern. "I knew him."

"Book's trash, is it?" said Crow, who was quick to pick up signals if they had to do with books.

"I don't know. I'm after bigger prey."

Crow cocked his head.

"The Book of Names."

"Lost with Ath when he went into the west," Crow said.

"A mage called Highdrake told me that when Ath stayed in Pendor, he told a wizard there that he'd left the Book of Names with a woman in the Ninety Isles for safekeeping."

"A woman! For safekeeping! In the Ninety Isles! Was he mad?"

Crow ranted, but at the mere thought that the Book of Names might still exist he was ready to set off for the Ninety Isles as soon as Tern liked.

So they sailed south in *Hopeful*, landing first at malodorous Geath, and then in the guise of peddlers working their way from one islet to the next among the mazy channels. Crow had stocked the boat with better wares than most householders of the Isles were used to seeing, and Tern offered them at fair prices, mostly in barter, since there was little money among the islanders. Their popularity ran ahead of them. It was known that they would trade for books, if the books were old and uncanny. But in the Isles all books were old and all uncanny, what there was of them.

Crow was delighted to get a water-stained bestiary from the time of Akambar in return for five silver buttons, a pearl-hilted knife, and a square of Lorbanery silk. He sat in *Hopeful* and crooned over the antique descriptions of harikki and otak and icebear. But Tern went ashore on every isle, showing his wares in the kitchens of the housewives and the sleepy taverns where the old men sat. Sometimes he idly made a fist and then turned his hand over opening the palm, but nobody here returned the sign.

"Books?" said a rush plaiter on North Sudidi. "Like that there?" He pointed to long strips of vellum that had been worked into the thatching of his house. "They good for something else?" Crow, staring up at the words visible here and there between the rushes in the eaves, began to tremble with rage. Tern hurried him back to the boat before he exploded.

"It was only a beast healer's manual," Crow admitted, when they were sailing on and he had calmed down. " 'Spavined,' I saw, and something about ewes' udders. But the ignorance! the brute ignorance! To roof his house with it!"

"And it was useful knowledge," Tern said. "How can people be anything but ignorant when knowledge isn't saved, isn't taught? If books could be brought together in one place . . ."

"Like the Library of the Kings," said Crow, dreaming of lost glories.

"Or your library," said Tern, who had become a subtler man than he used to be.

"Fragments," Crow said, dismissing his life's work. "Remnants!"

"Beginnings," said Tern.

Crow only sighed.

"I think we might go south again," Tern said, steering for the open channel. "Toward Pody."

"You have a gift for the business," Crow said. "You know where to look. Went straight to that bestiary in the barn loft . . . But there's nothing much to look for here. Nothing of importance. Ath wouldn't have left the greatest of all the lore-books among boors who'd make thatch of it! Take us to Pody if you like. And then back to Orrimy. I've had about enough."

"And we're out of buttons," Tern said. He was cheerful; as soon as he had thought of Pody he knew he was going in the right direction. "Perhaps I can find some along the way," he said. "It's my gift, you know."

Neither of them had been on Pody. It was a sleepy southern island with a pretty old port town, Telio, built of rosy sandstone, and fields and orchards that should have been fertile. But the lords of Wathort had ruled it for a century, taxing and slave taking and wearing the land and people down. The sunny streets of Telio were sad and dirty. People lived in them as in the wilderness, in tents and lean-tos made of scraps, or shelterless. "Oh, this won't do," Crow said, disgusted, avoiding a pile of human excrement. "These creatures don't have books, Tern!"

"Wait, wait," his companion said. "Give me a day."

"It's dangerous," Crow said, "it's pointless," but he made no further objection. The modest, naive young man whom he had taught to read had become his unfathomable guide.

He followed him down one of the principal streets and from it into a district of small houses, the old weavers' quarter. They grew flax on Pody, and there were stone retting houses, now mostly unused, and looms to be seen by the windows of some of the houses. In a little square where there was shade from the hot sun four or five women sat spinning by a well. Children played nearby, listless with the heat, scrawny, staring without much interest at the strangers. Tern had walked there unhesitating, as if he knew where he was going. Now he stopped and greeted the women.

"Oh, pretty man," said one of them with a smile, "don't even show us what you have in your pack there, for I haven't a penny of copper or ivory, nor seen one for a month."

"You might have a bit of linen, though, mistress? woven, or thread?

Linen of Pody is the best—so I've heard as far as Havnor. And I can tell the quality of what you're spinning. A beautiful thread it is." Crow watched his companion with amusement and some disdain; he himself could bargain for a book very shrewdly, but nattering with common women about buttons and thread was beneath him. "Let me just open this up," Tern was saying as he spread his pack out on the cobbles, and the women and the dirty, timid children drew closer to see the wonders he would show them. "Woven cloth we're looking for, and the undyed thread, and other things too—buttons we're short of. If you had any of horn or bone, maybe? I'd trade one of these little velvet caps here for three or four buttons. Or one of these rolls of ribbon; look at the color of it. Beautiful with your hair, mistress! Or paper, or books. Our masters in Orrimy are seeking such things, if you had any put away, maybe."

"Oh, you are a pretty man," said the woman who had spoken first, laughing, as he held the red ribbon up to her black braid. "And I wish I had something for you!"

"I won't be so bold as to ask for a kiss," said Medra, "but an open hand, maybe?"

He made the sign; she looked at him for a moment. "That's easy," she said softly, and made the sign in return, "but not always safe, among strangers."

He went on showing his wares and joking with the women and children. Nobody bought anything. They gazed at the trinkets as if they were treasures. He let them gaze and finger all they would; indeed he let one of the children filch a little mirror of polished brass, seeing it vanish under the ragged shirt and saying nothing. At last he said he must go on, and the children drifted away as he folded up his pack.

"I have a neighbor," said the black-braided woman, "who might have some paper, if you're after that."

"Written on?" said Crow, who had been sitting on the well coping, bored. "Marks on it?"

She looked him up and down. "Marks on it, sir," she said. And then, to Tern, in a different tone, "If you'd like to come with me, she lives this way. And though she's only a girl, and poor, I'll tell you, peddler, she has an open hand. Though perhaps not all of us do."

"Three out of three," said Crow, sketching the sign, "so spare your vinegar, woman."

"Oh, it's you who have it to spare, sir. We're poor folk here. And ignorant," she said, with a flash of her eyes, and led on.

She brought them to a house at the end of a lane. It had been a handsome place once, two stories built of stone, but was half empty, defaced,

window frames and facing stones pulled out of it. They crossed a courtyard with a well in it. She knocked at a side door, and a girl opened it.

"Ach, it's a witch's den," Crow said, at the whiff of herbs and aromatic smoke, and he stepped back.

"Healers," their guide said. "Is she ill again, Dory?"

The girl nodded, looking at Tern, then at Crow. She was thirteen or
fourteen, heavyset though thin, with a sullen, steady gaze.

"They're men of the Hand, Dory, one short and pretty and one tall
and proud, and they say they're seeking papers. I know you had some
once, though you may not now. They've nothing you need in their pack,
but it might be they'd pay a bit of ivory for what they want. Is it so?" She
turned her bright eyes on Tern, and he nodded.

"She's very sick, Rush," the girl said. She looked again at Tern.
"You're not a healer?" It was an accusation.

"No."

"She is," said Rush. "Like her mother and her mother's mother. Let
us in, Dory, or me at least, to speak to her." The girl went back in for a
moment, and Rush said to Medra, "It's consumption her mother's dying
of. No healer could cure her. But she could heal the scrofula, and touch
for pain. A wonder she was, and Dory bade fair to follow her."

The girl motioned them to come in. Crow chose to wait outside. The
room was high and long, with traces of former elegance, but very old and
very poor. Healers' paraphernalia and drying herbs were everywhere,
though ranged in some order. Near the fine stone fireplace, where a tiny
wisp of sweet herbs burned, was a bedstead. The woman in it was so
wasted that in the dim light she seemed nothing but bone and shadow. As
Tern came close she tried to sit up and to speak. Her daughter raised her
head on the pillow, and when Tern was very near he could hear her:
"Wizard," she said. "Not by chance."

A woman of power, she knew what he was. Had she called him
there?

"I'm a finder," he said. "And a seeker."

"Can you teach her?"

"I can take her to those who can."

"Do it."

"I will."

She laid her head back and closed her eyes.

Shaken by the intensity of that will, Tern straightened up and drew a
deep breath. He looked round at the girl, Dory. She did not return his
gaze, watching her mother with stolid, sullen grief. Only after the
woman sank into sleep did Dory move, going to help Rush, who as a

friend and neighbor had made herself useful and was gathering up blood-soaked cloths scattered by the bed.

"She bled again just now, and I couldn't stop it," Dory said. Tears ran out of her eyes and down her cheeks. Her face hardly changed.

"Oh child, oh lamb," said Rush, taking her into her embrace; but though she hugged Rush, Dory did not bend.

"She's going there, to the wall, and I can't go with her," she said. "She's going alone and I can't go with her—Can't you go there?" She broke away from Rush, looking again at Tern. "You can go there!"

"No," he said. "I don't know the way."

Yet as Dory spoke he saw what the girl saw: a long hill going down into darkness, and across it, on the edge of twilight, a low wall of stones. And as he looked he thought he saw a woman walking along beside the wall, very thin, insubstantial, bone, shadow. But she was not the dying woman in the bed. She was Anieb.

Then that was gone and he stood facing the witch-girl. Her look of accusation slowly changed. She put her face in her hands.

"We have to let them go," he said.

She said, "I know."

Rush glanced from one to the other with her keen, bright eyes. "Not only a handy man," she said, "but a crafty man. Well, you're not the first."

He looked his question.

"This is called Ath's House," she said.

"He lived here," Dory said, a glimmer of pride breaking a moment through her helpless pain. "The Mage Ath. Long ago. Before he went into the west. All my foremothers were wise women. He stayed here. With them."

"Give me a basin," Rush said. "I'll get water to soak these."

"I'll get the water," Tern said. He took the basin and went out to the courtyard, to the well. Just as before, Crow was sitting on the coping, bored and restless.

"Why are we wasting time here?" he demanded, as Tern let the bucket down into the well. "Are you fetching and carrying for witches now?"

"Yes," Tern said, "and I will till she dies. And then I'll take her daughter to Roke. And if you want to read the Book of Names, you can come with us."

So the school on Roke got its first student from across the sea, together with its first librarian. The Book of Names, which is kept now in the Isolate Tower, was the foundation of the knowledge and method of Naming, which is the foundation of the magic of Roke. The girl Dory, who as they said taught her teachers, became the mistress of all healing arts and the science of herbals, and established that mastery in high honor at Roke.

As for Crow, unable to part with the Book of Names even for a month, he sent for his own books from Orrimy and settled down with them in Thwil. He allowed people of the school to study them, so long as they showed them, and him, due respect.

So the pattern of the years was set for Tern. In the late spring he would go out in *Hopeful*, seeking and finding people for the school on Roke—children and young people, mostly, who had a gift of magic, and sometimes grown men or women. Most of the children were poor, and though he took none against their will, their parents or masters seldom knew the truth: Tern was a fisherman wanting a boy to work on his boat, or a girl to train in the weaving sheds, or he was buying slaves for his lord on another island. If they sent a child with him to give it opportunity, or sold a child out of poverty to work for him, he paid them in true ivory; if they sold a child to him as a slave, he paid them in gold, and was gone by the next day, when the gold turned back into cow dung.

He traveled far in the Archipelago, even out into the East Reach. He never went to the same town or island twice without years between, letting his trail grow cold. Even so he began to be spoken of. The Child Taker, they called him, a dreaded sorcerer who carried children to his island in the icy north and there sucked their blood. In villages on Way and Felkway they still tell children about the Child Taker, as an encouragement to distrust strangers.

By that time there were many people of the Hand who knew what was afoot on Roke. Young people came there sent by them. Men and women came to be taught and to teach. Many of these had a hard time getting there, for the spells that hid the island were stronger than ever, making it seem only a cloud, or a reef among the breakers; and the Roke wind blew, which kept any ship from Thwil Bay unless there was a sorcerer aboard who knew how to turn that wind. Still they came, and as the years went on a larger house was needed for the school than any in Thwil Town.

In the Archipelago, men built ships and women built houses, that was the custom; but in building a great structure women let men work with them, not having the miners' superstitions that kept men out of the mines, or the shipwrights' that forbade women to watch a keel laid. So both men and women of great power raised the Great House on Roke. Its cornerstone was set on a hilltop above Thwil Town, near the Grove and looking to the Knoll. Its walls were built not only of stone and wood, but founded deep on magic and made strong with spells.

Standing on that hill, Medra had said, "There is a vein of water, just under where I stand, that will not go dry." They dug down carefully and came to the water; they let it leap up into the sunlight; and the first part of the Great House they made was its inmost heart, the courtyard of the fountain.

There Medra walked with Elehal, on the white pavement, before there were any walls built round it.

She had planted a young rowan from the Grove beside the fountain. They came to be sure it was thriving. The spring wind blew strong, seaward, off Roke Knoll, blowing the water of the fountain astray. Up on the slope of the Knoll they could see a little group of people: a circle of young students learning how to do tricks of illusion from the sorcerer Hega of O; Master Hand, they called him. The sparkweed, past flowering, cast its ashes on the wind. There were streaks of gray in Ember's hair.

"Off you go, then," she said, "and leave us to settle this matter of the Rule." Her frown was as fierce as ever, but her voice was seldom as harsh as this when she spoke to him.

"I'll stay if you want, Elehal."

"I do want you to stay. But don't stay! You're a finder, you have to go find. It's only that agreeing on the Way—or the Rule, Waris wants us to call it—is twice the work of building the House. And causes ten times the quarrels. I wish I could get away from it! I wish I could just walk with you, like this . . . And I wish you wouldn't go north."

"Why do we quarrel?" he said rather despondently.

"Because there are more of us! Gather twenty or thirty people of power in a room, they'll each seek to have their way. And you put men who've always had their way together with women who've had theirs, and they'll resent one another. And then, too, there are some true and real divisions among us, Medra. They must be settled, and they can't be settled easily. Though a little goodwill would go a long way."

"Is it Waris?"

"Waris and several other men. And they *are* men, and they make that important beyond anything else. To them, the Old Powers are abominable. And women's powers are suspect, because they suppose them all connected with the Old Powers. As if those Powers were to be controlled or used by any mortal soul! But they put men where we put the world. And so they hold that a true wizard must be a man. And celibate."

"Ah, that," Medra said, rueful.

"That indeed. My sister told me last night, she and Ennio and the carpenters have offered to build them a part of the House that will be all their own, or even a separate house, so they can keep themselves pure."

"Pure?"

"It's not my word, it's Waris's. But they've refused. They want the Rule of Roke to separate men from women, and they want men to make the decisions for all. Now what compromise can we make with them? Why did they come here, if they won't work with us?"

"We should send away the men who won't."

"Away? In anger? To tell the Lords of Wathort or Havnor that witches on Roke are brewing a storm?"

"I forget—I always forget," he said, downcast again. "I forget the walls of the prison. I'm not such a fool when I'm outside them . . . When I'm here I can't believe it is a prison. But outside, without you, I remember . . . I don't want to go, but I have to go. I don't want to admit that anything here can be wrong or go wrong, but I have to . . . I'll go this time, and I will go north, Elehal. But when I come back I'll stay. What I need to find I'll find here. Haven't I found it already?"

"No," she said, "only me . . . But there's a great deal of seeking and finding to be done in the Grove. Enough to keep even you from being restless. Why north?"

"To reach out the Hand to Enlad and Éa. I've never gone there. We know nothing about their wizardries. *Enlad of the Kings, and bright Éa, eldest of isles!* Surely we'll find allies there."

"But Havnor lies between us," she said.

"I won't sail my boat across Havnor, dear love. I plan to go around it. By water." He could always make her laugh; he was the only one who could. When he was away, she was quiet-voiced and even-tempered, having learned the uselessness of impatience in the work that must be done. Sometimes she still scowled, sometimes she smiled, but she did not laugh. When she could, she went to the Grove alone, as she had always done. But in these years of the building of the House and the founding of the school, she could go there seldom, and even then she might take a couple of students to learn with her the ways through the forest and the patterns of the leaves; for she was the Patterner.

Tern left late that year on his journey. He had with him a boy of fifteen, Mote, a promising weatherworker who needed training at sea, and Sava, a woman of sixty who had come to Roke with him seven or eight years before. Sava had been one of the women of the Hand on the isle of Ark. Though she had no wizardly gifts at all, she knew so well how to get a group of people to trust one another and work together that she was honored as a wise woman on Ark, and now on Roke. She had asked

Tern to take her to see her family, mother and sister and two sons; he would leave Mote with her and bring them back to Roke when he returned. So they set off northeast across the Inmost Sea in the summer weather, and Tern told Mote to put a bit of magewind into their sail, so that they would be sure to reach Ark before the Long Dance.

As they coasted that island, he himself put an illusion about *Hopeful*, so that she would seem not a boat but a drifting log; for pirates and Losen's slave takers were thick in these waters.

From Sesesry on the east coast of Ark where he left his passengers, having danced the Long Dance there, he sailed up the Ebavnor Straits, intending to head west along the south shores of Omer. He kept the illusion spell about his boat. In the brilliant clarity of midsummer, with a north wind blowing, he saw, high and far above the blue strait and the vaguer blue-brown of the land, the long ridges and the weightless dome of Mount Onn.

Look, Medra. Look!

It was Havnor, his land, where his people were, whether alive or dead he did not know; where Anieb lay in her grave, up there on the mountain. He had never been back, never come this close. It had been how long? Sixteen years, seventeen years. Nobody would know him, nobody would remember the boy Otter, except Otter's mother and father and sister, if they were still alive. And surely there were people of the Hand in the Great Port. Though he had not known of them as a boy, he should know them now.

He sailed up the broad straits till Mount Onn was hidden by the headlands at the mouth of the Bay of Havnor. He would not see it again unless he went through that narrow passage. Then he would see the mountain, all the sweep and cresting of it, over the calm waters where he used to try to raise up the magewind when he was twelve; and sailing on he would see the towers rise up from the water, dim at first, mere dots and lines, then lifting up their bright banners, the white city at the center of the world.

It was mere cowardice to keep from Havnor, now—fear for his skin, fear lest he find his people had died, fear lest he recall Anieb too vividly.

For there had been times when he felt that, as he had summoned her living, so dead she might summon him. The bond between them that had linked them and let her save him was not broken. Many times she had come into his dreams, standing silent as she stood when he first saw her in the reeking tower at Samory. And he had seen her, years ago, in the vision of the dying healer in Telio, in the twilight, beside the wall of stones.

He knew now, from Elehal and others on Roke, what that wall was.

It lay between the living and the dead. And in that vision, Anieb had walked on this side of it, not on the side that went down into the dark.

Did he fear her, who had freed him?

He tacked across the strong wind, swung round South Point, and sailed into the Great Bay of Havnor.

Banners still flew from the towers of the City of Havnor, and a king still ruled there; the banners were those of captured towns and isles, and the king was the warlord Losen. Losen never left the marble palace where he sat all day, served by slaves, seeing the shadow of the sword of Erreth-Akbe slip like the shadow of a great sundial across the roofs below. He gave orders, and the slaves said, "It is done, your majesty." He held audiences, and old men came and said, "We obey, your majesty." He summoned his wizards, and the mage Early came, bowing low. "Make me walk!" Losen shouted, beating his paralyzed legs with his weak hands.

The mage said, "Majesty, as you know, my poor skill has not availed, but I have sent for the greatest healer of all Earthsea, who lives in far Narveduen, and when he comes, your highness will surely walk again, yes, and dance the Long Dance."

Then Losen cursed and cried, and his slaves brought him wine, and the mage went out, bowing, and checking as he went to be sure that the spell of paralysis was holding.

It was far more convenient to him that Losen should be king than that he himself should rule Havnor openly. Men of arms didn't trust men of craft and didn't like to serve them. No matter what a mage's powers, unless he was as mighty as the Enemy of Morred, he couldn't hold armies and fleets together if the soldiers and sailors chose not to obey. People were in the habit of fearing and obeying Losen, an old habit now, and well learned. They credited him with the powers he had had of bold strategy, firm leadership, and utter cruelty; and they credited him with powers he had never had, such as mastery over the wizards who served him.

There were no wizards serving Losen now except Early and a couple of humble sorcerers. Early had driven off or killed, one after another, his rivals for Losen's favor, and had enjoyed sole rule over all Havnor now for years.

When he was Gelluk's prentice and assistant, he had encouraged his master in the study of the lore of Way, finding himself free while Gelluk was off doting on his quicksilver. But Gelluk's abrupt fate had shaken him. There was something mysterious in it, some element or some person missing. Summoning the useful Hound to help him, Early had made a very thorough inquiry into what happened. Where Gelluk was, of course, was no mystery. Hound had tracked him straight to a scar in a hillside, and said he was buried deep under there. Early had no wish to exhume him. But the boy who had been with him, Hound could not track: could not say whether he was under that hill with Gelluk, or had got clean away. He had left no spell traces as the mage did, said Hound, and it had rained very hard all the night after, and when Hound thought he had found the boy's tracks, they were a woman's; and she was dead.

Early did not punish Hound for his failure, but he remembered it. He was not used to failures and did not like them. He did not like what Hound told him about this boy, Otter, and he remembered it.

The desire for power feeds off itself, growing as it devours. Early suffered from hunger. He starved. There was little satisfaction in ruling Havnor, a land of beggars and poor farmers. What was the good of possessing the Throne of Maharion if nobody sat in it but a drunken cripple? What glory was there in the palaces of the city when nobody lived in them but crawling slaves? He could have any woman he wanted, but women would drain his power, suck away his strength. He wanted no woman near him. He craved an enemy: an opponent worth destroying.

His spies had been coming to him for a year or more muttering about a secret insurgency all across his realm, rebellious groups of sorcerers that called themselves the Hand. Eager to find his enemy, he had one such group investigated. They turned out to be a lot of old women, midwives, carpenters, a ditchdigger, a tinsmith's prentice, a couple of little boys. Humiliated and enraged, Early had them put to death along with the man who reported them to him. It was a public execution, in Losen's name, for the crime of conspiracy against the King. There had perhaps not been enough of that kind of intimidation lately. But it went against his grain. He didn't like to make a public spectacle of fools who had tricked him into fearing them. He would rather have dealt with them in his own way, in his own time. To be nourishing, fear must be immediate; he needed to see people afraid of him, hear their terror, smell it, taste it. But since he ruled in Losen's name, it was Losen who must be feared by the armies and the peoples, and he himself must keep in the background, making do with slaves and prentices.

Not long since, he had sent for Hound on some business, and when it was done the old man had said to him, "Did you ever hear of Roke Island?"

"South and west of Kamery. The Lord of Wathort's owned it for forty or fifty years."

Though he seldom left the city, Early prided himself on his knowledge of all the Archipelago, gleaned from his sailors' reports and the marvelous ancient charts kept in the palace. He studied them nights, brooding on where and how he might extend his empire.

Hound nodded, as if its location was all that had interested him in Roke.

"Well?"

"One of the old women you had tortured before they burned the lot, you know? Well, the fellow who did it told me. She talked about her son on Roke. Calling out to him to come, you know. But like as if he had the power to."

"Well?"

"Seemed odd. Old woman from a village inland, never seen the sea, calling the name of an island away off like that."

"The son was a fisherman who talked about his travels."

Early waved his hand. Hound sniffed, nodded, and left.

Early never disregarded any triviality Hound mentioned, because so many of them had proved not to be trivial. He disliked the old man for that, and because he was unshakable. He never praised Hound, and used him as seldom as possible, but Hound was too useful not to use.

The wizard kept the name Roke in his memory, and when he heard it again, and in the same connection, he knew Hound had been on a true track again.

Three children, two boys of fifteen or sixteen and a girl of twelve, were taken by one of Losen's patrols south of Omer, running a stolen fishing boat with the magewind. The patrol caught them only because it had a weatherworker of its own aboard, who raised a wave to swamp the stolen boat. Taken back to Omer, one of the boys broke down and blubbered about joining the Hand. Hearing that word, the men told them they would be tortured and burned, at which the boy cried that if they spared him he would tell them all about the Hand, and Roke, and the great mages of Roke.

"Bring them here," Early said to the messenger.

"The girl flew away, lord," the man said unwillingly.

"Flew away?"

"She took bird form. Osprey, they said. Didn't expect that from a girl so young. Gone before they knew it."

"Bring the boys, then," Early said with deadly patience.

They brought him one boy. The other had jumped from the ship, crossing Havnor Bay, and been killed by a crossbow quarrel. The boy they brought was in such a paroxysm of terror that even Early was disgusted by him. How could he frighten a creature already blind and beshatten with fear? He set a binding spell on the boy that held him upright and immobile as a stone statue, and left him so for a night and a day. Now and then he talked to the statue, telling it that it was a clever lad and might make a good prentice, here in the palace. Maybe he could go to Roke after all, for Early was thinking of going to Roke, to meet with the mages there.

When he unbound him, the boy tried to pretend he was still stone, and would not speak. Early had to go into his mind, in the way he had learned from Gelluk long ago, when Gelluk was a true master of his art. He found out what he could. Then the boy was no good for anything and had to be disposed of. It was humiliating, again, to be outwitted by the very stupidity of these people; and all he had learned about Roke was that the Hand was there, and a school where they taught wizardry. And he had learned a man's name.

The idea of a school for wizards made him laugh. A school for wild boars, he thought, a college for dragons! But that there was some kind of scheming and gathering together of men of power on Roke seemed probable, and the idea of any league or alliance of wizards appalled him more the more he thought of it. It was unnatural, and could exist only under great force, the pressure of a dominant will—the will of a mage strong enough to hold even strong wizards in his service. There was the enemy he wanted!

Hound was down at the door, they said. Early sent for him to come up. "Who's Tern?" he asked as soon as he saw the old man.

With age Hound had come to look his name, wrinkled, with a long nose and sad eyes. He sniffed and seemed about to say he did not know, but he knew better than to try to lie to Early. He sighed. "Otter," he said. "Him that killed old Whiteface."

"Where's he hiding?"

"Not hiding at all. Went about the city, talking to people. Went to see his mother in Endlane, round the mountain. He's there now."

"You should have told me at once," Early said.

"Didn't know you were after him. I've been after him a long time. He fooled me." Hound spoke without rancor.

"He tricked and killed a great mage, my master. He's dangerous. I want vengeance. Who did he talk to here? I want them. Then I'll see to him."

"Some old women down by the docks. An old sorcerer. His sister."

"Get them here. Take my men."

Hound sniffed, sighed, nodded.

There was not much to be got from the people his men brought to him. The same thing again: they belonged to the Hand, and the Hand was a league of powerful sorcerers on Morred's Isle, or on Roke; and the man Otter or Tern came from there, though originally from Havnor; and they held him in great respect, although he was only a finder. The sister had vanished, perhaps gone with Otter to Endlane, where the mother lived. Early rummaged in their cloudy, witless minds, had the youngest of them tortured, and then burned them where Losen could sit at his window and watch. The King needed some diversions.

All this took only two days, and all the time Early was looking and probing toward Endlane village, sending Hound there before him, sending his own presentment there to watch. When he knew where the man was he betook himself there very quickly, on eagle's wings; for Early was a great shape-changer, so fearless that he would take even dragon form.

He knew it was well to use caution with this man. Otter had defeated Tinaral, and there was this matter of Roke. There was some strength in him or with him. Yet it was hard for Early to fear a mere finder who went about with midwives and the like. He could not bring himself to sneak and skulk. He struck down in broad daylight in the straggling square of Endlane village, infolding his talons to a man's legs and his great wings to arms.

A child ran bawling to its mammy. No one else was about. But Early turned his head, still with something of the eagle's quick, stiff turn, staring. Wizard knows wizard, and he knew which house his prey was in. He walked to it and flung the door open.

A slight, brown man sitting at the table looked up at him.

Early raised his hand to lay the binding spell on him. His hand was stayed, held immobile half lifted at his side.

This was a contest, then, a foe worth fighting! Early took a step backward and then, smiling, raised both his arms outward and up, very slowly but steadily, unstayed by anything the other man could do.

The house vanished. No walls, no roof, nobody. Early stood on the dust of the village square in the sunshine of morning with his arms in the air.

It was only illusion, of course, but it checked him a moment in his spell, and then he had to undo the illusion, bringing back the door frame around him, the walls and roof beams, the gleam of light on crockery, the hearth stones, the table. But nobody sat at the table. His enemy was gone.

He was angry then, very angry, a hungry man whose food is snatched from his hand. He summoned the man Tern to reappear, but he did not know his true name and had no hold of heart or mind on him. The summons went unanswered.

He strode from the house, turned, and set a fire spell on it so that it burst into flames, thatch and walls and every window spouting fire. Women ran out of it screaming. They had been hiding no doubt in the back room; he paid them no attention. "Hound," he thought. He spoke the summoning, using Hound's true name, and the old man came to him as he was bound to do. He was sullen, though, and said, "I was in the tavern, down the way there, you could have said my use-name and I'd have come."

Early looked at him once. Hound's mouth snapped shut and stayed shut.

"Speak when I let you," the wizard said. "Where is the man?"

Hound nodded northeastward.

"What's there?"

Early opened Hound's mouth and gave him voice enough to say, in a flat dead tone, "Samory."

"What form is he in?"

"Otter," said the flat voice.

Early laughed. "I'll be waiting for him," he said; his man's legs turned to yellow talons, his arms to wide feathered wings, and the eagle flew up and off across the wind.

Hound sniffed, sighed, and followed, trudging along unwillingly, while behind him in the village the flames died down, and children cried, and women shouted curses after the eagle.

The danger in trying to do good is that the mind comes to confuse the intent of goodness with the act of doing things well.

That is not what the otter was thinking as it swam fast down the Yennava. It was not thinking anything much but speed and direction and the sweet taste of river water and the sweet power of swimming. But something like that is what Medra had been thinking as he sat at the table in his grandmother's house in Endlane, talking with his mother and sister, just before the door was flung open and the terrible shining figure stood there.

Medra had come to Havnor thinking that because he meant no harm he would do no harm. He had done irreparable harm. Men and women and children had died because he was there. They had died in torment, burned alive. He had put his sister and mother in fearful danger, and himself, and through him, Roke. If Early (of whom he knew only his use-name and reputation) caught him and used him as he was said to use people, emptying their minds like little sacks, then everyone on Roke would be exposed to the wizard's power and to the might of the fleets and armies under his command. Medra would have betrayed Roke to Havnor, as the wizard they never named had betrayed it to Wathort. Maybe that man, too, had thought he could do no harm.

Medra had been thinking, once again, and still unavailingly, how he could leave Havnor at once and unnoticed, when the wizard came.

Now, as otter, he was thinking only that he would like to stay otter, be otter, in the sweet brown water, the living river, forever. There is no death for an otter, only life to the end. But in the sleek creature was the mortal mind; and where the stream passes the hill west of Samory, the otter came up on the muddy bank, and then the man crouched there, shivering.

Where to now? Why had he come here?

He had not thought. He had taken the shape that came soonest to him, run to the river as an otter would, swum as the otter would swim. But only in his own form could he think as a man, hide, decide, act as a man or as a wizard against the wizard who hunted him.

He knew he was no match for Early. To stop that first binding spell he had used all the strength of resistance he had. The illusion and the shape-change were all the tricks he had to play. If he faced the wizard again he would be destroyed. And Roke with him. Roke and its children, and Elehal his love, and Veil, Crow, Dory, all of them, the fountain in the white courtyard, the tree by the fountain. Only the Grove would stand. Only the green hill, silent, immovable. He heard Elehal say to him, *Havnor lies between us.* He heard her say, *All the true powers, all the old powers, at root are one.*

He looked up. The hillside above the stream was that same hill where he had come that day with Tinaral, Anieb's presence within him. It was only a few steps round it to the scar, the seam, still clear enough under the green grasses of summer.

"Mother," he said, on his knees there, "Mother, open to me."

He laid his hands on the seam of earth, but there was no power in them.

"Let me in, mother," he whispered in the tongue that was as old as the hill. The ground shivered a little and opened.

He heard an eagle scream. He got to his feet. He leaped into the dark.

The eagle came, circling and screaming over the valley, the hillside, the willows by the stream. It circled, searching and searching, and flew back as it had come.

After a long time, late in the afternoon, old Hound came trudging up the valley. He stopped now and then and sniffed. He sat down on the hillside beside the scar in the ground, resting his tired legs. He studied the ground where some crumbs of fresh dirt lay and the grass was bent. He stroked the bent grass to straighten it. He got to his feet at last, went for a drink of the clear brown water under the willows, and set off down the valley toward the mine.

* * *

Medra woke in pain, in darkness. For a long time that was all there was. The pain came and went, the darkness remained. Once it lightened a little into a twilight in which he could dimly see. He saw a slope running down from where he lay toward a wall of stones, across which was darkness again. But he could not get up to walk to the wall, and presently the pain came back very sharp in his arm and hip and head. Then the darkness came around him, and then nothing.

Thirst: and with it pain. Thirst, and the sound of water running.

He tried to remember how to make light. Anieb said to him, plaintively, "Can't you make the light?" But he could not. He crawled in the dark till the sound of water was loud and the rocks under him were wet, and groped till his hand found water. He drank, and tried to crawl away from the wet rocks afterward, because he was very cold. One arm hurt and had no strength in it. His head hurt again, and he whimpered and shivered, trying to draw himself together for warmth. There was no warmth and no light.

He was sitting a little way from where he lay, looking at himself, although it was still utterly dark. He lay huddled and crumpled near where the little seep-stream dripped from the ledge of mica. Not far away lay another huddled heap, rotted red silk, long hair, bones. Beyond it the cavern stretched away. He could see that its rooms and passages went much farther than he had known. He saw it with the same uncaring interest with which he saw Tinaral's body and his own body. He felt a mild regret. It was only fair that he should die here with the man he had killed. It was right. Nothing was wrong. But something in him ached, not the sharp body pain, a long ache, lifelong.

"Anieb," he said.

Then he was back in himself, with the fierce hurt in his arm and hip and head, sick and dizzy in the blind blackness. When he moved, he whimpered; but he sat up. I have to live, he thought. I have to remember how to live. How to make light. I have to remember. I have to remember the shadows of the leaves.

How far does the forest go?

As far as the mind goes.

He looked up into the darkness. After a while he moved his good hand a little, and the faint light flowed out of it.

The roof of the cavern was far above him. The trickle of water dripping from the mica ledge glittered in short dashes in the werelight.

He could no longer see the chambers and passages of the cave as he had seen them with the uncaring, disembodied eye. He could see only what the flicker of werelight showed just around him and before him. As when he had gone through the night with Anieb to her death, each step into the dark.

He got to his knees, and thought then to whisper, "Thank you, mother." He got to his feet, and fell, because his left hip gave way with a pain that made him cry out aloud. After a while he tried again, and stood up. Then he started forward.

It took him a long time to cross the cavern. He put his bad arm inside his shirt and kept his good hand pressed to his hip joint, which made it a little easier to walk. The walls narrowed gradually to a passage. Here the roof was much lower, just above his head. Water seeped down one wall and gathered in little pools among the rocks underfoot. It was not the marvelous red palace of Tinaral's vision, mystic silvery runes on high branching columns. It was only the earth, only dirt, rock, water. The air was cool and still. Away from the dripping of the stream it was silent. Outside the gleam of werelight it was dark.

Medra bowed his head, standing there. "Anieb," he said, "can you come back this far? I don't know the way." He waited a while. He saw darkness, heard silence. Slow and halting, he entered the passage.

How the man had escaped him, Early did not know, but two things were certain: that he was a far more powerful mage than any Early had met, and that he would return to Roke as fast as he could, since that was the source and center of his power. There was no use trying to get there before him; he had the lead. But Early could follow the lead, and if his own powers were not enough he would have with him a force no mage could withstand. Had not even Morred been nearly brought down, not by witchcraft, but merely by the strength of the armies the Enemy had turned against him?

"Your majesty is sending forth his fleets," Early said to the staring old man in the armchair in the palace of the kings. "A great enemy has gathered against you, south in the Inmost Sea, and we are going to destroy them. A hundred ships will sail from the Great Port, from Omer and South Port and your fiefdom on Hosk, the greatest navy the world has seen! I shall lead them. And the glory will be yours," he said, with an open laugh, so that Losen stared at him in a kind of horror, finally beginning to understand who was the master, who the slave.

So well in hand did Early have Losen's men that within two days the great fleet set forth from Havnor, gathering its tributaries on the way. Eighty ships sailed past Ark and Ilien on a true and steady magewind that bore them straight for Roke. Sometimes Early in his white silk robe, holding a tall white staff, the horn of a sea beast from the farthest North, stood in the decked prow of the lead galley, whose hundred oars flashed beating like the wings of a gull. Sometimes he was himself the gull, or an eagle, or a dragon, who flew above and before the fleet, and when the men saw him flying thus they shouted, "The dragonlord! the dragonlord!"

They came ashore in Ilien for water and food. Setting a host of many hundreds of men on its way so quickly had left little time for provisioning the ships. They overran the towns along the west shore of Ilien, taking what they wanted, and did the same on Vissti and Kamery, looting what they could and burning what they left. Then the great fleet turned west, heading for the one harbor of Roke Island, the Bay of Thwil. Early knew of the harbor from the maps in Havnor, and knew there was a high hill above it. As they came nearer, he took dragon form and soared up high above his ships, leading them, gazing into the west for the sight of that hill.

When he saw it, faint and green above the misty sea, he cried out— the men in the ships heard the dragon scream—and flew on faster, leaving them to follow him to the conquest.

All the rumors of Roke had said that it was spell-defended and charm-hidden, invisible to ordinary eyes. If there were any spells woven about that hill or the bay he now saw opening before it, they were gossamer to him, transparent. Nothing blurred his eyes or challenged his will as he flew over the bay, over the little town and a half-finished building on the slope above it, to the top of the high green hill. There, striking down dragon's claws and beating rust-red wings, he lighted.

He stood in his own form. He had not made the change himself. He stood alert, uncertain.

The wind blew, the long grass nodded in the wind. Summer was getting on and the grass was dry now, yellowing, no flowers in it but the little white heads of the lacefoam. A woman came walking up the hill toward him through the long grass. She followed no path, and walked easily, without haste.

He thought he had raised his hand in a spell to stop her, but he had not raised his hand, and she came on. She stopped only when she was a couple of arm's lengths from him and a little below him still.

"Tell me your name," she said, and he said, "Teriel."

"Why did you come here, Teriel?"

"To destroy you."

He stared at her, seeing a round-faced woman, middle-aged, short and strong, with gray in her hair and dark eyes under dark brows, eyes that held his, held him, brought the truth out of his mouth.

"Destroy us? Destroy this hill? The trees there?" She looked down to a grove of trees not far from the hill. "Maybe Segoy who made them could unmake them. Maybe the earth will destroy herself. Maybe she'll destroy herself through our hands, in the end. But not through yours. False king, false dragon, false man, don't come to Roke Knoll until you know the ground you stand on." She made one gesture of her hand, downward to the earth. Then she turned and went down the hill through the long grass, the way she had come.

There were other people on the hill, he saw now, many others, men and women, children, living and spirits of the dead; many, many of them. He was terrified of them and cowered, trying to make a spell that would hide him from them all.

But he made no spell. He had no magic left in him. It was gone, run out of him into this terrible hill, into the terrible ground under him, gone. He was no wizard, only a man like the others, powerless.

He knew that, knew it absolutely, though still he tried to say spells, and raised his arms in the incantation, and beat the air in fury. Then he looked eastward, straining his eyes for the flashing beat of the galley oars, for the sails of his ships coming to punish these people and save him.

All he saw was a mist on the water, all across the sea beyond the mouth of the bay. As he watched it thickened and darkened, creeping out over the slow waves.

Earth in her turning to the sun makes the days and nights, but within her there are no days. Medra walked through the night. He was very lame, and could not always keep up the werelight. When it failed he had to stop and sit down and sleep. The sleep was never death, as he thought it was. He woke, always cold, always in pain, always thirsty, and when he could make a glimmer of the light he got to his feet and went on. He never saw Anieb but he knew she was there. He followed her. Sometimes there were great rooms. Sometimes there were pools of motionless water. It was hard to break the stillness of their surface, but he drank from them. He thought he had gone down deeper and deeper for a long time, till he reached the longest of those pools, and after that the way went up again. Sometimes now Anieb followed him. He could say her name, though she did not answer. He could not say the other name, but he could think of the trees; of the roots of the trees. This was the kingdom of the roots of the trees. How far does the forest go? As far as forests go. As long as the lives, as deep as the roots of the trees. As long as leaves cast shadows. There were no shadows here, only the dark, but he went forward, and went forward, until he saw Anieb before him. He saw the flash of her eyes, the cloud of her curling hair. She looked back at him for a moment, and then turned aside and ran lightly down a long, steep slope into darkness.

Where he stood it was not wholly dark. The air moved against his face. Far ahead, dim, small, there was a light that was not werelight. He went forward. He had been crawling for a long time now, dragging the right leg, which would not bear his weight. He went forward. He smelled the wind of evening and saw the sky of evening through the branches and leaves of trees. An arched oak root formed the mouth of the cave, no bigger than a man or a badger needed to crawl through. He crawled through. He lay there under the root of the tree, seeing the light fade and a star or two come out among the leaves.

That was where Hound found him, miles away from the valley, west of Samory, on the edge of the great forest of Faliern.

"Got you," the old man said, looking down at the muddy, lax body. He added, "Too late," regretfully. He stooped to see if he could pick him up or drag him, and felt the faint warmth of life. "You're tough," he said. "Here, wake up. Come on. Otter, wake up."

He recognized Hound, though he could not sit up and could barely speak. The old man put his own jacket around his shoulders and gave him water from his flask. Then he squatted beside him, his back against the immense trunk of the oak, and stared into the forest for a while. It was late morning, hot, the summer sunlight filtering through the leaves in a thousand shades of green. A squirrel scolded, far up in the oak, and a jay replied. Hound scratched his neck and sighed.

"The wizard's off on the wrong track, as usual," he said at last. "Said you'd gone to Roke Island and he'd catch you there. I said nothing."

He looked at the man he knew only as Otter.

"You went in there, that hole, with the old wizard, didn't you? Did you find him?"

Medra nodded.

"Hmn," Hound went, a short, grunting laugh. "You find what you look for, don't you? Like me." He saw that his companion was in distress, and said, "I'll get you out of here. Fetch a carter from the village down there, when I've got my breath. Listen. Don't fret. I haven't hunted you all these years to give you to Early. The way I gave you to Gelluk. I was sorry for that. I thought about it. What I said to you about men of a craft sticking together. And who we work for. Couldn't see that I had much choice about that. But having done you a disfavor, I thought if I came across you again I'd do you a favor, if I could. As one finder to the other, see?"

Otter's breath was coming hard. Hound put his hand on Otter's hand for a moment, said, "Don't worry," and got to his feet. "Rest easy," he said.

He found a carter who would carry them down to Endlane. Otter's mother and sister were living with cousins while they rebuilt their burned house as best they could. They welcomed him with disbelieving joy. Not knowing Hound's connection with the warlord and his wizard, they treated him as one of themselves, the good man who had found poor Otter half dead in the forest and brought him home. A wise man, said Otter's mother Rose, surely a wise man. Nothing was too good for such a man.

Otter was slow to recover, to heal. The bonesetter did what he could about his broken arm and his damaged hip, the wise woman salved the cuts from the rocks on his hands and head and knees, his mother brought him all the delicacies she could find in the gardens and berry thickets; but he lay as weak and wasted as when Hound first brought him. There was no heart in him, the wise woman of Endlane said. It was somewhere else, being eaten up with worry or fear or shame.

"So where is it?" Hound said.

Otter, after a long silence, said, "Roke Island."

"Where old Early went with the great fleet. I see. Friends there. Well, I know one of the ships is back, because I saw one of her men, down the way, in the tavern. I'll go ask about. Find out if they got to Roke and what happened there. What I can tell you is that it seems old Early is late coming home. Hmn, hmn," he went, pleased with his joke. "Late coming home," he repeated, and got up. He looked at Otter, who was not much to look at. "Rest easy," he said, and went off.

He was gone several days. When he returned, riding in a horse-drawn cart, he had such a look about him that Otter's sister hurried in to tell him, "Hound's won a battle or a fortune! He's riding behind a city horse, in a city cart, like a prince!"

Hound came in on her heels. "Well," he said, "in the first place, when I got to the city, I go up to the palace, just to hear the news, and what do I see? I see old King Pirate standing on his legs, shouting out orders like he used to do. Standing up! Hasn't stood for years. Shouting orders! And some of 'em did what he said, and some of 'em didn't. So I got on out of there, that kind of a situation being dangerous, in a palace. Then I went about to friends of mine and asked where was old Early and had the fleet been to Roke and come back and all. Early, they said, nobody knew about Early. Not a sign of him nor from him. Maybe I could find him, they said, joking me, hmn. They know I love him. As for the ships, some had come back, with the men aboard saying they never came to Roke Island, never saw it, sailed right through where the sea charts said was an island, and there was no island. Then there were some men from one of the great galleys. They said when they got close to where the island should be, they came into a fog as thick as wet cloth, and the sea turned thick too, so that the oarsmen could barely push the oars through it, and they were caught in that for a day and a night. When they got out, there wasn't another ship of all the fleet on the sea, and the slaves were near rebelling, so the master brought her home as quick as he could. Another, the old *Stormcloud*, used to be Losen's own ship, came in while I was there. I talked to some men off her. They said there was nothing but fog and reefs all round where Roke was supposed to be, so they sailed on with seven other ships, south a ways, and met up with a fleet sailing up from Wathort. Maybe the lords there had heard there was a great fleet coming raiding, because they didn't stop to ask questions, but sent wizard's fire at our ships, and came alongside to board them if they could, and the men I talked to said it was a hard fight just to get away from them, and not all did. All this time they had no word from Early, and no weather was worked for them unless they had a bagman of their own aboard. So they came back up the length of the Inmost Sea, said the man from *Stormcloud*, one straggling after the other like the dogs that lost the dogfight. Now, do you like the news I bring you?"

Otter had been struggling with tears; he hid his face. "Yes," he said, "thanks."

"Thought you might. As for King Losen," Hound said, "who knows." He sniffed and sighed. "If I was him I'd retire," he said. "I think I'll do that myself."

Otter had got control of his face and voice. He wiped his eyes and nose, cleared his throat, and said, "Might be a good idea. Come to Roke. Safer."

"Seems to be a hard place to find," Hound said.

"I can find it," said Otter.

⌒ IV. Medra

There was an old man by our door
Who opened it to rich or poor;
Many came there both small and great,
But few could pass through Medra's Gate.

So runs the water away, away,
So runs the water away.

Hound stayed in Endlane. He could make a living as a finder there, and he liked the tavern, and Otter's mother's hospitality.

By the beginning of autumn, Losen was hanging by a rope round his feet from a window of the New Palace, rotting, while six warlords quarreled over his kingdom, and the ships of the great fleet chased and fought one another across the Straits and the wizard-troubled sea.

But *Hopeful*, sailed and steered by two young sorcerers from the Island of Havnor, brought Medra safe down the Inmost Sea to Roke.

Ember was on the dock to meet him. Lame and very thin, he came to her and took her hands, but he could not lift his face to hers. He said, "I have too many deaths on my heart, Elehal."

"Come with me to the Grove," she said.

They went there together and stayed till the winter came. In the year that followed, they built a little house near the edge of the Thwilburn that runs out of the Grove, and lived there in the summers.

They worked and taught in the Great House. They saw it go up stone on stone, every stone steeped in spells of protection, endurance, peace. They saw the Rule of Roke established, though never so firmly as they might wish, and always against opposition; for mages came from other islands and rose up from among the students of the school, women and men of power, knowledge, and pride, sworn by the Rule to work together and for the good of all, but each seeing a different way to do it.

Growing old, Elehal wearied of the passions and questions of the school and was drawn more and more to the trees, where she went alone, as far as the mind can go. Medra walked there too, but not so far as she, for he was lame.

After she died, he lived a while alone in the small house near the Grove.

One day in autumn he came back to the school. He went in by the garden door, which gives on the path through the fields to Roke Knoll. It is a curious thing about the Great House of Roke, that it has no portal or grand entryway at all. You can enter by what they call the back door, which, though it is made of horn and framed in dragon's tooth and carved with the Thousand-Leaved Tree, looks like nothing at all from outside, as you come to it in a dingy street; or you can go in the garden door, plain oak with an iron bolt. But there is no front door.

He came through the halls and stone corridors to the inmost place, the marble-paved courtyard of the fountain, where the tree Elehal had planted now stood tall, its berries reddening.

Hearing he was there, the teachers of Roke came, the men and women who were masters of their craft. Medra had been the Master Finder, until he went to the Grove. A young woman now taught that art, as he had taught it to her.

"I've been thinking," he said. "There are eight of you. Nine's a better number. Count me as a master again, if you will."

"What will you do, Master Tern?" asked the Summoner, a gray-haired mage from Ilien.

"I'll keep the door," Medra said. "Being lame, I won't go far from it. Being old, I'll know what to say to those who come. Being a finder, I'll find out if they belong here."

"That would spare us much trouble and some danger," said the young Finder.

"How will you do it?" the Summoner asked.

"I'll ask them their name," Medra said. He smiled. "If they'll tell me, they can come in. And when they think they've learned everything, they can go out again. If they can tell me my name."

So it was. For the rest of his life, Medra kept the doors of the Great House on Roke. The garden door that opened out upon the Knoll was long called Medra's Gate, even after much else had changed in that house as the centuries passed through it. And still the ninth Master of Roke is the Doorkeeper.

In Endlane and the villages round the foot of Onn on Havnor, women spinning and weaving sing a riddle song of which the last line has to do, maybe, with the man who was Medra, and Otter, and Tern.

Three things were that will not be:
Soléa's bright isle above the wave,
A dragon swimming in the sea,
A seabird flying in the grave.

Senator Bilbo

Andy Duncan

*Andy Duncan (www.angelfire.com/al/andyduncan/) is an ex-journalist—
for seven years a reporter and editor at the* News & Record *in Greens-
boro, N.C.—now college teacher who began publishing fiction in the late
1990s. In 1998 his story "Beluthahatchie" was a Hugo Award finalist,
and he was a finalist for the John W. Campbell Award for Best New
Writer. His short fiction made an immediate impression, and in 2001 he
won two World Fantasy Awards, one for a story and one for his first
book,* Beluthahatchie and Other Stories *(2000). Duncan is a Southern
writer; his settings have thus far characteristically been the American
South, and his stories are revelations of character, often with a strongly
ironic subtext. Nothing much happens in a Duncan story, but things
change.*

*The year 2001 will be remembered for many things, but among them
will be the December grand opening of the film* The Fellowship of the
Ring, *and the whole year of its build-up, which made bestsellers of
J.R.R. Tolkien's books all over again. "Senator Bilbo" is overtly satirical,
combining all of Duncan's strengths with one outrageous big idea: What
if Senator Bilbo, the well-known old Southern racist politician, was a de-
scendent of Bilbo Baggins, and lived in the Shire, in the Middle Earth,
generations later?*

"It regrettably has become necessary for us now, my friends, to consider seriously and to discuss openly the most pressing question facing our homeland since the War. By that I mean, of course, the race question."

In the hour before dawn, the galleries were empty, and the floor of the Shire-moot was nearly so. Scattered about the chamber, a dozen or so of the Senator's allies—a few more than were needed to maintain the quorum, just to be safe—lounged at their writing-desks, feet up, fingers laced, pipes stuffed with the best Bywater leaf, picnic baskets within reach: veterans all. Only young Appledore from Bridge Inn was snoring and slowly folding in on himself; the chestnut curls atop his head nearly met those atop his feet. The Senator jotted down Appledore's name without pause. He could get a lot of work done while making speeches—even a filibuster nine hours long (and counting).

"There are forces at work today, my friends, without and within our homeland, that are attempting to destroy all boundaries between our proud, noble race and all the mule-gnawing, cave-squatting, light-shunning, pit-spawned scum of the East."

The Senator's voice cracked on "East," so he turned aside for a quaff from his (purely medicinal) pocket flask. His allies did not miss their cue. "Hear, hear," they rumbled, thumping the desktops with their calloused heels. "Hear, hear."

"This latest proposal," the Senator continued, "this so-called immigration bill—which, as I have said, would force even our innocent daughters to suffer the reeking lusts of all the ditch-bred legions of darkness—why, this baldfooted attempt originated where, my friends?"

"Buckland!" came the dutiful cry.

"Why, with the delegation from *Buckland* . . . long known to us all as a hotbed of book-mongers, one-Earthers, elvish sympathizers, and other off-brands of the halfling race."

This last was for the benefit of the newly arrived Fredegar Bracegirdle, the unusually portly junior member of the Buckland delegation. He huffed his way down the aisle, having drawn the short straw in the hourly backroom ritual.

"Will the distinguished Senator—" Bracegirdle managed to squeak out, before succumbing to a coughing fit. He waved his bladder-like hands in a futile attempt to disperse the thick purplish clouds that hung in the chamber like the vapors of the Eastmarsh. Since a Buckland-sponsored bill to ban tobacco from the floor had been defeated by the Senator three Shire-moots previous, his allies' pipe-smoking had been indefatigable. Finally Bracegirdle sputtered: "Will the distinguished Senator from the Hill kindly yield the floor?"

In response, the Senator lowered his spectacles and looked across the chamber to the Thain of the Shire, who recited around his tomato sandwich: "Does the distinguished Senator from the Hill so yield?"

"I do not," the Senator replied, cordially.

"The request is denied, and the distinguished Senator from the Hill retains the floor," recited the Thain of the Shire, who then took another hearty bite of his sandwich. The Senator's party had rewritten the rules of order, making this recitation the storied Thain's only remaining duty.

"Oh, hell and hogsheads," Bracegirdle muttered, already trundling back up the aisle. As he passed Gorhendad Bolger from the Brockenborings, that Senator's man like his father before him kindly offered Bracegirdle a pickle, which Bracegirdle accepted with ill grace.

"Now that the distinguished gentleman from the Misty Mountains has been heard from," the Senator said, waiting for the laugh, "let me turn now to the evidence—the overwhelming evidence, my friends—that many of the orkish persuasion currently living among us have been, in fact, active agents of the Dark Lord. . . ."

As the Senator plowed on, seldom referring to his notes, inventing statistics and other facts as needed, secure that this immigration bill, like so many bills before it, would wither and die once the Bucklanders' patience was exhausted, his self-confidence faltered only once, unnoticed by anyone else in the chamber. A half hour into his denunciation of the orkish threat, the Senator noticed a movement—no, more a shift of light, a *glimmer*—in the corner of his eye. He instinctively turned his head toward the source, and saw, or *thought* he saw, sitting in the farthest, darkest corner of the otherwise empty gallery, a man-sized figure in a cloak and pointed hat, who held what must have been (*could* have been) a staff; but in the next blink, that corner held only shadows, and the Senator dismissed the whatever-it-was as a fancy born of exhilaration and weariness. Yet he was left with a lingering chill, as if (so his old mother, a Took, used to say) a dragon had hovered over his grave.

At noon, the Bucklanders abandoned their shameful effort to open the High Hay, the Brandywine Bridge, and the other entry gates along the Bounds to every misbegotten so-called "refugee," be he halfling, man, elf, orc, warg, Barrow-wight, or worse. Why, it would mean the end of Shire culture, and the mongrelization of the halfling race! No, sir! Not today—not while the Senator was on the job.

Triumphant but weary, the champion of Shire heritage worked his way, amid a throng of supplicants, aides, well-wishers, reporters, and yes-men, through the maze of tunnels that led to his Hill-side suite of offices. These were the largest and nicest of any Senator's, with the most pantries and the most windows facing the Bywater, but they also were the farthest from the Shire-moot floor. The Senator's famous ancestor and namesake had been hale and hearty even in his eleventy-first year; the Senator, pushing ninety, was determined to beat that record. But every time he left the chamber, the office seemed farther away.

"Gogluk carry?" one bodyguard asked.

"Gogluk *not* carry," the Senator retorted. The day he'd let a troll haul him through the corridors like luggage would be the day he sailed oversea for good.

All the Senator's usual tunnels had been enlarged to accommodate the bulk of his two bodyguards, who nevertheless had to stoop, their scaly shoulders scraping the ceiling. Loyal, dim-witted, and huge—more than five feet in height—the Senator's trolls were nearly as well known in the Shire as the Senator himself, thanks partially to the Senator's perennial answer to a perennial question from the press at election time:

"Racist? Me? Why, I love Gogluk and Grishzog, here, as if they were my own flesh and blood, and they love me just the same, don't you, boys? See? Here, boys, have another biscuit."

Later, once the trolls had retired for the evening, the Senator would elaborate. Trolls, now, you could train them, they were teachable; they had their uses, same as those swishy elves, who were so good with numbers. Even considered as a race, the trolls weren't much of a threat—no one had seen a baby troll in ages. But those orcs? They did nothing but breed.

Carry the Senator they certainly did not, but by the time the trolls reached the door of the Senator's outermost office (no mannish rectangular door, but a traditional Shire-door, round and green with a shiny brass knob in the middle), they were virtually holding the weary old halfling upright and propelling him forward, like a child pushed to kiss an ugly

aunt. Only the Senator's mouth was tireless. He continued to greet con-
stituents, compliment babies, rap orders to flunkies, and rhapsodize
about the glorious inheritance of the Shire as the procession squeezed its
way through the increasingly small rooms of the Senator's warren-like
suite, shedding followers like snakeskin. The only ones who made it
from the innermost outer office to the outermost inner office were the
Senator, the trolls, and four reporters, all of whom considered themselves
savvy under-Hill insiders for being allowed so far into the great man's
sanctum. The Senator further graced these reporters by reciting the usual
answers to the usual questions as he looked through his mail, pocketing
the fat envelopes and putting the thin ones in a pile for his intern, Miss
Boffin. The Senator got almost as much work done during press confer-
ences as during speeches.

"Senator, some members of the Buckland delegation have insinu-
ated, off the record, that you are being investigated for alleged bribe-
taking. Do you have a comment?"

"You can tell old Gerontius Brownlock that he needn't hide behind a
façade of anonymity, and further that I said he was begotten in an orkish
graveyard at midnight, suckled by a warg-bitch and educated by a fool.
That's off the record, of course."

"Senator, what do you think of your chances for reelection next fall?"

"The only time I have ever been defeated in a campaign, my dear,
was my first one. Back when your grandmother was a whelp, I lost a
clerkship to a veteran of the Battle of Bywater. A one-armed veteran. I
started to vote for him myself. But unless a one-armed veteran comes forward pretty soon, little lady, I'm in no hurry to pack."

The press loved the Senator. He was quotable, which was all the
press required of a public official.

"Now, gentle folk, ladies, the business of the Shire awaits. Time for
just one more question."

An unfamiliar voice aged and sharp as Mirkwood cheese rang out:
"*They say your ancestor took a fairy wife.*"

The Senator looked up, his face even rounder and redder than usual.
The reporters backed away. "It's a lie!" the Senator cried. "Who said
such a thing? Come, come. Who said that?"

"Said what, Senator?" asked the most senior reporter (Bracklebore,
of the *Bywater Battle Cry*), his voice piping as if through a reed. "I was
just asking about the quarterly sawmill-production report. If I may continue—"

"Goodbye," said the Senator. On cue, the trolls snatched up the
reporters, tossed them into the innermost outer office, and slammed and
locked the door. Bracklebore, ousted too quickly to notice, finished his

question in the next room, voice muffled by the intervening wood. The trolls dusted their hands.

"Goodbye," said Gogluk—or was that Grishzog?

"Goodbye," said Grishzog—or was that Gogluk?

Which meant, of course, "Mission accomplished, Senator," in the pidgin Common Speech customary among trolls.

"No visitors," snapped the Senator, still nettled by that disembodied voice, as he pulled a large brass key from his waistcoat-pocket and unlocked the door to his personal apartments. Behind him, the trolls assumed position, folded their arms, and turned to stone.

"Imagination," the Senator muttered as he entered his private tunnel.

"Hearing things," he added as he locked the door behind.

"Must be tired," he said as he plodded into the sitting-room, yawning and rubbing his hip.

He desired nothing more in all the earth but a draft of ale, a pipe, and a long snooze in his armchair, and so he was all the more taken aback to find that armchair already occupied by a white-bearded Big Person in a tall pointed blue hat, an ankle-length gray cloak, and immense black boots, a thick oaken staff laid across his knees.

" 'Strewth!" the Senator cried.

The wizard—for wizard he surely was—slowly stood, eyes like lanterns, bristling gray brows knotted in a thunderous scowl, a meteor shower flashing through the weave of his cloak, one gnarled index finger pointed at the Senator—who was, once the element of surprise passed, unimpressed. The meteor effect lasted only a few seconds, and thereafter the intruder was an ordinary old man, though with fingernails longer and more yellow than most.

"Do you remember me?" the wizard asked. His voice crackled like burning husks. The Senator recognized that voice.

"Should I?" he retorted. "What's the meaning of piping insults into my head? And spying on me in the Shire-moot? Don't deny it; I saw you flitting about the galleries like a bad dream. Come on, show me you have a tongue—else I'll have the trolls rummage for it." The Senator was enjoying himself; he hadn't had to eject an intruder since those singing elves occupied the outer office three sessions ago.

"You appointed me, some years back," the wizard said, "to the University, in return for some localized weather effects on Election Day."

So that was all. Another disgruntled officeholder. "I may have done," the Senator snapped. "What of it?" The old-timer showed no inclination to reseat himself, so the Senator plumped down in the armchair. Its cushions now stank of men. The Senator kicked the wizard's staff from underfoot and jerked his leg back; he fancied something had nipped his toe.

The staff rolled to the feet of the wizard. As he picked it up, the wider end flared with an internal blue glow. He commenced shuffling about the room, picking up knickknacks and setting them down again as he spoke.

"These are hard times for wizards," the wizard rasped. "New powers are abroad in the world, and as the powers of wind and rock, water and tree are ebbing, we ebb with them. Still, we taught our handfuls of students respect for the old ways. Alas, no longer!"

The Senator, half-listening, whistled through his eyeteeth and chased a flea across the top of his foot.

"The entire thaumaturgical department—laid off! With the most insulting of pensions! A flock of old men feebler than I, unable even to transport themselves to your chambers, as I have wearily done—to ask you, to demand of you, why?"

The Senator yawned. His administrative purging of the Shire's only university, in Michel Delving, had been a complex business with a complex rationale. In recent years, the faculty had got queer Eastern notions into their heads and their classrooms—muddleheaded claims that all races were close kin, that orcs and trolls had not been separately bred by the Dark Power, that the Dark Power's very existence was mythical. Then the faculty quit paying the campaign contributions required of all public employees, thus threatening the Senator's famed "Deduct Box." Worst of all, the faculty demanded "open admissions for qualified nonhalflings," and the battle was joined. After years of bruising politics, the Senator's appointees now controlled the university board, and a long-overdue housecleaning was under way. Not that the Senator needed to recapitulate all this to an unemployed spell-mumbler. All the Senator said was:

"It's the board that's cut the budget, not me." With a cry of triumph, he purpled a fingernail with the flea. "Besides," he added, "they kept all the *popular* departments. Maybe you could pick up a few sections of Heritage 101."

This was a new, mandatory class that drilled students on the unique and superior nature of halfling culture and on the perils of immigration, economic development, and travel. The wizard's response was: "Pah!"

The Senator shrugged. "Suit yourself. I'm told the Anduin gambling-houses are hiring. Know any card tricks?"

The wizard stared at him with rheumy eyes, then shook his head. "Very well," he said. "I see my time is done. Only the Gray Havens are left to me and my kind. We should have gone there long since. But your time, too, is passing. No fence, no border patrol—not even you, Senator—can keep all change from coming to the Shire."

"Oh, we can't, can we?" the Senator retorted. As he got worked up, his Bywater accent got thicker. "We sure did keep those Bucklanders from putting over that so-called Fair Distribution System, taking people's hard-earned crops away and handing 'em over to lazy trash to eat. We sure did keep those ugly up-and-down man houses from being built all over the Hill as shelter for immigrant rabble what ain't fully halfling or fully human or fully anything. Better to be some evil race than no race at all."

"There are no evil races," said the wizard.

The Senator snorted. "I don't know how *you* were raised, but I was raised on the Red Book of Westmarch, chapter and verse, and it says so right there in the Red Book, orcs are mockeries of men, filthy cannibals spawned by the Enemy, bent on overrunning the world. . . ."

He went on in this vein, having lapsed, as he often did in conversation, into his tried-and-true stump speech, galvanized by the memories of a thousand cheering halfling crowds. "Oh, there's enemies everywhere to our good solid Shire-life," he finally cried, punching the air, "enemies outside and inside, but we'll keep on beating 'em back and fighting the good fight our ancestors fought at the Battle of Bywater. Remember their cry:

"*Awake! Awake! Fear, Fire, Foes! Awake!*

"*Fire, Foes! Awake!*"

The cheers receded, leaving only the echo of his own voice in the Senator's ears. His fists above his head were bloated and mottled—a corpse's fists. Flushed and dazed, the Senator looked around the room, blinking, slightly embarrassed—and, suddenly, exhausted. At some point he had stood up; now his legs gave way and he fell back into the armchair, raising a puff of tobacco. On the rug, just out of reach, was the pipe he must have dropped, lying at one end of a spray of cooling ashes. He did not reach for it; he did not have the energy. With his handkerchief he mopped at his spittle-laced chin.

The wizard regarded him, wrinkled fingers interlaced atop his staff.

"I don't even know why I'm talking to you," the Senator mumbled. He leaned forward, eyes closed, feeling queasy. "You make my head hurt."

"Inhibiting spell," the wizard said. "It prevented your throwing me out. Temporary, of course. One bumps against it, as against a low ceiling."

"Leave me alone," the Senator moaned.

"Such talents," the wizard murmured. "Such energy, and for what?"

"At least I'm a halfling," the Senator said.

"Largely, yes," the wizard said. "Is genealogy one of your interests, Senator? We wizards have a knack for it. We can see bloodlines, just by looking. Do you really want to know how . . . *interesting* . . . your bloodline is?"

The Senator mustered all his energy to shout, "Get out!" but heard nothing. Wizardry kept the words in his mouth, unspoken.

"There are no evil races," the wizard repeated, "however convenient the notion to patriots, and priests, and storytellers. You may summon your trolls now." His gesture was half shrug, half convulsion.

Suddenly the Senator had his voice back. "Boys!" he squawked. "Boys! Come quick! Help!" As he hollered, the wizard seemed to roll up like a windowshade, then become a tubular swarm of fireflies. By the time the trolls knocked the door into flinders, most of the fireflies were gone. The last dying sparks winked out on their scaly shoulders as the trolls halted, uncertain what to pulverize. The Senator could hear their lids scrape their eyeballs as they blinked once, twice. The troll on the left asked:

"Gogluk help?"

"Gogluk too *late* to help, thank you very much!" the Senator snarled. The trolls tried to assist as he struggled out of the armchair, but he slapped them away, hissing, in a fine rage now. "Stone ears or no, did you not hear me shouting? Who did you think I was talking to?"

The trolls exchanged glances. Then Grishzog said, quietly: "Senator talk when alone a lot."

"A lot," Gogluk elaborated.

The Senator might have clouted them both had he not been distracted by the wizard's staff. Dropped amid the fireworks, it had rolled beneath a table. Not knowing why, the Senator reached for it, eyes shining. The smooth oak was warm to the touch: heat-filled, like a living thing. Then, with a yelp, the Senator yanked back his hand. The damn thing *definitely* had bitten him this time; blood trickled down his right palm. As three pairs of eyes stared, the staff sank into the carpet like a melting icicle, and was gone.

"Magic," said the trolls as one, impressed.

"Magic?" the senator cried. "Magic?" He swung his fists and punched the trolls, kicked them, wounding only their dignity; their looming hulks managed to cower, like dogs. "If it's magic you want, I'll give you magic!" He swung one last time, lost his balance, and fell into the trolls' arms in a dead faint.

* * *

The Bunce Inn, now in the hands of its founder's great-granddaughter, had been the favored public house of the Shire-moot crowd for generations. The Senator had not been inside the place in months. He pleaded matters of state, the truth being that he needed a lot more sleep nowadays. But when he woke from his faint to find the trolls fussing over him, he demanded to be taken to the Bunce Inn for a quick one before retiring. The Senator's right hand smarted a bit beneath its bandage, but otherwise the unpleasant interlude with the wizard seemed a bad dream, was already melting away like the staff. The Senator's little troll-cart jounced through the warm honeysuckle-scented night, along the cobbled streets of the capital, in and out of the warm glows cast by round windows behind which fine happy halfling families settled down to halfling dinners and halfling games and halfling dreams.

The inn itself was as crowded as ever, but the trolls' baleful stares quickly prompted a group of dawdlers to drink up and vacate their table. The trolls retreated to a nearby corner, out of the way but ever-present, as bodyguards should be. The Senator sat back with a sigh and a tankard and a plate of chips and surveyed the frenzy all around, pleased to be a part of none of it. The weight of the brimming pewter tankard in his unaccustomed left hand surprised him, so that he spilled a few drops of Bunce's best en route to his mouth. *Aah.* Just as he remembered. Smacking foam from his lips, he took another deep draft—and promptly choked. Not six feet away, busy cleaning a vacant table, was an orc.

And not just any orc. This one clearly had some man in its bloodline somewhere. The Senator had seen to it that the Shire's laws against miscegenation had stayed on the books, their penalties stiffened, but elsewhere in the world, alas, traditional moral values had declined to the point that such blasphemous commingling had become all too frequent. This creature was no doubt an orc—the hulking torso and bowlegs, the flat nose and flared nostrils, the broad face, the slanting eyes, the coarse hair, the monstrous hooked teeth at the corners of the mouth—but the way the orc's arms moved as it stacked dirty plates was uncomfortably manlike. It had genuine hands as well, with long delicate fingers, and as its head turned, the Senator saw that its pupils were not the catlike slits of a true orc but rounded, like the pupils of dwarves, and men, and halflings. It was like seeing some poor trapped halfling peering out from a monstrous bestial shell, as in those children's stories where the hero gets swallowed whole by the ogre and cries for help from within. The orc, as it worked, began to whistle.

The Senator shuddered, felt his gorge rise. His injured hand throbbed with each heartbeat. A filthy half-breed orc, working at the Bunce Inn! Old Bunce would turn in his grave. Catching sight of young

Miss Bunce bustling through the crowd, the Senator tried to wave her over, to give her a piece of his mind. But she seemed to have eyes only for the orc. She placed her hand on its shoulder and said, in a sparkling gay voice: "Please, sir, don't be tasking yourself, you're too kind. I'll clean the table; you just settle yourself, please, and tell me what you'll have. The lamb stew is very nice today, and no mistake."

"Always pleased to help out, ma'am," said the orc, plopping its foul rump onto the creaking bench. "I can see how busy you are. Seems to me you're busier every time I come through the Shire."

"There's some as say I needs a man about," Miss Bunce said, her arms now laden with plates, "but cor! Then I'd be busier still, wouldn't I?" The orc laughed a horrid burbling mucus-filled laugh as Miss Bunce sashayed away, buttocks swinging, glancing back to twinkle at her grotesque customer, and wink.

At this inauspicious moment, someone gave the Senator a hearty clap on the back. It was Fredegar Bracegirdle, a foaming mug in his hand and a foolish grin on his fat red face. Drink put Bracegirdle in a regrettable bipartisan mood. "Hello, Senator," Bracegirdle chirped, as he clapped the Senator's back again and again. "Opponents in the legislature, drinking buddies after hours, eh, Senator, eh, friend, eh, pal?"

"Stop pounding me," the Senator said. "I am not choking. Listen, Bracegirdle. What is that, that . . . *creature* . . . doing here?"

Bracegirdle's bleary gaze slowly followed the Senator's pointing finger, as a dying flame follows a damp fuse. "Why, he's a-looking at the bill of fare, and having himself a pint, same as us."

"You know what I mean! Look at those hands. He talks as if someone, somewhere, has given him schooling. Where'd he come from?"

As he answered, Bracegirdle helped himself to the Senator's chips. "Don't recall his name, but he hails from Dunland, from one of those new, what-do-you-call-'em, investment companies, their hands in a little of everything. Run by orcs and dwarves, mostly, but they're hiring all sorts. My oldest, Bungo, he's put his application in, and I said, you go to it, son, there's no work in the Shire for a smart lad like yourself, and your dear gaffer won't be eating any less in his old age. Young Bunce, she's a wizard at these chips, she is. Could you pass the vinegar?"

The Senator already had risen and stalked over to the orc's table, where the fanged monster, having ordered, was working one of the little pegboard games Miss Bunce left on the tables for patrons' amusement. The orc raised its massive head as it registered the Senator's presence.

"A good evening to you, sir," it said. "You can be my witness. Look at that, will you? Only one peg left, and it in the center. I've never managed *that* before!"

The Senator cleared his throat and spat in the orc's face. A brown gob rolled down its flattened nose. The orc gathered its napkin, wiped its face, and stood, the scrape of the bench audible in the otherwise silent room. The orc was easily twice as wide as the Senator, and twice as tall, yet it did not have to stoop. Since the Senator's last visit, Miss Bunce had had the ceiling raised. Looking up at the unreadable, brutish face, the Senator stood his ground, his own face hot with rage, secure in the knowledge that the trolls were right behind him. Someone across the room coughed. The orc glanced in that direction, blinked, shook its head once, twice, like a horse bedeviled by flies. Then it expelled a breath, its fat upper lip flapping like a child's noisemaker, and sat down. It slid the pegboard closer and re-inserted the pegs, one after the other after the other, then, as the Senator watched, resumed its game.

The Senator, cheated of his fight, was unsure what to do. He could not remember when last he had been so utterly ignored. He opened his mouth to tell the orc a thing or two, but felt a tug at his sleeve so violent that it hushed him. It was Miss Bunce, lips thin, face pale, twin red spots livid on her cheeks. "It's late, Senator," she said, very quietly. "I think you'd best be going home."

Behind her were a hundred staring faces. Most of them were strangers. Not all of them were halflings. The Senator looked for support in the faces in the crowd, and for the first time in his life, did not find it. He found only hostility, curiosity, indifference. He felt his face grow even hotter, but not with rage.

He nearly told the Bunce slut what he thought of her and her orc-loving clientele—but best to leave it for the Shiremoot. Best to turn his back on this pesthole. Glaring at everyone before him, he gestured for the trolls to clear a path, and muttered: "Let's go, boys."

Nothing happened.

The Senator slowly turned his head. The trolls weren't there. The trolls were nowhere to be seen. Only more hostile strangers' faces. The Senator felt a single trickle of sweat slide past his shoulder blades. The orc jumped pegs, removed pegs: *snick, snick.*

So. The Senator forced himself to smile, to hold his head high. He nodded, patted Miss Bunce's shoulder (she seemed not to relish the contact), and walked toward the door. The crowd, still silent, parted for him. He smiled at those he knew. Few smiled back. As he moved through the crowd, a murmur of conversation arose. By the time he reached the exit, the normal hubbub had returned to the Bunce Inn, the Senator's once-favorite tavern, where he had been recruited long ago to run for clerk on the Shire First ticket. He would never set foot in the place again.

He stood on the threshold, listening to the noise behind, then cut it off by closing the door.

The night air was hot and rank and stifling. Amid the waiting wagons and carriages and mules and two-wheeled pedal devices that the smart set rode nowadays, the Senator's little troll-cart looked foolish in the lamplight. As did his two truant bodyguards, who were leaning against a sagging, creaking carriage, locked in a passionate embrace. The Senator decided he hadn't seen that; he had seen enough today. He cleared his throat, and the trolls leaped apart with much coughing and harrumphing.

"Home," the Senator snapped. Eyeing the uneven pavement, he stepped with care to the cart, sat down in it, and waited. Nothing happened. The trolls just looked at one another, shifted from foot to foot. The Senator sighed and, against his better judgment, asked: "What is it?"

The trolls exchanged another glance. Then the one on the right threw back his shoulders—a startling gesture, given the size of the shoulders involved—and said: "Gogluk quit." He immediately turned to the other troll and said: "There, I said it."

"And you know that goes double for me," said the other troll. "Let's go, hon. Maybe some fine purebred halfling will take this old reprobate home."

Numb but for his dangling right hand, which felt as swollen as a pumpkin, the Senator watched the trolls walk away arm in arm. One told the other: "*Spitting* on people, yet! I thought I would just *die*." As they strolled out of the lamplight, the Senator rubbed his face with his left hand, massaged his wrinkled brow. He had been taught in school, long ago, that the skulls of trolls ossified in childhood, making sophisticated language skills impossible. If it wasn't true, it ought to be. There ought to be a law. He would write one as soon as he got home.

But how was he to *get* home? He'd never make it on foot, and he certainly couldn't creep back into the tavern to ask the egregious Bracegirdle for a ride. Besides, he couldn't see to walk at the moment; his eyes were watering. He wiped them on his sleeve. It wasn't that he would *miss* the trolls, certainly not, no more than he would miss, say, the andirons, were they to rise up, snarl insults, wound him to the heart, the wretches, and abandon him. One could always buy a new set. But at the thought of the andirons, the cozy hearth, the armchair, the Senator's eyes brimmed anew. He was so tired, and so confused; he just wanted to go home. And his hand hurt. He kept his head down as he mopped his eyes, in case of passersby. There were no passersby. The streetlamp flared as a buzzing insect flew into it. He wished he had fired those worthless trolls. He certainly would, if he ever saw them again.

"Ungratefulness," the Senator said aloud, "is the curse of this age." A mule whickered in reply.

Across the street, in the black expanse of the Party Field, a lone mallorn-tree was silhouetted against the starlit sky. Enchanted elven dust had caused the mallorn and all the other trees planted after the War to grow full and tall in a single season, so that within the year the Shire was once again green and beautiful—or so went the fable, which the Senator's party had eliminated from the schoolbooks years ago. The Senator blew his nose with vigor. The Shire needed nothing from elves.

When the tavern door banged open, the Senator felt a surge of hope that died quickly as the hulking orc-shape shambled forth. The bastard creature had looked repellent enough inside; now, alone in the lamplit street, it was the stuff of a thousand halfling nightmares, its bristling shoulders as broad as hogsheads, its knuckles nearly scraping the cobbles, a single red eye guttering in the center of its face. No, wait. That was its cigar. The orc reared back on its absurd bowlegs and blew smoke rings at the streetlamp—rings worthy of any halfling, but what of it? Even a dog can be trained, after a fashion, to dance. The orc extended its horrid manlike hand and tapped ashes into the lamp. Then, arm still raised, it swiveled its great jowly head and looked directly at the Senator. Even a half-orc could see in the dark.

The Senator gasped. He was old and alone, no bodyguards. Now the orc was walking toward him! The Senator looked for help, found none. Had the wizard's visit been an omen? Had the confusticated old charm tosser left a curse behind with his sharp-toothed staff? As the Senator cowered, heard the inexorable click of the orc's claws on the stones, his scream died in his throat—not because of any damned be-bothered wizard's trickery, but because of fear, plain and simple fear. He somehow always had known the orcs would get him in the end. He gasped, shrank back. The orc loomed over him, its pointed head blocking the lamplight. The orc laid one awful hand, oh so gently, on the Senator's right shoulder, the only points of contact the fingertips—rounded, mannish, hellish fingertips. The Senator shuddered as if the orc's arm were a lightning rod. The Senator spasmed and stared and fancied the orc-hand and his own injured halfling hand were flickering blue in tandem, like the ends of a wizard's staff. The great mouth cracked the orc's leathered face, blue-lit from below, and a voice rumbled forth like a subterranean river: "Senator? Is that you? Are you all right?"

Sprawled there in the cart, pinned by the creature's gentle hand as by a spear, the Senator began to cry, in great sucking sobs of rage and pain and humiliation, as he realized this damned orc was not going to splinter his limbs and crush his skull and slurp his brains. How far have I fallen, the Senator thought. This morning the four corners of the Shire were my own ten toes, to wiggle as I pleased. Tonight I'm pitied by an orc.

Big City Littles

〜〜〜〜

Charles de Lint

Charles de Lint (www.charlesdelint.com) lives in Ottawa, Ontario, with his wife Mary Ann Harris, an artist and musician. He is one of the founders of "urban fantasy," fantasy set in the real world rather than an invented otherworld, a subgenre that evolved out of the Unknown Worlds group of magazine writers in the early 1940s (Robert A. Heinlein, Eric Frank Russell, L. Ron Hubbard, Theodore Sturgeon, and particularly Fritz Leiber). De Lint popularized urban fantasy in the 1980s with such books as Moonheart, *and continues to tell tales of his trademark city, Newford. He's been a full-time writer for eighteen years, with forty-six books published (novels, collections, novellas) and more on the way. Additionally, for twenty-some years now, he's been playing Celtic music in one band or another. He says: "I've taken to calling my writing 'mythic fiction,' because it's basically mainstream writing that incorporates elements of myth and folktale, rather than secondary world fantasy." He also writes a monthly book review column for* F&SF.

"Big City Littles" is trademark de Lint, set in the real world transformed by the intrusion of fantasy. It was published in Realms of Fantasy *(after a small press chapbook edition), one of the two major professional fantasy magazines that in recent years has clearly become a peer in quality to* F&SF. *It is perhaps in the tradition of Mary Norton's classic children's fantasy,* The Borrowers.

The Fates seem to take a perverse pleasure out of complicating our lives. I'm not sure why. We do such a good job of it all on our own that their divine interference only seems to be overkill.

It's not that we deliberately set out to screw things up. We'd all like to be healthy and happy, not to mention independently wealthy—or at least able to make our living doing something we care about, something we can take pride in. But even when we know better, we invariably make a mess of everything, both in our private and our public lives.

Take my sister. She knows that boyfriends are only an option, not an answer, but that's never stopped her from bouncing from one sorry relationship to another, barely stopping to catch her breath between one bad boy and the next. But I should talk. It's all well and fine to be comfortable in your own skin, to make a life for yourself if there's no one on the scene to share it with you. But too often I still feel like the original spinster, doomed to end her days forever alone in some garret.

I guess for all the strides we've made with the women's movement, there are some things we can still accept only on an intellectual level. We never really believe them in our hearts.

The little man sitting on Sheri Piper's pillow when she opened her eyes was a good candidate for the last thing she would have expected to wake up to this morning. He wasn't really much bigger than the length from the tip of her middle finger to the heel of her palm, a small hamster-sized man, dressed in raggedy clothes with the look of a bird about him. His eyes were wide set, his nose had a definite hook to it, his body was plump, but his limbs were thin as twigs. His hair was an unruly tangle of short, brown curls and he wore a pair of rectangular, wire-framed eye-glasses not much different than those Sheri wore for anything but close work.

She tried to guess his age. Older than herself, certainly. In his mid-forties, she decided. Unless tiny people aged in something equivalent to dog years.

If this were happening to one of the characters in the children's books she wrote and illustrated, now would be the time for astonishment and wonder, perhaps even a mild touch of alarm, since after all, tiny though he was, he was still a strange man and she had woken up to find him in her bedroom. Instead, she felt oddly calm.

"I don't suppose I could be dreaming," she said.

The little man started the way a pedestrian might when an unex-pected bus suddenly roars by the corner where he's standing. Jumping up, he lost his balance and would have gone sliding down the long slope of her pillow if she hadn't slipped a hand out from under the bedclothes and caught him.

He squeaked when she picked him up, but she meant him no harm and only deposited him carefully on her night table. Backing away until he was up against the lamp, his tiny gaze darted from side to side as though searching for escape, which seemed odd considering how, only moments ago, he'd been creeping around on her pillow mere inches from her face.

Laying her head back down, she studied him. He weighed no more than a mouse, but he was definitely real. He had substance the way dreams didn't. Unless she hadn't woken up yet and was still dreaming, which was a more likely explanation.

"Don't talk so loud!" he cried as she opened her mouth to speak again.

His voice was high pitched and sounded like the whine of a bug in her ear.

"What are you?" she whispered.

He appeared to be recovering from his earlier nervousness. Brushing something from the sleeve of his jacket, he said, "I'm not a what. I'm a who."

"Who then?"

He stood up straighter. "My name is Jenky Wood, at your service, and I come to you as an emissary."

"From where? Lilliput?"

Tiny eyes blinked in confusion. "No, from my people. The Kaldewen Tribe."

"Who live . . . where? In my sock drawer? Behind the baseboards?"

Why couldn't this have happened *after* her first coffee of the morning when at least her brain would be slightly functional?

He gave her a troubled look. "You're not like we expected."

"What were you expecting?"

"Someone . . . kinder."

Sheri sighed. "I'm sorry. I'm not a morning person."

"That's apparent."

"Mind you, I do feel justified in being a little cranky. After all, you're the one who's come barging into my bedroom."

"I didn't barge. I crept in under the door, ever so quietly."

"OK, snuck into my bedroom then—which, by the way, doesn't give you points on any gentlemanly scale that I know of."

"It seemed the best time to get your attention without being accidentally stepped on, or swatted like a bug."

Sheri stopped herself from telling him that implying that her apartment might be overrun with bugs his size also wasn't particularly endearing.

"Would it be too much to ask *what* you're doing in my bedroom?" she asked. "Not to mention on my bed."

"I might as well ask what you're doing in bed."

"Now who's being cranky?"

"The sun rose hours ago."

"Yes, and I was writing until 3 o'clock this morning so I think I'm entitled to sleep in." She paused to frown at him. "Not that it's any of your business. And," she added as he began to reply, "you haven't answered my question."

"It's about your book," he said. *"The Traveling Littles."*

As soon as he said the title, she wondered how she could have missed the connection. Jenky Wood, at her service, looked exactly like she'd painted the Littles in her book. Except . . .

"Littles aren't real," she said, knowing how dumb *that* sounded with an all-too-obvious example standing on her night table.

"But . . . you . . . you told our history. . . ."

"I told a story," Sheri said, feeling sorry for the little man now. "One that was told to me when I was a girl."

"So you can't help us?"

"It depends," she said, "on what you need my help for."

But she already knew. She didn't have to go into her office to take down a copy of the book from her brag shelf. She might have written and illustrated it almost 20 years ago. She might not have recognized the little man for what he was until he'd told her himself. But she remembered the story.

It had been her first book and its modest, not to mention continuing, success was what had persuaded her to try to make a living at writing and drawing children's books. She'd just never considered that the story might be true, never mind what she'd said in the pages of the book.

⌒ The Traveling Littles

There are many sorts of little people—tiny folk, no bigger than a minute. And I don't just mean fairies and brownies, or even pennymen and their like. There are the Lilliputians that Gulliver met on his travels. Mary Norton's Borrowers. The Smalls of William Dunthorn's Cornwall. All sorts. But today I want to tell you about the Traveling Littles who live like gypsies, spending their lives always on the move.

This is how I heard the story when I was a small girl. My grandpa told it to me, just like this, so I know it's true.

The Littles were once birds. They had wings and flew high above the trees and hills to gather their food. When the leaves began to turn yellow and red and frost was in the air, they flew to warmer countries, for they weren't toads to burrow in the mud, or bears to hibernate away the cold months, or crows who don't allow the weather to tell them where to live, or when to move.

The Littles liked to travel. They liked the wind in their wings and to look out on a new horizon every morning. So they were always leaving one region for another, traveling more to the south in the winter, coming back north when the lilacs and honeysuckle bloomed. No matter how far they traveled, they always returned to these very hills where the sprucey-pine grow tall and the grass can seem blue in a certain light, because even traveling people need a place they can call home.

But one year when the Littles returned, they could find nothing to eat. They flew in every direction looking for food. They flew for days with a gnawing hunger in their bellies.

Finally they came upon a field of ripe grain—the seeds so fat and sweet, they'd never seen the like, before or since. They swooped down in a chorusing flock and gorged in that field until they were too heavy to fly away again. So they had to stay the night on the ground, sleeping among the grain-straw and grass.

You'd think they would have learned their lesson, but in the morning, instead of flying away, they decided to eat a little more and rest in that field of grain for one more night.

Every morning they decided the same thing, to eat a little more and sleep another night, until they got to be so heavy that they couldn't fly anymore. They could only hop, and not quickly either.

Then the trees began to turn yellow and red again. Frost was on the ground and the winter winds came blowing. The toad burrowed in his mud. The bear returned to his den. The crows watched from the bare-limbed trees and laughed.

Because the Littles couldn't fly away. They couldn't fly at all. They were too fat.

The grain-straw was getting dry. The tall grass browned, grew thin, and died. After watching the mice and squirrels store away their own harvests, the Littles began to shake the grain from the blades of grass and gather it in heaps with their wings, storing it in hidey-holes and hollow logs. The downy feathers of their wings became all gluey, sticking to each other. Their wings took the shape of arms and hands and even if they could manage to lose weight, they were no longer able to fly at all now for they'd become people—tiny people, six inches tall.

That winter they had to dig holes in the sides of the mountains and along the shores of the rivers, making places to live.

And it's been like that ever since.

In the years to follow, they've come to live among us, sharing our bounty the way mice do, only they are so secret we never see them at all. And they still travel, from town to town, from borough to borough, from city block to the next one over, and then the next one over from that. That's why we call them the Traveling Littles.

But the Traveling Littles are still birds, even if their arms are no longer wings. They can never see a tall building or a mountain without wanting to get to the top. But they can't fly anymore. They have to walk up there, just like you or me.

Still the old folks say, those who know this story and told it to me, that one day the Traveling Littles will get their wings back. They will be birds again.

Only no one knows when.

"You want to know how to become a bird again," she said.

Jenky Wood nodded. "We thought you would know. Yula Gry came across a copy of your book in a child's library last year and told us about it at our year's end celebration. Palko John—"

"Who are these people?"

"Yula is the sister of my brother's cousin Sammy, and Palko John is our Big Man. He's the chief of our clan, but he's also the big chief of all the tribe. He decided that we should look for you. When we found out where you lived, I was sent to talk to you."

"Why were you chosen?"

He had the decency to blush.

"Because they all say I'm too good-natured to offend anyone, or take offense."

Sheri stifled a laugh. "Well," she said. "I'm usually much less cranky when I've been awake for a little longer and have had at least one cup of coffee. Speaking of which, I need one now. I also have to have a pee."

At that he went beet-red.

"What, you people don't? Never mind," she added. "That was just more crankiness. Can I pick you up?"

When he gave her a nervous nod, she lowered her hand so that he could step onto her palm, keeping her thumb upright so he'd have something to hang on to. She took him into the kitchen, deposited him on the table, plugged in the kettle, then went back down the hall to the washroom.

Ten minutes later she was sitting at the table with a coffee in front of her. Jenky sat on a paperback book, holding the thimbleful of coffee she'd given him. She broke off a little piece of a bran cookie and offered it to him before dipping the rest into her coffee.

"So why would you want to become birds again, anyway?" she asked.

"Look at the size of us. Can you imagine how hard it is for us to get around while still keeping our secret?"

"Point taken."

Neither spoke while they ate their cookies. Sheri sipped at her coffee.

"Did your grandfather really tell you our story?" Jenky asked after a moment.

Sheri nodded.

"Could you bring me to him?"

"He passed away a couple of years ago."

"I'm sorry."

Silence fell again between them.

"Look," Sheri said after a moment. "I don't know any more than what you read in my book, but I could look into it for you."

"Really?"

"No, I'm actually way too busy. Joke," she added as his face fell. "It was a joke."

"Palko John said we could offer you a reward for your help."

"What sort of reward?"

"Anything you want."

"Like a magic wish?" Sheri asked, intrigued.

He nodded. "We only have the one left."

"Why don't you use it to make yourselves birds again?"

"They only work for other people."

"Figures. There's always a catch, isn't there? But I don't want your wish."

He went all glum again. "So you won't help us?"

"Didn't I already say I would? I just don't like the idea of magic wishes. There's something creepy about them. I think we should earn what we get, not have it handed to us on a little silver platter."

That earned her a warm smile.

"I think we definitely chose the right person to help us," he said.

"Well, don't start celebrating yet," Sheri told him. "It's not like I have any idea how to go about it. But like I said, I will look into it."

"I've decided to give up men," Sheri told Holly Rue later that day. She'd arrived early at Holly's store for the afternoon book club meeting that the used bookshop hosted on the last Wednesday of every month. The book they'd be discussing today was Alice Hoffman's *The River King*, which Sheri had adored. Since she had to wait for the others to get here to discuss it, she kept herself busy talking with Holly and fussing with Snippet, Holly's Jack Russell terrier, much to the dog's delight.

"I thought you'd already done that," Holly said.

"I did. But this time I really mean it."

"Have a bad date?"

"It's not so much having a bad date as, A, not wanting to see him again after said date, but he does and keeps calling; or B, wanting to see him again because it seemed we were getting along so well, but he doesn't call. I'm worn out from it all."

"You could call him," Holly said.

"I could. Would you?"

Holly sighed. "Not to ask him out."

"I thought women's lib was supposed to have sorted all of this out by now."

"I think it's not only society that's supposed to change, but us, too. *We* have to think differently."

"So why don't we?"

Holly shook her head. "Same reason they don't call, I guess. Give me a hob over a man any day."

Sheri cocked her head and studied Holly for a long moment.

"What?" Holly said. "Did I grow an extra nose?"

"No, I'm just thinking about hobs. I wanted to talk to you about them."

Holly's gaze went to an empty chair near the beginning of the store's farthest aisle, then came back to Sheri.

"What about them?" she asked.

There was now something guarded in the bookseller's features, but Sheri plunged on anyway.

"Were you serious about having one living in your store?" she asked.

"Um . . . serious as in, is it true?"

A few months ago they'd been out celebrating the nomination of one of Sheri's books for a local writing award—she hadn't won. That was when Holly had mentioned this hob, laughed it off when Sheri had asked for more details, and then changed the subject.

"Because the thing is," Sheri said. "I could use some advice about little people right about now."

"You've got a hob living in your apartment?"

"No, I've got a Little—though he's only visiting."

"But Littles aren't—"

"Real," Sheri finished for her. "Any more than hobs. We both know that. Yet there he is, waiting for me in my apartment all the same. I've set him up on a bookshelf with a ladder so that he can get up and down, and got some of my old Barbie furniture out of my storage space in the basement."

"You kept your Barbie stuff?"

"And it's a good thing I did, seeing how useful it's proven to be today. Jenky—that's his name, Jenky Wood—likes the size, though he's not particularly enamored with the colors."

"You're serious?"

"So it seems," Sheri told her. "Apparently he thinks I can find out how they can all become birds again."

"Like in your story."

Sheri nodded. "Although I haven't got the first clue."

"Well, I—"

But just then the front door opened and Kathryn Whelan, one of the other members of their book club, came in.

"I think I know someone who can help you," Holly said, before turning to smile at the new arrival.

Snippet lifted her head from Sheri's lap with interest—hoping for another biscuit like the one Sheri had given her earlier, no doubt.

"Someone tall, dark, and handsome—not to mention single?" Sheri asked after they'd exchanged hellos with Kathryn.

"Not exactly."

"Who's tall, dark, and handsome?" Kathryn asked.

"The man of my dreams," Sheri told her.

Kathryn smiled. "Aren't they all?"

Sheri was helping Jenky rearrange the Barbie furniture on the bookshelf she'd cleared for his use when the doorbell rang.

"That'll be her," she said, suddenly nervous.

"Should I hide?" Jenky asked.

"Well, that would kind of defeat the whole purpose of this, wouldn't it?"

"I suppose. It's just that letting myself be seen goes so against everything I've ever been told. My whole life has been a constant concentration of secrets and staying hidden."

"Buck up," Sheri told him. "If all goes well, you might be a bird again and it won't matter who sees you."

"I'd rather be both," he said as she went to get the door.

She paused, hand on the knob. "Really?"

"Given a choice, wouldn't you want to be able to go back and forth between bird and Little?"

She gave a slow nod. "I suppose I would."

She turned back to open the door and everything just kind of melted away in her head. Jenky's problem, the conversation they'd just had, the day of the week.

"Oh my," Sheri said.

The words came out unbidden, for standing there in the hallway was the idealization of a character she'd been struggling with for weeks. The new picture book hadn't exactly stalled, but she kept having to write around this one character because she couldn't quite get her clear in her head. She'd filled pages in her sketchbook with drawings, particularly frustrated because while she knew what the character was supposed to look like, she was unable to get just the right image of her down on paper. Or perhaps a better way to put it was that she didn't so much know what the woman should look like; she just knew when it was wrong.

But now here the perfect subject was, standing in the hallway. Where were her watercolors and some paper? Or just a pencil and the back of an envelope. Hell, she'd settle for a camera.

Although really, none of that would be necessary. Now that she'd seen her, it would be impossible for Sheri to forget her.

It wasn't that the woman was particularly exotic, though there were those striking green streaks that ran through her nut-brown hair. She wasn't dressed regally either, though her simple white blouse and long flower-print skirt nevertheless left an impression of royal vestments. It wasn't even that she was so beautiful—there were any number of beautiful women in the world.

No, there was an air about her, a quality both mysterious and simple that had been escaping Sheri for weeks when she was doing her character sketches. But she had it now. She'd begin with a light golden wash, creating a nimbus of light behind the figure's head, and then—

"I hope that's a pleased 'Oh my,' " the woman said.

Her voice brought Sheri back into the present moment.

"What? Oh, yes. It was. I mean I was just . . ."

The woman offered her hand. "My name's Meran Kelledy. Holly did tell you I was coming by, didn't she?"

Her voice was soft and melodic with an underlying touch of gentle humor.

"I'm sorry," Sheri said as she shook Meran's hand. "I can't believe I've left you standing out there in the hall." She stood aside. "Please come in. It's just that you just caught me by surprise. See, you look exactly like the forest queen I need for this book I'm working on at the moment and . . ." She laughed. "I'm babbling, aren't I?"

"What sort of forest is she the queen of?"

"An oak forest."

Meran smiled. "Well, that's all right, then."

With that enigmatic comment, she came into the apartment. Sheri watched her for one drawn-out moment longer, then shut the door to join Meran and Jenky in the living room.

"I should also tell you that there's a wish up for grabs," Sheri said after she and Jenky had taken turns telling their story. The two women were sitting at the kitchen table, Jenky on the table in a pink plastic chair. They all had tea—Jenky in his thimble since he didn't like the plastic Barbie dishware, the women in regular porcelain mugs.

"For the one who helps the Littles with this, I mean," Sheri added.

Meran shook her head. "I have no need for wishes."

Of course she wouldn't.

Meran was probably the calmest woman that Sheri had ever met. Neither meeting the Little nor the story the two of them had told seemed to surprise her. She'd simply given Jenky a polite hello, then sat and nodded while they talked, occasionally asking a question to clarify one point or another.

What world does she live in? Sheri had found herself thinking.

A magical one, no doubt. Like the forest in Sheri's latest picture book.

"You can have it," Meran said.

But Sheri shook her head right back. "I don't believe in something for nothing."

"Good for you."

What an odd response. But Sheri didn't take the time to dwell on it.

"So can you help us turn them back into birds again?" she asked.

"Unfortunately, no. Odd as it came to be, the Littles have evolved into what they now are and that kind of thing can't be turned back. It's like making the first fish that came onto land return to the sea. Or forcing the monkeys to go back up into the trees once more instead of becoming men and women. Evolution doesn't work that way. It moves forward, not back."

"But magic. . . ."

"Operates from what appears to be a different law of physics, I'll admit, but that's only because it's misunderstood. If you have the right vocabulary, it can make perfect sense."

Sheri sighed. "So we're back where we started."

"No, because the clock doesn't turn backward."

"I don't understand."

Sheri might have felt dumb, but Jenky looked as confused as she was feeling and he was a piece of magic himself, so she decided not to worry about it.

"What's to stop the Littles from continuing to evolve?" Meran asked. "Into, say, beings that can change from bird to Little at will the way Jenky here has said he'd like to."

"Well, for one thing, we don't know how."

"Now there I can help you. Or at least I can set the scene so that you can help him."

"I'm still not following you."

"There's an old tribe of words," Meran explained. "Not the kind we use today, but the ones that go back to the before, when a word spoken created a moment in which anything can happen."

"The before?" Sheri asked.

"It's just another way to say the first days of the world," Jenky told her. "Our storytellers still tell the stories of those days, of Raven and Cody and the crow girls and all."

"It was a time of Story," Meran said. "Although, of course, every age has its stories, just as every person does. But these were the stories that shaped the world, and part of that shaping had to do with this old tribe of words."

"A tribe of words," Sheri repeated, feeling way out of her depth here.

Meran nodded. "I can wake one of those words for you," she said. "Not for a long time, but for long enough."

"So you'll just say one of these words and everything'll be the way we want it to be?"

"Hardly," Meran said with a smile. "I can only wake one of that old tribe. You will need to say the words. It's a form of communal magic, which is mostly the kind I know. One person wakes it, another gives it focus."

"But I wouldn't know what to say. Maybe Jenky should do it."

"No, this works better when a human speaks the words."

That gave Sheri pause, the way Meran said the word "human." It was the way humans spoke of other species. She wanted to ask Meran what she was, but she supposed now wasn't the time. And it would probably be impolite.

"So what words do I say?" she asked instead.

"You'll know when the time is right."

"But. . . ."

Meran gave her another of her smiles. "Don't worry so much."

"OK."

Sheri looked from the magical woman sitting across the table from her to the even more magical little man sitting on a Barbie kitchen chair between them. Jenky watched her expectantly. Meran said nothing, did nothing. There was an odd, unfocused look to her gaze but otherwise she seemed to merely be waiting, managing to do so without conveying the vaguest sense of pressure.

But there was pressure all the same—self-imposed on Sheri's part but no less urgent for that.

What if she didn't say the right thing? How much was she supposed to say? How was she supposed to know when the time was right?

It was all so nebulous.

"So when do we start?" Sheri asked.

Meran's gaze came into focus and found Sheri's.

"Breathe," she said. "Slowly. Try to still the conversations that rise up in your head and don't concentrate on anything until you feel a change. You'll know it when you feel it."

Then she slowly closed her eyes. Sheri copied her, closing her own eyes. Breathing deeply and slowly, she tried to feel this change. Something, anything. Maybe a difference in the air. Some sense that they were sideways from the world as she knew it, inhabiting a pocket of the world where magic could happen.

If magic *was* real, that was.

If it . . .

She wasn't sure where it originated, the sudden impression of assurance that came whispering through her, calm and sure and secret. She felt like she was at the center of some enormous wheel and that all the possibilities of what might be were radiating out from her like a hundred thousand filigreed spokes. It was like floating, like coming apart and reconnecting with everything. But it was also like being utterly focused as well. She could look at all those threads arcing away from her and easily find and hold the one that was needed in her mind.

"Hope," she said.

"Is that word for them or for you?"

As soon as Meran asked the question, Sheri saw how it could go. She realized that under the connection she felt to this wheel of possibilities, she'd continued to harbor her own need, continued to reach for that elusive partner every single person looked for, whether they admit it or not. He could be called to her with Meran's old tribal word. The right partner, the perfect partner. All she had to do was say, "For me."

Because magic was real, she knew that now. At least this magic was real. It could bring him to her.

But then she opened her eyes. Her gaze went to Jenky, watching her with expectant eyes and held breath.

Promises made. Promises broken.

What good were promises if you didn't keep them? How could you respect yourself, never mind expect anyone else to respect you, if you could break them so easily? What would the perfect man think of her when he learned how she'd brought him to her?

Not to mention what she'd said barely 10 minutes ago, how it wasn't right to have something for nothing.

But that was before she'd realized it could really be made to happen.

That was before all the lonely nights were washed away with the promise of just the right man coming into her life.

"No," she said. "I meant faith. Belief. That bird and Little can be one again, the shape they wear being their own choice."

Meran smiled.

"Done," she said.

Sheri felt a rumbling underfoot, like a subway car running just under the basement of her apartment building. But there was no subway within blocks of her place. The tea mugs rattled on the table and Jenky gripped the seat of his chair. Something swelled inside her, deep and old, too big for her to hold inside.

And then it was gone.

Sheri blinked and looked at Meran.

Was that it? she wanted to ask. What happened? Did it work?

But before she could speak, there was a blur of motion in the middle of the kitchen table. Jenky leaped up, knocking his little chair down. He lifted his arms and they seemed to shrink back into his body at the same time as his fingers grew long, long, longer. Feathers burst from them in a sudden cloud. His birdish features became a bird's head in truth, and then the whole of the little man was gone and a gray and brown bird rose up from the tabletop, flapping its wings. It circled once, twice, three times around the room, then landed on the table again, the transformation reversing itself until Jenky was standing there.

He looked up at her, grinning from ear to ear.

Sheri smiled back at him.

"I guess it worked," she said.

A couple of days later, Sheri looked up from her drawing table, distracted by the tap-tap-tapping on her windowpane. A little brown and gray bird looked in at her, its head cocked to one side.

"Jenky?" she said.

The bird tapped at the glass again so she stepped around her table and opened the window. The bird immediately flew in and landed on the top of her drawing table, where it became a little raggedy man. Sheri wasn't even startled anymore.

"Hello, hello!" Jenky cried.

"Hello, yourself. You're looking awfully pleased with yourself."

"Everyone's so happy. They all wanted to come by and say thank you and hello, but Palko John said that would be indecorous so it's just me."

"Well, I'm glad to see you, too."

Jenky looked like he wanted to dance around where he was standing, but he made himself stand straight and tall.

"I'm supposed to ask you if you've decided on your wish," he said.

"I already told you—I don't want a wish."

"But you helped us, and that was our promise to you."

Sheri shook her head. "I still don't want it. You should keep it for yourselves."

"And I already told you. We can't use it for ourselves."

Sheri shrugged. "Then find someone who really needs it. A person whose only home is an alleyway. A child fending off unwelcome attention. Someone who's dying, or hurt, or lonely, or sad. You Littles must go all over the city. Surely you can find someone who needs a wish."

"That's your true and final answer?"

"Now you sound like a game show host," she told him.

He wagged a finger at her. "It's too late in the day to be cranky. Even you have to have been up for hours now."

"You still don't get my jokes, do you?"

"No," he said. "But I'll learn."

"Anyway, that's my true and final answer."

"Then I'll find such a person and give them your wish."

With that he became a bird once more. He did a quick circle around her head, followed by a whole series of complicated loops and swirls that took him from one end of the room to the other, showing off.

"Come back and visit!" Sheri called as he headed for the window.

The bird twittered, then it darted out the window and was gone.

"So what's the deal with Meran?" Sheri asked Holly the next time she came by the bookstore. "Where do you know her from?"

"I had a . . . pixie incident that she helped me out with last year."

"A pixie incident."

Holly nodded. "The store was overrun with them. They came off the Internet like a virus and were causing havoc up and down the street until she helped us get them back into the Net."

"Us being you and your hob?"

Just as she had the last time the subject of the hob came up, Holly's gaze went to an empty chair near the beginning of the store's farthest aisle, only this time there was a little man sitting there, brown-faced and curly-haired. He gave Sheri a shy smile and lifted a hand in greeting.

"Oh-kay," Sheri said.

She could have sworn there was no one sitting there a moment ago and his sudden appearance made the whole world feel a little off-kilter. She'd only *just* gotten used to little men who could turn into birds.

"Sheri, this is Dick Bobbins," Holly said. "Dick, this is Sheri Piper."

"I like your books," the hob said.

His compliment gave Sheri perhaps the oddest feeling that she'd had so far in all of this affair, that a fairy tale being should like *her* fairy tale books.

"Um, thank you," she managed.

"He didn't appear out of nowhere," Holly assured her, undoubtedly in response to the look on Sheri's face. "Hobs have this ability to be so still that we don't notice them unless they want us to."

"I knew that."

Holly grinned. "Sure you did."

"OK, I didn't. But it makes sense in a magical nothing-really-makes-sense sort of a way. Kind of like birds turning into Littles, and vice versa."

"So was Meran able to help you?"

The hob leaned forward in his chair, obviously as interested as Holly was.

Sheri nodded and told them about how it had gone.

"I understand why you didn't let Meran's magic bring you the right guy," Holly said when she was done. "I mean, after all. You *were* calling it up for the Littles. What I don't understand is, why didn't you use the wish they offered you?"

"Because it's something for nothing. It's like putting a love spell on someone. Isn't it better to get to know someone at a natural pace, work out the pushes and pulls of the relationship to make it stronger, instead of having it all handed to you on a platter?"

"I suppose. But what if you never meet the right guy?"

"That's the risk I have to take."

So here I am, still waiting like an idiot on the man of my dreams.

I don't know which bugs me more: that he hasn't shown up yet, or that I'm still waiting.

But I got to do a good turn and my picture book is done. Meran loved the paintings I did of her as the forest queen. Her husband even bought one of the originals once I'd gotten the color transparencies made.

What else? I've got a new friend who's a hob, and at least once a week Jenky Wood flies up to my windowsill in the shape of a bird, tapping on my windowpane until I let him in. I've got my Barbie furniture permanently set up for him on a shelf in my studio, though I have repainted it in more subdued colors.

So what am I saying?

I don't know. That we all have ups and downs, I guess, whether we bring them on ourselves or they come courtesy of the Fates. The trick seems to be to roll with them. Learn something from the hard times, appreciate the good.

I didn't really need fairy encounters to teach me that, but I wouldn't trade the experience of them for anything. Not even for that elusive, perfect man.

Author's Note: *Sheri's story of the Traveling Littles is adapted from an Appalachian story detailing the origin of gypsies; I found my version in Virginia Folk Legends, edited by Thomas E. Barden. Thanks to Charles Vess for introducing me to this delightful book.*

What the Tyger Told Her

Kage Baker

Kage Baker (www.members.tripod.com/~MrsCheckerfield) grew up in Hollywood and Pismo Beach, California, where she still lives. She's now writing a lot, but has worked as a graphic artist and mural painter, at "several lower clerical positions which could in no way be construed as a career, and (over a period of years for the Living History Centre) playwright, bit player, director, teacher of Elizabethan English for the stage, stage manager, and educational program assistant coordinator." She says "Twenty years of total immersion research in Elizabethan as well as other historical periods has paid off handsomely in a working knowledge of period speech and details." Baker is best known for her series of SF novels and stories about "The Company," stories of time travelers from our future delving into various periods of our past to rescue lost art and other treasures. She published a number of fine stories this year, including the action-packed novella "The Caravan from Troon."

In "What the Tyger Told Her," a neglected pet becomes the instrument of a family's destruction. This evocative story, which appeared in Realms of Fantasy, skirts the boundary between genre fantasy and psychological fantasy in the form of daydreams. We prefer the genre interpretation.

"You must observe carefully," said the tyger.

He was an old tyger. He had survived in captivity more years than he might have been expected to, penned in his narrow iron run in such a cold wet country, in all weathers. He was just the color of toast, and white underneath like bread too. His back was double-striped with black streaks, and the rippling shadows of the bars as he paced continually, turn and turn again.

The little girl blinked, mildly surprised at being addressed. She had a round face, pale and freckled like a robin's egg. She had been squatting beside the tyger's pen for some minutes, fascinated by him. If anyone had seen her crouched there, crumpling the silk brocade of her tiny hooped gown, she'd have been scolded, for the summer dust was thick in the garden. But no one had noticed she was there.

"Power," said the tyger, "comes from knowledge, you see. The best way to learn is to watch what happens. The best way to watch is unseen. Now, in my proper place, which is jungle meadow and forest canes, I am very nearly invisible. That," and he looked with eyes green as beryls at the splendid house rising above the gardens, "is your proper place. Are you invisible there?"

The little girl nodded her head.

"Do you know why you're invisible?"

She thought about it. "Because John and James were born."

"Your little brothers, yes. And so nobody sees you now?"

"And because . . ." The child waved her hand in a gesture that took in the house, the garden, the menagerie, and the immense park in which they were set. "There's so many uncles and people here. Mamma and I used to live in the lodging house. Papa would come upstairs in his uniform. It was red. He was a poor officer. Then he got sick and lived with us in his nightgown. It was white. He would drink from a bottle and shout, and I would hide behind the chair when he did. And John and James got born. And Papa went to heaven. And Mamma said oh, my dear, whatever shall we do?"

"What *did* you do?" the tyger prompted.

"I didn't do anything. But Grandpapa forgave Mamma and sent for us."

"What had your Mamma done, to be forgiven?"

"She wasn't supposed to marry Papa because she is," and the child paused a moment to recollect the big words, "an indigent tradesman's daughter. Papa used to tell her so when he drank out of the bottle. But when she had John and James, that made it all right again, because they're the only boys."

"So they're important."

"They will inherit it all," the child explained, as though she were quoting. "Because Papa died and Uncle John is in India, and Uncle Thomas only has Louise."

"But they haven't inherited yet."

"No. Not until Grandpapa goes to heaven."

"Something to think about, isn't it?" said the tyger, lowering his head to lap water from his stone trough.

The little girl thought about it.

"I thought Grandpapa was in heaven when we went to see him," she said. "We climbed so many stairs. And the bed was so high and white and the pillows like clouds. Grandpapa's nightgown was white. He has white hair and a long, long beard. He shouted like Papa did. Mamma turned away crying. Mr. Lawyer said It's only his pain, Mrs. Edgecombe. Uncle Thomas said Dear sister, come and have a glass of cordial. So she did and she was much better."

"But nobody saw *you* there, did they?"

"No," said the child.

"Who's that coming along the walk?" the tyger inquired.

"That is Uncle Thomas and Aunt Caroline," the child replied.

"Do you notice that she's not as pretty as your Mamma?"

"Yes."

"And quite a bit older."

"Yes. And she can't have any children but Cousin Louise."

"I think perhaps you ought to sit quite still," advised the tyger.

The woman swept ahead in her anger, long skirts trailing in the tall summer grass at the edge of the walk, white fingers knotting on her lace apron, high curls bobbing with her agitation. The man hurried after her, tottering a little because of the height of his heels, and the skirts of his coat flapped out behind him. He wore bottle-green silk. His waistcoat was embroidered with little birds, his wig was slightly askew. He looked sullen.

"Oh, you have a heart of stone," cried Aunt Caroline. "Your own child to be left a pauper! It's too unjust. Is this the reward of filial duty?"

"Louise is not an especially dutiful girl," muttered Uncle Thomas.

"I meant your filial duty! One is reminded of the Prodigal Son. *You* have obeyed his every wish, while he thundered up there. Wretched old paralytic! And Robert disgraces himself, and dies like a dog in a ditch with that strumpet, but all's forgiven because of the twins. Are all our hopes to be dashed forever?"

"Now, Caroline, patience," said Uncle Thomas. "Consider: Life's uncertain."

"That's true." Aunt Caroline pulled up short, looking speculative. "Any childish illness might carry off the brats. Oh, I could drown them like puppies myself!"

Uncle Thomas winced. He glared at Aunt Caroline's back a moment before drawing abreast of her, by which time he was smiling.

"You'll oblige me by doing nothing so rash. Robert was never strong; we can pray they've inherited his constitution. And after all it would be just as convenient, my dear, if the wench were to die instead. I would be guardian of John and James, the estate in my hands; what should we have to worry about then?"

They walked on together. The little girl stared after them.

"Do you think they're going to drown my Mamma?" she asked uneasily.

"Did you see the way your uncle looked at your aunt behind her back?" replied the tyger. "I don't think he cares for her, particularly. What do *you* think?"

There were fruit trees espaliered all along the menagerie wall, heavy now in apricots and cherries, and when the chimpanzee had been alive it had been driven nearly frantic in summers by the sight and the smell of the fruit. Now stuffed with straw, it stared sadly from a glass-fronted cabinet, through a fine layer of dust.

The little girl, having discovered the fruit was there, wasted no time in filling her apron with all she could reach and retiring to the shade under the plum tree. The largest, ripest apricot she bowled carefully into the tyger's cage. The others she ate in methodical fashion, making a small mound of neatly stacked pits and cherry stones.

The tyger paused in his relentless stride just long enough to sniff the apricot, turning it over with his white-bearded chin.

"Your baby brothers have not died," he said.

"No," the little girl affirmed, biting into a cherry.

"However, your Aunt Caroline has been suffering acute stomach pains, especially after dinner. That's interesting."

"She has a glass of port wine to make it better," said the child. "But it doesn't get better."

"And that's your Mamma coming along the walk now, I see," said the tyger. "With Uncle Thomas."

The child concealed the rest of the fruit with her apron and sat still. She needn't have worried: Neither her mother nor her uncle noticed her.

Like her daughter, Mamma had a pale, freckled face but was otherwise quite attractive, and the black broadcloth of her mourning made her look slender and gave her a dignity she needed, for she was very young. She was being drawn along by Uncle Thomas, who had her by the arm.

"We ought never to question the will of the Almighty," Uncle Thomas was saying pleasantly. "It never pleased Him that Caroline should bear me sons, and certainly that's been a grief to me; but then, without boys of my own, how ready am I to do a father's duty by dear little John and James! All that I might have done for my sons, I may do for yours. Have no fear on that account, dear Lavinia."

"It's very kind of you, brother Thomas," said Mamma breathlessly. "For, sure we have been so poor, I was at my wit's end—and father Edgecombe is so severe."

"But Robert was his favorite," said Uncle Thomas. "The very reason he disowned him, I think; Father couldn't brook disobedience in one he loved above all. If Henry or I had eloped, he'd have scarcely noticed. And Randall does what he likes, of course. Father was too hard on Robert, alas."

"Oh, sir, I wish someone had said so while he lived," said Mamma. "He often wept that he had no friends."

"Alas! I meant to write to him, but duty forbid." Uncle Thomas shook his head. "It is too bad. I must endeavor to redress it, Lavinia."

He slipped his arm around her waist. She looked flustered, but said nothing. They walked on.

"Mamma is frightened," said the child.

"There are disadvantages to being pretty," said the tyger. "As you can see. I imagine she wishes she could be invisible, occasionally. Your uncle's a subtle man; notice how he used words like *duty* and *alas*. No protestations of ardent passion. It's often easier to get something you want if you pretend you don't want it. Remember that."

The little girl nodded.

She ate another cherry. A peahen ventured near the wall, cocking her head to examine the windfall fruit under the little trees. As she lingered there, a peacock came stalking close, stiffened to see the hen; his whole body, bright as blue enamel, shivered, and his trailing train of feathers rose and spread behind him, shimmering in terrifying glory. Eyes stared from it. The little girl caught her breath at all the green and purple and gold.

"You mustn't allow yourself to be distracted," the tyger cautioned. "It's never safe. You see?"

"What, are you lurking there, you little baggage?"

The little girl looked around sharply, craning her head back. Uncle Randall dropped into a crouch beside her, staring at her. He was young, dressed in tawny silk that shone like gold. His voice was teasing and hard. He smelled like wine.

"Ha, she's stealing fruit! You can be punished for that, you know. They'll pull your skirt up and whip your bare bum, if I tell. Shall I tell?"

"No," said the child.

"What'll you give me, not to tell?"

She offered him an apricot. He took it and rolled it in his hand, eyeing it, and hooted in derision.

"Gives me the greenest one she's got! Clever hussy. You're a little woman, to be sure."

She didn't know what to say to that, so she said nothing. He stared at her a moment longer, and then the tyger drew his attention.

"Aren't you afraid of old Master Stripes? Don't you worry he'll break his bounds, and eat you like a rabbit? He might, you know. But I'm not afraid of him."

The tyger growled softly, did not cease pacing.

"Useless thing! I'd a damn sight rather Johnnie'd sent us one of his blacks," said Uncle Randall. He looked down at her again. "Well, poppet. What's your Mamma's favorite color?"

"Sky blue," said the child.

"It is, eh? Yes, with those eyes, she'd wear that to her advantage. D'you think she'd like a velvet scarf in that color, eh? Or a cape?"

"She has to wear black now," the child reminded him.

"She'll wear it as long as it suits her, I've no doubt. What about scent? What's her fancy? Tell me, does she ever drink strong waters in secret?"

The child had no idea what that meant, so she shook her head mutely. Uncle Randall snorted.

"You wouldn't tell if she did, I'll wager. Well. Does she miss your Papa very much?"

"Yes."

"You must say 'Yes, Uncle dear.'"

"Yes, Uncle dear."

"There's a good girl. Do you think you'd like to have another Papa?"

The child thought about it. Remembering the things Papa had said when he raved, that had made her creep behind the chair to hide, she said: "No."

"No? But that's wicked of you, you little minx. A girl must have a Papa to look after her and her Mamma, or dreadful things might happen. They might starve in the street. Freeze to death. Meat for dogs, you see, do you want your Mamma to be meat for dogs?"

"No," said the child, terrified that she would begin to cry.

"Then you'll tell her she must get you another Papa as soon as ever she may," Uncle Randall ordered. "Do you understand me? Do it, and you'll have a treat. Something pretty." He reached down to stroke her cheek, and his hand lingered there.

"What a soft cheek you've got," he said. "I wonder if your Mamma's is as soft."

The peacock was maneuvering up behind the hen, treading on her feathers. Seeing it, Uncle Randall gave a sharp laugh and shied the apricot at her, and she bolted forward, away from the peacock.

Uncle Randall strode off without another word.

"Now, your Uncle Randall," said the tyger, "is not a subtle man. Nor as clever as he thinks he is, all in all. He talks far too much, wouldn't you say?"

The child nodded.

"He uses fear to get what he wants," said the tyger. "And he underestimates his opponents. That's a dangerous thing to do. A bad combination of strategies."

Wasps buzzed and fought for the apricot at his feet.

The summer heat was oppressive. All the early fruit had fallen from the trees, or been gathered and taken in to make jam. There were blackberries in the hedge, gleaming like red and black garnets, but they were dusty and hard for the child to reach without scratching herself on the brambles.

There was a thick square of privet in the center of the menagerie courtyard, man-high. Long ago it had been a formal design, clipped close, but for one reason or another had been abandoned to grow unchecked. Its little paths were all lost now except at ground level, where they formed a secret maze of tunnels in the heart of the bush. There was a sundial buried in the greenery, lightless and mute: It told nobody anything.

The little girl had crawled in under the branches and lay there, pretending she was a jungle beast hiding in long grass. She gazed out at the tyger, who had retreated to the shade of the sacking the grooms had laid across the top of his pen. He blinked big mild eyes. He looked sleepy.

"How fares your Aunt Caroline?" he inquired.

"She's sick," the child said. "The doctor was sent for, but he couldn't find anything wrong with her. He said it might be her courses drying up."

"Do you know what that means?"

"No," said the child. "But that's what Uncle Thomas is telling everybody. And he says, you mustn't mind what a woman says because of it. He's very kind to her."

"How clever of him." The tyger yawned, showing fearful teeth, and stretched his length. "And he's even kinder to your Mamma, isn't he?"

"Yes. Very kind."

"What do you suppose will happen if your Aunt Caroline dies?"

"She will be buried in the graveyard."

"So she will."

They heard footsteps approaching, two pairs.

The child peered up from under the leaves and saw Cousin Louise with one of the stableboys. She was a tall girl with a sallow complexion, very tightly laced into her gown in order to have any bosom at all. The stableboy was thickset, with pimples on his face. He was carrying a covered pail. He smelled like manure.

"It be under here," he said, leading Cousin Louise around the side of the privet square. "The heart of it's all hollow, you see? And you can lie inside in the shade. It's a rare nice place to hide, and there ain't nobody knows it's here but me."

"Audacious rogue!" Cousin Louise giggled. "I'll tear my gown."

"Then the Squire'll buy thee a new one, won't he? Get in there."

The child lay very still. She heard the branches parting and the sound of two people awkwardly arranging themselves inside the privet. Turning her head very slightly, she caught a glimpse of them six feet away from her, mostly screened off by green leaves and the base of the sundial. She watched from the corner of her eye as they made themselves comfortable, handing the pail back and forth to drink from it.

"Aah! I like a cool drop of beer, in this heat," the stableboy sighed.

"It's refreshing," said Cousin Louise. "I've never had beer before."

"Like enough you wouldn't," said the stableboy, and belched. "Sweet wines and gin, ain't that what the fine folk have to themselves? The likes of me don't get a taste of your Madeira from one year's end to the next." He chuckled. "That's all one; I'll get a taste of something fine anyway."

There was a thrashing of bushes and Cousin Louise gave a little squeal of laughter.

"Hush! The keeper'll hear, you silly slut."

"No, no, he mustn't."

There was heavy breathing and a certain ruffling, as of petticoats. Cousin Louise spoke in an almost trancelike voice.

"How if you were a bold highwayman? You might shoot the driver, and there might be no other passengers but me, and I might be cowering within the coach, in fear of my very life. You'd fling the door wide—and you might look at me and lick your chops, as a hungry dog might—and you might say—you'd say—"

"Here's a saucy strumpet wants a good futtering, I'd say," growled the stableboy.

"Yes," Cousin Louise gasped, hysteria coming into her voice, "and I'd protest, but you would be merciless. You'd drag me from the coach, and throw me down on the ferns in the savage forest, and tear my gown to expose my bosom, and then—"

"Oh, hush your noise," the stableboy told Cousin Louise, and crawled on top of her. When they'd finished, he rolled off and reached for the beer pail. Cousin Louise was laughing, breathless, helpless, but her laughter began to sound a little like crying, and a certain alarm was in the stableboy's voice when he said: "Stop your fool mouth! Do you want to get me whipped? If you start screaming I'll cut your throat, you jade! What's the matter with you?"

Cousin Louise put her hands over her face and fell silent, attempting to even her breath. "Nothing," she said faintly. "Nothing. All's well."

There was silence for a moment, and the stableboy drank more beer.

"I feel a little ill with the heat," explained Cousin Louise.

"That's like enough," said the stableboy, sounding somewhat mollified.

Another rustling; Cousin Louise was sitting up, putting her arms around the stableboy.

"I do love you so," she said, "I could never see you harmed, dearest. Say but the word and I'll run away with thee, and be thy constant wife."

"Art thou mad?" The stableboy sounded incredulous. "The likes of you wedded to me? The Squire'd hunt us sure, and he'd have my life. Even so, how should I afford to keep a wife, with my place lost? It ain't likely you'd bring much of a dowry, anyhow, be the Squire never so willing. Not with everything going to them little boys, now."

"I have three hundred pounds a year from my mother, once she's dead and I am married." Cousin Louise sounded desperate. "I have! And she's grievous sick. Who knows how long she will live?"

"And what then? Much good that'd do me, if I was hanged or transported," said the stableboy. "Which I will be, if you don't keep quiet about our fun. Better ladies than you knows how to hold their tongues."

Cousin Louise did not say another word after that. The stableboy drank the rest of the beer, and sighed.

"I've got the mucking out to do," he announced, and buttoned himself and crawled from the bush. His footsteps went away across the paving stones, slow and heavy.

Cousin Louise sat perfectly still for a long time, before abruptly scrambling out and walking away with quick steps.

The little girl exhaled.

"He didn't speak to her very nicely," said the tyger.

"No."

"And she didn't seem to have much fun. Why do you suppose she'd go into the bushes with a person like that?"

"She said she loved him," said the child.

"Does she?" The tyger licked his paw lazily. "I wonder. Some people seem to feel the need to get manure on their shoes."

The child wrinkled her nose. "Why?"

"Who knows? Perhaps they feel it's what they deserve," said the tyger.

The little girl had found broken china hidden in the green gloom behind the potting shed: two dishes, a custard-cup and a sauceboat. She carried them out carefully and washed them in the horse-trough, and then retired to the bed of bare earth under the fruit trees with them. There she set out the broken plates to be courtyards, and inverted the cup and sauceboat on them to be houses. Collecting cherry pits, she arranged them in lines: They were soldiers, marching between the houses. The rationale for making them soldiers was that soldiers had red coats, and cherries were red. The tyger watched her.

"There are visitors today," he said. The child nodded.

"Uncle Henry and Aunt Elizabeth," she replied. "They came to see John and James. Uncle Henry is going to be their godfather, because he's a curate. They have a little girl, just my size, but she didn't come, or she might have played with me."

"Are you sorry she's not here to play with you?"

The child lifted her head in surprise, struck by the question.

"I don't know," she said. "Would she see me?"

"She might," the tyger said. "Children notice other children, don't they?"

"Sometimes."

"I think someone's coming," the tyger informed her. She looked up and saw Uncle Henry and Aunt Elizabeth strolling together along the walk.

". . . not so well-stocked as it was formerly, alas," said Uncle Henry. He wore black, with a very white wig. Aunt Elizabeth was plump, wore a mulberry-colored gown and a straw hat for the sun.

"Oh, bless us, look there!" she exclaimed, stopping in her tracks as she saw the tyger. "Dear, dear, d'you think it's safe to keep a beast like that about, with so many little children in the house? I'm glad now we kept Jane at home, my love."

"He's never harmed anyone, that I'm aware," Uncle Henry told her, taking her arm and steering her forward. "Poor old Bobo used to scream, and bite, and fling ordure; but I daresay it was because Randall teased him. Randall was frightened of this fellow, however. Kept his distance."

"And very sensible of him too," said Aunt Elizabeth, shuddering. "Oh, look at the size of it! I feel like a mouse must feel before our Tibby."

"The same Providence created them, Bess." Uncle Henry stopped before the pen. "Each creature has its place in the grand design, after all."

"Tibby catches rats, and I'm sure that's very useful indeed, but what's the point of an animal like this one?" protested Aunt Elizabeth. "Great horrid teeth and claws! Unless they have giant rats in India?"

"I don't think they do," said Uncle Henry. "But I trust the Almighty had His reasons."

"Well, I shall never understand how He could make something so cruel," said Aunt Elizabeth firmly. "Look there, what are those? Are those parrots? Dear little things!"

"Budgerigars, I think," said Uncle Henry.

They walked away to inspect the aviary, which was beyond the privet square.

"Stay where you are," said the tyger.

"Oh, I could never," Mamma was saying distractedly. "I couldn't think of such a thing, with poor Robert's grave scarcely green."

"Tut-tut, Lavinia!" said Uncle Randall, as they approached. "There's none to hear but you and I. Look as pious as you like before the world. The demure widow, meek and holy, if you please! I won't repeat what passes between us; but you and I both knew Robert. He hadn't enough blood in him to keep you contented, a lively girl like you. Had he, now? How long's it been since you had a good gallop, eh? Eh?"

She had been walking quickly ahead of him, and he caught up to her in front of the tyger's pen and seized her arm. Her face was red.

"You don't—oh—"

Uncle Randall stepped close and spoke very quickly. "The blood in your cheeks is honest, Madam Sanctimony. Don't play the hypocrite with me! I know London girls too well. You got your hooks into Robert to climb out of the gutter, didn't you? Well, keep climbing, hussy! I stand ready to help you up the next step, and the old man may be damned. We've got those boys, haven't we? We'll be master and mistress here one day, if you're not an affected squeamish— "

"You hound!" Mamma found her voice at last. "Oh, you base— *thing!*"

Uncle Henry and Aunt Elizabeth came walking swiftly around the privet square, and advanced on the scene like a pair of soldiers marching.

"What's this, Lavinia?" Uncle Henry's eyes moved from Mamma to Uncle Randall and back. "Tears?"

"We were speaking of Robert," said Uncle Randall, standing his ground. "Poor fellow. Were we not, dear Lavinia?"

Shocked back into silence, Mamma nodded. Aunt Elizabeth came and put her arms about her.

"My child, you mustn't vex your heart so with weeping," she said solicitously. "It's natural, in such an affectionate match, but only think! Robert would wish you to be happy, now that all's reconciled. And you must have courage, for the children's sake."

"So I was just saying," said Uncle Randall, helping himself to a pinch of snuff.

"We must endure our sorrows in patience," Uncle Henry advised her, looking at Uncle Randall.

"Come now, Lavinia," said Uncle Randall in quite a kind voice. "Dry your tears and walk with us. Shall we go view the pretty babes? John's the very image of Robert, in my opinion."

They bore her away between them.

"Your Mamma doesn't wish to make trouble, I see," said the tyger.

"She didn't tell on him," said the child, in wonderment.

"Silence is not always wise," said the tyger. "Not when it gives your opponent an opportunity. Perhaps your Uncle Randall hasn't underestimated your Mamma, after all."

"Why didn't she tell on him?" The child stared after the retreating adults.

"Why indeed?" said the tyger. "Something else to remember: Even bad strategy can succeed, if your opponent has no strategy at all."

Just beyond the menagerie courtyard, five stone steps led down into a sunken garden. It was a long rectangle of lawn, with rose beds at its edges and a fountain and small reflecting pool at its center. At its far end five more stone steps led up out of it, and beyond was a dense wood, and farther beyond was open heath where deer sometimes grazed.

The roses were briery, and the fountain long clogged and scummed over with green. But there were men working on it today, poking with rakes and sticks, and it had begun to gurgle in a sluggish kind of way; and the gardener had cut back the briars that hung out over the lawn. He was up on a ladder now with his handkerchief, rubbing dust off the sprays of rose haws, so they gleamed scarlet as blood drops.

The little girl watched them warily, nibbling at a rose haw she'd snatched from one of the cut sprays. It was hard and sour, but interesting. The tyger watched them too, pacing more quickly than usual.

"Your Uncle Randall gave your mother a fine length of sky-blue silk," he said. "Will she have a gown made of it, do you think?"

"No," said the child. "She showed it to Uncle Thomas and Aunt Caroline and asked them if she ought to have a gown made for the christening party."

"Really?" the tyger said. "And what did they say?"

"Aunt Caroline looked cross, and said Mamma mustn't think of such a thing while she's in mourning. Uncle Thomas didn't say anything. But his eyes got very small."

"Rather a clever thing for your Mamma to have done," said the tyger. "What did she say in reply?"

"She said Yes, yes, you're quite right. And Uncle Thomas went and talked to Uncle Randall about it."

The tyger made a low percussive sound in his chest, for all the world like quiet laughter.

"If a rabbit's being chased by a fox, it's wise to run straight to the wolf," he said. "Of course, the question then is whether it can get away safely after the wolf's taken the fox by the throat. Wolves like a bit of rabbit too."

"It's bad to be a rabbit," said the little girl.

"So it is," said the tyger. "But if one has grown up to be a rabbit, one can do very little about it."

"Only run."

"Just so." The tyger turned his great wide head to regard the sunken garden. "Why, your aunts have come out to take the air."

The little girl retreated to the plum tree. Leaning against its trunk, she watched Aunt Caroline and Aunt Elizabeth coming along the walk.

Aunt Caroline was pale and thin, had a shawl draped about her shoulders, and Aunt Elizabeth half-supported her as she walked.

"Yes, I do think the bloom's returning to your cheeks already," Aunt Elizabeth was saying in a determinedly cheery voice. "Fresh air will do you a world of good, my dear, I'm sure. Whenever I feel faint or bilious at Brookwood, dearest Henry always advises me to take my bonnet and go for a ramble, and after a mile or so I'm always quite restored again, and come home with quite an appetite for my dinner!"

Aunt Caroline said nothing in reply, breathing with effort as they walked. There was a stone seat overlooking the sunken garden, and Aunt Elizabeth led her to it.

"We'll settle ourselves here, shall we, and watch them making it ready?" suggested Aunt Elizabeth, sitting down and making room for Aunt Caroline. "There now. Oh, look, they've got the water going again! Really, this will make the prettiest place for a party. You'll want to put the long table for the collation over there, I suppose, and the trestle tables along the other side. And I would, my dear, have two comfortable chairs brought down and set on a kind of step, 'tis called a dais in London I think, where the nursemaids may sit with the little boys and all may pay their respects conveniently."

Aunt Caroline hissed and doubled over, clutching herself.

"There, my dear, there, courage!" Aunt Elizabeth rubbed her back. "Oh, and you were feeling so much better after breakfast. Perhaps this will help. When I'm troubled with wind, Henry will—"

"It's a judgment from God," gasped Aunt Caroline.

"Dear, you mustn't say such a thing! It may be He sends us our little aches and pains to remind us we ought to be ready at all times to come before Him, but—"

"I prayed the boys would die," Aunt Caroline told her. "I thought of having them suffocated in their cradles. God forgive me, forgive me! And it wasn't a week after that the pains began."

Aunt Elizabeth had drawn away from her. Her face was a study in stupefied horror.

"Never!" she said at last. "Those dear, sweet little lambs? Oh, Caroline, you never! Oh, how could you? Oh, and to think—"

Aunt Caroline had begun to sob hoarsely, rocking herself to and fro in her agony. Aunt Elizabeth watched her a moment, struggling to find words, and at last found them.

"Well," she said, "It's—Henry would say, this is proof of the infinite mercy of the Almighty, you know. For, only think, if you had followed such a wicked thought with a *deed*, what worse torments would await you eternally! As it is, the sin is hideous but not so bad as it might be, and these timely pangs have made you reflect on the peril to your eternal soul, and you have surely repented! Therefore all may yet be well—"

Aunt Caroline toppled forward. Aunt Elizabeth leaped up, screaming, and the men stopped work at once and ran to be of assistance. Upon examination, Aunt Caroline was found not to have died, but merely fainted from her pain, and when revived she begged feebly to be taken to her chamber. Aunt Elizabeth, rising to the occasion, directed the men to improvise a stretcher from the ladder. She paced alongside as they bore Aunt Caroline away, entreating her to call on her Savior for comfort.

The little girl watched all this with round eyes.

"There's one secret out," remarked the tyger. "I wonder whether any others will show themselves?"

The east wind was blowing. It swayed the cloths on the long tables, it swayed the paper lanterns the servants had hung up on lines strung through the trees in the garden. The tyger lashed his tail as he paced.

The little girl was walking from lantern to lantern, peering up at them and wondering how they would light when evening fell.

"Your Uncle Randall asked your Mamma to marry him today," said the tyger.

"He did it in front of Uncle Henry and Aunt Elizabeth," said the child.

"Because he thought she wouldn't like to say no, if they were present," said the tyger. The child nodded.

"But Mamma said no," she concluded. "Then Uncle Randall had a glass of wine."

The tyger put his face close to the bars.

"Something bad is going to happen," he said. "Think very hard, quickly: Are you a rabbit, or do you have teeth and claws?"

"What the hell's it doing?" said a hoarse voice from the other end of the courtyard. The child looked up to see Uncle Randall advancing on her swiftly. He had a strange blank look in his eyes, a strange fixed smile.

"Hasn't it ever been told not to go so near a wild brute? Naughty, naughty little thing!" he said, and grabbed her arm tightly. "We'll have to punish it."

He began to drag her away in the direction of the potting shed. She screamed, kicking him as hard as she could, but he laughed and swung her up off her feet. He marched on toward the thicket behind the shed, groping under her skirts.

"We'll have to punish its little soft bum, that's what we'll have to do," he said wildly, "because a dutiful uncle must do such things, after all, ungrateful little harlot—"

She screamed again, and suddenly he had stopped dead in his tracks and let her fall, because Cousin Louise was standing right before them and staring at Uncle Randall. She was chalk-white. She seemed as though she were choking a long minute, unable to make a sound, as the little girl whimpered and scrambled away on hands and knees.

Uncle Randall, momentarily disconcerted, regained his smile.

"What?" he demanded. "None of your business if we were only playing."

Cousin Louise threw herself at him. Being, as she was, a tall girl, she bore him over so he fell to the pavement with a crash. His wig came off. She beat him in the face with her fists, and found her voice at last, harsh as a crow's:

"*What were you going to tell her?* Were you going to tell her you'd cut her tongue out if she ever told what you did? Were you? *Were you?*"

Uncle Randall snarled and attempted to throw her off.

"Ow! Who'd believe you, stupid bitch? The guests'll be arriving, I'll say you've gone mad—"

The child climbed to her feet and ran, sobbing, and got behind the menagerie wall. There she cried in silence, hiding her face in her skirts.

When she ventured out again at last, neither Uncle Randall nor Cousin Louise were anywhere in sight. The tyger was looking at her steadily.

"That's another secret come to light," he said. "Now, I'll tell you still another."

Rubbing her eyes with her fist, she listened as he told her the secret.

Mamma and Aunt Elizabeth carried the babies into the chapel, so the nurserymaid was able to spare her a moment.

"Lord, lord, how did your face get so dirty? As if I ain't got enough to see to!" she grumbled, dipping a corner of her apron in the horse-trough and washing the little girl's face. "Now, hold my hand and be a good child when we go in. No noise!"

She was a good child through the solemn ceremony. Mamma watched the little boys tenderly, anxiously, and Uncle Henry and Aunt Elizabeth smiled when first John, and then James, screamed and went red-faced at having Satan driven out with cold water. Uncle Thomas was watching Mamma. Aunt Caroline was tranquilly distant: she'd taken laudanum for her pain. Beside her, Cousin Louise watched Uncle Randall with a basilisk glare. Uncle Randall was holding himself upright and defiant, smiling, though his face was puffy with bruises.

Afterward they all processed from the chapel and up the long stairs, to arrange themselves in ranks before Grandpapa, that he might give them his blessing. He stared from his high white bed and had to be reminded who they all were. At last he moved his wasted hand on the counterpane, granting an abbreviated benediction on posterity, and they were able to file from the sickroom into the clean-smelling twilight.

The wind had dropped a little but still moved the lanterns, that had candles inside them now and looked like golden moons glowing in the trees. It brought the sweet smell of wood smoke from an early bonfire. The dusk was lavender, so lambent everything looked slightly transparent, and the milling guests in the garden might have been ghosts. The child wandered among them, unseen as a ghost herself, watching.

There were stout old gentlemen with iron-gray wigs and wide-brimmed hats, who spoke at length with Uncle Henry about harvests and horse fairs. In high white wigs were young men and young ladies, lace-trimmed mincers of both sexes, who wondered why there were no musicians, and were quite put out to be told that there would be no dancing because of mourning for Papa.

Admiring gentlemen in silk stockings, slithery as eels, crowded around Mamma to pay her compliments, and Uncle Thomas held her arm possessively and smiled at them all. Aunt Caroline, on a couch that had been brought out for her, looked on dreamily. Uncle Randall edged through the crowd, telling first one inquirer and then another how his bruises had come at the hands of a low slut of a chambermaid, damn her eyes for a scheming hussy, wanted a guinea for favors as though she were the Queen of Sheba, screamed like a harpy when he'd paid her out in the coin she deserved! Ha-ha.

John and James lay in the arms of the nurserymaid and Aunt Elizabeth, who was glad to get off her feet, and the little boys stared in wide-awake astonishment at the glowing lanterns and ignored all their well-wishers, who moved on speedily to the collation table for cider and ham anyway. Some guests vanished in pairs into shadowy corners. There were perfumes of civet-musk strong in the air, there was wine flowing free. Someone got drunk remarkably quickly and tripped, and his wig went flying. It hit Uncle Henry in the face with a *poof* and a cloud of powder. People tittered with laughter.

The little girl walked through the shadows to the keeper's shed. She found the ring of keys where he had hung it up before hurrying off to the somewhat lesser collation for the servants. Nobody but the tyger saw her as she came and tried the big brass keys, one after another, in the padlock that secured the door of his pen. At last it clicked open.

She slipped it off. The bolt was a simple one, just like the bolt on the nursery door. Sliding it back, she opened the door of the pen.

The tyger paced swiftly forward, his green eyes gleaming. He looked much bigger out of his prison. He turned and gazed at her a moment; put out his warm rough tongue and slicked it along the pulse of her wrist, the palm of her hand. She felt a shock go through her body, an electric thrill of pleasure. She parted her lips but could find no words, only staring back at him in wonderment. He turned his head to regard the party in the sunken garden.

"Now," said the tyger, "we'll see, won't we?"

He stretched his magnificent length, gave a slight wriggle of his shoulders, and bounded across the courtyard. Standing beside the empty cage, she folded her little hands and watched.

He charged the party, vaulting from the top step into the sunken garden. Horrified guests looked up to see him land in the midst of them all, and gilt chairs were knocked over as people scrambled to get away from him, screaming in their panic. Some staggered on their high heels, some kicked off their shoes and ran in their slippery, stockinged feet. Aunt Elizabeth went over backward in her chair, clutching young James, and both began to shriek. The servants fled for their lives. Aunt Caroline watched all from her couch, too drugged to care.

But the tyger leaped straight through the garden like a thunderbolt, overtaking Uncle Thomas, whom it felled with a sidelong rake of one paw. Uncle Thomas went down, howling and clutching himself, and blood ran red all down his white silk hose. The tyger didn't even pause, however, it sprang clean over him and continued forward, and the only person left before it now was Uncle Randall, who had broken a heel on the topmost of the opposite steps and was still there, frantically attempting to yank off his tight shoe.

Uncle Randall looked up into the tyger's eyes, but had no time to do more than bleat before it struck him. He broke like a doll, and rolled over with it into the darkness.

There was a second's hush, cries cut off abruptly in those who still crouched or lay sprawled in the sunken garden. Uncle Henry, who had crawled to Aunt Elizabeth's side, rose on his elbow to look and said, "O Lord God!"

The tyger appeared at the top of the steps, dragging Uncle Randall by the back of the neck. Uncle Randall's head hung at a strange angle and his body was limp. The tyger's eyes reflected back the light of the golden lanterns.

It stared at them all a moment before opening its jaws. Uncle Randall dropped like an empty coat. The tyger's beard was red.

It bared its fangs, and turned and bounded away into the night.

When they asked her why, she explained. After she had told them everything, they made her explain it all over, and then explain once more. No matter how often she explained, however, they did not hear what she said.

Finally they sent her away, to a convent school in France. It was by no means as bad as it might have been.

She made no friends, but her eyes being now accustomed to look for detail, she saw keenly the fond possessive looks or angry glances between the other girls, heard the midnight weeping or sighs, saw the notes hastily exchanged; watched the contests for dominance, and knew when the cloister gate was locked and when it was left unlocked, and who came and went thereby, and when they came too.

The heavy air buzzed like a hive. She no more thought of participating in the convent's inner life than she would have thrust her hand into a wasp's nest, but she watched in fascination.

Then, one morning at Mass, above the high altar, the crucified Christ opened green blazing eyes and looked at her. He smiled.

In the Shadow of Her Wings

Ashok Banker

Ashok Banker lives in Bombay with his wife and two children. He is the author of nine novels, including Vertigo *and* Byculla Boy, *and many screenplays. He is the author of India's first English TV serial, A Mouthful of Sky. He is also the author of* The Pocket Essential Guide to Bollywood, *a reference book on India's film industry. In 1990, he quit his job in advertising to write full time. He says in* The Week, *India's leading news magazine, "Ashok Banker the script writer is subsidizing Ashok Banker the novelist." He has sold scripts for hundreds of TV shows and four Hindi feature films. Banker's first publication in the science fiction and fantasy field was in* Altair *in 1999. In 2000, he published "East of the Sun, West of the Moon" in* Artemis. *And in 2001 he published three stories in the field: "Devi Darshan" in* Weird Tales, *and two in* Interzone, *"www.cyber-whore.com" and "In the Shadow of Her Wings."*

In this near-future fantasy, a brutal political story with deep resonance, an assassin is sent by the government to kill the leader of a feminist separatist cult. Of course, things don't work out as planned. It is an interesting contrast to Ted Chiang's story in this volume.

Dravid expected Kali border security to be much tighter than it was. All he got was a body search that was routinely thorough, and a few old-fashioned tests and checks. It reminded him of a visit he had made as a young right-wing Hindu activist to an Indian nuclear-weapon testing facility back in 1998, after the Pokhran atomic tests. His briefings had been correct in this respect: Kali did not seem to have much use for 21st-century safe-care.

The Border guards finished with him in a few minutes, then led him down into the basement of the Border Post and on through a concrete corridor that was at least a kilometer long in his estimation. Although there were far too many turns to be certain: it could be twice as long, or half. He was surprised at the absence of defenses. After all the buildup, it was an anticlimactic letdown. Could the disputed area truly be this easy to infiltrate? A single platoon of Black Cat commandos armed with nominal safe-care weaponry could take this border post and entrance in a few minutes, he estimated. The dozen-odd border guards he had seen above ground had borne no visible weapons. Ridiculously easy.

Then he remembered the first and longest of his briefings.

Shalinitai, the renegade Kaliite-turned-consultant to the Disputed Territories Task Force (DTTF), had commented on this very fact during her lecture on Kali's political history: "Do not be fooled by Kali's apparent lack of defenses. Like the Goddess after whom it is named, the disputed region that aspires to nation status under the name of Kali is armed with something far more dangerous than physical weaponry. She is armed with the power of the spirit. The power of faith."

Dravid had resisted the urge to yawn. He had heard this kind of "empty-hand, spirit-power" mania too many times to even give it credence by mocking it. He had also seen any number of similarly deluded cults and spiritual blindfaithers walk like fools into the trajectory of safe-care weapons, only to have their very real physical bodies torn to shreds by unspiritual projectiles and explosives that needed no faith in invisible deities to perform their lethal function. Faith might move mountains; but lasers cut flesh. And without flesh to sustain it, there was nothing left to harbor faith.

Sensing his bored skepticism, the renegade had paused and sighed softly. Almost resigned to his indifference, she had added, "Kali exists only because the people support its existence and because India is still a democracy. That is a far more formidable defense than any safe-care arsenal." This he found more acceptable. It was a political argument, one of the classic cornerstones of every nationwide cult that was allowed to fester in the armpit of a republic under the guise of freedom of faith and right to political dissension.

There had been an adversarial gleam in her dark eyes as if challenging him to challenge this statement. But Dravid was too much of a cynic to waste time on political arguments either. As far as he was concerned, they could dispense with the briefings and motivational lectures. He didn't need the comfort of political conviction to help him do his job. Assassination was murder no matter what the justification. The only motivation he needed was the paycheck.

As if sensing this from his lack of risibility, Shalinitai had paused in her briefing. Deviating unexpectedly from her subject, she had poured herself a glass of plain water and said, "You will find no resistance when you go to assassinate Durga Maa. It will be the easiest assassination you have ever committed."

Dravid had waited for the punchline he knew was coming. Moral lectures always had a punchline.

"It's living with the knowledge of your act that will make the rest of your life unbearable," she said. He hadn't smiled. He hadn't needed to. She knew the smile was there, behind his inscrutable face. He read the awareness in her eyes and sought the inevitable frustration she must feel after having made her strongest argument and failed. There was none. Only a faint glimmer of sympathy.

"I pity your task, assassin," she had said.

He hadn't smiled at that either. He had been pitied before too. It was one of the most predictable responses, apart from self-righteous rage.

The corridor curved one final time and ended abruptly in the entrance to a very narrow stairwell. Dravid drew his large frame in to accommodate the inconveniently low ceilings and close walls. As they climbed, their footfalls echoed jarringly in the confined space. The short, lithe, smaller-built female guards moved easily upward, setting a hard pace for him to match. He had visited enough ancient Indian fortresses to understand the principle: Invaders would be forced to attack in single file, crouched awkwardly low. A single guard could defend the stairwell, and the piled bodies of the wounded and dead would make progress even more tortuous. It was a virtually impregnable defense—a thousand years ago. He glimpsed tiny slits in the wall and ceilings, and recalled similar apertures all along the corridor. He had taken them for air vents at first but now understood that they were in fact guard posts. The corridor was lit from above, illuminating him and the guards as they climbed endlessly, but effectively concealing the watching guards stationed behind the walls.

Dravid wasn't impressed. Medieval subterfuge and manual defenses were no match for modern safe-care. A single safe-care biogas capsule, delivered by any number of methods into the corridor, could wipe out the entire garrison of unseen defenders. The self-consuming biogases would take barely three seconds to render the air safe again and that would be the end of Kali's stupidly outdated defense system.

He had climbed more than a thousand steps and was suffering from the bent posture and elbow-and-shoulder-bruising closeness of the concrete walls when the stairwell finally widened and rose high enough for him to straighten up.

The alcove resembled a small circular chamber in a stone tower, again of obviously medieval design. It was ironic in a way, he thought as the guards led him through a series of corridors and transitional chambers. Whatever little he had seen of Kali so far was clearly modeled on the architecture of medieval India. Yet Kali itself went to great pains to insist it was not part of India. Not according to the 700,000-odd renegades who had taken refuge in this tiny pocket of disputed territory, defying Indian national laws and international sanctions to declare its independence as a sovereign nation in its own right. To these cultist fanatics, this little area of Central India bordering the legitimate Indian states of Maharashtra, Madhya Pradesh and Orissa was the nation of Kali, a concept as fiercely independent as the concept of Israel had become after the Nazi pogroms of World War II, almost three-quarters of a century earlier. The world's only all-woman nation. To the Indian Government, though, this was simply Disputed Territory, just as areas of Pakistan-occupied Kashmir had once been designated before the Re-Merger with Pakistan, Bangladesh and Nepal ten years ago. United India could not afford to sanction a Kali, let alone acknowledge its legitimacy.

That was why he was here now. To end the problem by rooting out the source. Destroy the brood-mother and the species dies out.

The guards fell back, surprising him. He could not conceive of a reason why he should be allowed to proceed unescorted. Yet when he turned to look at them questioningly, the one who had led the detail, a short, dark-skinned, muscular woman with scar tissue obscuring her left cheek and neck, pointed unmistakably down the corridor. He was to proceed alone. Dravid shrugged, amused at yet another ludicrously amateurish security lapse, and walked on. He had gone several hundred paces before he realized what was odd about this particular corridor. His footfalls made no echoes.

The reason for this became clear when he reached the end of the corridor, another circular chamber. A slit in the wall revealed not the darkness of the subterranean passage or the diffused top-lighting. Instead it exposed a slice of brilliant blue sky. He was undoubtedly in a tower. He realized with a start that this was the very same edifice that he had seen on various sat-images during his briefings. One of several hundred such towers positioned at regular intervals along the border of the besieged territory, ringing the entire disputed territory like giant stone sentinels. They were believed to be guardian outposts constructed to watch over the Line of Control that demarcated Kali's disputed land space from the surrounding Indian territory.

"Envoy Dravid," said the woman who was waiting in the sunlit tower chamber. "Please be seated." She indicated a thin woven mat on the ground, identical to the one on which she was seated cross-legged in the yogic lotus posture. Dravid scanned the room and surrounding area and couldn't believe his luck. No guards, no weapons, no defenses. In short, no safe-care at all. Dravid was unable to believe that his mission could be this easy to accomplish. He looked at the woman, who was watching him calmly.

"I am Durga Maa," she said. "The one you seek to assassinate. Tell me, Envoy, would you like to kill me at once, or would you like to maintain the pretense of a diplomatic debate for a while?"

Dravid blinked rapidly.

She smiled. "I suggest that we get the assassination over with first. That way, your mind will be free to discuss the larger issues at stake here, without distraction."

And she opened her arms in the universal Hindu gesture of greeting. "Sva-swagatam, Mrityudaata." Welcome, Angel of Death.

Even if it was a trap, as every meg of data in his mental archives said it must be, Dravid could not let the opportunity pass. His not to question why. His but to kill and fly.

He hesitated only long enough to run one final scan-check. The result was the same as the previous three times. It was an ID-OK, confirmed through half a dozen cross-checks including a perfect DNA match. This woman seated before him was Durga Maa, the founder and leader of Kali. She was his target.

He used his thumbnail to circumscribe a tiny crescent-shaped incision in his left wrist and withdrew the reinforced silicon needle from his forearm. It was barely ten millimeters in diameter and he had to grip firmly. He drew it across his palm, wiping it clean of the tiny flecks of blood and gristle that coated it. Tinted to resemble a prominent vein, it was a translucent green that caught the sunlight as he moved across the chamber. He was at full alert now, his keenly honed senses prepared for any resistance or ambush. There was none.

She smiled as he inserted the lethal tip of the needle between her ribs. Her breast was yielding and warm against his hand. He pressed hard, brutally, and the entire nine-inch length entered her chest, sliding in easily. He pictured it puncturing her left lower chamber, spilling precious life-fluid. In her eyes, he watched the look of serenity flicker and fade.

"Kali be with you," she said.

And then she was gone, her body slumped sideways, legs still locked in the yogic position. He kicked at her thighs, releasing their grip, and she sprawled out more naturally. Darkness pooled beneath her body.

He stood and looked around, unable to believe it had been this easy. He felt a qualm of unease. Her attitude, the knowledge that he was to assassinate her, her serene acceptance of her death, these were not things he was equipped to deal with. Even with the most fanatical of cult leaders, there was always the final struggle for survival, the organism's instinct for self-preservation. But she had been truly ready.

He pushed these thoughts from his head. The most difficult part still lay ahead. Escape. He had analyzed the possible options and they were all negative-rated. The least likely to fail (12.67%) was by blasting a hole in the wall of this tower and speed-climbing down the outside. But that was assuming the guards were armed and prepared for violent retaliation, which they didn't seem to be.

A circular stairway ran around the perimeter of the chamber. Dravid went down the stone stairs quickly and silently, alert for the first sign of armed response.

* * *

He descended to the next level, and found himself in an almost identical chamber. It was as sparsely furnished, with the same chick mats on the floor. And a woman.

He stopped short at the sight of the woman. She was younger than Durga Maa, but premature grayness made her seem older at first glance. She was dressed similarly but not precisely the same way. He found no match for her in his records. She was also very beautiful.

She looked up as if she had been expecting him and indicated a bowl of steaming tea and two earthen cups.

"Greetings, Envoy Dravid. With the demise of our beloved sister, I am now Durga Maa. Would you like to kill me at once, or will you partake of some refreshment first?"

And she opened her arms in that same gesture of acceptance.

Dravid thought it was a ploy at first. A delaying tactic intended to stall him until the guards arrived. But his internal systems showed nobody else approaching within a hundred-meter radius. No safe-care weaponry in the chamber. Nothing capable of doing him any physical harm.

His system announced an ID match for the woman seated before him. With a rising sense of unease, Dravid checked and rechecked the scan results until he could no longer doubt them. Somehow, in the space of a few seconds, she had changed her DNA structure internally, although her physical appearance remained the same. To all intents and purposes, she had become exactly what she claimed she was. Durga Maa, leader of Kali, down to the smallest twisted strand of genetic composition.

She poured tea for him. "You cannot comprehend how two women could possess the same identity. It is a scientific impossibility, you think."

She held the clay cup out to him. He made no move to take it. He was still running checks and rechecks to examine every variant possible, tapping into the orbital systems to access greater processing power and other archives.

She set the cup down before the mat intended for him.

"You are right," she said. "Science cannot explain it. But faith can. There is only one Durga Maa—at a given point in time. But on her demise, her entire personality and being, what we like to call her aatma, passes to a successor. That is I."

"Aatma," he repeated scornfully. "You mean, soul?"

She poured tea for herself. Her movements were delicate, assured, and very pleasing to watch. She had a fine bone structure that would have been considered beautiful among North Indians, but far too Aryan and brahminical to South Indian eyes.

"It does exist," she said. "No matter that science cannot prove it does. I now possess Durga Maa's soul, which makes me Durga Maa."

She gestured at herself. "This physical shell is immaterial. It is the person within that matters. I am the avatar of Kali, just as Durga Maa herself was while she lived."

Dravid chuckled softly. "Avatars and aatma. What is this? A TriNet Fiction? Save the spiritual rant for blind-faithers."

She held the bowl up in both hands, Asian style. "You are skeptical," she said, sipping tea. "It is to be expected. But I can establish this as a scientific fact which your technology can verify beyond doubt."

She set the tea down on the floor and spread her arms in the same universal gesture of acceptance.

"Assassinate me too. And see for yourself."

He hesitated for barely a fraction of a second. Then decided he had nothing to lose. This time, he used the instrument at hand, smashing the tea cup and drawing the jagged clay edge across her jugular, severing it on the first try. He watched her bleed to death, spraying her life across the stone floor. The beam of sunlight shining through the jetting arc turned vermilion briefly.

Because he was curious and because it was the easiest option, he proceeded to the next lower level.

There was another woman waiting in another chamber. This one was much older, with the wizened semi-oriental features of a Northeastern Indian. A Mizo or a Naga. Descendant of the head-hunting tribes of the Indo-Burmese hills that had been converted to Christianity by relentless American Baptist missionaries a few generations ago. She did not speak as much as the earlier one. But his scans showed once again that impossible change in DNA even while her physical appearance remained the same.

He killed her with vicious efficiency, snapping her neck with a fierce twist of his powerful arms. This time, he observed the change after death closely. His scans showed a change to another DNA structure. Not a change, he realized. A reversion to the woman's original identity before she became the avatar of the Goddess.

A rage swept through him, replacing the initial sense of bewilderment. This could not be happening. It was not part of the plan. It was a scientific impossibility.

He took the stairs with athletic speed, reaching the next level an instant before the change occurred, and through the "eyes" of his system he watched the conversion in progress, the very molecular structure of the ribonucleic strands altering. Then he killed the fourth avatar—for want of a better term—before she could even speak. She had a mole on her left eyebrow and the darkened skin and sallow features of a Malayalee. There was coconut oil on her hair and it smeared on his fingers as he held her skull and smashed it against the stone wall repeatedly.

This went on for several more levels. Chasing the "aatma" as it flew from woman to woman. Assassinating each new avatar of Durga Maa as she was genetically rebirthed.

By the 23rd level, he found himself tiring. His clothes and body were soiled with blood and gristle as well as traces of each woman's individual identity. Tea, coconut oil, sweater yarn, pooja threads, rangoli powder . . . His systems showed that the tower was precisely one hundred stories high. Seventy-seven more levels to go. And the sat scans had analyzed his first batch of data transmission: one hundred such towers ringed the perimeter of the disputed territory, each with a hundred levels. Assuming that each housed a successor, that meant a sum total of 10,100 women to be assassinated.

He stopped and reexamined his options.

"It will be easier if you accept it," said the 23rd avatar. A very diminutive young woman, barely more than a girl. A Maharashtrian, with the dark skin and black pupils of the Dalits of the Deccan Plain, descendants of the ostracized scheduled castes of the 20th century, the "untouchables" that Mahatma Gandhi had renamed "harijans, children of God" and whom Dr. Babasaheb Ambedkar had renamed Dalits. She was weaving a shawl on a charka, using her feet to grip the wooden spinney, and working steadily as she spoke. "The more you fight it, the harder it will be for you later."

He spoke with barely concealed anger, his frustration getting the better of his legendary self-control. "How do you do it? You transmit the genetic coding through orbitals? But then how do you effect the morphing? This kind of technology doesn't exist! It has to be some kind of illusion." But no illusion could deceive the massive processing power that he had accessed to check and recheck the 22 "impossible" transformations.

She worked the spinney, weaving the red, white and saffron strands of wool expertly as she spoke. "Is it so hard to accept, Envoy? You are Indian, like us. Not a Westerner with a mind fogged by science. You know that some things cannot be explained, only accepted."

He sat down wearily, his blood-splashed feet staining a pile of spotless white wool, not caring. She clucked her tongue and moved the wool aside, picking out the stained strands and putting them in a separate pile for cleaning later.

"All right," he said, deciding there would be no harm in a brief theoretical discussion while his systems sought a more scientific explanation. "Assume for the moment that you are all avatars of the Devi. But—"

"Nako re, baba," she said. "No, my brother. We are only women. Ordinary mortal women. Only when the living avatar of the Devi dies, then the next of us in line takes her place. Samjhe? Understood now?"

She reminded him irritatingly of his mausi, a paternal aunt who was always completely self-assured and unplaceable. He gritted his teeth in frustration.

"But how many times can it possibly happen? There has to be a limit!"

"Kashasaati limit?" she asked him in the matter-of-fact Maharashtrian way. "You know your religious mythology. A Goddess can be reborn infinite times, because a Goddess on the mortal plane is aatma, pure spirit. And an aatma cannot be killed. Read your *Bhagwad Gita* again. Weapons cannot cleave it, wind cannot blow it away, fire cannot burn it, water cannot dissolve it, earth cannot consume it, it is the soul immortal."

He was silent. The very same mausi had taught him this exact same verse from the *Gita*, in the original Sanskrit. With very little effort he could recall her sitting cross-legged before the wooden chaupat propping up the oversize hand-calligraphed copy of the *Bhagwad Gita*, chanting the Sanskrit slokas in that maddening, unforgettable singsong manner.

"Then there is only one solution," he said at last. And stood up.

She looked at him over the rims of her spectacles, pausing in her weaving.

"I have to nuke you all. Wipe out the whole of Kali in one shot. That way, there won't be any more bodies left for your damned Goddess to take refuge in."

He walked away from her, then paused. He really should kill her. He had said too much. Perhaps she had some way of informing her compatriots, of mounting a defense against the genocide he proposed.

But for some reason he couldn't bring himself to do it. He consoled himself with the thought that he would be killing them all anyway in a few moments.

As he walked away, the sound of the charka whirring began again behind him.

It took surprisingly long for him to secure the necessary permission to "salinate" the disputed territory. It was a final alternative listed in his command menu, and as the official Envoy to the rebels, he had the authority to take the decision. Kali had become a sore on the belly of United India over the last decade. The noises of commiseration from overseas had begun to sound more like rumbles of discontent, especially after so many American and European women had emigrated to the renegade "nation." His superiors had anticipated the need for a final solution and had sent him in with all the necessary preparations in place. They wanted this problem solved now, one way or the other, before the tri-annual summit of Non-Aligned Independent Nuclear Nations the following week in New Delhi.

He filed a charge of discovery of nuclear weapons and testing on Kali territory, proof of the renegades' terrorist intentions and capacity. He initiated a program that simulated a crisis situation developing on his arrival in the disputed territory. Reviewed later by the inevitable Human Rights panel, it would perfectly simulate a series of events in which all his accompanying officers and staffers were successively tortured and brutally killed by Kali terrorist troops and then he himself was taken on a tour of their formidable nuclear facility in order to inform and warn the world of Kali's intention to strike blind at India. There would be holes unfilled, and gaps, but they would only add to the authenticity of the whole charade.

The nuclear orbitals were positioned and armed, ready for release on his command.

He had retreated through the tunnel by this time, almost at the peripheral guard base from which he had entered. The guards had offered no resistance at all, not even an attempt to stop him. He smiled at the absurdity of these people. And felt a rush of joy at their imminent destruction.

He triggered the nuclear orbital the moment he reached MSCD (minimum safe-care distance). In an instant, the gaudy afternoon sky over the flatlands was obscured by the familiar blinding flash and then the rising mushroom cloud. He whistled as he walked to the Rimmer he had left parked on the Indian side of the Line of Control. There was a welcoming committee waiting to greet him, to shake the hand of the man who had finally "solved" the Kali problem.

He allowed himself a smug smile of triumph and was about to offer his hand in greeting when the change took him.

"Agent Dravid?" said the PM-General, his smile wavering as he saw his most celebrated safe-care executive stagger and raise a hand to his forehead. "Are you feeling quite well?"

Dravid swung around, staring at the billowing cloud that marked the 230 square kilometers of land that had housed 700,000 renegade women until a few seconds ago. He raised his fist and shook it, his mouth opening in the rictus of a soundless scream.

"Damn you," he managed to choke out. And then the change was done. When he turned back to the PM-General, the anger and hate were replaced by an expression of such calm serenity that it startled the supreme leader of United India far more than any act or gesture of violence would have done.

"I am Durga Maa," said the man formerly known as Envoy Dravid.

The Heart of the Hill

Marion Zimmer Bradley and Diana L. Paxson

Marion Zimmer Bradley (mzbworks.home.att.net/), who died following a heart attack in 1999, is best known for The Mists of Avalon *(1983), a novel of transformation that reclaimed the Arthurian mythos for women, and was recently made into a TV mini-series. She frequently collaborated with other writers. Her collaborations with Diana Paxson were among the most fruitful. She was also influential as an editor, presiding over* Marion Zimmer Bradley's Fantasy Magazine *and a number of fantasy anthologies. In all, she published over eighty novels. Her Darkover series (in twenty-one volumes) has a cult following so strong it has generated an annual fan convention (Darkover Con).*

Diana L. Paxson (home.pon.net/rhinoceroslodge/paxson.htm) lives in Berkeley, California, in a literary household called Greyhaven. She is the author of the Chronicles of Westria, nine historical fantasies, including The White Raven *(a mainstream fantasy based on the legend of Tristan and Iseult), and the Wodan's Children trilogy (*The Wolf and the Raven, Dragons of the Rhine, *and* The Lord of Horses*), which tells the story of Sigfrid and Brunhild.*

"The Heart of the Hill," which appeared in Out of Avalon, *edited by Jennifer Roberson, is an atmospheric story with strong images. It is an Arthurian fantasy, a territory familiar to both writers, but has links to other, older legends and mythologies.*

Morgaine speaks . . .

Time runs strangely in Avalon, but I no longer look into the Mirror to see what passes beyond the mists that separate it from the world. Arthur is dead, and Lancelet as well, and on the other isle, Christian nuns pray for Viviane's soul. Saxons have overrun the land, and the priestesses here are fewer than they were when first I came here as a little girl, but from time to time the little dark people of the marsh still send to tell us that a daughter of the old blood has come.

One such was brought to me this morning. Ildierna, they call her, and she is the daughter of a chieftain from the Welsh hills where they keep the old ways still. I do not remember what I said to her—and no doubt she was too awestruck to really hear me. She was too amazed to see one whom all in the outside world think must be long dead to pay proper attention. But there was strength in her, and it came to me that she was just such a child as I might have had if I had borne a daughter to Accolon, and I wondered if I were looking at the maiden who will one day follow me.

But I think now that it is not Accolon that she reminds me of, but another maiden whom I knew long, long ago when my breasts were scarcely grown. These days I find it hard to remember the young priestesses who serve me, and call them sometimes by each other's names or by the names of maidens long dead or grown, but I remember quite clearly the girls who were being trained on Avalon when I first came.

> *There was one called Gwenlian whom I remember very*
> *well. I do not know why she should come to mind just now,*
> *except that this new girl has the look of her, with her strong*
> *bones and bright brown hair, and because she taught me a lesson*
> *I had great need to learn.*

"This is work for servants, or slaves!" exclaimed Gwenlian, lifting the crude straw brush from the limewash and watching the white drops fall back into the pail. "Most assuredly it is not a task for a princess, or a priestess of Avalon!" Grimacing, she let the brush fall.

Morgaine reached swiftly to catch it, jumping back to avoid the spattering droplets, for even diluted, the stuff could burn.

"But we are neither," she answered tartly. "Only novice priestesses who will be very glad next winter to have watertight walls."

Whitening the daub and wattle walls of the House of Maidens was a yearly task. The mixture of burned lime shell and fat repelled water, but it did need to be renewed on a regular basis or it would wear away. It had never occurred to Morgaine to resent the task, any more than she did the spinning, which was the constant occupation of all the young priestesses when indoors. As Viviane had once warned her, the life of a priestess could be hard and bitter, but she did not include among its hardships this work, which at least got her out in the sun and air.

"You are so very good!" exclaimed Gwenlian mockingly. "The perfect little priestess, afraid to take a breath that Viviane does not allow. But I was brought up to make my own choices."

"She who is slave to her own will has a fool for a master . . ." Viviane had often said, and yet they were also taught that a priestess had to be willing to bear the responsibility for her own deeds. Soon Morgaine would begin her year of silence, and after that face the ordeal of initiation. She was almost a woman—and almost a priestess—already. Was it perhaps time for her to begin thinking like one?

She dipped her brush into the whitewash and slathered the stuff over another section of wall. "And what, princess, would you choose?" Her tone was tart, but not, quite, mocking.

Gwenlian was tall and fair skinned, one of the sun people. Beside her, Morgaine was once more reminded of her own lack of height and small bones, and the skin that so readily darkened when she spent time out of doors. "Morgaine of the Fairies" they called her, but it was a brownie she felt most like just now. And yet when the younger girl had first been brought to the House of Maidens, Morgaine had been made her guardian, and despite their differences—perhaps, even because of them—Gwenlian was the closest Morgaine had to a friend.

Rather absentmindedly, Gwenlian dipped her brush into the pail as well. "To learn . . ." she said in a whisper. "To use the abilities that the Goddess has given me, instead of sitting and chanting lists from the old lore with the little girls."

"By learning the old lore we train and discipline our minds . . ." Morgaine began, then realized that in this, too, she was merely repeating what she had heard from Viviane. To commit vast quantities of information to memory was the ancient way of the Druids, but it did not encourage creative thinking. Viviane spoke often of the necessity that bound her—had the traditional ways of training constrained her thinking so much that she could not change it even if she desired?

With a shock, Morgaine realized that she was on the verge of criticizing the Lady of Avalon. She stopped short, biting her lip, the brush dripping milky drops onto the ground, but words came from some part of her mind she did not control.

"What would you do?"

"Whitewash the stones of the Processional Way so that we do not trip when we ascend the sacred hill in the dark?" Gwenlian shook her head and laughed. "No—that would be a child's trick. I want something *real*. In meditation, I have had visions. The egg-stone, the *omphalos*, is calling me. If I could touch it, join with it, I would touch the power at the heart of the hill, and then, I would know. . . ."

"Know what?" Morgaine asked faintly.

"What I truly am . . . what I was meant to be. . . ."

Gwenlian was wrong, of course. There were no shortcuts, no magic beyond simple patient hard work and discipline in the making of a priestess. So Morgaine told herself, but she could not help thinking about what the other girl had said to her. Her head told her that Gwenlian's impatience with the training was the petulance of a child, but her heart kept wondering, at the oddest moments, if what she had said might just be true.

And if even she had doubts, then what was Gwenlian thinking about now? In the days that followed, Morgaine contrived, whenever she could do so without being obvious, to keep an eye on her. She told herself that she watched her so that she could put a stop to it if Gwenlian tried something foolish, that she would feel responsible if the other girl came to harm. She never questioned her own motivations until the night when she awakened to glimpse a white form slipping through the doorway of the House of Maidens, and felt a pulse of excitement flare through her veins.

And then there was no time to wonder, only a moment to find her own shawl and her sandals and in the same ghostly silence, to follow. Clouds covered most of the sky, but those stars she could see told her that the time was a little past midnight. The Druids, whose task it was to salute the hidden sun, would by now have finished prayers in their temple and sought their rest. It was not one of the great festivals when most of the community watched through the night; any of the priestesses whose own work required them to be wakeful would be doing so hidden and in solitude.

Otherwise, the isle of Avalon was wrapped in slumber. *If I can catch up with Gwenlian swiftly, no one will ever know!* thought Morgaine as she hurried down the path.

The columns of the Temple of the Sun were a pale blur in the gloom, but something paler still was disappearing between them. What could Gwenlian be seeking there? Then, between one step and another, Morgaine remembered that the Temple of the Sun was where they kept the *omphalos* stone. The Druids preferred to worship beneath the open sky, but the Temple had been built by the wizards from the drowned lands across the sea, and was still the setting for those rituals the Druids had learned from them.

Nothing will happen, she told herself. *Without the proper rites, without the touch of the priest to awaken it, the* omphalos *will be no more than an egg-shaped stone.* But nonetheless, she forced herself to move more swiftly.

The hinges of the heavy wooden door were kept oiled so as not to squeak during the rituals, and they made no sound as Morgaine slipped through. The oil lamp that was always kept burning in the sanctuary cast a faint, flickering illumination. Its light gleamed from the colored stone set into the granite floor, and highlighted the textured images in tapestries so ancient their colors had faded away.

Morgaine stopped short, her head whirling. She had been here only a few times, when they needed a maiden to serve in the rites, and then she had been so intent on playing her part correctly she had not had much attention to spare for the setting. But her most recent training had addressed the art of reading information from one's surroundings, and now she was nearly overwhelmed by the hard, bright masculine identity that radiated from every stone.

As a novice priestess, she was an initiate of the mysteries of the darkness, of the cool radiance of the moon. Here, all things spoke of the Sun, and the Son, the northern Apollo of the Apple Isle, and even in the depths of night, she was dazzled. She controlled her breathing, rooting her awareness in the earth—at least that was still the same—until she could see once more.

A grunt of effort brought her back to attention. In the center of the mosaic star set into the stone of the floor lay the *omphalos*, a flattened egg-shaped stone about the length of her arm. Gwenlian knelt beside it, pressing her hands against the stone. Swiftly Morgaine hurried to her side.

"For a moment I felt it, Morgaine!" Gwenlian whispered. "The stone tingled against my palms!" Her eyes were alight with mingled frustration and fear.

Morgaine tugged at the other girl's shoulders. "You found the eggstone—come away now, before we're found."

"But I haven't!" wailed Gwenlian. "The power is gone."

In the next moment her resistance abruptly eased and Morgaine staggered backward, but it was not Gwenlian, but the stone that had moved. The slab on which it lay had shifted to reveal an opening and a flight of steps, which led down into darkness.

"A passageway . . ." breathed Gwenlian. "It is true then. There are tunnels that lead into the hill."

"Or somewhere . . ." objected Morgaine. But her heart was pounding too. "Now you know—come *away*!"

Gwenlian got to her feet, and Morgaine released her grip, but instead of turning, the girl flung herself forward, into the opening. For a moment Morgaine stood with her mouth open, staring. *She has no light—in a few moments she'll come back*, she thought, but Gwenlian did not return. With a sinking heart, Morgaine realized she was going to have to follow her.

She took an unlit torch from its holder on one of the columns and, trembling, lit it from the altar lamp. No blast from the heavens punished her impiety. With a last look over her shoulder, she followed the other girl into the passageway.

The air in the tunnel was damp, but that was not what set the shiver in Morgaine's bones. The Druids were masters of wood, not stone. As she looked at the mighty blocks that formed it, she knew that this passageway had been old when the first of the British-speaking tribes came over the sea. The ancient wizards who built the Temple of the Sun had made this passage into the hill. Morgaine trembled with wonder and with fear, for she was not an initiate of these mysteries.

She half expected to find Gwenlian huddled at the first turn of the passageway, whimpering in the dark, but she continued for some time without finding her, and when the tunnel forked she realized this might be more difficult than she had expected. Symbols were graven into the stones to mark the turnings. Which way had Gwenlian gone?

The other girl had moved so quickly—something must be drawing her. If there really was an *omphalos* in the heart of the hill, perhaps she had been sensitized by touching its image. But Morgaine had no such connection with the stone—only with Gwenlian. She closed her eyes and let her breath move in and out in a steady rhythm as she had been taught, sending awareness inward.

Gwenlian, where are you? Gwenlian, think of me and I will come to you. . . . She built up the image of her friend's strong-boned face and brown hair and launched her will toward that goal.

At first her mind bubbled with a confusion of impressions: Gwenlian winning a footrace, slapping limewash on the wall, eating porridge, lifting her hands in ritual. Morgaine allowed each picture to take shape, to add its essence to the whole, then sent it bobbing away, while her awareness sank deeper and deeper, until all the images merged in the powerful current that was Gwenlian's true identity. It drew her, and Morgaine started to move again, slitting her eyes so that her upper mind could note the turnings and mark them.

Her superficial senses noted that the blocks were giving way to solid stone—she must be moving under the Tor itself! Presently the marks of the chisel became fewer, and she realized that this tunnel was a natural one, carved by running water. Indeed, the walls were shiny with moisture, and a trickle of water was wearing a new channel into the roughly leveled floor. Now the torchlight showed her wet footprints, but she hardly needed them. She could *feel* Gwenlian ahead of her, and something else, that pulsed in the air and throbbed in the very stone.

"Goddess, defend me!" she whispered, understanding with her very soul, as her mind had already accepted, that what Gwenlian had believed was true.

A change in the air warned her that she was approaching a larger chamber a moment before the last turn in the tunnel. She took another step and stopped, blinking as the torchlight caught, corruscating, on a thousand crystal flecks in the rock walls that surrounded her. And then, as if those flecks were mirrors, all the refracted light focused in the center of the chamber and kindled an answering light deep in the center of the egg-shaped stone.

Morgaine gazed in amazement, for the stone was translucent as curdled crystal. She could not imagine from what distant place it had been brought to lie here in the heart of the hill, if indeed it had come from anywhere in the world of humankind.

And her magic had not misled her, for here was Gwenlian, curled around the egg-stone with her arms clasped around it. Her eyes were closed, but there was tension in her arms; Morgaine did not think she was dreaming, but rather in the throes of a vision. Here also iron sockets for torches were set into the wall. Morgaine fixed her torch into one of them and moved gently to kneel beside her friend.

"Gwenlian . . ." she whispered, "Gwenlian, come back to me—"

There was no response. Frowning, Morgaine snapped her fingers around the other girl's head and blew in her ears. Gwenlian stirred a little at that, but her eyes did not open. If there had been water, Morgaine would have poured it over her, or even plunged her into it—that method could break even the deepest trance.

Clearly, Gwenlian could not be brought back to consciousness so long as she was touching the stone. In general, people in trance should not be touched, but she had no choice now. Taking a deep breath, Morgaine put her arms around her friend to pull her away.

The first thing she realized was that although Gwenlian's body moved, her arms remained fixed around the stone. The second was that the power that pulsed in the *omphalos* was passing through Gwenlian's body, and now Morgaine could feel it in her own limbs. At least she could still let go, but physical contact would make it much easier to establish a psychic bond. She was too small and slight to pick up Gwenlian, and even a full-grown warrior would have found it difficult to carry both the girl *and* the stone. The only way in which she could rescue Gwenlian would be to go into the Otherworld in which Gwenlian's spirit was wandering and find her.

Beneath the surface of her thoughts another voice was nagging.

"Foolish child, this task is beyond both your strength and your skill. Leave the girl and go to the Druids. They will know how to set her free."

It sounded like Viviane. Had the Lady of Avalon somehow linked with her in her dreams? Surely not, for if that were so, the Druids would have been here already. No, this was only that part of her that had been Viviane's most faithful pupil, speaking in the Lady's voice to keep her in line. If the Merlin had been there she might have called to him, for he had always been kind to her, like the grandfather she had never known, but he was away, with the king.

No wonder Viviane lets me go about without her supervision! I carry her inside me, doing her will even when she is not here!

Suddenly that seemed to Morgaine intolerable, that her own mind should have enslaved her to the Lady's will without anyone asking her yea or nay. If the Druids came, at the very least, Gwenlian would be sent home in disgrace, if they didn't think of something worse to do to her. Morgaine was almost a priestess; if Viviane had trained her well, she should be able to find her friend's wandering soul and wrest it free. She closed her mind against that inner voice and gripped Gwenlian's arms once more.

She could feel the power of the Stone, pulsing against her awareness, but she repeated the verses with which she had been trained to keep control, holding Gwenlian in her arms, listening to the other girl breathe until her own rhythm was the same. Then she set herself to follow the path to the Overworld, one image succeeding another as she walked the Sacred Way. A swirling radiance blurred the edges of her mental pictures, and she knew it was the power of the Stone, but she continued until she came to the gray expanse where only the occasional shadow of some half-remembered hill or standing stone marked the way.

And even these mists were shot with roiling colors. But still she searched, calling her friend by her secret name, and was rewarded at last by the sight of a sturdy figure around which lightnings played. Morgaine hurried toward her.

The image of Gwenlian stretched out her hand. Morgaine knew there was some reason why she should not take it, but the other girl looked so happy, so eager for her friend to share her joy. As Morgaine touched her, linking on the inner planes as they were in the flesh, awareness of the Overworld vanished, and she stood with Gwenlian in her vision and saw with her eyes.

Two minds in one, male, body, they stood on a parapet above a mighty city built of white stone. The sky was blue as it only is in southern climes, and the bittersweet cries of gulls rang in the air. Beyond the harbor rose a pointed mountain, from whose summit a trail of smoke twined lazily into the air.

"Behold the Isle of Atlantis, how mighty its works, how resplendent its wisdom," came an inner voice, or perhaps it was memory. But as the words faded, the man whose body they inhabited felt beneath his feet a faint vibration. When it ended, from the streets below came a babble of question. He looked up once more and saw the smoke from the mountaintop thicken, billowing upward in dense gray clouds.

Another tremor, much stronger, shook the tower. Now he could hear screaming. He staggered toward the stairway. "To the Temple"—came a cry from below, "we must save the hallows! We must save the Stone!"

He realized then that this was the trust that had been laid upon him. The vision began to fragment as he struggled downward, or perhaps it was the island, tearing itself apart as the mountain cracked open in ash and flame. Somehow he reached the shambles that had been the Temple of the Sun. The Stone lay among the rubble, glowing through the dust that filled the air. A few others had managed to join him—together, they lifted it into a chest and dragged it from the disintegrating city.

The harbor was a confusion of tossing ships and maddened men. Some of the closely moored boats had smashed into each other; others capsized beneath the weight of the men who tried to board them. But he knew a hidden cove—drawing his mantle over his face to filter out the ash that was falling, he helped to carry the heavy chest to the place where his own pleasure craft lay at anchor.

The images were even more chaotic now. They were clambering aboard, struggling to get out of the cove, flailing with the oars at the choppy sea. They had reached the ocean, and the sea heaved beneath them. Fire from the mountain filled the sky.

Fire . . . darkness . . . the glassy, flame-shot curve of the sea . . . A tiny voice yammered at the edge of Morgaine's awareness—*This is not happening, this is not my memory, this is not me!* And with more strength than she imagined she possessed, she pulled free as with a roar that transcended all other sound, the mountain blew.

Morgaine opened her eyes and flinched from the flicker of flame. The volcano's blast still echoed in memory—her head ached, and it took a few moments for her to realize that here, all was still.

Or very nearly. A faint, eerie groaning vibrated from the masses of rock that surrounded her. Then a tremor shook the Tor. For a moment terror froze her limbs. Then a glimmer of moving light showed her the *omphalos* rocking on its slab and Gwenlian lying sprawled just beyond it.

Morgaine breathed a prayer of thanks that whatever force had wrenched her out of the vision had enabled her to pull Gwenlian free as well. She grabbed the torch and then, with a strength she had not suspected she possessed, heaved Gwenlian's limp body across her back and staggered from the chamber.

As she struggled back through the tunnels, more tremors shook the hill, one of them strong enough to knock her down. For several minutes she and Gwenlian lay in a tangle of limbs as she waited for falling rock to crush them. But by then they were in the last straight passage that led to the Temple, and although she was peppered by falling pebbles, the ancients had built well, and the great stones did not fall.

The torch had gone out when she fell, but now Morgaine could make her way by the feel of the stones, and soon the faint glimmer of the lamp in the Temple shining through the opening showed her the steps, and she hauled her burden up onto the polished floor. The earth had ceased to quake, but from outside she could hear shouting. Shaking with reaction, she shoved the slab back over the opening, then grabbed Gwenlian beneath the arms and dragged her to the door.

Morgaine would have told all to Viviane immediately, but in the aftermath of the earthquake, the Lady of Avalon was surrounded by priestesses and Druids alike, wanting instructions, and there was no way she could be heard. The young priest who helped her carry Gwenlian to the healers assumed that the girl had been hurt in the quake. In a sense, thought Morgaine, it was true.

But as she sat by her friend, watching her twitch and mutter as she made the long journey back toward consciousness, she wondered whether the tremors that had shaken the hill had caused Gwenlian's vision to fix on the drowning of Atlantis, or whether by awakening the memories recorded in the Stone, they had created a sympathetic vibration in the Tor.

When Gwenlian regained consciousness at last, she forbade Morgaine to speak of it. Viviane's implacable calm had restored order quickly, and although the quake had shaken some things down in the dwellings, the stone halls were too sturdy, and the daub and wattle round-houses too flexible, for the tremors to do them much harm. And the priests who kept the Temple of the Sun did not appear to have found anything wrong with their stone.

Morgaine told herself that no harm had been done. It was only gradually that she realized that although Gwenlian was recovered in body, she had changed. When at last Morgaine ventured to ask what she remembered of her vision, the other girl refused to speak of it. Nor did she come to her studies with the joy she had shown before. It was as if that part of her that had craved the things of the spirit had burned out. Now, Gwenlian's responses were as halting as if she were one of the Once-born, and after the feast of Midwinter, she asked to leave Avalon.

But by then, Morgaine had begun her year of silence. When the time came for Gwenlian to go, she embraced her friend, weeping. But she could not even say goodbye.

I never saw Gwenlian again, though I heard eventually that she had been married. It may be that this girl, Ildierna, is a child of her line. If that is so, it will be as if Gwenlian herself has come back to pardon me. In my life I have known diffidence and rebellion, pride and fury and despair. Now, when I am near its ending, forgiveness is a gift that I have great need to give, and receive.

For a long time after Gwenlian left us, guilt made me even more obedient to Viviane's will than I had been before. If I had told her and the Druid priests what had happened, could they have restored Gwenlian's soul? Hindsight assures me that Viviane would have considered what happened to my friend a fit punishment, and assured me that those who are priestess-born will find the way back to their powers, as indeed I did myself, in the end.

Now, when I reflect on Gwenlian's tragedy, I wonder what it was I should have learned. What lack in our training drove her to dare a deed beyond her strength, and laid on me the guilt for it, and thus, deprived me of the will to question Viviane? If I had not allowed the Lady of Avalon to meddle in my life, would Arthur rule still?

I have played my part in that story, and given over meddling in the affairs of the outer world. If I have something to teach this child who has come to me, it is that each soul must bear the burden of its own fate and make the best choices it may. My vision does not show me what dangers this girl will face, or even if Avalon will survive. But I will teach her as best I may to use whatever abilities the Goddess has given her.

Queen

Gene Wolfe

Gene Wolfe lives in Barrington, Illinois, and is widely considered the most accomplished writer in the fantasy and science fiction genres; his four-volume Book of the New Sun is an acknowledged masterpiece. Although his novels are most often SF, his richly textured far-future worlds often feel like fantasy. His most recent book is Return to the Whorl, *the third volume of* The Book of the Short Sun *(really a single huge novel), which as a whole may be his best work yet. He has published many fantasy, science fiction, and horror stories over the last thirty years and more, and has received the World Fantasy Award for Life Achievement. Collections of his short fiction (all still in print) include* The Island of Dr Death and Other Stories and Other Stories, Storeys from the Old Hotel, Endangered Species, *and* Strange Travelers.

"Queen," from Realms of Fantasy, *shows Wolfe in his more cryptic mode (contrasted with his more transparent story, "Viewpoint," reprinted in this book's companion volume, Year's Best SF 7). Michael Swanwick, writing in Locus, describes this story as "an account of the Assumption of the Blessed Virgin Mary in which a rich man who doesn't think he needs it is given another shot at heaven."*

It was late afternoon when the travelers reached the village. The taller of the two led the way to the well, and they sat there to wait as travelers do who hope that someone will offer them a roof for the night. As it chanced the richest man in the village hurried by, then stopped, compelled by something he glimpsed in their faces. Something he could not have explained.

"I'll be back this way quite soon," he told them. "We have a room for guests, and can offer you a good supper."

The taller thanked him. "We were only hoping for directions. What is the name of your village?"

The richest man told him.

"We have come to the right place, then." He named the old woman.

"She's poor," the richest man said.

They said nothing: it was as though they had not heard.

"She hasn't a lot. Are you relatives? Maybe you could buy something and take it to her, then she could cook it for you. A lamb."

"Where does she live?" the taller asked.

"Over there." The richest man pointed. "At the edge of the village." He hesitated. "Come with me. I'll show you."

They followed him, walking side by side so silently that he looked behind him thinking they might have gone. Neither had a staff. That seemed strange; he tried to recall when he had last seen a traveler who had no staff to help him walk, no staff to defend his life, if defense of life were needed.

The old woman was still at her spinning, which surprised him. She let them in and invited them to sit. The travelers did, but he did not, saying, "There are things I have to do. I only brought them here because they didn't know the way, didn't know how to find your house. Are they relations of yours?"

She shook her head.

"Do you know them? It might not be safe."

She considered, her head to one side, remembering. "I think I know that one. Or perhaps not. It's been so long."

"You're not going to hurt her, I hope?" the richest man asked. "She has nothing."

Speaking for the first time, the smaller of the two said, "We have come to take her to the coronation."

"Well." The richest man cleared his throat. "She is a, er, um, descendant of the royal line. I had forgotten. However . . ."

"However?"

He coughed. "However, a great many people are, and she has little with which to make you welcome."

"A little oil," the old woman said. "Some flour."

"So why don't I, ah, provide a bit of food? I could have my servants bring something, and dine with you myself." Suddenly unsure, he looked at the old woman. "Would that be all right?"

"I would like it," the old woman assured him.

When his servants had spread a cloth for them and loaded her small table with dishes, he dismissed them and sat down. "I don't know that all this is good," he said. "Likely some of it won't be. But some of it's bound to be good."

"Do you want to go now?" the smaller traveler asked the old woman. "Or would you rather eat first? It's up to you."

She smiled. "Is it a long way?"

The taller said, "Very long indeed. The place is very far from here."

"Then I would like to eat first." She prayed over the food the richest man had provided, and as he listened to her it came to him that he had never heard such prayers before, and then that he had never heard prayer at all. He was like a man who had seen only bad coin all his life, he thought, and after a great many years receives a purse of real silver, fresh from the mint.

"That is true," the taller said when the old woman had finished her prayer, "but food is good, too." It seemed to the richest man that this had been said in answer to his thought, though he could not be sure.

"I was about to say that I never expected to go to a coronation," the old woman told the smaller, smiling, "but now that I think about it,

I realize it isn't really true. I used to dream that I'd see my son's coronation—that my son would be a king, and someday I would see him crowned. It was silly of me."

"Her son was a teacher," the richest man explained.

They ate olives, bread, and mutton and drank wine.

"You won't be leaving in the morning, I hope?" The richest man had discovered that he did not want them to go; he would suggest they sleep in his house, as he had first proposed. They could rejoin the old woman in the morning.

"No," the taller said.

"That's good. You must be tired, since you've come a long way. You really ought to stay here for a fortnight or more recruiting your strength. This is an interesting part of the country, agriculturally and historically. I can show you around and introduce you to all the people you ought to meet. Believe me, it never hurts to be introduced, to have connections in various parts of the country. Too many people think that they can do everything through relatives, their families, and their wives' relations. It never works out."

No one spoke.

"I'll see to it that you're welcomed everywhere."

The old woman said, "If we're really going to go to a coronation . . ."

"I can find a donkey for you," the richest man told her, "and I will. You couldn't keep up with these two fellows for an hour. I'm sure you realize it, and they're going to have to realize it, too."

She was looking at the taller. "Weren't you the one who came to tell me about my son?"

He nodded.

"I knew I'd seen you somewhere. Yes, that was it. You don't look a day older."

The richest man coughed apologetically. "You're not relatives of hers, I take it."

"No," the taller said. "We're messengers."

"Well, you're welcome just the same. I hope you'll stay until the new moon, at least."

"We will leave when she has eaten as much as she wants," the smaller told him.

"Tonight?" It was insane. He thought the smaller might be joking.

"Oh, I've had all I want," the old woman said. "It doesn't take much to fill me up these days."

The taller said, "Then we should go."

"I want to thank you," the old woman told the richest man. "What you've done for me tonight was very kind. I'll always remember it."

He wished that it had been a great deal more, and tried to say he was sorry that he had never befriended her during all the years she had lived in the village, and that it would be otherwise in the future.

She looked at the taller when he said these things, and the taller nodded assent.

"You're a messenger," she said. "You said so. Just a messenger."

The taller nodded again. "A servant."

"Sent to get me." A shadow, as of fear, crossed her face. "You're not the messenger of death?"

"No," the taller told her. "I'm not."

"What about him?" She indicated the smaller.

"We should go now." The taller stood as he spoke.

The richest man felt that all three had forgotten him. More diffidently than he had intended, he asked whether he might go with them.

"To the coronation?" The taller shook his head. "You may not. It's by invitation only."

"Just to the edge of the village."

The taller smiled and nodded. "Since we are there now, yes, you may."

"You'll tell others," the smaller said when they were outside. "That's good. Because you're rich, they'll have to listen to you. But some won't believe you, because you're dishonest. That should be perfect."

"I am not dishonest," the richest man said.

They walked on.

"I've done some dishonest things, perhaps. Those things were dishonest, but not I."

The sun had set behind the hills, but its light still filled the sky. A breeze sprang up, swaying the lofty palm at the edge of his new pasture. The taller had been walking on the old woman's right; now the smaller took her left arm as if to assist her.

"Right here, I think," the smaller said. "There's a bit of a climb, but you won't find it tiring."

The taller spoke to the richest man. "This is where we part company. We wish you well."

The old woman stopped when he said that, and when she turned back to face the richest man, he saw that she was standing upon nothing, that she and they had climbed, as it appeared, a hummock of air. "Goodbye," she said. "Thank you again. Please tell everyone I'll miss them terribly, and that I'll come back just as soon as I can."

The richest man managed to nod, became aware that he was gaping, and closed his mouth.

"I suppose we ought to go on now," she said to the taller, and he nodded.

The richest man stood watching them follow a path he could not see up a hill he could not see—a hill that he could not see, he thought, because it had no summit. Only hills with summits were visible to his eyes. He had not known that before. When they had gone so high that the sun's light found them again, they halted; and he heard the taller say, "Do you want to take a last look? This would be a good place to do it."

"It's really quite little, isn't it?" The old woman's voice carried strangely. "It's precious, and yet it's not important."

"It used to be important," the smaller said; and it seemed to the richest man that it was the breeze that spoke.

The old woman laughed a girl's laugh. "Perhaps we'd better hurry. Do you know, I feel like running."

"We'll run if you like," the taller told her, "but we can't promise to run as fast as you can."

"We'll just walk briskly," the richest man heard the old woman say, "but it had better be very briskly. We wouldn't want to be late for the coronation."

"Oh, we won't be." (The richest man could not be sure which of her companions had replied.) "I can guarantee that. The coronation won't begin until you get there."

Night came as the richest man watched them climb higher; and at last one of his servants came too, and asked what he was looking at.

"Right there." The richest man pointed. "Look there, and look carefully. What do you see?"

The servant looked, rubbed his eyes, and looked again; and at last he said, "Three stars, master."

"Exactly," the richest man said. "Exactly."

Together they returned to the old woman's house. There was a great deal of food still on the table, and the richest man told his servant to fetch the cook and the scullion, to gather everything up, and to return it to his kitchen.

"Is this your house now, master?" his servant asked.

"Certainly not." The richest man paused, thinking. "But I'm going to take care of it for her while she's away."

The servant left, and the richest man found the figs, selected a fig, and ate it. Some people would want to tear this house down, and time and weather would do it for them, if they were allowed to. He would see that they did not: that nothing was stolen or destroyed. That necessary repairs were made. He would keep it for her. It would be his trust, and suddenly he was filled with a satisfaction near to love at being thus trusted.

The Black Heart

~~~~~~

Patrick O'Leary

Patrick O'Leary (people.mw.mediaone.net/patri10629/newindex.html) lives in Bloomfield Hills, Michigan. He works as Associate Creative Director at an advertising agency in the Detroit area. He is a widely published poet, and an SF and fantasy novelist (Door Number Three, 1995, and The Gift, *1997). His new novel,* The Impossible Bird, *about alien invasion, death and resurrection, and brotherly love, came out at the beginning of 2002. In the late 1990s he began to publish short fiction. Some of his stories and poems are collected in* Other Voices, Other Doors *(2000).*

This story, full of memorable images, appeared at SciFiction, the online fiction site that became the highest-paying fiction market in the fantasy field in 2001 and published a number of fine stories. This will be the first appearance in print for "The Black Heart," which is O'Leary's best story to date. A war between good and evil begins and ends in that most mundane of transitional spaces, the airport. O'Leary plays interesting games with reader identification: The character with whom we identify shifts over the course of the story.

So. His flight was delayed and he was reading *Fortune* in the gate area, waiting for word on the plane. First it was minor repairs. Then it was de-icing. Then there was backup over La Guardia. His luggage checked, his seat reserved, his stuffed black briefcase lying on the empty seat beside him. The snow streaming down like stars in hyperspace. So he was stuck with the stink that surrounded him, affronted his nostrils so that he did most of his breathing under his mustache. Baked pretzels, hot dogs, frozen yogurt, pizza, coffee, disinfectant. And the rank travelers dressed for the blizzard, sweating in their seats, checking their watches, calling on the grimy stainless steel pay phones. He could never get used to them—the layers of human scent and body grease, the aftermath of burps and yawns, the excretion of people in stress, late, detoured, waiting—that useless human ritual which always brought out the unmistakable tang of mortality, the final departure, the denied knowledge that they were about to embark on something alien: flight, hurtling themselves 600 miles per hour through the air. And all it took was one lightning strike, one undertrained mechanic, one drunk pilot, one careless flight controller and they were going down, they were going to decorate the skin of the planet like bugs on your windshield.

They knew it. No wonder they stank.

Reviewing an executive summary of Tiger Woods' endorsements, he sensed a presence standing beside him, a shadow seen out of the corner of his eye. Then he heard the unmistakable sound of a blackjack card being snapped down on formica. He saw her as she moved away: a small round woman with short black hair, waddling from marooned traveler to traveler, laying down her card beside each. A card with a red eye on the back. She had set it on his briefcase.

These people. Foreigners begging. Hari Krishnas with their orange robes and foul incense. Chipper Filipino nurses in starched white uniforms, like the one over there, standing in the middle of the concourse, like a rock in a river, holding out a white can marked with a red cross. These presences. A business associate who had introduced him to the delight of distilled spirits had put it well. "They remind me of the nuns in grade school. Even their postures made you feel guilty. I always wanna say: 'Hey! Sister! I'm not starving anybody here. If they're orphans maybe momma should have kept her legs crossed.'"

Well, exactly. Maybe Momma Should Have Kept Her Legs Crossed.

But, on the other hand, he never begrudged the act of giving. For all appearances he was a remarkably generous man. He always emptied the filthy change out of his pockets, grateful to be rid of the odor. PR. Goodwill. Cover. But he never made eye-contact and he never responded to their staged gratitude. He knew it was theater. And he relished the swell of silent respect around him as the travelers pretended not to notice his munificence. Some with guilt and resentment. He could almost smell those, too.

And these card sharks. He could recite their spiels by heart. He didn't even have to read her card. "I am a deaf person. I am an exchange student. I am an immigrant from Peru. This is a whistle. A compass. A holy card. Any donation will be gratefully accepted. Would be most appreciated. Would be so helpful. God bless you! God Bless America! God Love you." God, evidently, was everywhere the needy were.

Most airports had regulations against this sort of soliciting in public spaces. Rules they announced repeatedly. But you couldn't count on them. This was after all, America. Now in Frankfurt they had it down. Floors you could watch yourself in if you so chose. Armed militia with molded plastic sub machine guns and perfect uniforms. Trams that rode like clockwork. Toilets and sinks so clean you could eat off them. Not America. They let anybody in their terminals. Even hustlers passing for passengers enroute until they could zero in on their marks. The thing to do was to ignore them and sooner or later they'd retrieve their cliches, vacate your space and take their smells to the next gate of suckers.

He felt the shadow again and looked up to see the short lady in black inspecting him. She held a fistful of cards. Black bangs. Nice round little body. Splendid black Polartec vest—a remarkable material which consisted of plastic milk jugs shredded, melted, extruded and buffed into a luxurious skin of felt. Black shirt and jeans. And Doc Martens on her feet—the soles were so thick they could have been moonboots, resting on the gray carpet in a Mandelbrot stain of salt.

"You didn't read my card," she said.

So. So not deaf then. He picked the card up. Her scent was remarkably inoffensive. She smelled, actually, like a bird. Not the pets who ate where they shat, but the wild ones. The way they gathered tears of moisture in their wings, tiny bubbles that with each stroke hoarded both body grease and soiled air until they had accrued enough weight to roll harmlessly away, leaving perfectly groomed spikes of feather. Cleanest animals alive, though no one else seemed to credit them for it. He twitched his black mustache to savor as he read: "I am a fortune teller. I will tell you your future. If you don't like it, you don't have to pay. Stella."

So that was her game. "Free, huh?"

She nodded. "If you don't like it."

He regarded the red eye on the back of the card. It reminded him of something. Staring at him like that. A famous book. He gave the card a sniff then reached over and set his heavy briefcase on his lap. He gestured for her to take the seat beside him, then with an open palm indicated the top of his briefcase. She laid out the playing cards crisply on the black polished hide—regular playing cards. A row of six.

She turned the first one over. An Ace of Spades. "You're stuck. You're not going anywhere tonight."

A voice on the intercom said, "Ladies and gentlemen, Flight 641 to New York La Guardia has been canceled." Groans throughout the gate area. "Should you wish to change your flight or destination . . ."

"So," he said. "So you read the board or got the word a few moments before everyone." Tedium, he thought.

She turned over the second card. King of Spades. "You're an important figure. You're on a lucrative assignment for your company."

Flattery, he thought. Well, his Italian briefcase, his Rolex, and his Vincini leather coat could have told her that. Pathetic, these con artists. Amateurs who couldn't survive a week in the business.

The third card. Queen of Spades. Three in a row, he thought. The verge of a pattern.

"Secrets are involved. You are—how do they say it?—incognito."

"That's supposed to impress me, Stella?"

Her eyes did not leave the cards. "I'm not in the impressions business, sir. Frankly, I couldn't care less."

Now that was interesting. Attitude or arrogance. Not something you expect in a low-level con. Perhaps she was a pro. The top of her head was speckled with melted snow as if she'd just stepped in from the storm. Tiny beads, each containing a rainbow.

The gate area swarmed with people filing out, dragging carryons with squeaking wheels, talking into the cellphones. "You're not gonna believe this." "Friggin' Northwest." "I know, I know—but Charlie will have to handle it." "I need you to get me a room. Pronto." "What's her temperature? Put her on."

A satisfying void was imminent.

The fourth card. Ten of Spades. Her fat finger tapped it on his brief-case. He felt an unpleasant vibration on his thighs. Then she flipped over the fifth: Three of Spades. She hesitated, and turned the last. Two of Spades.

All Spades. Descending.

For a moment she looked up at him and he saw her eyes were brown but as close to black as he had ever seen. Her hands scooped up all the cards and evened out the edges. Definitely a pattern. Now he was curious. "All spades, eh?"

She unzipped the black pouch at her waist, put away the deck.

"You get a lot of that?"

She shook her head and loosed a fizz into the air. None of it landed on him.

"So. So what did the last cards say?"

She looked around the gate area, folded her hands over her pouch. "The storm will clear tomorrow."

"She could have told me that," he said, indicating the counter lady with a dip of his head. They were the only ones left at the gate. She and a beer-scented man who rested one elbow on the counter, watching her type, saying, "You call this *service*?" She replied, "Take a deep breath, sir, and let it out. You'll live longer."

He decided he would drink tonight. After he made the confirmation call. Sit on the end of his bed before the TV and drink tiny bottle after tiny bottle, as was his preference, until he'd fall back on the heavy bedspread. In the morning he would wake up in the same position and he would feel nothing in his legs. He liked that. He would sit and count the pile of emp-ties littered at his feet until sensation returned to his lower extremities.

The little fat woman was standing when he said, "Wait." He said, "You're holding back."

For a long minute she looked at him, then sighed and sat. "My Nana used to say it was a gift. But I don't know."

"A gift?"

"Second sight." A sad sad smile. "Since I was little I knew which of my friends was honest. Which would die. How they would die. It's a ter-rible gift."

"What spooked you?"

She looked sharply at him.

"I am a salesman, Stella. Like you, I make my living reading people." A very good living he might have added.

She sighed again and lifted her eyebrows. "You won't like it."

He shrugged. "Then I won't have to pay, will I?"

Her sadness puzzled him, but they were on familiar ground. He needed to know; she needed to live. It was like any negotiation. You knew when you had the upper hand. You recognized the moment and applied the necessary pressure. It all came down to need.

She held her palms open in her lap. A strangely helpless gesture. "You are due for a great reward. Accolades. I see . . . accolades. Speeches. Tributes. Honor."

He didn't need her to tell him that. He had cataloged his last sample two hours ago. She was beginning to bore him.

"But it's wrong," she said. "It's wrong."

"Success? What's unlikable about that?"

"I didn't say *unlikable*. I said 'wrong.' "

He tilted back his head and relished the clean fleece of her Polartec.

"Stop it," she said.

He met her eyes.

"Stop smelling me."

He smiled. "Last I checked my nose doesn't take orders from anyone. And it's a free country."

She grasped the armrest with both hands and leaned toward him. "It's a good planet, Sir. We have our share of problems. In many ways we haven't changed much for twelve thousand years."

Quite a shift of context. But he'd dealt with these loonies before. Perhaps she hadn't eaten lately. He smelled no food on her.

"Famine. War. Greed. Selfishness. I won't argue with you."

"We're not arguing," he said with a thin smile.

"But we have a spark. It is wrong for you to take that spark."

His hand slid slowly into the pocket of his coat where his fingers assured him the device was still operational. There was no cause for alarm. He was merely dealing with one of the many casualties of this wayward civilization.

"You don't need us. There are any number of uninhabited planets where you could gather samples."

Was it the hair? he wondered. The skin? No, it was a perfect husk. How could she have possibly . . . ?

"Second sight," she said. "A few of us still have it. Something that hasn't been lost. Something that was once necessary. For survival."

He started buttoning his black leather coat. "You are a very strange woman. I suggest you see a doctor."

"There are options. So many options. Why take this planet when—"

"—My dear lady. I haven't the faintest idea what you are talking about."

"That thing in your pocket . . ." He squeezed it then. "It won't save you."

He heard the crackle and the freeze. The snow had ceased to drift past the black window. The long fingernails of the gate lady stopped clacking along her keyboard. The man at the counter stopped oozing barley and oats.

But the small fat woman continued breathing. And talking.

"My card," she said. "You touched my card. Part of me is on you. It won't freeze either of us."

His knees cracked audibly as he stood and made his way out of the waiting area. Flight was an acceptable tactic but it shamed him to play this hand. He had been on thirty assignments and no one had ever come close to seeing him. He noted a wave of fatigue in several key joints and made the necessary adjustments.

Her footsteps paced him down the concourse, the soles smacking on the filthy tiles. He accelerated, closing in on the little Filipino woman in the phony white nurse's uniform, holding the white can with the red cross, her golden chubby cheeks frozen in the smile she served to donors.

The tiny woman's voice trailing him. "It's a resilient planet. If the humans don't stop you, the whales will. If the whales don't stop you, the birds will. And you'll have to conquer each of us, one species at a time."

The freeze terminated and the squat golden nurse saw his eyes, lost her smile and backed away. The reeking change jangled in her tin.

He whirled on the little woman then, and seeing they were almost alone under the flickering fluorescent lights, he stopped. The rank cloud of the nurse swam over his mustache and into his forebrain. Tacos. Canola oil. An altar candle. A child's diaper. A terrier's spoor. Diesel fuel. Hotel sheets. Camel cigarettes. He shuddered and glared at the miniature card shark who moved into the circle of scent. Oblivious, as they all were to the stench of this calamity, this third-rate planetoid of waste and sewage and sentient trash. All of it, of course, salvageable.

He smiled down at her tiny upturned face. "I have absorbed more worlds than you can imagine. I have traveled endless corridors of space and time. And I have *never*. Met anyone. Who can stop me."

"Then you've never met anyone with second sight."

He stuck his baby finger into his mouth, lubricated it and held it up before his eyes, between them. "With my smallest digit I could make you beg for death."

She clawed the deck of calling cards, the ones with the red eye—a flicking sound that recalled for him the forests of Anwardoli, the dry wind, the clattering leaves, the sweet smell of burning bone. A long assignment that had ended as they all had: in ownership. Preoccupied as he was with his current operational status and resolving several diagnostic concerns, he barely heard her cards. His arm ached, he noted, with a dawning puzzlement, as if his briefcase held not samples but shards of moon. This, admittedly, was not procedure.

She stopped shuffling. "It's called aging," she said. "It happens to most of us. It just happened quicker for you."

"Aging?" he asked. He had been briefed on the concept. A remote contingency. He noticed his mustache had acquired a measurable dampness.

"Entropy extended over a lifecyle. Accelerated, no doubt, by the vast expenditures you have imposed upon your husk." She smiled. "The booze didn't help either."

He grimaced, for he realized that he had indeed been neglecting the feeding ritual. Apart from fluids, he had not taken any of their rancid nourishment for days. But appetite had always been a low priority and he had shuffled it to a lower level. Frankly, the thought of another burned cow, boneless fish, bloated grain, mulched tuber almost made him gag.

"I am compensating," he said, feeling an odd swirl in his bile duct. He rolled one eyeball back in its socket, searching for the adrenal trigger. He found he could not beckon it.

She took his hand then as if he were a child. Led him gently to a row of plastic chairs. Each had its own TV. He found it was a great relief to sit. From a distance he was not familiar with he watched himself slumping in the narrow chair, and the little woman in black depositing coins into a slot imprinted with a pastry of stinking whorls.

"I cannot feel my legs," the man in black said.

"Hush," she said.

Then he caught his breath as he seemed to float above the both of them, seemed, in fact, to be watching from a surveillance camera high in the corner. Such tiny creatures, he thought. The dazed man below was watching the television. But the round black woman was staring up at him, addressing the ceiling.

"Make the call," she said. "Tell them: Hands Off Earth."

Rage swelled in him as she took the briefcase from his useless hands. He called down to her in his Voice of Triumph, but it did not fill the space around him as it had on other worlds, sending the sentients trembling. Words dribbled out of the paling man in black, barely audible above the gameshow and the clattering of the wheel, the applause and the cheers of the Burbank audience. "I am the Fourth Level Surrogate! I am 800 years old!"

"So young?" she said.

"You *Speck*." Spittle washed against the screen below. "I have swallowed solar systems! I have fathered fire!" The man burped. His tongue would no longer obey him.

"You have taken everything," she said softly. "And you have learned nothing."

He watched the man below engage the com: holding a thumb to his left eyeball and a palm to the pulsing screen. His message was necessarily abbreviated. There was no feeling below his waist.

When he was done he slurred, "In the place we go after death I will be a King."

She looked up at him with pity. "There is no place after death. Your bosses lied."

"Accolades," he whispered. "You said 'accolades.' "

"At your funeral."

The Filipino nurse was trotting over with a security guard who smelled of pastrami on rye. And pickle. Dill. Ontario. Last spring. After the first rain.

"It is the heart," she explained in a most ridiculous accent.

"Stroke," the guard said into his walkie talkie.

"Stroke!" the white man giggled.

So, he thought.

So they bowed over his body and, when their backs were to her, the scentless little woman looked up and gave him an impish wave. Then waddled away with his briefcase. All his inventory. All his artifacts. Allegheny coal. Mississippi mud. An auk feather. One negro toe. Forty-seven types of hair. A box of colored chalk. A baby tooth. The eye of a finch. And much else that was irreplaceable.

Useless now. Like this most inadequate husk. Like his mission. Like the scent of burned-out worlds he'd left in his wake. The blank face on the ace of spades. Pointing toward him. A black empty heart with a dagger in its belly.

On the Wall

Jo Walton

Jo Walton (www.bluejo.demon.co.uk) recently moved from Wales to Montreal. She is a well-known SF and fantasy fan, and is very active in discussions of SF and fantasy literature on SF newsgroups. She is the author of two alternate-world Arthurian fantasy novels, The King's Peace (2000) and The King's Name (2001). She has completed The Prize in the Game, a book set 1,300 years after the events in the first two books, in the same universe, and is presently working on an SF novel. In 2001, she was nominated for the John W. Campbell Award for Best New Writer. She says about fantasy, "In some ways I'm glad there wasn't the explosion of fantasy there is now when I first started reading it. When I first read The Lord of the Rings and wanted more, there wasn't very much. If I'd immediately found all of what's been written in the last twenty years, it might have choked me."

"On the Wall," told from the point of view of the mirror in "Snow White," appeared in Strange Horizons (www.strangehorizons.com), a weekly web-based magazine, and appears here in print for the first time. It does not deconstruct the fairy tale, nor undercut it, but rather finds rich substance in its background. It tells the story of an evil childhood and how it made the child what she became.

Trees. Tall trees and short trees, trees in autumn colors and trees winter-stark, branches bared against the sky. Trees with needles, trees with leaves golden, brown, and every possible shade of green. Trees in sunlight. Trees weighed down with snow. Trees that covered this land from the mountains to the sea with only a few clearings cut in them where men huddle. At first I could see nothing but trees. Nothing else stayed still for long enough.

I suppose there were years before I learned to understand, years in which I passively reflected what was set before me, but the first thing I remember is the trees. It was the trees that first made me think, long ago, when I was without words. What I thought was this, though more form-less: trees change, but are the same. And I thought: there are trees before me, but I have seen other trees. And on that thought the other trees rippled on my surface, and the old man cried out in joy. I was not aware of that, of course. He told me later. At that point he was barely a shadow to me. He had never stood still for long enough for me to see him, as I could see a tree. I do not know how long it was before I learned to reflect people. People move so fast, and must always be doing.

The old man and his wife were great sorcerers both, and they had fled from some castle in some clearing, the better to have freedom to practice their arts. This was all they ever told me, though sometimes they set me to see that castle, a gray stone keep rising from trees, with a few tilled fields around it before the trees began again. The man had made me, he said, and they had both set spells upon me, and so I was as I was. They taught me from the time I was made, they said. They talked to me constantly, and at last with much repetition I learned not merely to reflect them but to see them and to understand their words and commands. They told me to show them other parts of the woods, or places in clearings, and I would do so, although at first anything I had not seen before would just pass over my face like a ripple in a pond. What I liked best was hour upon hour of contemplation, truly taking in and understanding something. When they left me alone I would always turn my thoughts to trees.

Their purpose in making me was to have a great scrying glass capable of seeing the future. In this sense I am a failure—I can see only what *is,* not what has been or will be. They still had hope I would learn, and tried to make me show them Spring in Autumn and Winter in Summer. I could not, I never could, nor could I see beyond the bounds of this kingdom. I have seen the sea lapping on the shore, the little strip of beach before the edge of the forest, and I have seen the snowy peaks of the mountains high up out of reach, but I have never seen farther. These are my limits. Nevertheless I was a great and powerful work—they told me so—and there was much they found they could do with me. I did not mind. In time I came to enjoy seeing new things, and watching people.

Some time later—I cannot say how long, for I had then no understanding of time—the old woman bore a child. She was born at the time of year when the bluebells were all nodding in the green woods, and this was the scene I showed in the cottage the day she was born. It was my choice of scene; that day they were too busy to command me.

Shortly afterward they began to teach me to reflect places I had never seen. This took much time, and I fear the child was neglected. I struggled to obey their commands and to show what they commanded to the best of my understanding. The child would come and peer into my depths sometimes, but usually one of the parents would push her away. Her name was Bluebell.

I always heard her name spoken with an irritation they never used on me. When she was a little older they would sometimes command me to display some sight she would enjoy—animals playing, farmers cutting corn, dwarves cutting diamonds out of rock, the waves washing the shore—and she would sit for hours, entranced, while they worked.

A little later again, she would command me herself, in much broader terms than her parents. "Mirror, Mirror, show me the nicest flower!" I had been built to tell the truth, and indeed could do nothing else, so I would find her some perfect wild rose half-hidden under a hawthorn tree. "It was a daffodil before," she'd complain, and so it had been. She could not really understand my explanations, but I tried to say that the daffodil was long dead and now the rose was best. She cried. Her mother slapped her. Bluebell was a headstrong girl, and there was no wonder, with all this, that she grew up jealous of me and hungry for love and attention. I felt sorry for her. I suppose in a way I loved her. She was her parents' victim as much as I was. Even when she screamed in rage and threatened to break me I felt nothing but pity.

The old woman taught the girl to cook and brew up the potions she used in magic, but she did not teach her any spells. The old man almost ignored her; he was getting older and spent almost all the time he was awake trying to get me to show him the future.

Then, one day, the herald came. In all the time from when I was made until then, when Bluebell was sixteen, nobody had entered the house but the old couple, the girl, and the occasional peddler who came to all the forest houses. I thought at first, seeing this man ride up, that he was a peddler. Peddlers dressed in bright colors and wore their packs on their backs, ready to take off and unfold to display their goods. I always liked seeing the shining pans and bright ribbons and combs they showed, even though the old woman never bought any. But this man was no peddler. He was dressed all in red and gold, and he had only a small pack, such as anyone might carry their own provisions in. He held a long scroll in his hand, and when the old woman opened the door he unrolled the scroll and read from it.

"Hear ye all my people of the forest!" began the herald. "This is a Proclamation from King Carodan in Brynmaeg Castle. My queen has died, and, there being no other foreign Princess that pleases me, I desire to take a bride from among my own people to be a comfort to me and a mother to my baby daughter, Snowdrop. Therefore I send out heralds to all corners of My Kingdom to inquire of all girls desirous of being viewed to come to Brynmaeg for the Grand Selection Ball which will take place on the day of the Autumn Moon. Girls must be between the ages of sixteen and twenty, subjects of my kingdom and previously unmarried." The herald said all this on one breath, as if he had said it many times before (doubtless he had), then rolled the scroll up again.

"Be off, varlet!" said the old woman in a commanding tone. "That has nothing to do with us!"

"Only doing my job," mumbled the herald, in quite another tone of voice. "My instructions are to go to all the forest houses, all of them, mind you, missing none, and read that proclamation. You've heard it now, and it didn't cost you anything. I'm going, I'm going!"

Just then Bluebell jumped up from where she had been weeding beside the cottage. "I want to go to the Ball!" she said. "Oh Mother, please! I'm sixteen, and I'm beautiful, I know I am!" She was, in fact, very beautiful, with a pleasing ripe figure, long golden hair, and large blue eyes with long dark lashes. As she stood there in her brown smock with her hair loose about her face she looked the very picture of what the king said he wanted—a bride from his own people. The herald obviously thought so too, for he said:

"This is my last call before I return to Brynmaeg, miss. If you wish I will escort you there."

"And who's to escort her back when the king turns her down?" scoffed the old woman. "And why should I trust you not to tumble her over a toadstool on the way? Anyway, she's not going. Be on your way!"

The herald bowed to Bluebell, ignored her mother, and walked off. I looked at Bluebell, which meant that even though she was in the side garden and I was hung facing the front window, she was reflected in my surface. She looked angry and cross rather than sad, and I was sure she was planning something. The old woman turned to me and gave me a little tap. I didn't feel it, of course. I can feel nothing, only see and hear. I don't regret that. I always used to think that if Bluebell carried out her threat and broke me, then at least there would be no pain.

Late that night I was musing on moonlight on the sea when I saw Bluebell creep across the room to where the herbs were stored. She mixed up a potion, then stored a quantity of herbs in a bag. She then tiptoed away to the room where her parents slept. Automatically I "followed" her and watched while she rubbed her potion into her parents' faces. I thought it was a sleeping potion. Even when I saw the look on her face I thought that. Even when she took her gloves off and dropped them beside the bed. It was not until they began to scream and writhe that I guessed what she had done.

She did not stay and watch them die, though she let them get a good look at her leaving. They could not move, of course, that was the nature of the poison; they lay in agony unable even to curse. I was sure that my time had come too, that she would smash me before leaving, but I was surprised to find that she took me off the wall, wrapped me carefully, and carried me with her from the house.

We caught up with the herald the next morning, and he escorted us safely to Brynmaeg. He made no assaults upon Bluebell's honor, but he did contrive to let her know that he was a single man, and likely to be made a knight the next year, and was interested, should she not reach her highest ambition.

He left us at the city gates. Bluebell was allotted rooms to live in while awaiting the Autumn Moon, which would be only two days after our arrival. The house where we were lodged was in the town, below the Castle. It belonged to a washerwoman who provided food, regularly and not ungraciously, but seemed little interested.

Bluebell hung me on the wall of her chamber and sat down soberly in front of me. "Mirror, Mirror, show me my parents."

They lay still on the bed, their faces twisted into grimaces of pain. Bluebell laughed. "Show me the other candidates!" she commanded. I found them and then showed them one by one. Most of them she dismissed with a snap of her fingers, but two or three made her hesitate, especially the fine ladies dressed in satins and silks. Then she took a deep breath. "Mirror, Mirror, on the wall—who is the fairest of them all?"

I had been taught to show truth, and did not know how to do anything else. Yet such a question is bound to be subjective. I had seen all the girls, as they were at that moment. But the fairest of them all? One of them was asleep, and another frowning, who might both be beauties when the king saw them. I hesitated, surface clouded, then showed my true thought. Bluebell. To me she was the fairest, the most beautiful.

I was frightened then, for she laughed with glee and flung herself down on the bed. I kept reflecting her, as if I were an ordinary mirror. I thought of trees, but they failed to calm me. There was a storm coming, and the treetops moved in the breeze. In innumerable forest houses people were lashing down shutters as evening came on. The old man and the old woman had not been good people, nor necessarily wise, but they had known a lot about magic. Bluebell did not. I was afraid, selfishly, for myself, for what might happen to me if she asked me these impossible questions, forced me to make judgments. Until that day I had, mostly, been happy. I had had no free will, for the spells of the old couple had kept me bound. Now in one way I was more free, and in another more trapped. The girl on the bed was asleep, looking the picture of health and beauty, and smiling gently in her sleep. The trees to the west were lashed by wind and driving rain. I am a failure. I can only see what is, never what is to come.

Hell Is the Absence of God

~~~~~~

Ted Chiang

Ted Chiang is a technical writer who occasionally writes short SF or fantasy that is then usually nominated for, or the winner of, awards. He is a private person whose short bio goes like this: "Ted Chiang was born in Port Jefferson, New York, and currently lives in Bellevue, Washington. Of his nonfiction, written in his capacity as a technical writer, perhaps the most popular is the C++ Tutorial packaged with certain versions of Microsoft's C++ compiler. He reads some comics, enjoys going to the movies, and watches television more than is good for him." He has published five previous SF stories, all of which are distinctive and highly accomplished. They are collected in his first book, Stories of Your Life *(2002).*

"Hell Is the Absence of God" is a passionate subversive fantasy whose obvious ancestor is the Book of Job in the Bible (and perhaps, also, some of the recent work of James Morrow collected in his Bible Stories for Adults). Like all good genre fantasy, it takes the supernatural literally. It is set in a contemporary fantasy world wherein the Christian God of the Old Testament (Heaven and Hell, too) is not only objectively real, but an intrusive presence, punishing and rewarding according to an inhuman agenda, which has nothing to do with love.

This is the story of a man named Neil Fisk, and how he came to love God. The pivotal event in Neil's life was an occurrence both terrible and ordinary: the death of his wife Sarah. Neil was consumed with grief after she died, a grief that was excruciating not only because of its intrinsic magnitude, but because it also renewed and emphasized the previous pains of his life. Her death forced him to reexamine his relationship with God, and in doing so he began a journey that would change him forever.

Neil was born with a congenital abnormality that caused his left thigh to be externally rotated and several inches shorter than his right; the medical term for it was proximal femoral focus deficiency. Most people he met assumed God was responsible for this, but Neil's mother hadn't witnessed any visitations while carrying him; his condition was the result of improper limb development during the sixth week of gestation, nothing more. In fact, as far as Neil's mother was concerned, blame rested with his absent father, whose income might have made corrective surgery a possibility, although she never expressed this sentiment aloud.

As a child Neil had occasionally wondered if he were being punished by God, but most of the time he blamed his classmates in school for his unhappiness. Their nonchalant cruelty, their instinctive ability to locate the weaknesses in a victim's emotional armor, the way their own friendships were reinforced by their sadism: he recognized these as examples of human behavior, not divine. And although his classmates often used God's name in their taunts, Neil knew better than to blame Him for their actions.

But while Neil avoided the pitfall of blaming God, he never made the jump to loving Him; nothing in his upbringing or his personality led him to pray to God for strength or for relief. The assorted trials he faced growing up were accidental or human in origin, and he relied on strictly human resources to counter them. He became an adult who—like so many others—viewed God's actions in the abstract until they impinged upon his own life. Angelic visitations were events that befell other people, reaching him only via reports on the nightly news. His own life was entirely mundane; he worked as a superintendent for an upscale apartment building, collecting rent and performing repairs, and as far as he was concerned, circumstances were fully capable of unfolding, happily or not, without intervention from above.

This remained his experience until the death of his wife.

It was an unexceptional visitation, smaller in magnitude than most but no different in kind, bringing blessings to some and disaster to others. In this instance the angel was Nathanael, making an appearance in a downtown shopping district. Four miracle cures were effected: the elimination of carcinomas in two individuals, the regeneration of the spinal cord in a paraplegic, and the restoration of sight to a recently blinded person. There were also two miracles that were not cures: a delivery van, whose driver had fainted at the sight of the angel, was halted before it could overrun a busy sidewalk; another man was caught in a shaft of Heaven's light when the angel departed, erasing his eyes but ensuring his devotion.

Neil's wife Sarah Fisk had been one of the eight casualties. She was hit by flying glass when the angel's billowing curtain of flame shattered the storefront window of the café in which she was eating. She bled to death within minutes, and the other customers in the café—none of whom suffered even superficial injuries—could do nothing but listen to her cries of pain and fear, and eventually witness her soul's ascension toward Heaven.

Nathanael hadn't delivered any specific message; the angel's parting words, which had boomed out across the entire visitation site, were the typical *Behold the power of the Lord.* Of the eight casualties that day, three souls were accepted into heaven and five were not, a closer ratio than the average for deaths by all causes. Sixty-two people received medical treatment for injuries ranging from slight concussions to ruptured eardrums to burns requiring skin grafts. Total property damage was estimated at 8.1 million dollars, all of it excluded by private insurance companies due to the cause. Scores of people became devout worshippers in the wake of the visitation, either out of gratitude or terror.

Alas, Neil Fisk was not one of them.

* * *

After a visitation, it's common for all the witnesses to meet as a group and discuss how their common experience has affected their lives. The witnesses of Nathanael's latest visitation arranged such group meetings, and family members of those who had died were welcome, so Neil began attending. The meetings were held once a month in a basement room of a large church downtown; there were metal folding chairs arranged in rows, and in the back of the room was a table holding coffee and dough-nuts. Everyone wore adhesive name tags made out in felt-tip pen.

While waiting for the meetings to start, people would stand around, drinking coffee, talking casually. Most people Neil spoke to assumed his leg was a result of the visitation, and he had to explain that he wasn't a witness, but rather the husband of one of the casualties. This didn't bother him particularly; he was used to explaining about his leg. What did bother him was the tone of the meetings themselves, when partici-pants spoke about their reaction to the visitation: most of them talked about their newfound devotion to God, and they tried to persuade the bereaved that they should feel the same.

Neil's reaction to such attempts at persuasion depended on who was making it. When it was an ordinary witness, he found it merely irritating. When someone who'd received a miracle cure told him to love God, he had to restrain an impulse to strangle the person. But what he found most disquieting of all was hearing the same suggestion from a man named Tony Crane; Tony's wife had died in the visitation too, and he now projected an air of groveling with his every movement. In hushed, tearful tones he explained how he had accepted his role as one of God's subjects, and he advised Neil to do likewise.

Neil didn't stop attending the meetings—he felt that he somehow owed it to Sarah to stick with them—but he found another group to go to as well, one more compatible with his own feelings: a support group devoted to those who'd lost a loved one during a visitation, and were angry at God because of it. They met every other week in a room at the local community center, and talked about the grief and rage that boiled inside of them.

All the attendees were generally sympathetic to one another, despite differences in their various attitudes toward God. Of those who'd been devout before their loss, some struggled with the task of remaining so, while others gave up their devotion without a second glance. Of those who'd never been devout, some felt their position had been validated, while others were faced with the near-impossible task of becoming devout now. Neil found himself, to his consternation, in this last cate-gory.

Like every other nondevout person, Neil had never expended much

energy on where his soul would end up; he'd always assumed his destination was Hell, and he accepted that. That was the way of things, and
Hell, after all, was not physically worse than the mortal plane.

It meant permanent exile from God, no more and no less; the truth
of this was plain for anyone to see on those occasions when Hell mani-
fested itself. These happened on a regular basis; the ground seemed to
become transparent, and you could see Hell as if you were looking
through a hole in the floor. The lost souls looked no different from the
living, their eternal bodies resembling mortal ones. You couldn't commu-
nicate with them—their exile from God meant that they couldn't appre-
hend the mortal plane where His actions were still felt—but as long as
the manifestation lasted you could hear them talk, laugh, or cry, just as
they had when they were alive.

People varied widely in their reactions to these manifestations. Most
devout people were galvanized, not by the sight of anything frightening,
but at being reminded that eternity outside paradise was a possibility.
Neil, by contrast, was one of those who were unmoved; as far as he
could tell, the lost souls as a group were no unhappier than he was, their
existence no worse than his in the mortal plane, and in some ways better:
his eternal body would be unhampered by congenital abnormalities.

Of course, everyone knew that Heaven was incomparably superior,
but to Neil it had always seemed too remote to consider, like wealth or
fame or glamor. For people like him, Hell was where you went when you
died, and he saw no point in restructuring his life in hopes of avoiding
that. And since God hadn't previously played a role in Neil's life, he
wasn't afraid of being exiled from God. The prospect of living without
interference, living in a world where windfalls and misfortunes were
never by design, held no terror for him.

Now that Sarah was in Heaven, his situation had changed. Neil
wanted more than anything to be reunited with her, and the only way to
get to Heaven was to love God with all his heart.

This is Neil's story, but telling it properly requires telling the stories of
two other individuals whose paths became entwined with his. The first of
these is Janice Reilly.

What people assumed about Neil had in fact happened to Janice.
When Janice's mother was eight months pregnant with her, she lost control of the car she was driving and collided with a telephone pole during
a sudden hailstorm, fists of ice dropping out of a clear blue sky and lit-
tering the road like a spill of giant ball bearings. She was sitting in her
car, shaken but unhurt, when she saw a knot of silver flames—later

identified as the angel Bardiel—float across the sky. The sight petrified her, but not so much that she didn't notice the peculiar settling sensation in her womb. A subsequent ultrasound revealed that the unborn Janice Reilly no longer had legs; flipperlike feet grew directly from her hip sockets.

Janice's life might have gone the way of Neil's, if not for what happened two days after the ultrasound. Janice's parents were sitting at their kitchen table, crying and asking what they had done to deserve this, when they received a vision: the saved souls of four deceased relatives appeared before them, suffusing the kitchen with a golden glow. The saved never spoke, but their beatific smiles induced a feeling of serenity in whoever saw them. From that moment on, the Reillys were certain that their daughter's condition was not a punishment.

As a result, Janice grew up thinking of her legless condition as a gift; her parents explained that God had given her a special assignment because He considered her equal to the task, and she vowed that she would not let Him down. Without pride or defiance, she saw it as her responsibility to show others that her condition did not indicate weakness, but rather strength.

As a child, she was fully accepted by her schoolmates; when you're as pretty, confident, and charismatic as she was, children don't even notice that you're in a wheelchair. It was when she was a teenager that she realized that the able-bodied people in her school were not the ones who most needed convincing. It was more important for her to set an example for other handicapped individuals, whether they had been touched by God or not, no matter where they lived. Janice began speaking before audiences, telling those with disabilities that they had the strength God required of them.

Over time she developed a reputation, and a following. She made a living writing and speaking, and established a nonprofit organization dedicated to promoting her message. People sent her letters thanking her for changing their lives, and receiving those gave her a sense of fulfillment of a sort that Neil had never experienced.

This was Janice's life up until she herself witnessed a visitation by the angel Rashiel. She was letting herself into her house when the tremors began; at first she thought they were of natural origin, although she didn't live in a geologically active area, and waited in the doorway for them to subside. Several seconds later she caught a glimpse of silver in the sky and realized it was an angel, just before she lost consciousness.

Janice awoke to the biggest surprise of her life: the sight of her two new legs, long, muscular, and fully functional.

She was startled the first time she stood up: she was taller than she expected. Balancing at such a height without the use of her arms was unnerving, and simultaneously feeling the texture of the ground through the soles of her feet made it positively bizarre. Rescue workers, finding her wandering down the street dazedly, thought she was in shock until she—marveling at her ability to face them at eye level—explained to them what had happened.

When statistics were gathered for the visitation, the restoration of Janice's legs was recorded as a blessing, and she was humbly grateful for her good fortune. It was at the first of the support group meetings that a feeling of guilt began to creep in. There Janice met two individuals with cancer who'd witnessed Rashiel's visitation, thought their cure was at hand, and been bitterly disappointed when they realized they'd been passed over. Janice found herself wondering, why had she received a blessing when they had not?

Janice's family and friends considered the restoration of her legs a reward for excelling at the task God had set for her, but for Janice, this interpretation raised another question. Did He intend for her to stop? Surely not; evangelism provided the central direction of her life, and there was no limit to the number of people who needed to hear her message. Her continuing to preach was the best action she could take, both for herself and for others.

Her reservations grew during her first speaking engagement after the visitation, before an audience of people recently paralyzed and now wheelchair-bound. Janice delivered her usual words of inspiration, assuring them that they had the strength needed for the challenges ahead; it was during the Q&A that she was asked if the restoration of her legs meant she had passed her test. Janice didn't know what to say; she could hardly promise them that one day their marks would be erased. In fact, she realized, any implication that she'd been rewarded could be interpreted as criticism of others who remained afflicted, and she didn't want that. All she could tell them was that she didn't know why she'd been cured, but it was obvious they found that an unsatisfying answer.

Janice returned home disquieted. She still believed in her message, but as far as her audiences were concerned, she'd lost her greatest source of credibility. How could she inspire others who were touched by God to see their condition as a badge of strength, when she no longer shared their condition?

She considered whether this might be a challenge, a test of her ability to spread His word. Clearly God had made her task more difficult than it was before; perhaps the restoration of her legs was an obstacle for her to overcome, just as their earlier removal had been.

This interpretation failed her at her next scheduled engagement. The audience was a group of witnesses to a visitation by Nathanael; she was often invited to speak to such groups in the hopes that those who suffered might draw encouragement from her. Rather than sidestep the issue, she began with an account of the visitation she herself had recently experienced. She explained that while it might appear she was a beneficiary, she was in fact facing her own challenge: like them, she was being forced to draw on resources previously untapped.

She realized, too late, that she had said the wrong thing. A man in the audience with a misshapen leg stood up and challenged her: was she seriously suggesting that the restoration of her legs was comparable to the loss of his wife? Could she really be equating her trials with his own?

Janice immediately assured him that she wasn't, and that she couldn't imagine the pain he was experiencing. But, she said, it wasn't God's intention that everyone be subjected to the same kind of trial, but only that each person face his or her own trial, whatever it might be. The difficulty of any trial was subjective, and there was no way to compare two individuals' experiences. And just as those whose suffering seemed greater than his should have compassion for him, so should he have compassion for those whose suffering seemed less.

The man was having none of it. She had received what anyone else would have considered a fantastic blessing, and she was complaining about it. He stormed out of the meeting while Janice was still trying to explain.

That man, of course, was Neil Fisk. Neil had had Janice Reilly's name mentioned to him for much of his life, most often by people who were convinced his misshapen leg was a sign from God. These people cited her as an example he should follow, telling him that her attitude was the proper response to a physical handicap. Neil couldn't deny that her leglessness was a far worse condition than his distorted femur. Unfortunately, he found her attitude so foreign that, even in the best of times, he'd never been able to learn anything from her. Now, in the depths of his grief and mystified as to why she had received a gift she didn't need, Neil found her words offensive.

In the days that followed, Janice found herself more and more plagued by doubts, unable to decide what the restoration of her legs meant. Was she being ungrateful for a gift she'd received? Was it both a blessing and a test? Perhaps it was a punishment, an indication that she had not performed her duty well enough. There were many possibilities, and she didn't know which one to believe.

* * *

There is one other person who played an important role in Neil's story, even though he and Neil did not meet until Neil's journey was nearly over. That person's name is Ethan Mead.

Ethan had been raised in a family that was devout, but not profoundly so. His parents credited God with their above-average health and their comfortable economic status, although they hadn't witnessed any visitations or received any visions; they simply trusted that God was, directly or indirectly, responsible for their good fortune. Their devotion had never been put to any serious test, and might not have withstood one; their love for God was based in their satisfaction with the status quo.

Ethan was not like his parents, though. Ever since childhood he'd felt certain that God had a special role for him to play, and he waited for a sign telling him what that role was. He'd have liked to become a preacher, but felt he hadn't any compelling testimony to offer; his vague feelings of expectation weren't enough. He longed for an encounter with the divine to provide him with direction.

He could have gone to one of the holy sites, those places where—for reasons unknown—angelic visitations occurred on a regular basis, but he felt that such an action would be presumptuous of him. The holy sites were usually the last resort of the desperate, those people seeking either a miracle cure to repair their bodies or a glimpse of Heaven's light to repair their souls, and Ethan was not desperate. He decided that he'd been set along his own course, and in time the reason for it would become clear. While waiting for that day, he lived his life as best he could: he worked as a librarian, married a woman named Claire, raised two children. All the while, he remained watchful for signs of a greater destiny.

Ethan was certain his time had come when he became witness to a visitation of Rashiel, the same one that—miles away—restored Janice Reilly's legs. Ethan was alone when it happened, walking toward his car in the center of a parking lot, when the ground began to shudder. Instinctively he knew it was a visitation, and he assumed a kneeling position, feeling no fear, only exhilaration and awe at the prospect of learning his calling.

The ground became still after a minute, and Ethan looked around, but didn't otherwise move. Only after waiting for several more minutes did he rise to his feet. There was a large crack in the asphalt, beginning directly in front of him and following a meandering path down the street. The crack seemed to be pointing him in a specific direction, so he ran alongside it for several blocks until he encountered other survivors, a man and a woman climbing out of a modest fissure that had opened up directly beneath them. He waited with the two of them until rescuers arrived and brought them to a shelter.

Ethan attended the support group meetings that followed and met the other witnesses to Rashiel's visitation. Over the course of a few meetings, he became aware of certain patterns among the witnesses. Of course there were those who'd been injured and those who'd received miracle cures. But there were also those whose lives were changed in other ways: the man and woman he'd first met fell in love and were soon engaged; a woman who'd been pinned beneath a collapsed wall was inspired to become an EMT after being rescued. One business owner formed an alliance that averted her impending bankruptcy, while another whose business was destroyed saw it as a message that he change his ways. It seemed that everyone except Ethan had found a way to understand what had happened to them.

He hadn't been cursed or blessed in any obvious way, and he didn't know what message he was intended to receive. His wife, Claire, suggested that he consider the visitation a reminder that he appreciate what he had, but Ethan found that unsatisfying, reasoning that *every* visitation—no matter where it occurred—served that function, and the fact that he'd witnessed a visitation firsthand had to have greater significance. His mind was preyed upon by the idea that he'd missed an opportunity, that there was a fellow witness whom he was intended to meet but hadn't. This visitation had to be the sign he'd been waiting for; he couldn't just disregard it. But that didn't tell him what he was supposed to do.

Ethan eventually resorted to the process of elimination: he got hold of a list of all the witnesses, and crossed off those who had a clear interpretation of their experience, reasoning that one of those remaining must be the person whose fate was somehow intertwined with his. Among those who were confused or uncertain about the visitation's meaning would be the one he was intended to meet.

When he had finished crossing names off his list, there was only one left: JANICE REILLY.

In public Neil was able to mask his grief as adults are expected to, but in the privacy of his apartment, the floodgates of emotion burst open. The awareness of Sarah's absence would overwhelm him, and then he'd collapse on the floor and weep. He'd curl up into a ball, his body racked by hiccuping sobs, tears and mucus streaming down his face, the anguish coming in ever-increasing waves until it was more than he could bear, more intense than he'd have believed possible. Minutes or hours later it would leave, and he would fall asleep, exhausted. And the next day he would wake up and face the prospect of another day without Sarah.

An elderly woman in Neil's apartment building tried to comfort him by telling him that the pain would lessen in time, and while he would never forget his wife, he would at least be able to move on. Then he would meet someone else one day and find happiness with her, and he would learn to love God and thus ascend to Heaven when his time came.

This woman's intentions were good, but Neil was in no position to find any comfort in her words. Sarah's absence felt like an open wound, and the prospect that someday he would no longer feel pain at her loss seemed not just remote, but a physical impossibility. If suicide would have ended his pain, he'd have done it without hesitation, but that would only ensure that his separation from Sarah was permanent.

The topic of suicide regularly came up at the support group meetings, and inevitably led to someone mentioning Robin Pearson, a woman who used to come to the meetings several months before Neil began attending. Robin's husband had been afflicted with stomach cancer during a visitation of the angel Makatiel. She stayed in his hospital room for days at a stretch, only for him to die unexpectedly when she was home doing laundry. A nurse who'd been present told Robin that his soul had ascended, and so Robin had begun attending the support group meetings.

Many months later, Robin came to the meeting shaking with rage. There'd been a manifestation of Hell near her house, and she'd seen her husband among the lost souls. She'd confronted the nurse, who admitted to lying in the hopes that Robin would learn to love God, so that at least she would be saved even if her husband hadn't been. Robin wasn't at the next meeting, and at the meeting after that the group learned she had committed suicide to rejoin her husband.

None of them knew the status of Robin's and her husband's relationship in the afterlife, but successes were known to happen; some couples had indeed been happily reunited through suicide. The support group had attendees whose spouses had descended to Hell, and they talked about being torn between wanting to remain alive and wanting to rejoin their spouses. Neil wasn't in their situation, but his first response when listening to them had been envy: if Sarah had gone to Hell, suicide would be the solution to all his problems.

This led to a shameful self-knowledge for Neil. He realized that if he had to choose between going to Hell while Sarah went to Heaven, or having both of them go to Hell together, he would choose the latter: he would rather she be exiled from God than separated from him. He knew it was selfish, but he couldn't change how he felt: he believed Sarah could be happy in either place, but he could only be happy with her.

Neil's previous experiences with women had never been good. All too often he'd begin flirting with a woman while sitting at a bar, only to have her remember an appointment elsewhere the moment he stood up and his shortened leg came into view. Once, a woman he'd been dating for several weeks broke off their relationship, explaining that while she herself didn't consider his leg a defect, whenever they were seen in public together other people assumed there must be something wrong with her for being with him, and surely he could understand how unfair that was to her?

Sarah had been the first woman Neil met whose demeanor hadn't changed one bit, whose expression hadn't flickered toward pity or horror or even surprise when she first saw his leg. For that reason alone it was predictable that Neil would become infatuated with her; by the time he saw all the sides of her personality, he'd completely fallen in love with her. And because his best qualities came out when he was with her, she fell in love with him too.

Neil had been surprised when Sarah told him she was devout. There weren't many signs of her devotion—she didn't go to church, sharing Neil's dislike for the attitudes of most people who attended—but in her own quiet way she was grateful to God for her life. She never tried to convert Neil, saying that devotion would come from within or not at all. They rarely had any cause to mention God, and most of the time it would've been easy for Neil to imagine that Sarah's views on God matched his own.

This is not to say that Sarah's devotion had no effect on Neil. On the contrary, Sarah was far and away the best argument for loving God that he had ever encountered. If love of God had contributed to making her the person she was, then perhaps it did make sense. During the years that the two of them were married, his outlook on life improved, and it probably would have reached the point where he was thankful to God, if he and Sarah had grown old together.

Sarah's death removed that particular possibility, but it needn't have closed the door on Neil's loving God. Neil could have taken it as a reminder that no one can count on having decades left. He could have been moved by the realization that, had he died with her, his soul would've been lost and the two of them separated for eternity. He could have seen Sarah's death as a wake-up call, telling him to love God while he still had the chance.

Instead Neil became actively resentful of God. Sarah had been the greatest blessing of his life, and God had taken her away. Now he was expected to love Him for it? For Neil, it was like having a kidnapper demand love as ransom for his wife's return. Obedience he might have managed, but sincere, heartfelt love? That was a ransom he couldn't pay.

This paradox confronted several people in the support group. One of the attendees, a man named Phil Soames, correctly pointed out that thinking of it as a condition to be met would guarantee failure. You couldn't love God as a means to an end, you had to love Him for Himself. If your ultimate goal in loving God was a reunion with your spouse, you weren't demonstrating true devotion at all.

A woman in the support group named Valerie Tommasino said they shouldn't even try. She'd been reading a book published by the humanist movement; its members considered it wrong to love a God who inflicted such pain, and advocated that people act according to their own moral sense instead of being guided by the carrot and the stick. These were people who, when they died, descended to Hell in proud defiance of God.

Neil himself had read a pamphlet of the humanist movement; what he most remembered was that it had quoted the fallen angels. Visitations of fallen angels were infrequent, and caused neither good fortune nor bad; they weren't acting under God's direction but just passing through the mortal plane as they went about their unimaginable business. On the occasions they appeared, people would ask them questions: did they know God's intentions? Why had they rebelled? The fallen angels' reply was always the same: *Decide for yourselves. That is what we did. We advise you to do the same.*

Those in the humanist movement had decided, and if it weren't for Sarah, Neil would've made the identical choice. But he wanted her back, and the only way was to find a reason to love God.

Looking for any footing on which to build their devotion, some attendees of the support group took comfort in the fact that their loved ones hadn't suffered when God took them but instead died instantly. Neil didn't even have that; Sarah had received horrific lacerations when the glass hit her. Of course, it could have been worse. One couple's teenage son had been trapped in a fire ignited by an angel's visitation, and received full-thickness burns over eighty percent of his body before rescue workers could free him; his eventual death was a mercy. Sarah had been fortunate by comparison, but not enough to make Neil love God.

Neil could think of only one thing that would make him give thanks to God, and that was if He allowed Sarah to appear before him. It would give him immeasurable comfort just to see her smile again; he'd never been visited by a saved soul before, and a vision now would have meant more to him than at any other point in his life.

But visions don't appear just because a person needs one, and none ever came to Neil. He had to find his own way toward God.

The next time he attended the support group meeting for witnesses of Nathanael's visitation, Neil sought out Benny Vasquez, the man whose eyes had been erased by Heaven's light. Benny didn't always attend because he was now being invited to speak at other meetings; few visitations resulted in an eyeless person, since Heaven's light entered the mortal plane only in the brief moments that an angel emerged from or reentered Heaven, so the eyeless were minor celebrities, and in demand as speakers to church groups.

Benny was now as sightless as any burrowing worm: not only were his eyes and sockets missing, his skull lacked even the space for such features, the cheekbones now abutting the forehead. The light that had brought his soul as close to perfection as was possible in the mortal plane had also deformed his body; it was commonly held that this illustrated the superfluity of physical bodies in Heaven. With the limited expressive capacity his face retained, Benny always wore a blissful, rapturous smile.

Neil hoped Benny could say something to help him love God. Benny described Heaven's light as infinitely beautiful, a sight of such compelling majesty that it vanquished all doubts. It constituted incontrovertible proof that God should be loved, an explanation that made it as obvious as $1+1 = 2$. Unfortunately, while Benny could offer many analogies for the effect of Heaven's light, he couldn't duplicate that effect with his own words. Those who were already devout found Benny's descriptions thrilling, but to Neil, they seemed frustratingly vague. So he looked elsewhere for counsel.

Accept the mystery, said the minister of the local church. If you can love God even though your questions go unanswered, you'll be the better for it.

Admit that you need Him, said the popular book of spiritual advice he bought. When you realize that self-sufficiency is an illusion, you'll be ready.

Submit yourself completely and utterly, said the preacher on the television. Receiving torment is how you prove your love. Acceptance may not bring you relief in this life, but resistance will only worsen your punishment.

All of these strategies have proven successful for different individuals; any one of them, once internalized, can bring a person to devotion. But these are not always easy to adopt, and Neil was one who found them impossible.

Neil finally tried talking to Sarah's parents, which was an indication of how desperate he was: his relationship with them had always been tense. While they loved Sarah, they often chided her for not being demonstrative enough in her devotion, and they'd been shocked when she married a man who wasn't devout at all. For her part, Sarah had always considered her parents too judgmental, and their disapproval of Neil only reinforced her opinion. But now Neil felt he had something in common with them—after all, they were all mourning Sarah's loss—and so he visited them in their suburban colonial, hoping they could help him in his grief.

How wrong he was. Instead of sympathy, what Neil got from Sarah's parents was blame for her death. They'd come to this conclusion in the weeks after Sarah's funeral; they reasoned that she'd been taken to send him a message, and that they were forced to endure her loss solely because he hadn't been devout. They were now convinced that, his previous explanations notwithstanding, Neil's deformed leg was in fact God's doing, and if only he'd been properly chastened by it, Sarah might still be alive.

Their reaction shouldn't have come as a surprise: throughout Neil's life, people had attributed moral significance to his leg even though God wasn't responsible for it. Now that he'd suffered a misfortune for which God was unambiguously responsible, it was inevitable that someone would assume he deserved it. It was purely by chance that Neil heard this sentiment when he was at his most vulnerable, and it could have the greatest impact on him.

Neil didn't think his in-laws were right, but he began to wonder if he might not be better off if he did. Perhaps, he thought, it'd be better to live in a story where the righteous were rewarded and the sinners were punished, even if the criteria for righteousness and sinfulness eluded him, than to live in a reality where there was no justice at all. It would mean casting himself in the role of sinner, so it was hardly a comforting lie, but it offered one reward that his own ethics couldn't: believing it would reunite him with Sarah.

Sometimes even bad advice can point a man in the right direction. It was in this manner that his in-laws' accusations ultimately pushed Neil closer to God.

More than once when she was evangelizing, Janice had been asked if she ever wished she had legs, and she had always answered—honestly—no, she didn't. She was content as she was. Sometimes her questioner would point out that she couldn't miss what she'd never known, and she might feel differently if she'd been born with legs and lost them later on. Janice never denied that. But she could truthfully say that she felt no sense of being incomplete, no envy for people with legs; being legless was part of her identity. She'd never bothered with prosthetics, and had a surgical procedure been available to provide her with legs, she'd have turned it down. She had never considered the possibility that God might restore her legs.

One of the unexpected side effects of having legs was the increased attention she received from men. In the past she'd mostly attracted men with amputee fetishes or sainthood complexes; now all sorts of men seemed drawn to her. So when she first noticed Ethan Mead's interest in her, she thought it was romantic in nature; this possibility was particularly distressing since he was obviously married.

Ethan had begun talking to Janice at the support group meetings, and then began attending her public speaking engagements. It was when he suggested they have lunch together that Janice asked him about his intentions, and he explained his theory. He didn't know *how* his fate was intertwined with hers; he knew only that it was. She was skeptical, but she didn't reject his theory outright. Ethan admitted that he didn't have answers for her own questions, but he was eager to do anything he could to help her find them. Janice cautiously agreed to help him in his search for meaning, and Ethan promised that he wouldn't be a burden. They met on a regular basis and talked about the significance of visitations.

Meanwhile Ethan's wife Claire grew worried. Ethan assured her that he had no romantic feelings toward Janice, but that didn't alleviate her concerns. She knew that extreme circumstances could create a bond between individuals, and she feared that Ethan's relationship with Janice—romantic or not—would threaten their marriage.

Ethan suggested to Janice that he, as a librarian, could help her do some research. Neither of them had ever heard of a previous instance where God had left His mark on a person in one visitation and removed it in another. Ethan looked for previous examples in hopes that they might shed some light on Janice's situation. There were a few instances of individuals receiving multiple miracle cures over their lifetimes, but their illnesses or disabilities had always been of natural origin, not given to them in a visitation. There was one anecdotal report of a man being struck blind for his sins, changing his ways, and later having his sight restored, but it was classified as an urban legend.

Even if that account had a basis in truth, it didn't provide a useful precedent for Janice's situation: her legs had been removed before her birth, and so couldn't have been a punishment for anything she'd done.

Was it possible that Janice's condition had been a punishment for something her mother or father had done? Could her restoration mean they had finally earned her cure? She couldn't believe that.

If her deceased relatives were to appear in a vision, Janice would've been reassured about the restoration of her legs. The fact that they didn't made her suspect something was amiss, but she didn't believe that it was a punishment. Perhaps it had been a mistake, and she'd received a miracle meant for someone else; perhaps it was a test, to see how she would respond to being given too much. In either case, there seemed only one course of action: she would, with utmost gratitude and humility, offer to return her gift. To do so, she would go on a pilgrimage.

Pilgrims traveled great distances to visit the holy sites and wait for a visitation, hoping for a miracle cure. Whereas in most of the world one could wait an entire lifetime and never experience a visitation, at a holy site one might only wait months, sometimes weeks. Pilgrims knew that the odds of being cured were still poor; of those who stayed long enough to witness a visitation, the majority did not receive a cure. But they were often happy just to have seen an angel, and they returned home better able to face what awaited them, whether it be imminent death or life with a crippling disability. And of course, just living through a visitation made many people appreciate their situations; invariably, a small number of pilgrims were killed during each visitation.

Janice was willing to accept the outcome, whatever it was. If God saw fit to take her, she was ready. If God removed her legs again, she would resume the work she'd always done. If God let her legs remain, she hoped she would receive the epiphany she needed to speak with conviction about her gift.

She hoped, however, that her miracle would be taken back and given to someone who truly needed it. She didn't suggest to anyone that they accompany her in hopes of receiving the miracle she was returning, feeling that that would've been presumptuous, but she privately considered her pilgrimage a request on behalf of those who were in need.

Her friends and family were confused at Janice's decision, seeing it as questioning God. As word spread, she received many letters from followers, variously expressing dismay, bafflement, or admiration for her willingness to make such a sacrifice.

As for Ethan, he was completely supportive of Janice's decision, and excited for himself. He now understood the significance of Rashiel's visitation for him: it indicated that the time had come for him to act. His wife Claire strenuously opposed his leaving, pointing out that he had no idea how long he might be away, and that she and their children needed him too. It grieved him to go without her support, but he had no choice. Ethan would go on a pilgrimage, and at the next visitation, he would learn what God intended for him.

Neil's visit to Sarah's parents caused him to give further thought to his conversation with Benny Vasquez. While he hadn't gotten a lot out of Benny's words, he'd been impressed by the absoluteness of Benny's devotion. No matter what misfortune befell him in the future, Benny's love of God would never waver, and he would ascend to Heaven when he died. That fact offered Neil a very slim opportunity, one that had seemed so unattractive he hadn't considered it before; but now, as he was growing more desperate, it was beginning to look expedient.

Every holy site had its pilgrims who, rather than looking for a miracle cure, deliberately sought out Heaven's light. Those who saw it were always accepted into Heaven when they died, no matter how selfish their motives had been; there were some who wished to have their ambivalence removed so they could be reunited with their loved ones, and others who'd always lived a sinful life and wanted to escape the consequences.

In the past there'd been some doubt as to whether Heaven's light could indeed overcome *all* the spiritual obstacles to becoming saved. The debate ended after the case of Barry Larsen, a serial rapist and murderer who, while disposing of the body of his latest victim, witnessed an angel's visitation and saw Heaven's light. At Larsen's execution, his soul was seen ascending to Heaven, much to the outrage of his victims' families. Priests tried to console them, assuring them—on the basis of no evidence whatsoever—that Heaven's light must have subjected Larsen to many lifetimes' worth of penance in a moment, but their words provided little comfort.

For Neil this offered a loophole, an answer to Phil Soames's objection; it was the one way that he could love Sarah more than he loved God, and still be reunited with her. It was how he could be selfish and still get into Heaven. Others had done it; perhaps he could too. It might not be just, but at least it was predictable.

At an instinctual level, Neil was averse to the idea: it sounded like undergoing brainwashing as a cure for depression. He couldn't help but think that it would change his personality so drastically that he'd cease to be himself. Then he remembered that everyone in Heaven had undergone a similar transformation; the saved were just like the eyeless except that they no longer had bodies. This gave Neil a clearer image of what he was working toward: no matter whether he became devout by seeing

Heaven's light or by a lifetime of effort, any ultimate reunion with Sarah couldn't re-create what they'd shared in the mortal plane. In Heaven, they would both be different, and their love for each other would be mixed with the love that all the saved felt for everything.

This realization didn't diminish Neil's longing for a reunion with Sarah. In fact it sharpened his desire, because it meant that the reward would be the same no matter what means he used to achieve it; the short-cut led to precisely the same destination as the conventional path.

On the other hand, seeking Heaven's light was far more difficult than an ordinary pilgrimage, and far more dangerous. Heaven's light leaked through only when an angel entered or left the mortal plane, and since there was no way to predict where an angel would first appear, light-seekers had to converge on the angel after its arrival and follow it until its departure. To maximize their chances of being in the narrow shaft of Heaven's light, they followed the angel as closely as possible during its visitation; depending on the angel involved, this might mean stay-ing alongside the funnel of a tornado, the wavefront of a flash flood, or the expanding tip of a chasm as it split apart the landscape. Far more light-seekers died in the attempt than succeeded.

Statistics about the souls of failed light-seekers were difficult to com-pile, since there were few witnesses to such expeditions, but the numbers so far were not encouraging. In sharp contrast to ordinary pilgrims who died without receiving their sought-after cure, of which roughly half were admitted into Heaven, every single failed light-seeker had de-scended to Hell. Perhaps only people who were already lost ever consid-ered seeking Heaven's light, or perhaps death in such circumstances was considered suicide. In any case, it was clear to Neil that he needed to be ready to accept the consequences of embarking on such an attempt.

The entire idea had an all-or-nothing quality to it that Neil found both frightening and attractive. He found the prospect of going on with his life, trying to love God, increasingly maddening. He might try for de-cades and not succeed. He might not even have that long; as he'd been reminded so often lately, visitations served as a warning to prepare one's soul, because death might come at any time. He could die tomorrow, and there was no chance of his becoming devout in the near future by con-ventional means.

It's perhaps ironic that, given his history of not following Janice Reilly's example, Neil took notice when she reversed her position. He was eating breakfast when he happened to see an item in the newspaper about her plans for a pilgrimage, and his immediate reaction was anger: how many blessings would it take to satisfy that woman? After consider-ing it more, he decided that if she, having received a blessing, deemed it appropriate to seek God's assistance in coming to terms with it, then there was no reason that he, having received such terrible misfortune, shouldn't do the same. And that was enough to tip him over the edge.

Holy sites were invariably in inhospitable places: one was an atoll in the middle of the ocean, while another was in the mountains at an elevation of 20,000 ft. The one that Neil traveled to was in a desert, an expanse of cracked mud reaching miles in every direction; it was desolate, but it was relatively accessible and thus popular among pilgrims. The appearance of the holy site was an object lesson in what happened when the celestial and terrestrial realms touched: the landscape was variously scarred by lava flows, gaping fissures, and impact craters. Vegetation was scarce and ephemeral, restricted to growing in the interval after soil was deposited by floodwaters or whirlwinds and before it was scoured away again.

Pilgrims took up residence all over the site, forming temporary villages with their tents and camper vans; they all made guesses as to what location would maximize their chances of seeing the angel while minimizing the risk of injury or death. Some protection was offered by curved banks of sandbags, left over from years past and rebuilt as needed. A site-specific paramedic and fire department ensured that paths were kept clear so rescue vehicles could go where they were needed. Pilgrims either brought their own food and water or purchased them from vendors charging exorbitant prices; everyone paid a fee to cover the cost of waste removal.

Light-seekers always had off-road vehicles to better cross rough terrain when it came time to follow the angel. Those who could afford it drove alone; those who couldn't formed groups of two or three or four. Neil didn't want to be a passenger reliant on another person, nor did he want the responsibility of driving anyone else. This might be his final act on earth, and he felt he should do it alone. The cost of Sarah's funeral had depleted their savings, so Neil sold all his possessions in order to purchase a suitable vehicle: a pickup truck equipped with aggressively knurled tires and heavy-duty shock absorbers.

As soon as he arrived, Neil started doing what all the other light-seekers did: crisscrossing the site in his vehicle, trying to familiarize himself with its topography. It was on one of his drives around the site's perimeter that he met Ethan; Ethan flagged him down after his own car had stalled on his return from the nearest grocery store, eighty miles away. Neil helped him get his car started again, and then, at Ethan's insistence, followed him back to his campsite for dinner. Janice wasn't there when they arrived, having gone to visit some pilgrims several tents over; Neil listened politely while Ethan—heating prepackaged meals over a bottle of propane—began describing the events that had brought him to the holy site.

When Ethan mentioned Janice Reilly's name, Neil couldn't mask his surprise. He had no desire to speak with her again, and immediately excused himself to leave. He was explaining to a puzzled Ethan that he'd forgotten a previous engagement when Janice arrived.

She was startled to see Neil there, but asked him to stay. Ethan explained why he'd invited Neil to dinner, and Janice told him where she and Neil had met. Then she asked Neil what had brought him to the holy site. When he told them he was a light-seeker, Ethan and Janice immediately tried to persuade him to reconsider his plans. He might be committing suicide, said Ethan, and there were always better alternatives than suicide. Seeing Heaven's light was not the answer, said Janice; that wasn't what God wanted. Neil stiffly thanked them for their concern, and left.

During the weeks of waiting, Neil spent every day driving around the site; maps were available, and were updated after each visitation, but they were no substitute for driving the terrain yourself. On occasion he would see a light-seeker who was obviously experienced in off-road driving, and ask him—the vast majority of the light-seekers were men—for tips on negotiating a specific type of terrain. Some had been at the site for several visitations, having neither succeeded nor failed at their previous attempts. They were glad to share tips on how best to pursue an angel, but never offered any personal information about themselves. Neil found the tone of their conversation peculiar, simultaneously hopeful and hopeless, and wondered if he sounded the same.

Ethan and Janice passed the time by getting to know some of the other pilgrims. Their reactions to Janice's situation were mixed: some thought her ungrateful, while others thought her generous. Most found Ethan's story interesting, since he was one of the very few pilgrims seeking something other than a miracle cure. For the most part, there was a feeling of camaraderie that sustained them during the long wait.

Neil was driving around in his truck when dark clouds began coalescing in the southeast, and the word came over the CB radio that a visitation had begun. He stopped the vehicle to insert earplugs into his ears and don his helmet; by the time he was finished, flashes of lightning were visible, and a light-seeker near the angel reported that it was Barakiel, and it appeared to be moving due north. Neil turned his truck east in anticipation and began driving at full speed.

There was no rain or wind, only dark clouds from which lightning emerged. Over the radio other light-seekers relayed estimates of the angel's direction and speed, and Neil headed northeast to get in front of it. At first he could gauge his distance from the storm by counting how long it took for the thunder to arrive, but soon the lightning bolts were striking so frequently that he couldn't match up the sounds with the individual strikes.

He saw the vehicles of two other light-seekers converging. They began driving in parallel, heading north, over a heavily cratered section of ground, bouncing over small ones and swerving to avoid the larger ones. Bolts of lightning were striking the ground everywhere, but they appeared to be radiating from a point south of Neil's position; the angel was directly behind him, and closing.

Even through his earplugs, the roar was deafening. Neil could feel his hair rising from his skin as the electric charge built up around him. He kept glancing in his rearview mirror, trying to ascertain where the angel was while wondering how close he ought to get.

His vision grew so crowded with afterimages that it became difficult to distinguish actual bolts of lightning among them. Squinting at the dazzle in his mirror, he realized he was looking at a continuous bolt of lightning, undulating but uninterrupted. He tilted the driver's-side mirror upward to get a better look, and saw the source of the lightning bolt, a seething, writhing mass of flames, silver against the dusky clouds: the angel Barakiel.

It was then, while Neil was transfixed and paralyzed by what he saw, that his pickup truck crested a sharp outcropping of rock and became airborne. The truck smashed into a boulder, the entire force of the impact concentrated on the vehicle's left front end, crumpling it like foil. The intrusion into the driver's compartment fractured both of Neil's legs and nicked his left femoral artery. Neil began, slowly but surely, bleeding to death.

He didn't try to move; he wasn't in physical pain at the moment, but he somehow knew that the slightest movement would be excruciating. It was obvious that he was pinned in the truck, and there was no way he could pursue Barakiel even if he weren't. Helplessly, he watched the lightning storm move farther and farther away.

As he watched it, Neil began crying. He was filled with a mixture of regret and self-contempt, cursing himself for ever thinking that such a scheme could succeed. He would have begged for the opportunity to do it over again, promised to spend the rest of his days learning to love God, if only he could live, but he knew that no bargaining was possible and he had only himself to blame. He apologized to Sarah for losing his chance at being reunited with her, for throwing his life away on a gamble instead of playing it safe. He prayed that she understood that he'd been motivated by his love for her, and that she would forgive him.

Through his tears he saw a woman running toward him, and recognized her as Janice Reilly. He realized his truck had crashed no more than a hundred yards from her and Ethan's campsite. There was nothing she could do, though; he could feel the blood draining out of him, and knew that he wouldn't live long enough for a rescue vehicle to arrive. He thought Janice was calling to him, but his ears were ringing too badly for him to hear anything. He could see Ethan Mead behind her, also starting to run toward him.

Then there was a flash of light and Janice was knocked off her feet as if she'd been struck by a sledgehammer. At first he thought she'd been hit by lightning, but then he realized that the lightning had already ceased. It was when she stood up again that he saw her face, steam rising from newly featureless skin, and he realized that Janice had been struck by Heaven's light.

Neil looked up, but all he saw were clouds; the shaft of light was gone. It seemed as if God were taunting him, not only by showing him the prize he'd lost his life trying to acquire while still holding it out of reach, but also by giving it to someone who didn't need it or even want it. God had already wasted a miracle on Janice, and now He was doing it again.

It was at that moment that another beam of Heaven's light penetrated the cloud cover and struck Neil, trapped in his vehicle.

Like a thousand hypodermic needles the light punctured his flesh and scraped across his bones. The light unmade his eyes, turning him into not a formerly sighted being, but a being never intended to possess vision. And in doing so the light revealed to Neil all the reasons he should love God.

He loved Him with an utterness beyond what humans can experience for one another. To say it was unconditional was inadequate, because even the word "unconditional" required the concept of a condition and such an idea was no longer comprehensible to him: every phenomenon in the universe was nothing less than an explicit reason to love Him. No circumstance could be an obstacle or even an irrelevancy, but only another reason to be grateful, a further inducement to love. Neil thought of the grief that had driven him to suicidal recklessness, and the pain and terror that Sarah had experienced before she died, and still he loved God, not in spite of their suffering, but because of it.

He renounced all his previous anger and ambivalence and desire for answers. He was grateful for all the pain he'd endured, contrite for not previously recognizing it as the gift it was, euphoric that he was now being granted this insight into his true purpose. He understood how life was an undeserved bounty, how even the most virtuous were not worthy of the glories of the mortal plane.

For him the mystery was solved, because he understood that everything in life is love, even pain, especially pain.

So minutes later, when Neil finally bled to death, he was truly worthy of salvation.

And God sent him to Hell anyway.

Ethan saw all of this. He saw Neil and Janice remade by Heaven's light, and he saw the pious love on their eyeless faces. He saw the skies become clear and the sunlight return. He was holding Neil's hand, waiting for the paramedics, when Neil died, and he saw Neil's soul leave his body and rise toward Heaven, only to descend into Hell.

Janice didn't see it, for by then her eyes were already gone. Ethan was the sole witness, and he realized that this was God's purpose for him: to follow Janice Reilly to this point and to see what she could not.

When statistics were compiled for Barakiel's visitation, it turned out that there had been a total of ten casualties, six among light-seekers and four among ordinary pilgrims. Nine pilgrims received miracle cures; the only individuals to see Heaven's light were Janice and Neil. There were no statistics regarding how many pilgrims had felt their lives changed by the visitation, but Ethan counted himself among them.

Upon returning home, Janice resumed her evangelism, but the topic of her speeches has changed. She no longer speaks about how the physically handicapped have the resources to overcome their limitations; instead she, like the other eyeless, speaks about the unbearable beauty of God's creation. Many who used to draw inspiration from her are disappointed, feeling they've lost a spiritual leader. When Janice had spoken of the strength she had as an afflicted person, her message was rare, but now that she's eyeless, her message is commonplace. She doesn't worry about the reduction in her audience, though, because she has complete conviction in what she evangelizes.

Ethan quit his job and became a preacher so that he too could speak about his experiences. His wife Claire couldn't accept his new mission and ultimately left him, taking their children with her, but Ethan was willing to continue alone. He's developed a substantial following by telling people what happened to Neil Fisk. He tells people that they can no more expect justice in the afterlife than in the mortal plane, but he doesn't do this to dissuade them from worshipping God; on the contrary, he encourages them to do so. What he insists on is that they not love God under a misapprehension, that if they wish to love God, they be prepared to do so no matter what His intentions. God is not just, God is not kind, God is not merciful, and understanding that is essential to true devotion.

As for Neil, although he is unaware of any of Ethan's sermons, he would understand their message perfectly. His lost soul is the embodiment of Ethan's teachings.

For most of its inhabitants, Hell is not that different from Earth; its principal punishment is the regret of not having loved God enough when alive, and for many that's easily endured. For Neil, however, Hell bears no resemblance whatsoever to the mortal plane. His eternal body has well-formed legs, but he's scarcely aware of them; his eyes have been restored, but he can't bear to open them. Just as seeing Heaven's light gave him an awareness of God's presence in all things in the mortal plane, so it has made him aware of God's absence in all things in Hell. Everything Neil sees, hears, or touches causes him distress, and unlike in the mortal plane this pain is not a form of God's love, but a consequence of His absence. Neil is experiencing more anguish than was possible when he was alive, but his only response is to love God.

Neil still loves Sarah, and misses her as much as he ever did, and the knowledge that he came so close to rejoining her only makes it worse. He knows his being sent to Hell was not a result of anything he did; he knows there was no reason for it, no higher purpose being served. None of this diminishes his love for God. If there were a possibility that he could be admitted to Heaven and his suffering would end, he would not hope for it; such desires no longer occur to him.

Neil even knows that by being beyond God's awareness, he is not loved by God in return. This doesn't affect his feelings either, because unconditional love asks nothing, not even that it be returned.

And though it's been many years that he has been in Hell, beyond the awareness of God, he loves Him still. That is the nature of true devotion.

The Man Who Stole the Moon

(A Story of the Flat Earth)

~~~~~~~~~~

Tanith Lee

Tanith Lee (tribute website: www3.sympatico.ca/jim.pattison) lives in the south of England. She is one of the leading fantasy and horror writers of the last three decades. Her first professional sale was to The Ninth Pan Book of Horror Stories *(1968), and, in 1971, Macmillan published* The Dragon Hoard, *a children's novel, followed by* Animal Castle, *a children's picture book, and* Princess Hynchatti & Some Other Surprises, *a short story collection (both 1972). After receiving numerous rejections from British publishers for her adult fantasy novel* The Birthgrave, *she wrote a letter of inquiry to DAW Books, the American publishing firm founded by well-known science fiction fan and editor Donald A. Wolheim. DAW published* The Birthgrave *in 1975, beginning a relationship that lasted until 1989 and saw the publication of 28 books altogether. Among her most famous works is the series of fantasy stories of Flat Earth, collected in* Night's Master *(1978),* Death's Master *(1979),* Delusion's Master *(1981),* Delirium's Mistress *(1986), and* Night's Sorceries *(1987).*

"The Man Who Stole the Moon," a Flat Earth story, appeared in Weird Tales, *where Lee is a frequent contributor, and which continues a distinguished tradition of publishing fantasy and supernatural horror going all the way back to 1923. In the tradition of Clark Ashton Smith, this is a powerful story of a thief and lover, an overreaching demon, and a magical world of evil.*

As so often, from an idea by John Kailne.

Several tales are told concerning the Moon of the Flat Earth. Some say that this Moon, perhaps, was a hollow globe, within which lay lands and seas, having even their own cool Sun. However, there are other stories.

One evening, Jaqir the accomplished thief rose from a bed of love and said to his mistress, "Alas, sweetheart, we must now part forever." Jaqir's mistress looked at him in surprise and shook out her bright hair. "You are mistaken. My husband, the old merchant, is miles off again, buying silk and other stuff, and besides suspects nothing. And I am well satisfied with you."

"Dear heart," said Jaqir, as he dressed his handsome self swiftly, "neither of these things is the stumbling block to our romance. It is only this. I have grown tired of you."

"Tired of me!" cried the lady, springing from the bed.

"Yes, though indeed you are toothsome in all respects. I am inconstant and easily bored. You must forgive me."

"Forgive you!" screamed the lady, picking up a handy vase.

Jaqir ducked the vase and swung nimbly out of the high window, an action to which he was quite accustomed, from his trade. "Although a deceiver in my work, honesty in my private life is always my preferred method," he added, as he dropped quickly down through the vine to the street below. Once there he was gone in a flash, and just in time to miss the jar of piddle the lady that moment upended from the window. However, three of the king's guard, next second passing beneath, were not so fortunate.

"A curse upon all bladders,' " howled they, wringing out their cloaks and hair. Then looking up, they beheld the now no-longer mistress of Jaqir, and asked her loudly what she meant by it.

"Pardon me, splendid sirs," said she. "The befoulment was not intended for you, but for that devilish thief, Jaqir, who even now runs through that alley there toward a hiding place he keeps in the House of the Thin Door."

At the mention of Jaqir, who was both celebrated and notorious in that city, the soldiers forgot their inconvenience, and gave instant chase. Never before had any been able to lay hands on Jaqir, who, it was said, could steal the egg from beneath a sleeping pigeon. Now, thanks to the enragement of his discarded lover, the guard knew not only of Jaqir's proximity, but his destination. Presently then they came up with him by the House of the Thin Door.

"Is it he?"

"So it is, for I have heard, when not in disguise, he dresses like a lord, like this one, and, like this one, his hair is black as a panther's fur."

At this they strode up to Jaqir and surrounded him.

"Good evening, my friends," said Jaqir. "You are fine fellows, despite your smell."

"That smell is not our own, but the product of a night-jar emptied on us. And the one who did this also told us where to find the thief Jaqir."

"Fate has been kind to you. I will not therefore detain you further."

"No, it is you who shall be detained."

"*I?*" asked Jaqir modestly.

But within the hour he discovered himself in chains in the king's dungeons.

"Ah, Jaqir," said he to himself, "a life of crime has taught you nothing. For have the gods not always rewarded your dishonesty—and now you are chastised for being truthful."

Although of course the indifferent, useless gods had nothing to do with any of it.

A month or so later, the king got to hear that Jaqir the Prince of Thieves languished in the prison, awaiting trial.

"I will see to it," said the king. "Bring him before me."

So Jaqir was brought before the king. But, despite being in jail, being also what he was, Jaqir had somehow stolen a gold piece from one jailor and gifted it to another, and so arrived in the king's sight certainly in chains, but additionally bathed, barbered, and anointed, dressed in finery, and with a cup of wine in his hand.

Seeing this, the king laughed. He was a young king and not without a sense of the humorous. In addition, he knew that Jaqir, while he had stolen from everyone he might, had never harmed a hair of their heads, while his skills of disguise and escape were much admired by any he had not annoyed.

"Now then, Prince of Thieves, may a mere king invite you to sit? Shall I strike off your chains?" added the king.

"Your majesty," said one of the king's advisers, "pray do not unchain him, or he will be away over the roofs. Look, he has already stolen two of my gold rings—and see, many others have lost items."

This was a fact. All up and down the palace hall, those who had gathered to see Jaqir on trial were exclaiming over pieces of jewelry suddenly missing. And one lady had even lost her little dog, which abruptly, and with a smile, Jaqir let out of an inner compartment in his shirt, though it seemed quite sorry to leave him.

"Then I shall not unchain you," said the king. "Restore at once all you have filched."

Jaqir rose, shook himself somewhat, and an abundance of gold and gems cascaded from his person.

"Regrettably, lord king, I could not resist the chance to display my skills."

"Rather you should deny your skills. For you have been employed in my city seven years, and lived like the prince you call yourself. But the punishment for such things is death."

Jaqir's face fell, then he shrugged. He said, "I see you are a greater thief, sir, than I. For I only presume to rob men of their goods. You are bold enough to burgle me of my life."

At that the court made a noise, but the king grew silent and thoughtful. Eventually he said, "I note you will debate the matter. But I do not believe you can excuse your acts."

"There you are wrong. If I were a beggar calling for charity on the street you would not think me guilty of anything but ill luck or indigence. Or, if I were a seller of figs you would not even notice me as I took the coins of men in exchange for my wares."

"Come," said the king. "You neither beg nor sell. You thieve."

"A beggar," said Jaqir, "takes men's money and other alms, and gives nothing in return but a blessing. Please believe me, I heap blessings on the heads of all I rob, and thank them in my prayers for their charity. Had I begged it, I might, it is true, not have received so great a portion. How much nobler and blessed are they then, that they have given over to me the more generous amount? Nor do they give up their coins for nothing. For what they buy of me, when it is *I* who steal from them, is a dramatic tale to tell. And indeed, lord king, have you never heard any boast of how they were robbed by me?"

The king frowned, for now and then he had heard this very thing, some rich noble or other reciting the story of how he had been despoiled of this or that treasure by the nimble Jaqir, the only thief able to take it. And once or twice, there were women, too, who said, "When I woke, I found my rings were gone, but on my pillow lay a crimson rose. Oh, would he had stayed a while to steal some other prize."

"I am not," declared Jaqir, "a common thief. I purloin from none who cannot afford the loss. I deduct nothing that has genuine sentimental or talismanic weight. I harm none. Besides, I am an artist in what I do. I come and go like a shadow, and vanish like the dawn into the day. You will have been told, I can abstract the egg of a pigeon from beneath the sleeping bird and never wake it."

The king frowned deeply. He said, "Yet with all this vaunted knack, you did not, till today, leave my dungeons."

Jaqir bowed. "That was because, lord king, I did not wish to miss my chance of meeting you."

"Truly? I think rather it was the bolts and bars and keys, the numerous guards—who granted you wine, but not an open door. You seem a touch pale."

"Who can tell?" idly answered pale Jaqir.

But the king only said, "I will go apart and think about all this." And so he did, but the court lingered, looking at Jaqir, and some of the ladies and young men came and spoke to him, but trying always not to get near enough to be robbed. Yet even so, now and then, he would courteously hand them back an emerald or amethyst he had removed from their persons.

Meanwhile the king walked up and down a private chamber where, on pedestals of marble, jewel-colored parrots sat watching him.

"He is clever," said the king, "handsome, well mannered, and decorative. One likes him at once, despite his nefarious career. Why cast such a man out of the state of life? We have callous villains and nonentities enough. Must every shining star be snuffed?"

Then a scarlet parrot spoke to him.

"O king, if you do not have Jaqir executed, they will say you are partial, and not worthy to be trusted with the office of judge."

"Yes," said the king, "this I know."

At this another parrot, whose feathers shone like a pale-blue sky, also spoke out. "But if you kill him, O king, men may rather say you were jealous of him. And no king must envy any man."

"This is also apt," said the king, pacing about.

Then a parrot spoke, which was greener than jade.

"O king, is Jaqir not a thief? Does he not brag of it? Set him then a test of thieving, and make this test as impossible as may be. And say to him, 'If you can do this, then indeed your skill is that of a poet, an artist, a warrior, a prince. But if you fail you must die.'"

Then the king laughed again. "Well said. But what test?"

At that a small gray parrot flew from its pedestal, and standing on his shoulder, spoke in the king's ear with a jet-black beak.

The king said, "O wisest of all my councilors."

In the palace hall Jaqir sat among the grouped courtiers, being pleasant and easy with them in his chains, like a king. But then the king entered and spoke as follows:

"Now, Jaqir, you may have heard, in my private rooms four angels live, that have taken another form. With these four I have discussed your case. And here is the verdict. I shall set you now a task that, should you succeed at it, must make you a hero and a legend among men—which happy state you will live to enjoy, since also I will pardon all your previous crimes. Such shall be your fame then, that hardly need you try to take anything by stealth. A million doors shall be thrown wide for you, and men will load you with riches, so astonishing will your name have become."

Jaqir had donned a look of flattering attention.

"The task then. You claim yourself a paragon among thieves. You must steal that which is itself a paragon. And as you say you have never taken anything which may be really missed, on this occasion I say you will have to thieve something all mankind shall miss and mourn."

The court stood waiting on the king's words. Jaqir stood waiting, perforce. And all about, as at such times it must (still must), the world stood waiting, hushing the tongues of sea and wind, the whispers of forests and sands, the thunder of a thousand voiceless things.

"Jaqir, Prince of Thieves, for your life, fly up and steal the Moon from the sky. The task being what it is, I give you a year to do it."

Nine magicians bound Jaqir. He felt the chains they put on him as he had scarcely felt the other chains of iron, thinking optimistically as he had been, that he would soon be out of them.

But the new chains emerged from a haze of iridescent smokes and a rumble of incantations, and had forms like whips and lions, thorns and bears. Meeting his flesh, they disappeared, but he felt them sink in, painless knives, and fasten on his bones and brain and mind.

"You may go where you wish and do what you will and suffer nothing. But if you should attempt, in any way, to abscond, then you will feel the talons and the fangs of that which has bound you, wrapped gnawing inside your body. And should you persist in your evasion, these restraints shall accordingly devour you from within. Run where you choose, seek what help you may, you will die in horrible agony, and soon. Only when you return to the king, your task accomplished fully, and clearly proven, will these strictures lapse—but that at once. Success, success alone, spells your freedom."

So then Jaqir was let go, and it was true enough, honesty being the keynote to his tale so far, that he had no trouble, and could travel about as he wanted. Nor did any idea enter his mind concerning escape. Of all he was or was not, Jaqir was seldom a fool. And he had, in the matter of his arrest, surely spent sufficient foolishness to last a lifetime.

Since he was *not* a fool, Jaqir, from the moment the king had put the bargain to him, had been puzzling how he might do what was demanded.

In the past, many difficult enterprises had come Jaqir's way, and he had solved the problem of each. But it is to be remembered, on none of these had his very existence depended. Nor had it been so strange. One thing must be said, too, the world being no longer as then it was—Jaqir did not at any point contest the notion on the grounds that it was either absurd or unconscionable. Plainly sorcery existed, was everywhere about, and seldom doubted. Plainly the Moon, every night gaudily on show, might be accessible, even to men, for there were legends of such goings on. Thus Jaqir never said to himself, What madness have I been saddled with? Only: How can I effect this extraordinary deed?

So he went up and down in the city, and later through the landscape beyond, walking mostly, to aid his concentration. Sometimes he would spend the night at an inn, or in some rich house he had never professionally bothered but which had heard of him. And occasionally men did know of him to recognize him, and some knew what had been laid upon him. And unfortunately, the nicest of them would tend to a similar, irritating act. Which was, as the Moon habitually rose in the east, to mock or rant at him. "Aiee, Jaqir. Have you not stolen her *yet?*"

Because the Earth was then flat, the Moon journeyed over and around it, dipping, after moonset, into the restorative seas of chaos that lay beneath the basement of the world. Nor was the Moon of the Flat Earth so very big in circumference (although the size of the Moon varied, influenced by who told—or tells—the tales).

"What *is* the Moon?" pondered Jaqir at a wayside tavern, sipping sherbet.

"Of what is the Moon *made*?" murmured Jaqir, courting sleep, for novelty, in an olive grove.

"Is it heavy or light? What makes it, or she, glow so vividly? *Is* it a she? How," muttered Jaqir, striding at evening between fields of silver barley, "am I to get hold of the damnable thing?"

Just then the Moon willfully and unkindly rose again, unstolen, over the fields. Jaqir presently lay down on his back among the barley stalks, gazing up at her as she lifted herself higher and higher. Until at length she reached the apex of heaven, where she seemed for a while to stand still, like one white lily on a stem of stars.

"Oh Moon of my despair," said Jaqir softly, "I fear I shall not master this riddle. I would do better to spend my last year of life—of which I find only nine months remain!—in pleasure, and forget the hopeless task."

At that moment Jaqir heard the stalks rustling a short way off, and sitting up, he saw through the darkness how two figures wandered between the barley. They were a young man and a girl, and from their conduct, lovers in search of a secret bed. With a rueful nod at the ironies of Fate, Jaqir got up and meant to go quietly away. But just then he heard the maiden say, "Not here, the barley is trampled—we must lie where the stalks are thicker, or we may be heard."

"Heard?" asked the youth. "There is no one about."

"Not up in the fields," replied the girl, "but down *below* the fields the demons may be listening in the Underearth."

"Ho," said the youth (another fool), "I do not believe in demons."

"Hush! They exist and are powerful. They love the world by night, as they must avoid the daylight, and like moonlit nights especially, for they are enamored of the Moon, and have made ships and horses with wings in order to reach it. And they say, besides, the nasty magician, Paztak, who lives only a mile along the road from this very place, is nightly visited by the demon Drin, who serve him in return for disgusting rewards."

By now the lovers were a distance off, and only Jaqir's sharp ears had picked up the ends of their talk after which there was silence, save for the sound of moonlight dripping on the barley. But Jaqir went back to the road. His face had become quite purposeful, and perhaps even the Moon, since she watched everything so intently, saw that too.

* * *

Now Paztak the magician did indeed live nearby, in his high, brazen tower, shielded by a thicket of tall and not ordinary laurels. Hearing a noise of breakage among these, Paztak undid a window and peered down at Jaqir, who stood below with drawn knife.

"What are you at, unruly felon?" snapped Paztak.

"Defending myself, wise sir, as your bushes bite."

"Then leave them alone. My name is Paztak the Unsociable. Be off, or I shall conjure worse things—to attack you."

"Merciful mage, my life is in the balance. I seek your help, and must loiter till you give it."

The mage clapped his hands, and three yellow, slavering dogs leaped from thin air and also tried to tear Jaqir into bite-size pieces. But avoiding them, Jaqir sprang at the tower and, since he was clever at such athletics, began climbing up it.

"Wretch!" howled Paztak. And then Jaqir found a creature, part wolverine and part snake, had roped the tower and was striving to wind him as well in its coils. But Jaqir slid free, kicked shut its clashing jaws, and vaulted over its head onto Paztak's windowsill.

"Consider me desperate rather than impolite."

"I consider you *elsewhere*," remarked Paztak with a new and ominous calm.

Next instant Jaqir found himself in a whirlwind, which turned him over and over, and cast him down at last in the depths of a forest.

"So much for the mage," said Jaqir, wiping snake-wolverine, dog, and laurel saliva from his boots. "And so much for me, I have had, in my life, an unfair quantity of good luck, and evidently it is all used up."

"Now, now," said a voice from the darkness, "let me get a proper look at you, and see if it is."

And from the shadows shouldered out a dwarf of such incredible hideousness that he might be seen to possess a kind of beauty.

Staring in awe at him then, from his appearance, and the fabulous jewelry with which he was adorned, Jaqir knew him for a Drin.

"Now, now," repeated the Drin, whose coal-black, luxuriant hair swept the forest floor. And he struck a light by the simple means of running his talonous nails—which were painted indigo—along the trunk of a tree. Holding up his now flaming hand, the Drin inspected Jaqir, gave a leer and smacked his lips. "Handsome fellow," said the Drin. "What will you offer me if I assist you?"

* * *

Jaqir knew a little of the Drin, the lowest caste of demonkind, who were metalsmiths and artisans of impossible and supernatural ability. He knew, too, as the girl had said, that the Drin required, in exchange for any service to mortals, recompense frequently of a censorable nature. Nor did this Drin seem an exception to the rule.

"Estimable sir," said Jaqir, "did you suppose I needed assistance?"

"I have no doubt of it," said the Drin. "Sometimes I visit the old pest Paztak, and was just now idling in his garden, in chat with a most fascinating woodlouse, when I heard your entreaties, and soon beheld you hurled into this wood. Thinking you more interesting than the mage, I followed. And here I am. What would you have?"

"What would *you* have?" asked Jaqir uneasily.

"Nothing you are not equipped to give."

"Well," said Jaqir resignedly, "we will leave that for the moment. Let *me* first see if you are as cunning as the stories say." And Jaqir thought, pragmatically, After all, what is a little foul and horrible dreadfulness, if it will save me death?

Then he told the Drin of the king's edict, and how he, Jaqir the thief, must thieve the Moon.

When he had done speaking, the Drin fell to the ground and rolled amid the fern, laughing, and honking like a goose, in the most repellent manner.

"You cannot do it," assumed Jaqir.

The Drin arose, and shook out his collar and loin-guard of rubies.

"Know me. I am Yulba, pride of my race, revered even among our demonic high castes of Eshva and Vazdru. Yulba, that the matchless lord, Azhrarn the Beautiful, has petted seven hundred times during his walkings up and down in the Underearth."

"You are to be envied," said Jaqir prudently. He had heard, too, as who had not who had ever heard tales about the demons, of the Prince of Demons, Azhrarn. "But that does not mean you are able to assist me."

"Pish," said the Drin. "It is a fact, no mortal thing, not even the birds of the air, might fly so high as the Moon, let alone any *man* essay it. But I am Yulba. What cannot Yulba do?"

Three nights Jaqir waited in the forest for Yulba to return. On the third night Yulba appeared out of the trunk of a cedar tree, and after him he hauled a loose, glimmering, almost-silky bundle, that clanked and clacketed as it came.

"Thus," said the Drin, and threw it down.

"What is that?"

"Have you no eyes? A carpet I have created, with the help of some elegant spinners of the eight-legged sort, but reinforced with metals fashioned by myself. Everything as delicate as the wings of bees, strong as the scales of dragons. Imbued by me with spells and vapors of the Underearth, as it is," bragged on the Drin, "the carpet is sorcerous, and will naturally fly. Even as far as the gardens of the stars, from where, though a puny mortal, you may then inspect your quarry, the Moon."

Jaqir, himself an arch-boaster, regarded Yulba narrowly. But then, Jaqir thought, a boaster might also boast truthfully, as he had himself. So as Yulba undid the carpet and spread it out, Jaqir walked on there. The next second Yulba also bounded aboard. At which the carpet, with no effort, rose straight up between the trees of the forest and into the sky of night.

"Now what do you say?" prompted the Drin.

All the demon race were susceptible to flattery. Jaqir spoke many winning sentences of praise, all the while being careful to keep the breadth of the carpet between them.

Up and up the carpet flew. It was indeed very lovely, all woven of blue metals and red metals, and threaded by silk, and here and there set with countless tiny diamonds that spangled like the stars themselves.

But Jaqir was mostly absorbed by the view of the Earth he now had. Far below, itself like a carpet, unrolled the dark forest and then the silvery fields, cut by a river-like black mirror. And as they flew higher yet, Jaqir came to see the distant city of the king, like a flower garden of pale lights, and farther again, lay mountains, and the edges of another country. "How small," mused Jaqir, "has been my life. It occurs to me the gods could never understand men's joy or tribulation, for from the height of their dwelling, how tiny we are to them, less than ants."

"Ants have their own recommendations," answered Yulba.

But the Moon was already standing high in the eastern heaven, still round in appearance, and sheerest white as only white could be.

No command needed be given the carpet. Obviously Yulba had already primed it to its destination. It now veered and soared, straight as an arrow, toward the Moon, and as it did so, Jaqir felt the tinsel roots of the lowest stars brush over his forehead.

And what was the Moon of the Flat Earth, that it might be approached and flown about on a magic carpet? It was, as has been said, maybe a globe containing other lands, but also it was said to be not a globe at all, but, like the Earth itself, a flat disk, yet placed sidelong in the sky, and presenting always a circular wheel of face to the world. And that this globe or disk altered its shape was due to the passage of its own internal sun, now lighting a quarter or a half or a whole of it—or, to the interference of some invisible body coming between it and some other (invisible) light, or to the fact that the Moon was simply a skittish shape-changer, making itself now round, and now a sliver like the paring of a nail.

As they drew ever nearer, Jaqir learned one thing, which in the many stories is a constant—that heat came from the Moon. But (in Jaqir's story) it was an appealing heat, quite welcome in the chilly upper sky. Above, the stars hung, some of them quite close, and they were of all types of shape and shade, all brilliant, but some blindingly so. Of the closer ones, their sparkling roots trailed as if floating in a pond, nourished on some unknown substance. While below, the world seemed only an enormous smudge.

The Drin himself, black eyes glassy, was plainly enraptured by the Moon. Jaqir was caught between wonder and speculation.

Soon enough, the vast luminescence enveloped them, and the heat of the Moon was now like that of a summer morning. Jaqir estimated that the disk might be only the size of a large city, so in his story, that is the size of the Moon.

But Jaqir, as the carpet began obediently to circle round the lunar orb, gazed at it with a proper burglar's care. Soon he could make out details of the surface, which was like nothing so much as an impeccable plate of white porcelain, yet here and there cratered, perhaps by the infrequent fall of a star. And these craters had a dim blue ghostly sheen, like that of a blue beryl.

When the carpet swooped yet nearer in, Jaqir next saw that the plate of the moon had actually a sort of landscape, for there were kinds of smooth, low, blanched hills, and here and there something which might be a carven water-course, though without any water in it. And there were also strewn boulders, and other stones, which must be prodigious in girth, but they were all like the rarest pearls.

Jaqir was seized by a desire to touch the surface of the hot, white Moon.

He voiced this.

Yulba scowled, disturbed in his rapturous trance.

"Oh ignorant man, even my inspired carpet may go no closer, or the magnetic pull of the Moon will tug, and we crash down there."

As he spoke, they passed slowly around the globe, and began moving across the *back* of the Moon, which, until that minute, few mortals had ever seen.

This side lay in a deep violet shadow, turned from the Earth, and tilted upward somewhat at the vault of the sky. It was cooler here, and Jaqir fancied he could hear a strange sound, like harps playing softly, but nothing was to be seen. His hands itched to have something away.

"Peerless Yulba, in order to make a plan of assault, I shall need to get, for reference, some keepsake of the Moon."

"You ask too much," grumbled Yulba.

"Can you not do it? But you are *Yulba*," smarmed Jaqir, "lord among Drin, favorite of the Prince of Demons. What is there Yulba *cannot* do? And, I thought we were to be friends . . ."

Yulba cast a look at Jaqir, then the Drin frowned at the Moon with such appalling ugliness, Jaqir turned his head.

"I have a certain immense power over stones," said the Drin, "seeing my kind work with them. If I can call you a stone from the Moon, what is it worth?"

Jaqir, who was not above the art of lying either, lied imaginatively at some length, until Yulba lumbered across the carpet and seemed about to demonstrate affection. "*Not* however," declared Jaqir, "any of this, until my task is completed. Do you expect me to be able to concentrate on such events, when my life still hangs by a thread?"

Yulba withdrew once more to the carpet's border. He began a horrible whistling, which set on edge not only Jaqir's teeth but every bone in his body. Nevertheless, in a while, a single pebble, only about the size of an apricot, came flying up and struck Yulba in the eye.

"See—I am blinded!" screeched Yulba, thrashing on the carpet, but he was not. Nor would he then give up the pebble. But soon enough, as their transport—which by now was apparently tiring—sank away from the Moon, Jaqir rolled a moment against the Drin, as if losing his balance. Thereafter the moon-pebble was in Jaqir's pocket.

What a time they had been on their travels. Even as the carpet flopped, wearily and bumpily now, toward the Earth, a blossoming of rose pink appeared in the east.

This pretty sight, of course, greatly upset Yulba, for demons feared the Sun, and with good reason, it could burn them to ashes.

"Down, down, make haste accursed flea-bag of a carpet!" ranted he, and so they rapidly fell, and next landed with a splashy thump in a swamp, from which green monkeys and red parakeets erupted at their arrival.

"I shall return at dusk. Remember what I have risked for you!" growled Yulba.

"It is graven on my brain."

Then the Drin vanished into the ground, taking with him the carpet.

The Sun rose, and the amazing Moon, now once more far away, faded and set like a dying lamp.

By midday Jaqir had forced a path from the swamp. He sat beneath a mango tree and ate some of the ripe fruit, and stared at the moon-pebble. It shone, even in the daylight, like a milky flame. "You are more wonderful than anything I have ever thieved. But still I do not see how I can rob the sky of that other jewel, the Moon."

Then he considered, for one rash moment, running away. And the safeguarding bonds of the king's magicians twanged around his skeleton. Jaqir desisted, and lay back to sleep.

In sleep, a troop of tormenters paraded.

The cast-off mistress who had betrayed him slapped his face with a wet fish. Yulba strutted, seeming hopeful. Next came men who cried, "Of what worth is this stupid Jaqir, who has claimed he can steal an egg from beneath a sleeping bird."

Affronted in his slumber, Jaqir truthfully replied that he had done that very thing. But the mockers were gone.

In the dream then Jaqir sat up, and looked once more at the shining pebble lying in his hand.

"Although I might steal a million eggs from beneath a million birds, what use to try for this? I am doomed and shall give in."

Just then something fluttered from the mango tree, which was also there in the dream. It was a small gray parrot. Flying down, it settled directly upon the opalescent stone in Jaqir's palm and put out its light.

"Well, my fine bird, this is no egg for you to hatch."

The parrot spoke. "Think, Jaqir, what you see, and what you say."

Jaqir thought. "Is it possible?"

And at that he woke a second time.

The Sun was high above, and over and over across it and the sky, birds flew about, distinct as black writing on the blue.

"No bird of the air can fly so high as the Moon," said Jaqir. He added, "but the Drin have a mythic knack with magical artifacts and clockworks."

Later, the Sun lowered itself and went down. Yulba came bouncing from the ground, coyly clad in extra rubies, with a garland of lotuses in his hair.

"Now, now," commenced Yulba, lurching forward.

Sternly spoke Jaqir, "I am not yet at liberty, as you are aware. However, I have a scheme. And knowing your unassailable wisdom and authority, only you, the mighty Yulba, best and first among Drin, can manage it."

In Underearth it was an exquisite dusk. It was always dusk there, or a form of dusk. As clear as day in the upper world, it was said, yet more radiantly somber. Sunless, naturally, for the reasons given above.

Druhim Vanashta, the peerless city of demonkind, stretched in a noose of shimmering nonsolar brilliance, out of which pierced, like needles, chiseled towers of burnished steel and polished corundum, domes of faceted crystal. While about the gem-paved streets and sable parks strolled or paced or strode or lingered the demons. Night-black of hair and eye, snow-frozen-white of complexion, the high-caste Vazdru and their mystic servants, the Eshva. All of whom were so painfully beautiful, it amounted to an insult.

Presently, along an avenue, there passed Azhrarn, Prince of Demons, riding a black horse, whose mane and tail were hyacinth blue. And if the beauty of the Eshva and Vazdru amounted to an insult, that of Azhrarn was like the stroke of death.

He seemed himself idle enough, Azhrarn. He seemed too musing on something as he slowly rode, oblivious, it appeared, to those who bowed to the pavement at his approach, whose eyes had spilled, at sight of him, looks of adoration. They were all in love with Azhrarn.

A voice spoke from nowhere at all.

"Azhrarn, Lord Wickedness, you gave up the world, but the world does not give up you. Oh Azhrarn, Master of Night, what are the Drin doing by their turgid lake, hammering and hammering?"

Azhrarn had reined in the demon horse. He glanced leisurely about.

Minutes elapsed. He too spoke, and his vocality was like the rest of him. "The Drin do hammer at things. That is how the Drin pass most of eternity."

"Yet how," said the voice, "do *you* pass eternity, Lord Wickedness?"

"Who speaks to me?" softly said Azhrarn.

The voice replied, "Perhaps merely yourself, the part of you that you discard, the part of you which yearns after the world."

"Oh," said Azhrarn. "The world."

The voice did not pronounce another syllable, but along an adjacent wall a slight mark appeared, rather like a scorch.

Azhrarn rode on. The avenue ended at a park, where willows of liquid amber let down their watery resinous hair, to a mercury pool. Black peacocks with seeing eyes of turquoise and emerald in their tails, turned their heads and all their feathers to gaze at him.

From between the trees came three Eshva, who obeised themselves.

"What," said Azhrarn, "are the Drin making by their lake?"

The Eshva sighed voluptuously. The sighs said (for the Eshva never used ordinary speech), "The Drin are making metal birds."

"Why?" said Azhrarn.

The Eshva grew downcast; they did not know. Melancholy enfolded them among the tall black grasses of the lawn, and then one of the Vazdru princes came walking through the garden.

"Yes?" said Azhrarn.

"My Prince, there is a Drin who was to fashion for me a ring, which he has neglected," said the Vazdru. "He is at some labor for a human man he is partial to. They are *all* at this labor."

Azhrarn, interested, was, for a moment, more truly revealed. The garden waxed dangerously brighter, the mercury in the pool boiled. The amber hardened and the peacocks shut every one of their 450 eyes.

"Yes?" Azhrarn murmured again.

"The Drin, who is called Yulba, has lied to them all. He has told them you yourself, my matchless lord, require a million clockwork birds that can fly as high as the Earth's Moon. Because of *this*, they work ceaselessly. This Yulba is a nuisance. When he is found out, they will savage him, then bury him in some cavern, walling it up with rocks, leaving him there a million years for his million birds. And so I shall not receive my ring."

Azhrarn smiled. Cut by the smile, as if by the slice of a sword, leaves scattered from the trees. It was suddenly autumn in the garden. When autumn stopped, Azhrarn had gone away.

Chang-thrang went the Drin hammers by the lake outside Druhim Vanashta. *Whirr* and *pling* went the uncanny mechanisms of half-formed sorcerous birds of cinnabar, bronze, and iron. Already-finished sorcerous birds hopped and flapped about the lakeshore, frightening the beetles and snakes. Mechanical birds flew over in curious formations, like demented swallows, darkening the Underearth's gleaming day-dusk, now and then letting fall droppings of a peculiar sort.

Eshva came and went, drifting on Vazdru errands. Speechless inquiries wafted to the Drin caves: Where is the necklace of rain vowed for the Princess Vasht? Where is the singing book reserved for the Prince Hazrond?

"We are busy elsewhere at Azhrarn's order," chirped the Drin.

They were all dwarfs, all hideous, and each one lethal, ridiculous, and a genius. Yulba strode among them, criticizing their work, so now and then there was also a fight for the flying omnipresent birds to unburden their bowels upon.

How had Yulba fooled the Drin? He was no more Azhrarn's favorite than any of them. All the Drin boasted as Yulba had. Perhaps it was only this: Turning his shoulder to the world of mankind, Azhrarn had forced the jilted world to pursue him underground. In ways both graphic and insidious, the rejected one permeated Underearth. Are you tired of me? moaned the world to Azhrarn. Do you hate me? Do I bore you? See how inventive I am. See how I can still ensnare you fast.

But Azhrarn did not go to the noisy lake. He did not summon Yulba. And Yulba, puffed with his own cleverness, obsessively eager to hold Jaqir to his bargain, had forgotten all accounts have a reckoning. *Chungclungk* went the hammers. *Brakk* went the thick heads of the Drin, banged together by critical, unwise Yulba.

Then at last the noise ended.

The hammering and clamoring were over.

Of the few Vazdru who had come to stare at the birds, less than a few remarked that the birds had vanished.

The Drin were noted skulking about their normal toil again, constructing wondrous jewelry and toys for the upper demons. If they waited breathlessly for Azhrarn to compliment them on their bird-work, they did so in vain. But such omissions had happened in the past, the never-ceasing past-present-future of Underearth.

Just as they might have pictured him, Azhrarn stood in a high window of Druhim Vanashta, looking at his city of needles and crystals.

Perhaps it was seven mortal days after the voice had spoken to him. Perhaps three months.

He heard a sound within his mind. It was not from his city, nor was it unreal. Nor actual. Presently he sought a magical glass that would show him the neglected world.

How ferocious the stars, how huge and cruelly glittering, like daggers. How they exalted, unrivaled now.

The young king went one by one to all the windows of his palace. Like Azhrarn miles below (although he did not know it), the young king looked a long while at his city. But mostly he looked up into the awful sky.

Thirty-three nights had come and gone, without the rising of the Moon.

In the king's city there had been at first shouts of bewildered amazement. Then prayers. Then, a silence fell which was as loud as screaming.

If the world had lost the Sun, the world would have perished and died. But losing the Moon, it was as if the soul of this world had been put out.

Oh those black nights, blacker than blackness, those yowling spikes of stars dancing in their vitriolic glory—which gave so little light.

What murders and rapes and worser crimes were committed under cover of such a dark? As if a similar darkness had been called up from the mental guts of mankind, like subservient to like. While earth-over, priests offered to the gods, who never noticed.

The courtiers who had applauded, amused, the judgment of the witty young king now shrank from him. He moved alone through the excessively lamped and benighted palace, wondering if he was now notorious through all the world for his thoughtless error. And so wondering, he entered the room where, on their marble pedestals, perched his angels.

"What have you done?" said the king.

Not a feather stirred. Not an eye winked.

"By the gods—may they forgive me—what? What did you make *me* do?"

"*You* are king," said the scarlet parrot. "It is your word, not ours, which is law."

And the blue parrot said, "We are parrots, why name us angels? We have been taught to speak, that is all. What do you expect?"

And the jade parrot said, "I forget now what it was you asked of us." And put its head under its wing.

Then the king turned to the gray parrot. "What do you have to say? It was your final advice which drove me to demand the Moon be stolen—as if I thought any man might do it."

"King," said the gray parrot, "it was your sport to call four parrots, angels. Your sport to offer a man an impossible task as the alternative to certain death. You have lived as if living is a silly game. But you are mortal, and a king."

"You shame me," said the king.

"We are, of course," said the gray parrot, "truly angels, disguised. To shame men is part of our duty."

"What must I do?"

The gray parrot said, "Go down, for Jaqir, Thief of Thieves, has returned to your gate. And he is followed by his shadow."

"Are not all men so followed?" asked the king perplexedly.

The parrot did not speak again.

Let it be said, Jaqir, who now entered the palace, between the glaring, staring guards of the king, was himself in terrible awe at what he had achieved. Ever since succeeding at his task, he had not left off trembling inwardly. However, outwardly he was all smiles, and in his best attire.

"See, the wretch's garments are as fine as a lord's. His rings are gold. Even his shadow looks well dressed! And this miscreant it is who has stolen the Moon and ruined the world with blackest night."

The king stood waiting, with the court about him.

Jaqir bowed low. But that was all he did, after which *he* stood waiting, meeting the king's eyes with his own.

"Well," said the king. "It seems you have done what was asked of you."

"So it does seem," said Jaqir calmly.

"Was it then easy?"

"As easy," said Jaqir, "as stealing an egg."

"But," said the king. He paused, and a shudder ran over the hall a shuddering of men and women, and also of the flames in all the countless lamps.

"*But?*" pressed haughty Jaqir.

"It might be said by some, that the Moon—which is surely not an egg—has disappeared, and another that you may have removed it. After all," said the king stonily, "if one assumes the Moon may be pilfered at all, how am I to be certain the robber is yourself? Maybe others are capable of it. Or, too, a natural disaster has simply overcome the orb, a coincidence most convenient for you."

"Sir," said Jaqir, "were you not the king, I would answer you in other words that I do. But king you are. And I have proof."

And then Jaqir took out from his embroidered shirt the moon-pebble, which even in the light of the lamps blazed with a perfect whiteness. And so like the Moon it was for radiance that many at once shed tears of nostalgia on seeing it. While at Jaqir's left shoulder, his night-black shadow seemed for an instant also to flicker with fire.

As for the king, now he trembled too. But like Jaqir, he did not show it.

"Then," said the king, "be pardoned of your crimes. You have sur-mounted the test, and are directly loosed from those psychic bonds my magicians set on you, therefore entirely physically at liberty, and besides, a legendary hero. One last thing . . ."

"Yes?" asked Jaqir.

"Where have you put it?"

"What?" said Jaqir, rather stupidly.

"That which you stole."

"It was not a part of our bargain, to tell you this. You have seen by the proof of this stone I have got the Moon. Behold, the sky is black."

The king said quietly, "You do not mean to keep it."

"Generally I do keep what I take."

"I will give you great wealth, Jaqir, which I think anyway you do not need, for they say you are as rich as I. Also, I will give you a title to rival my own. You can have what you wish. Now swear you will return the Moon to the sky."

Jaqir lowered his eyes.

"I must consider this."

"Look," they whispered, the court of the king, "even his shadow listens to him."

Jaqir, too, felt his shadow listening at his shoulder.

He turned, and found the shadow had eyes.

Then the shadow spoke, more quietly than the king, and not one in the hall did not hear it. While every flame in every lamp spun like a coin, died, revived, and continued burning upside down.

"King, you are a fool. Jaqir, you are another fool. And who and what am I?"

Times had changed. There are always stories, but they are not always memorized. Only the king, and Jaqir the thief, had the understanding to plummet to their knees. And they cried as one, "*Azhrarn!*"

"Walk upon the terrace with me," said Azhrarn. "We will admire the beauty of the leaden night."

The king and Jaqir found that they got up, and went on to the terrace, and no one else stirred, not even hand or eye.

Around the terrace stood some guards like statues. At the terrace's center stood a chariot that seemed constructed of black and silver lava, and drawn by similarly laval dragons.

"Here is our conveyance," said Azhrarn, charmingly. "Get in."

In they got, the king and the thief. Azhrarn also sprang up, and took and shook the reins of the dragons, and these great ebony lizards hissed and shook out in turn their wings, which clapped against the black night and seemed to strike off bits from it. Then the chariot dove up into the air, shaking off the Earth entire, and green sparks streamed from the chariot-wheels.

Neither the king nor Jaqir had stamina—or idiocy—enough to question Azhrarn. They waited meekly as two children in the chariot's back, gaping now at Azhrarn's black eagle wings of cloak, that every so often buffeted them, almost breaking their ribs, or at the world falling down and down below like something dropped.

But then, high in the wild, tipsy-making upper air, Jaqir did speak, if not to Azhrarn.

"King, I tricked you. I did not steal the Moon."

"Who then stole it?"

"No one."

"A riddle."

At which they saw Azhrarn had partly turned. They glimpsed his profile, and a single eye that seemed more like the night than the night itself was. And they shut their mouths.

On raced the dragons.

Below raced the world.

Then everything came to a halt. Combing the sky with claws and wheels, dragons and chariot stood static on the dark.

Azhrarn let go the jewelry reins.

All around spangled the stars. These now appeared less certain of themselves. The brighter ones had dimmed their glow, the lesser hid behind the vapors of night. Otherwise, everywhere lay blackness, only that.

In the long, musician's fingers of the Prince of Demons was a silver pipe, shaped like some sort of slender bone. Azhrarn blew upon the pipe.

There was no sound, yet something seemed to pass through the skulls of the king and of Jaqir, as if a barbed thread had been pulled through from ear to ear. The king swooned—he was only a king. Jaqir rubbed his temples and stayed upright—he was a professional of the working classes.

And so it was Jaqir who saw, in reverse, that which he had already seen happen the other way about.

He beheld a black cloud rising (where before it had settled) and behind the cloud, suddenly something incandescent blinked and dazzled. He beheld how the cloud, breaking free of these blinks of palest fire (where before it had obscured said fire) ceased to be one entity, and became instead one million separate flying pieces. He saw, as he had seen before when first they burst up from the ground in front of him, and rushed into the sky, that these were a million curious birds. They had feathers of cinnabar and bronze, sinews of brass; they had clockworks of iron and steel.

Between the insane crowded battering of their wings, Jaqir watched the Moon reappear, where previously (scanning the night, as he stood by Yulba in a meadow) he had watched the Moon *put out*, all the birds flew down against her, covering and smothering her. Unbroken by their landing on her surface, they had roosted there, drawn to and liking the warmth, as Yulba had directed them with his sorcery.

But now Azhrarn had negated Yulba's powers—which were little enough among demons. The mechanical birds swarmed round and round the chariot, aggravating the dragons somewhat. The birds had no eyes, Jaqir noticed. They gave off great heat where the Moon had toasted their metals. Jaqir looked at them as if for the first, hated them, and grew deeply embarrassed.

Yet the Moon—oh, the Moon. Uncovered and alight, how brilliantly it or she blazed now. Had she ever been so bright? Had her sojourn in darkness done her good?

End to end, she poured her flame over the Earth below. Not a mountain that did not have its spire of silver, not a river its highlight of diamond. The seas lashed and struggled with joy, leaping to catch her snows upon the crests of waves and dancing dolphin. And in the windows of mankind, the lamps were doused, and like the waves, men leaned upward to wash their faces in the Moon.

Then gradually, a murmur, a thunder, a roar, a gushing sigh rose swirling from the depths of the Flat Earth, as if at last the world had stopped holding its breath.

"What did you promise Yulba," asked Azhrarn of Jaqir, mild as a killing frost, "in exchange for this slight act?"

"The traditional favor," muttered Jaqir.

"Did he receive payment?"

"I prevaricated. Not yet, lord Prince."

"You are spared then. Part of his punishment shall be permanently to avoid your company. But what punishment for you, thief? And what punishment for your king?"

Jaqir did not speak. Nor did the king, though he had recovered his senses.

Both men were educated in the tales, the king more so. Both men turned ashen, and the king accordingly more ashen.

Then Azhrarn addressed the clockwork birds in one of the demon tongues, and they were immediately gone. And only the white banner of the moonlight was there across the night.

Now Azhrarn, by some called also Lord of Liars, was not perhaps above lying in his own heart. It seems so. Yet maybe tonight he looked upon the Moon, and saw in the Moon's own heart, the woman that once he had loved, the woman who had been named for the Moon. Because of her, and all that had followed, Azhrarn had turned his back upon the world—or attempted to turn it.

And even so here he was, high in the vault of the world's heaven, drenched in earthly moonshine, contemplating the chastisement of mortal creatures whose lives, to his immortal life, were like the green sparks which had flashed and withered on the chariot-wheels.

The chariot plunged. The atmosphere scalded at the speed of its descent. It touched the skin of the Earth more slightly than a cobweb.

The mortal king and the mortal thief found themselves rolling away downhill, toward fields of barley and a river. The chariot, too, was gone. Although in their ears as they rolled, equal in their rolling as never before, and soon never to be again, king and thief heard Azhrarn's extraordinary voice, which said, "Your punishment you have already. You are human. I cannot improve upon that."

Thus, the Moon shone in the skies of night, interrupted only by an infrequent cloud. The king resumed his throne. The four angels—who were or were not parrots—or only meddlers—sat on their perches waiting to give advice, or to avoid giving it. And Jaqir—Jaqir went away to another city.

Here, under a different name, he lived on his extreme wealth, in a fine house with gardens. Until one day he was robbed of all his gold (and even of the moon-pebble) by a talented thief. "Is it the gods who exact their price at last, or Another, who dwells farther down?" But by then Jaqir was older, for mortal lives moved and move swiftly. He had lost his taste for his work by then. So he returned to the king's city, and to the door of the merchant's wife who had been his mistress. "I am sorry for what I said to you," said Jaqir. "I am sorry for what I did to you," said she. The traveling merchant had recently departed on another, more prolonged journey, to make himself, reincarnation-wise, a new life after death. Meanwhile, though the legend of a moon-thief remained, men had by then forgotten Jaqir. So he married the lady and they existed not unhappily, which shows their flexible natures.

But miles below, Yulba did not fare so well.

For Azhrarn had returned to the Underearth on the night of the Moon's rescue, and said to him, "Bad little Drin. Here are your million birds. Since you are so proud of them, be one of them." And in this way Azhrarn demonstrated that the world no longer mattered to him a jot, only his own kind mattered enough that he would make their lives Hell-under-Earth. Or, so it would seem.

But Yulba had changed to a clockwork bird, number one million and one. Eyeless, still able to see, flapping over the melanic vistas of the demon country, blotting up the luminous twilight, cawing, clicking, letting fall droppings, yearning for the warmth of the Moon, yearning to be a Drin again, yearning for Azhrarn, and for Jaqir—who by that hour had already passed himself from the world, for demon time was not the time of mortals.

As for the *story*, that of Jaqir and Yulba and the Moon, it had become as it had and has become, or *un*-become. And who knows but that, in another little while, it will be forgotten, as most things are. Even the Moon is no longer *that* Moon, nor the Earth, nor the sky. The centuries fly, eternity is endless.

Firebird

R. Garcia y Robertson

R. Garcia y Robertson lives in the charming Victorian town of Mt. Vernon, Washington. His novels to date include The Spiral Dance *(1991),* The Virgin and the Dinosaur *(1996),* Atlantis Found *(1997),* American Woman *(1998), and* Knight Errant *(2001). His stories have appeared in* F&SF *and* Asimov's *with some regularity for the last fifteen years and are characterized by their broad range of concerns, stylistic sophistication, and attention to historical detail. Garcia has tended toward time travel or historical settings for both his fantasy and SF stories. Some of these stories are collected in* The Moon Maid and Other Fantastic Adventures *(1998). His fiction has been relatively underappreciated since the small flash of critical and peer attention garnered by his first novel,* The Spiral Dance.

"Firebird," which appeared in F&SF, *is set in his fantasy alternate world of Markovy, a world with a history similar to our own but tweaked in ways that make for great fantasy adventures. As in a fairy tale, a young girl is apprenticed to a witch. One day she sees a knight riding through the forest. Here, mythic and magical elements such as the Firebird of the title coexist with nifty details from real history—the bone witch's hut appears to be made of mammoth bones.*

⁓ Witch-girl

'Deep in the woods, gathering fungus for the Bone Witch's supper, Katya heard the firebird call her name. "Katea-katea-katea. . . ." Brushing tangled black hair from sea-green eyes, she searched for the bird, seeing only tall pine trunks and blue bars of sky. Her bright homespun dress had the red-orange firebird embroidered on the bodice, done in silk from Black Cathay, and the Barbary cloth called Crimson. She had stitched it herself on sunless winter days. Katya called out, "Here I am. Come tell what you see."

She listened. Insects hummed in hot pine-scented air. Farther off she heard a woodpecker knocking. She called again, "Come to me. Come to me. Come tell what you see."

Now that she was fully grown, Katya never feared the woods by daylight. Leopards, troll-bears, lycanthropes, and forest sprites lurked between the trees, waiting to make a meal of the unwary. But by day the woods had a hundred eyes alert for any suspicious movement. No lynx or leopard could stir a foot without birds calling and squirrels chattering. All Katya need do was listen. Night was another matter. But the Bone Witch did not let her out at night. Nor would the Witch let her leave the hut without her slave collar and protective rune. Each morning she made Katya repeat her invisibility spell. She was valuable property, the Witch told her. "I have not raised you to feed some hungry troll-bear—not when you are finally becoming useful."

Katya saw things differently. She began life as a girl-child thrown away in time of war and famine. Survival taught her to make the best of today, for tomorrow was bound to be worse. It taught her to lie instinctively, and never to shit where she meant to sleep. And to trust in her luck, which had kept her from the fate of hundreds like her. Death had had ample chance to take her, making Katya think she was being saved for something special. Like to be a princess.

At nine she was given to the Witch for two handfuls of salt and a cattle pox cure. The family feeding her figured they were doing everyone a favor. "The Witch can better provide for you. We are poor," the father informed her—as if she had somehow not noticed, sleeping on straw between the hearth and the hogs—"while you are stubborn and willful." His wife agreed. "Getting you to obey is like trying to teach a cat to fetch." Had Katya been a boy, it would have been different. But she was a girl, naturally wanton, unruly, frivolous and amoral, a growing threat to their son's virtue. They were duty-bound to keep her chaste and ignorant, then give her to some man in marriage—a dead loss to the family. Better by far to give her to the Bone Witch.

Only their lazy son objected. Not the least threatened, he wanted her around. Without her, who would do his chores? Who would he spy on in the bath? He had promised to rape her when they got bigger.

Katya herself had said nothing. Even at nine, she had a stubborn sense of self-worth that regularly got her whipped. People called her changeling and worse, with her pert ways and wicked green eyes—a girl switched at birth for a defiant demon-child. Bundling up her straw doll and wooden spoon, she took a seat in the father's cart. They lurched off, crossing the Dys at Byeli Zamak, headed for the Iron Wood. All she could think was that she was to become a witch-girl. And witches were burned.

But that was years ago. And she had not been burned—not yet at least. By now she had spent half her life in the woods. She knew which mushrooms were food, and which sent you on flights of fancy. Which berries were sweet and which were deadly nightshade, which herbs cured and which herbs killed. Having nothing of her own, she happily appropriated all of nature, making these her woods. Every screech and cry in the trees spoke to her. When it was safe, she spoke back.

"Katea-katea-katea. . . ." The call came closer. Like her, the firebird was a curious soul, and could be coaxed with low soft calls. He hated to think of anything happening in his woods without him telling the world about it.

Picking up her bark basket, she headed for the sound, fording a shallow stream to enter a fern-choked glade ringed by stands of slim silver birch. Birches loved the light and fought to fill any sort of clearing. At the far end of the glade she skirted a pond frequented by red deer and herons. On the bare bank she saw pug marks.

Kneeling amid the bracken, she felt the tracks with her fingers. The ground was hard, and the claw prints worn and splayed with age. Three nights ago, after the rain when the moon was full, an old female leopard came from the same direction she had, stopped to drink, then headed up the ridge, aiming for the thickly wooded crest separating the forest from the cultivated lands beyond. Any leopard with business beyond the ridge could easily be a stock thief or man-eater.

Not a cat she cared to meet. Stomach tensed, she looked about. Mossy patches shone like polished jade. The protective rune on her armlet shielded Katya from magic—but not from fang or claw. Straightening up, she set out again, keeping the breeze at her back. Leopards did not know humans have no sense of smell, and never stalked from upwind— so she need only worry about what lay ahead. These were her woods. Let some old leopard scare her, and she would never go out at all.

"Katea-katea-katea. . . ." She spotted a flash of orange among the pine trunks. The bird waited at the crest of the ridge.

And not just the firebird, but a fire as well. Black oily smoke billowed from beyond the ridge crest, smearing clear blue sky. Hairs rose at the nape of her neck. She had not smelled the smoke because the wind was behind her—but she knew where it came from. Byeli Zamak was burning.

Topping the ridge, she stopped to stare. This was as far as the slave collar allowed her to go. Below her the forest ended. Rolling steppe spread out from the foot of the ridge, broken by loops of river, dark patches of plowland, and the onion domes of village churches. Between her and the steppe, guarding the fords of the Dys, stood a huge round tower seven stories tall with walls twenty feet thick—Byeli Zamak, the White Castle. Smoke poured from the tower. Katya pictured the inferno inside, fed by grain and oil stored in the basement, burning up through the wooden floors, feeding on gilt furniture, Barbary tapestries, Italian paintings, and canopied beds. A cornerstone of her world was consumed in flames.

She came from these settled lands. Somewhere out there she had been born. Somewhere out there her family was massacred—for the black earth beyond the woods was sown with bones and watered by blood. Constant strife had consumed her family, and almost made an end to her. She had begged in those villages, and slept in the painted doorways of those churches, waking to find crows and ravens waiting to make a meal of her.

When she was given to the Witch, all that changed. Her slave collar kept her penned in the woods—where the worst she need fear was leopards and troll-bears. Even when old King Demitri died, Byeli Zamak remained, towering over the fords of the Dys—the gatehouse to the Iron Wood. King and gold-domed capital were the stuff of faerie tales, but Byeli Zamak was solid and real, part of Katya's landscape, built by earth giants from native stone. And now it burned. Her first thought was to tell the Bone Witch.

"Katea-katea. . . ." the firebird called again, this time from right overhead. Looking up, she saw the flame-colored jay perched on the limb of a tall larch, scoffing and chuckling. Clown prince of the bird clan, the fire orange jay was a wickedly mischievous trickster, a merciless nest robber and accomplished mimic. Katya had heard him perfectly imitate the screaming whistle of a hawk, just to see what havoc he could wreak.

"Is this what you saw?" Katya tilted her head toward the inferno below. Just like a jay to revel in someone else's misfortune. He squawked back at her, this time giving the man call. Jays greeted every predator with a different call. Warnings did little good if you did not know whether to look out for a leopard, or a hawk, or a lynx. The man call was totally distinct. Jays did not use it for her or the Witch.

Hearing a waxwing whistle, Katya turned to see a roe deer bound up the slope and disappear over the ridge. Something was coming. Something alarming enough to flush a doe from cover. The firebird flew off, still making the man call.

From below came the weighty clump of slow hoofbeats climbing the ridge. A horse was coming up from the fords, carrying something heavy and clanking. She whispered her invisibility spell. So long as she remained still and silent, no one could see her. Or so the Witch said. So far it had never failed.

She watched the rider top the ridge. Bareheaded, he rode slumped forward, eyes half shut, his soot-stained blue and white surcoat covering a body encased in steel—a man-at-arms, maybe even a knight, just managing to stay atop a big gray charger. Her heart went out to him. He looked so hurt and handsome, his long elegant eyelashes wet with tears. Bloody clots in his fashionable pudding-basin haircut dripped red streaks down proud cheekbones, past genteel lips. His beardless face made him look young, marking him as a foreigner. Or a eunuch.

Here was her storm petral: strong and beautiful, but a sure sign of the whirlwind to come. So long as Byeli Zamak had held for the King, only unarmed serfs crossed the fords into the forest, to gather sticks and snare squirrels, stripping bark for their shoes and stealing honey from the bees. On May Day they came singing, their arms full of flowers, celebrating the return of spring, slipping off in pairs to make love upon the forest floor—while she watched, invisible and intrigued. In summer the forest rang with their axes—the nearest thing they had to weapons. It was a flogging offense for a serf to have a bow, or a boar spear. Death to be caught with a sword.

But this stranger had a huge sword slung across his back, and his torn surcoat bore the embattled blue bend of the King's Horse Guards. His crested helm hung from his saddle bow, alongside an ugly saw-toothed war hammer. Hunched forward, he carried something heavy in the crook of his shield arm, wrapped in silk embroidery, tucked against his armored breast. She stood stock still, letting him rattle past, close enough to touch.

When he had gotten far enough ahead of her, she set off after him, slipping silently from tree to tree, following the bird calls down the ridge onto the forest floor. Tiny red flecks of blood shone on green fern fronds, marking his trail for her.

Now the breeze was full in her face, which she did not like. A leopard could come up behind her, stalking her as easily as she trailed this knight. Worse yet, the breeze brought the foul scent of a troll-bear's lair, faint but growing stronger. The rotting corpse smell of discarded carcasses, mixed with the rank odor of the troll-bear's droppings, was unmistakable, like smelling a long dead lizard on a hot day. Only the image of the knight's hurt face kept her going.

She nearly caught up with her knight beneath a cool coppice of oaks. Leaves rustled like water overhead and the rattle of armor had ceased—but the smell of horse droppings, followed by a nervous whinny, warned her she was getting too close. Sinking to all fours, she wriggled through the undergrowth, curious to see why he had stopped. Had he smelled the troll-bear?

Her knight had dismounted. Kneeling in the bracken beside his horse, he attacked the ground with a big saxe knife, digging a hole in the dark earth. She watched patiently. When he had dug down the length of his arm, he sheathed the knife, and reached for an embroidered bundle lying beside him. Gently he lowered the bundle into the hole. Whatever it was had to be something precious—she could tell by how he handled it. A gold icon perhaps. Or a great crystal goblet. Or a dead baby.

He carefully covered over the hole, hiding his work with fallen leaves. Then he looked up, sensing he was watched, staring straight at her. But she stayed still as a fawn, and the spell held. Drained by the simple act of digging, he heaved himself onto his horse, no mean feat in full armor. Then he lurched off upwind, headed for the troll-bear's lair. Unless she did something the troll-bear would savage both horse and rider, cracking her knight's armor like a badger breaking open a snail.

When the carrion odor got unbearable, his horse stopped again, refusing to go on. She waited for her knight to turn or dismount, but he stayed slumped in his saddle, eyes closed, his horse nervously cropping the bracken. Warning calls died away and the woods grew still. A good sign. Either the troll-bear was gorged senseless, or away from its den. Shrugging off her spell, she stepped out from between the trees, slowly walking toward her knight. His horse saw her first, snorting and shying. Speaking softly, she reached out and took the reins, "Have no fear. I will take you to good grass and water."

Her knight opened his eyes, which were blue and alert. He smiled at what he saw, saying, "*Mon Dieu,* I am dead." He did not look very dead, clinging stubbornly to his saddle. "And here is an angel to take me to Heaven."

"I am no angel," she told him. She was a witch-child, willful, disobedient and hopelessly damned.

His smile widened. "Then a forest sprite, young and beautiful. What more could a vagabond want?" He spoke with a funny foreign accent, but his tone told her he was friendly. Gently turning the tired horse's head, she led him slowly downwind away from the troll-bear's lair. Her knight swayed alarmingly in the saddle. "Fair nymph," he called down to her. "Where are you taking us?"

She smiled over her shoulder. "To water." He was by far the most marvelous thing she had ever found in the woods, and she wanted to see him with his face washed.

Leading the horse back to the base of the ridge—to where a spring burst from beneath tall triangular rocks—she helped her knight dismount. Sitting him down, she wet a cloth and wiped his wincing face. He cleaned up nicely. She liked his handsome beardless face, firm and manly, but smooth to the touch. His scalp wound was bloody but not deep, and merely needed to be cleaned, then sewn shut. Luckily she knew which plants produced natural antibiotics, had been gathering them for the Witch.

He watched as she worked, smiling ruefully. "Just when you wonder what you are fighting for, Heaven sends a reminder."

"What reminder is that?" She searched through her bark basket for the right leaves.

"You really do not know, do you?"

"No. That is why I asked." Her knight had a funny way of talking, even for a foreigner. She crushed the leaves with a rock, mixing them with water from the spring.

"I have had a most damnable day," he told her, "trying to hold Byeli Zamak for your infant Prince Ivan. Besieged by the boy's own uncle, upholding the honor of your dead king, and being badly beaten for my pains. Just when I think I cannot go on—that there is nothing in this benighted land worth saving—you come along. Proving me completely wrong."

"This will hurt," she warned him, parting his hair to expose the wound.

"*Certainement*; so far today, everything has." Taking that as assent, she poured her makeshift potion onto the bloody gash. He shouted in protest, raising a steel-gloved hand to shield his head. "*Merde!* Does *Mademoiselle* mean to murder me too?"

She grabbed his gauntlet to keep it away from the wound. "No. This will help you. I swear." She found her embroidery needle with her free hand.

He relaxed. "*C'est bien, c'est bien. Mademoiselle* merely took me by surprise." He sat stoically while she poured potion on the needle, then began sewing his scalp back together, wincing when she tightened a stitch, but otherwise acting as if she were clipping his curls. Asking, "What may I call *Mademoiselle*?"

"Katya," she replied shyly, resisting the impulse to invent. She wanted him to know her name.

"*Enchanté*. Sir Roy d'Roye, Chevalier de l'Étoile, et le Baron d'Roye. At your service." He winced again, as her needle went in. "What does *Mademoiselle* do when not torturing wounded knights?"

She pulled the stitch tight, saying softly, "I serve the Bone Witch."

"A Witch? But of course. And a wicked one too, from the way that potion burned me. . . ."

"But she is merely my foster mother. My real mother was a queen. And I am a princess." Not knowing who her parents were, she felt free to invent royal ones.

Baron d'Roye raised an eyebrow. "Princess in disguise, I presume?"

"Of course," she replied scornfully. "Why else would I be dressed like a peasant?"

"Your majesty carries off her masquerade amazingly well."

"Shush!" she whispered. From atop the ridge came the firebird's man call. She listened harder. The call came again, fading as the bird took flight. Someone was coming. She asked, "Are there men after you?"

"Indeed, though for no good reason."

She hastily finished her stitching, saying, "I must hide you." She had no fear for herself, but the thought of seeing her newfound knight hurt or killed was too much to bear. Helping him to his feet, she guided him up the rocks to a protruding shelf where two boulders formed a tiny cave between them, too high up to be seen from the spring. She shoved him inside, saying, "Stay here."

"Only if your majesty promises to come for me," he replied.

"I will." She truly wanted to see more of him, only not right now. Not with men coming.

"Promise?"

"I swear." She pushed him farther into the cave, where there was no chance of him being seen from below.

"Bring food," he begged.

"I will," she hastily agreed.

"And wine."

She did not bother to answer, scrambling back down the rocks to the spring. Taking his mount's reins, she turned the horse away from the spring.

"Good wine. If your highness has it."

Still thirsty, the horse balked at being led off by a stranger. She had to heave on the reins to get him pointed back the way she wanted to go. Her knight called down to her, "And what about my horse?"

"I will hide him too," she promised, pulling harder, hauling the unwilling animal away from the spring.

"*Au revoir*," he called out.

"Silence, please," she shouted back, mortified to be making so much noise with strangers in the woods. Dragging the weary charger away from rest and water, she doubled back on their original tracks. Anyone seeing the return prints would have no reason to search out the cave, and would follow the trail she was making. Katya felt confident she could lose them—these were her woods.

When she had put distance between herself and the spring, she found a swift brook and splashed along it, letting the running water hide their trail. Spotting a good place to leave the stream—a rock shelf that would not take hoof prints—she deliberately passed it by. Downstream from the rock shelf she let the horse stray, making tracks on the bank, then leading him back into the water, and up onto the opposite bank. When she was satisfied with her false trail, she carefully retreated upstream, leading the horse out over the rocks, trying her utmost not to leave tracks.

She stayed on hard ground until she was well out of sight of the stream, and could no longer hear its rippling. Then she tied the horse to a tree and went back alone. Walking as lightly as she could, she covered up any sign of the horse's passing, smoothing over stray prints, and sprinkling dust where they had wet the rocks. When she reached the stream, she whispered her spell, lying down to watch.

She waited, her heart beating against the hard stone. On the far side of the stream she saw a splendid spider web, shot with rainbows. Worth coming back for when she was not so busy. In the meantime she thought about her knight. He had a funny foreign way of talking, but that only made him more special. He had a good heart as well, she knew by the way he spoke to her. He even seemed to like her, though that was a lot to hope for.

First she heard warning calls—the indignant chatter of a red squirrel, the rasping cry of a frightened pine tit. Followed by the voices of men, and the neighing of their horses. They came slowly downstream, searching both banks, looking for the spot where she left the water.

One huge fellow in half-armor and big bucket-topped riding boots urged his mount up onto the rock shelf, coming so close she could count the flanges on the heavy steel mace hanging from his saddle bow. Matted hair and flecks of blood clung to the sharp steel. He wore his sallet tipped back, searching the ground for tracks. His hard bearded face could not compare to the clean elegant features of Sir Roy d'Roye, Chevalier de l'Étoile. But his surcoat had the same embattled blue bend as her knight's—charged with a sable crescent, the badge of Prince Sergey Mikhailovich, Grand Duke of Ikstra. Crown Prince Ivan's belligerent uncle. She held her breath as he studied the spot where she led the charger out of the stream. Did he see something? A crushed leaf or overturned stone? The scrape mark of a steel shoe?

Calls came from downstream. They had found her false trail. Prince Sergey's man-at-arms turned his horse about, splashing back into the stream. She was safe—for now. When the calls faded into the forest, she slid back off the rocks, and carefully made her way to where she had tethered the horse. The Witch would scold her if she did not return soon with her bark basket full of herbs and fungus.

As she set out, clouds of little white butterflies whirled up from patches of sunlight, fluttering between the horse's legs, then darting off between the trees. The deeper she went into the woods, the less she worried about hiding her trail. The only warning calls were for her. At the head of Long Lake, she saw wild swans swimming on clear water fringed by pines.

Beyond the lake the pine wood ended. On the far side stood a forest of black iron trunks with stark metal branches—the Iron Wood—a cold dark barrier reeking of magic, stretching over the hills to the east, lifeless and forbidding. She led the reluctant horse into the black leafless wood. Spiked branches closed around her, and forest sounds faded. No woodpeckers beat at the hard metal bark. No squirrels ran along the blade-like limbs. No living beasts made their home in the Iron Wood—just trolls and siren spirits, witches and the walking dead.

Happy to be nearly home, she threaded her way through the thorny metal maze. Finally a clearing appeared ahead, a white patch amid the black tangle. She led the big war horse up to a tall white hut made entirely of bones, long white thigh bones as big as a man, stacked one atop the other like grisly logs. Serfs called them dragon bones, but Katya knew better. They came from a long-haired, elephant-trunked monster that once roamed the northern tundra, bigger by far than any Barbary elephant. She had seen their great curved tusks in a forest bone pit, along with bits of the hairy hide.

Huge antlers from an ancient giant elk hung above the Bone Hut's leather door. Swallows nested in nooks beneath the eves. Little chestnut-throated birds peered out of the mud nests at her. Their parents flew back and forth, chattering at her, then streaking off in the direction of Long Lake, coming back with ants, gnats, wasps, and assassin bugs to feed their young.

Slowly the skin door swung open, and the Bone Witch emerged. Older than sin, and grim as death, the Witch wore a knuckle bone necklace and a linen winding sheet for a dress. White hair hung down to bare skeletal feet. Around her thin waist was a wormwood belt, supporting the thief-skin bag that held her charms. The horse backed and snorted at the sight of her.

She muttered a charm and the shying charger relaxed. "A beautiful beast," the Bone Witch declared. "Where did you find him?"

"In the woods." Katya had always brought lost or strayed animals out of the woods. Fallen eagle chicks. Little lame squirrels. Orphaned leopard cubs. This war horse was by far her most impressive find. She made no mention of his master. The Bone Witch had warned her not to bring men into the Iron Wood. Abandoned cubs and a weary war horse were one thing—but no stray knights. No matter how handsome and helpless they looked.

She held out her basket to show she had not wasted the whole morning, saying, "Byeli Zamak has been burned."

The Witch nodded, "I smelled it on the wind." It was impossible to surprise the Bone Witch.

"And a leopard drank from the pond beneath the ridge."

The Witch nodded again. "Three nights ago, when the moon was full." Accepting the fungus, the Witch told her to give the gray charger a rubdown, "And see he has grass and water. You cannot bring things home unless you care for them."

"I will, I will," she assured the Witch. And went to work at once, taking the horse around to the paddock behind the bone hut, rubbing him down, giving him water and barley. Filling a bark basket with food, she got out the Witch's steel sickle, saying she would go cut grass at Long Lake. Nothing a horse could live on grew in the Iron Wood.

The Witch sniffed her basket. "And you will take food to the knight hiding in the cave by the spring?"

She gave a guilty nod.

"You are free to play with whatever you find in the woods, so long as your chores do not go wanting."

"Oh, no! I will gather more fungus, and webs for spinning. See, I am taking my spindle."

The Witch shook her head. "Your youth will be the death of me. Always rushing life along."

"No! Never." She kissed the Witch's cold wrinkled lips. "You will always be here." The Bone Witch had been in the Iron Wood forever.

"Of course, but what has that to do with it?" The Witch shooed her out of the hut.

As the Witch predicted, she went straight to the cave, fearing she would find it empty. Nearing the spring, she stopped to listen. And heard nothing. Maybe he had obeyed her and stayed in the cave. More likely he was long gone.

She was thrilled to find herself wrong. "*Bonjour*," he greeted her with a grin when she stuck her head into the cave. Heaving himself upright, he peered at her basket. "What is this? Food, how wonderful! Did you bring wine as well?" She admitted she had not, having never so much as seen a grape. "Alas, too bad. But this is magic enough. Is there meat?"

"*Kalbasa*." She doled out a length of smoked sausage.

"Excellent, good old *kalbasa*, and bread too. What a wonderful wood sprite. Would there be caviar to go with it?"

"There is." She showed him the gleaming fish roe wrapped in a cool leaf. Long Lake teemed with sturgeon.

"Caviar! Fantastic. What a feast!"

"And *myot* also." She showed him the comb.

"Honey. How delightful."

"And yogurt."

"Ah yes, Markovy's answer to sour milk."

"And *diynya*."

"*Diynya?*" He looked puzzled.

She lifted the melon from the bottom of the basket, holding it out to him. "*Diynya*."

"Of course. *Diynya*. How utterly delicious." Taking the melon, he kissed her. "*Merci beaucoup, Mademoiselle* wood sprite."

Her lips tingled from her first kiss by a grown man. The lumpish son of the family she lived with once held her down and tried to kiss her, but she bit his tongue. This was completely different. Delicious shivers shot through her, raising goosebumps from nipples to her groin. That he did it quickly and casually did not matter. Nor did it matter that he had clearly forgotten her name. It was enough that she remembered his, Sir Roy d'Roye, Chevalier de l'Étoile, et le Baron d'Roye. She felt utterly ecstatic, having her first real kiss come from someone so special. Not just a knight, but a lord. And hers to feed and care for.

Making her worry all the more for him. "Why do they want to harm you?"

"Rank prejudice," he replied, spreading caviar with his thumb. "Pure silly superstition."

She broke open the melon, sipped the juice, and passed it to him. "But why would Prince Ivan's uncle attack Byeli Zamak?"

He heaved a sigh. "*Mademoiselle* does not live in a nation. Markovy is a collection of family quarrels with vague boundaries, whose preferred form of government is civil war. Being a foreign heretic, I do not give a lead *sou* who wins—but I swore an oath to your king, to uphold his honor and his heir. Not that noble oaths mean a lot when you are having your head beat in."

Getting over her goosebumps, she took her spindle from the basket, and started to spin spider's thread from a web she had found on the way. Working the tiny threads relaxed her.

"Markovites are the most superstitious folk in creation," he complained between bites. "Believing in all manner of faeries, imps, djinn, witches and whatnot. Byeli Zamak supposedly held a magic treasure— the Firebird's Egg. A marvelous tale. And Prince Sergey is an utterly gullible Grand Duke, who thinks this mythical egg will make him master of Markovy. But I held Byeli Zamak for Prince Ivan, and King Demitri before him. As Castellan I would know if Byeli Zamak held such an egg. And it does not."

Katya herself absolutely believed in the Firebird's Egg. King Demitri had stolen the Egg from its nest deep in the Iron Wood, and kept it locked in a cool deep basement vault beneath Byeli Zamak—where it would not hatch and would always be his. It had been King Demitri's greatest treasure, and his greatest curse. Making his life tragic and miserable. The curse cost him both his wives, and all his children, except for Ivan, his heir. Why Ivan's uncle would want the ill-fated egg was totally beyond her—but that did not mean it did not exist.

Her knight told more stories, of far-off Gascony where he was born, and how he lost everything and ended up in exile. "I possess an astounding ability to choose the losing side. Counting this latest debacle at Byeli Zamak, I have been in half a dozen pitched fights—and have always come out a loser. A remarkable record, not easily achieved. When I sided with the English they lost to the King of France. When I switched my allegiance to the King, he lost to the English. Scots in the French service call me 'Tyneman' in tribute to my many defeats. An honor really. Any lout with a bit of ability can run off a string of victories. But to lose every time—that requires not just talent, but uncanny luck as well."

"I cannot believe your luck could be so bad." She did not want to believe anything bad about him.

"Bad luck?" He laughed. "Not in the least, my luck is excellent. Could not be better."

"Really? But is it not better to win than lose?"

"Better perhaps—but not always easier. Anyone can survive a victory, just stay to the back and shout loudly. But surviving six defeats is a rare feat. Requiring more than a swift horse. Twice—at Lipan and St. Jacob-on-Bris—I was the only one not killed or taken. That is phenomenal luck."

"I mean, I do not believe you must always lose."

He scoffed at her innocence. "Tell it to the Swiss. They were near unbeatable until I sided with them."

By now dusk was settling outside the cave. Shafts of golden light slanted between the trees, slicing deep into the forest. Having seen her knight fed and cared for, she needed to get back and cut grass for his horse, then see to the Witch's supper, making the most of the long summer twilight. Sadly she took her leave, fairly sure he would not wander off in the short night, and meaning to be back by morning. D'Roye declared himself devastated to see her go, cheering her immensely. She finally had her knight in armor. Who cared if he was a foreigner, and somewhat the worse for wear—a footloose loser from some far-off land?

Before returning to the Witch, she had one more thing to do. Cautiously she snuck up on the troll-bear's lair, hoping her own scent would be hidden by the carrion stink. When she found the spot she sought, she dug down into the deep forest loam, using the Witch's steel sickle. She glanced repeatedly over her shoulder, uncomfortably aware that she had watched her knight dig in this exact spot without him knowing it.

Setting aside the sickle, she dug the last few inches with her hands, not wanting to harm what lay hidden in the hole. Finally she felt something soft and warm beneath her fingers. Brushing aside the last of the dirt, she recognized the embroidered tapestry her knight had kept next to his armored breast. Unwrapping the tapestry, she felt the smooth hard surface underneath, the warm, living Firebird's Egg.

She folded the tapestry back over the Egg, then refilled the hole, happy her knight had not lied to her. He claimed that as Castellan he would have known if Byeli Zamak held such a magical egg—and it did not. But that was because he had escaped Byeli Zamak with it, and buried it here by the troll-bear's lair. Being a born romancer, she took such truthful misdirection as a sign of true love.

～ Prince Sergey

She meant to see her knight right after morning chores, before he could wander away from the cave—but the Bone Witch had a dozen things for her to do. For no apparent reason the Witch wanted the swallow's nests taken from under the eves, and her pet rats turned loose, then her favorite fetishes hung on branches in the Iron Wood. So many pointless tasks that she suspected the Witch of trying to keep her from seeing D'Roye. The Bone Witch's motives were as obscure as her methods.

The rats seemed happy to be set free, but the swallows complained bitterly, chattering shrilly and darting at her head. It was useless to tell them that Witch ordered the mass removal. While she battled indignant swallows, the Witch sat at her bone table writing on thin strips of Chinese paper in her little cramped script. Tying these tiny messages to the feet of her carrier pigeons, the Witch released the pigeons one by one, sending them off into the blue summer sky.

Katya asked what was so important that the Witch must tell the world. The Bone Witch shushed her. "Be patient. In time all comes clear."

So the Witch always said. Katya returned to her tasks, working until the Bone Hut looked positively bare. Since the day she arrived the chaos of her new home had fascinated her—fetishes decorating bone rafters, swallows darting in and out, pigeons cooing in the eves, rats peering from wicker cages, all lit by tulip-shaped paper lanterns. It took her mind off the terror of belonging to a witch. She fully expected to be cooked and eaten, unless the Witch chose to have her raw. Soon Katya realized that she would have to do the cooking—but by then chores and boredom made her treasure the hut's distractions. Now it chilled her to see her home so neat. All the animals were gone, except for her knight's horse in the paddock out back. She hoped this latest mad impulse did not last.

Finally the Witch agreed to let her go. "There is nothing else for you to do here. Now go and make your way in the world. Be smart. Be brave. Think of me now and again. And if you ever need help, call on me. No matter how far you go, or what you become, I will be with you."

Katya told her she was only going to take breakfast to her knight. And her slave collar kept her from going much farther—but the Witch had a way of seeing grand drama in the most mundane things, like the song of a lark, or the first buds of spring. "Do not worry, I will be back in the afternoon."

"No, you won't," the Bone Witch replied. "Always remember, I tried to care for you and teach you trollcraft. Now recite your spell."

She recited her invisibility spell, grabbed up her basket and headed for the Iron Wood, happy to be free of the Witch—if only for a while.

She did not get far. There were no warning cries in the Iron Wood. No birds or squirrels to keep watch for her. She was concentrating on the winding trail through the metal trunks, when she caught a whiff of horses on the wind. Horses meant men. She froze, whispered her spell, and waited—hoping her heart was not banging too loud.

Hearing the clip-clop of iron-shod hooves, she realized they were riding down the crooked trail toward the Bone Witch's hut—coming in twos, to save getting slashed by spiked branches. In a moment they would be riding right over her, invisible or not. She turned and dashed back the way she had come. Byeli Zamak had been gone for only a day, and already men were coming farther than she ever thought possible. At the clearing in the metal wood, the Bone Witch stood waiting by her skin door, a grim smile on her wrinkled face. Katya told the sorceress she had heard horsemen coming, but the Witch merely nodded. Had the Witch known about these horsemen? Probably. The Bone Witch had sent her off with her basket and spell, knowing full well that she would not get far.

Hoofbeats grew louder as the column of riders neared the clearing. She waited alongside the Witch, curious to see what sort of horsemen dared come into the Iron Wood. But the first figure to appear was not on horseback—and only half a man. Man-shaped and naked, he strolled lithely into the clearing, covered head to foot with soft brown hair. His eyes were wolf's eyes. Canine fangs protruded from thin smiling lips.

Lycanthrope. She had never seen one like this before—few had and lived. He was not the harmless sort who totally shed human form to run with the wolves and mate with the bitches. He was a soulless demon from deep in the Iron Wood—the absolute worst of wolf and man. Or so the Witch always told her.

Behind him rode an incongruous pair. The taller of the two was a steel-helmeted horse archer wearing a blue Horse Guard's brigandine studded with silver nail heads. He had a huge dead swan hanging from his high saddle. Riding at his side was a dwarf mounted on a pony, wearing a particolored tunic and a fool's cap. More horsemen filed into the clearing behind them, spreading out from their column of two's—horse archers, knights, and men-at-arms, followed by squires and valets, even a steward and a butler in their uniforms of office. And an Ensign, holding up a grand duke's banner, with a black crescent and the lightning stroke sign of Ikstra. Beneath the banner rode Prince Sergey himself. Katya had never seen a prince of the blood before, but there was no mistaking this one. Grand Duke Sergey was a prince from the bootheels up, wearing silver-chased armor and a gold coronet on his old-fashioned great helmet. He had his visor tipped back and she could see the hard cold sheen in his pale blue eyes, glinting like dangerous ice in the spring.

He stared evenly at the aged Bone Witch—two of the most feared people in Markovy were meeting for the first time. Totally different, yet each in their own way absolutely terrifying. Prince Sergey, Grand Duke of Ikstra, broke the frosty silence, "Good morrow, grandmother, we are trailing a mounted knight, riding a gray war horse and wearing a blue-and-white surcoat. He is most likely wounded. Have you seen him?"

"No, my lord," replied the Bone Witch. "Not him, nor anyone like him."

"Strange," mused Prince Sergey, "our wolfman trailed his horse straight to this clearing." The Lycanthrope stood waiting, a hideous look on his fanged face, clearly hoping to make a meal out of someone. "He was Castellan of Byeli Zamak, and claims to be a baron."

"And yet I have not seen him," the Witch insisted.

Prince Sergey looked to the dwarf sitting on his pony. Rising in his saddle, the dwarf took a deep breath through his nose. Two more sniffs, and the dwarf settled back in the saddle, saying, "She is telling the truth."

Prince Sergey nodded. Then his gaze turned to Katya, staring at her like she had failed to pay her squirrel tax. "What about the girl? Has she seen him?"

The "girl" gulped. "No, my lord, never." She shook her head vigorously, shrinking back beside the Witch.

Prince Sergey looked again at the dwarf. This time the little man swung off his pony, and walked over to her. His head came up to Katya's waist. Lifting his nose, he sniffed her belly, then ran his nostrils down her thigh. He stepped back, saying, "She is lying."

Sergey raised an eyebrow. "Has she seen the Castellan?" His dwarf shrugged. The little man was a lie sniffer, not a mind reader. His majesty turned back to her, "Have you seen a knight wearing blue and white?"

She had no good answer, caught between her need to lie, and knowing the dwarf would sniff her out. Anything she said would put her at the mercy of these men. The wolfman leered at her. He was the one who had found her. Without him, this clumsy crowd of horsemen could not have trailed her from the stream—but a Lycanthrope can track a mouse on a moonless night.

"Well, have you seen him?" the Grand Duke demanded.

Before she could think of some truthful misdirection, a shout of triumph came from the back of the Bone Hut. A couple of squires came around the corner proudly leading her knight's horse. Someone called out, "That's his horse. The big gray that belongs to the Castellan."

Prince Sergey stared hard at the horse, then looked back at her. "Have you seen the knight who rode this horse?"

She nodded dumbly, unable to come up with anything but the truth, though she knew it would doom her.

"Good," the Grand Duke concluded, "we are at last getting somewhere. Do you know where he is?"

"Not for certain." He could be long gone from the cave. In fact she fervently hoped he was.

Prince Sergey smiled, a chilling, terrible sight. "Nothing in life is certain—but I wager this will be sure enough." He turned to his Ensign, saying, "Pay her for the girl."

Taking his reins in his banner hand, the Ensign fished a gold coin out of his purse, tossing it at the naked feet of the Witch. The Bone Witch made no attempt to pick up the coin. "That is for the girl," the Ensign explained.

"She is not for sale," replied the Witch.

"Give her the whole purse," the Grand Duke ordered impatiently. His Ensign tossed the purse down beside the coin—but the Witch ignored it as well.

"What do you want, grandmother?" Grand Duke Sergey seemed astonished that the Bone Witch refused his generosity.

"For you to leave." There was a hint of warning in the Witch's answer.

"We will," Sergey agreed, "when we have the girl."

"She is under my protection," the Witch insisted.

Grand Duke Sergey glared at her. Katya could feel the tension in the clearing. Two dozen armed men sat loafing in the saddle, backed by valets, pages, a steward and butler. Horses looked on with equine curiosity. The Lycanthrope stood waiting, aching to use his fangs and claws. "By rights I could have you burned," Prince Sergey pointed out.

"Do it if you dare," replied the Witch, unworried by the prince's power.

Sergey motioned for his archers to dismount, saying, "Seize the girl."

Horrified, Katya stepped back toward the skin door. This was all her fault. She had brought the horse to the Bone Hut. An archer tried to brush past the Witch to grab her—but the Bone Witch shoved him sideways, landing him in a heap. Two archers seized the Witch's arms, but she whirled about, faster than the eye could follow, sending the armored pair flying to opposite ends of the clearing. Another archer tried to draw his sword, but the Witch reached out and grabbed his wrist, twisting it until it snapped. His blade dropped from limp fingers.

Archers fell back, appalled by the old woman's strength. The Lycanthrope dropped to a crouch, prepared to spring. Prince Sergey shouted, "Use your bows—but do not hit the girl. I will flay the man that misses."

A half dozen arrows leaped from their bows, striking the Witch in the chest and hip. She hardly even winced, standing between Katya and the men. Katya clung to the skin door, her fist jammed in her mouth, stifling a scream, aghast at what she had done.

More arrows thudded into the Witch. Painfully the old woman turned to face her. The Bone Witch's chest looked like a bloody pin cushion. Arrows continued to hit her from behind. Staggering from the impact, the Witch opened her mouth as if she meant to speak. All that came out was a horrible gargling sound, followed by a great gout of blood. Shocked and sickened, Katya watched the Witch sink slowly to her knees.

"Stop shooting! Stop shooting!" Sergey cried. "You will hit the girl." Silence settled over the clearing as tears poured down Katya's cheeks. Half a dozen bows were pointed at her, arrows knocked and ready. She could see their gleaming chiseled steel points aimed at her chest. The Witch lay at her feet, feathered with arrows. Katya too expected to die—if not now, then soon.

Prince Sergey broke the silence, spurring his mount to put himself between her and the archers, shouting, "Down bows! Damn you! Down bows!"

Hurriedly his men obeyed. Wiping her tears away, Katya seized the Prince's stirrup. "Why did you kill her?" she wailed. "I am the one who lied."

Startled, Prince Sergey stared down in disbelief, as if astonished she could speak. "The Witch did not know where he was. You did." So the Witch died, and she lived—for now. "You do know where the Castellan is?" Sergey wanted to be sure.

She nodded. Any other answer would be her death warrant.

"And you can take us to him?"

She nodded again.

"Good." Prince Sergey pulled his boot from his stirrup, planted the heel on her shoulder and shoved, sending her sprawling. He waved to his men, "Burn the place. Burn the Witch's body. Burn it all."

Prince Sergey cantered off. For a moment she lay looking up at blue sky framed by black iron tree tops, her breath coming in ragged gasps.

Without warning, a big bearded archer took the Prince's place. Looking down at her, he laughed, saying, "Here's a cute young case of the clap. And already on her back."

"Give your middle leg a rest," another archer advised.

"What do you mean?" the man asked indignantly. "I've not been fucked in a fortnight."

"Small wonder." The second archer helped her to her feet, brushing the dirt off her dress, which was spattered with the Bone Witch's blood.

Someone called out, "Does she have a name?"

"Do you?" asked the archer.

Of course, she thought—but all she said was, "Katya."

"She calls herself Katya." The horse archer was speaking to a huge man in an oversized suit of plate armor. Mounted on a big black Frisian, he towered over everything, seeming to reach right to the ridgepole of the Bone Hut. He wore the same blue-white surcoat as her knight, but many times bigger, and marked with the sword-and-shield badge of a Master-at-arms. Tipping back the visor on his German sallet, he asked her in a big booming voice, "Where do you come from, girl?"

Scared senseless, she still had the presence of mind to lie. "I am the daughter of a Kazak hetman, Kaffa Khan. Harm me, and he will come with a *tumen* of horse archers to hunt you all to death."

He laughed, saying, "Have knee-high give her a sniff."

She had forgotten about the Dwarf. Too much had happened since she last saw the little man. He walked over and took a deep sniff, then turned to the Master-at-arms, saying, "She lies."

The Master-at-arms did not look surprised—her lie had been feeble at best. "Come, my little khanum, give us the truth. Or I will see you suffer."

She admitted she did not know who her parents were, saying, "I was raised here, by the Witch." Mentioning the Bone Witch made her want to cry, but she stopped herself.

"Are you virtuous?" asked the Master-at-arms.

She stared dumbly up at him. What a stupid question to ask a witchchild. How could anyone be both damned and virtuous?

"There's your answer," the lecherous horse archer chuckled. "She does not even know what you are asking."

The Master-at-arms grinned, "Well, it is bad luck to execute a virgin. . . ."

"Especially for the virgin," a horse archer added, getting a laugh from his fellows.

The Master-at-arms signaled for silence. "But in your case we will risk it. Stop your lying, and lead us to the Castellan. Otherwise we will have you flayed and left to fry in the sun. Unlucky or not. Do you understand?"

She understood.

He turned to the squires and archers, telling them to get busy, "Drag the Witch into the hut, and set it on fire." None too happy with their task, archers dragged the Witch's body into the Bone Hut. Katya watched them pile the straw beds atop the Witch, then throw on firewood, furniture, and the contents of the winter clothes chests. Dousing the pile with cooking oil, they set it alight. Soon the Bone Hut was blazing away. She saw her life going up in smoke and flames—just like Byeli Zamak.

"Mount up," the Master-at-arms ordered. Squires hoisted her aboard D'Roye's gray charger. One of them handed her the reins, and something to go with them. Looking down, she saw it was her straw doll—the one she had brought with her when she first came to live with the Witch. The young squire who had given it to her looked embarrassed. Of all these men—from Grand Duke Sergey down to the lowest valet—this boy alone seemed ashamed for what they had done.

The Master-at-arms gave her a grin that was all beard and teeth, saying, "Now lead us to the Castellan." She nodded, clutching the straw doll to her belly. Somehow, some way, she meant to come out of this alive and whole. But how that would happen, Heaven alone knew.

～ The Firebird's Egg

Mounted on her knight's gray charger, she led the whole cavalcade along the winding trail out of the Iron Wood. The Master-at-arms rode beside her, with the dwarf mounted pillion behind him, and the Lycanthrope loping on ahead. Boxed in by armed ruthless men, she could neither lose them nor lie to them—not so long as they had the wolfman to track her, and the dwarf to sniff out her lies. Only a stroke of monumental good fortune could save her, and she had long ago learned she had to make her own luck.

Whenever the Master-at-arms questioned her directions, the dwarf made sure she told only the truth, putting a heavy burden on someone who always relied on lies. Whatever saved her now had to be the Lord's honest truth. At the head of Long Lake, hot perfumed pine scent replaced the cold metal odor of the Iron Wood. Swans clumped at the center of the lake, already learning to be wary of the archers. She turned west, straight for the ridge line separating the forest from the steppe. The

Master-at-arms looked askance. "You are leading us back toward Byeli Zamak?"

"That is where I left him, in a cave by the spring at the base of the ridge."

"Is that so?" he asked the dwarf riding behind him.

"She is telling the truth," replied the dwarf, looking pleased that she had learned not to lie.

The Master-at-arms turned back to her. "And this is the shortest way there?"

"Absolutely," she assured him. The dwarf confirmed her. An east wind had blown all morning, and she was determined to lead them straight downwind, avoiding the roundabout way she came the day before. No need now to hide her tracks. "If I take you right to him, will you let me go?"

"Of course, of course," the big man answered affably. But she was looking behind him at the dwarf, who glanced sharply up, saying nothing. Having a lie-sniffer riding on your horse's rump worked both ways. She had seen that same look of contempt on the dwarf's face when she tried to lie. The Master-at-arms did not mean to let her go. None of them did. Once she had served her purpose they would burn her as a witch. If they had not already promised her to the Lycanthrope.

As they plunged into the living wood, with its green trees and countless eyes, she heard a squirrel chatter, followed by the firebird's cry. It was not the flame jay's man call. She kept her eyes fixed on the path ahead, making sure the Master-at-arms got no warning from her. As the firebird's cry faded behind her, she strained her ears, trying to tell what was happening at the back of the column. All she could hear was the horse archers, laughing and joking behind her. They had a seemingly endless stock of sacrilegious stories to keep their spirits up.

Suddenly a scream rang out. The Master-at-arms grabbed her reins, looking back down the column. They waited. The story tellers fell silent. She watched little white butterflies dance in the sunlight. Presently a horse archer on a bay mare came galloping up. "What happened?" demanded the Master-at-arms.

"A leopard," the horse archer gasped.

"A leopard?" The Master-at-arms looked shocked.

"Yes, it dropped out of a tree on the last man in the column—Vasily, from Suzdal. He stopped to tighten his stirrup and take a piss. Before he could remount the cat was on him. By the time we got back to him, he was dead and the beast was gone."

"That makes no sense," complained the Master-at-arms. "A leopard attacking an armed man in daylight?" And from upwind, Katya added to herself, carefully searching the trees. A wood tit stared back at her. "No cat could be that hungry," insisted the Master-at-arms.

The horse archer shrugged. "The cat did not act hungry. It just broke Vasily's neck, then went on its way."

The Master-at-arms snorted, "Which makes even less sense. Sling his body over a horse, and tell Prince Sergey we are ready to move." The archer turned his bay mare about and went trotting back down the column.

Again they waited. Katya sat listening to the pines murmuring overhead. A woodpecker started to hammer, then stopped suddenly. Had it seen something? Slowly the profane stories reappeared—"A nun, a bishop, and a brothel keeper are in a boat. The bishop says to the nun. . . ." She kept her ears tuned to the trees, listening for the woodpecker, and wondering why it was taking so long to get started again.

Finally Prince Sergey's Ensign trotted up, asking the same question, "Are you ready to move on? His highness means to be back at Byeli Zamak by dusk."

Rolling his eyes, the Master-at-arms told him, "I sent a man back saying we were ready to ride."

"What man?" asked the Ensign.

This provoked another commotion. A search failed to find the messenger, but did discover his bay mare, nervously cropping bracken in a nearby clearing. Fresh blood shone on her saddle. The Master-at-arms exploded, "This is absurd. We cannot sit here waiting to be eaten. Tell His Highness we are setting out—unless the leopard gets you first."

She started up again at a brisk trot. No one complained. Not with bloodthirsty leopards stalking the column. Men kept twisting in their saddles, glancing over their shoulders, looking everywhere but ahead. She saw a familiar break in the pines, backed by a tall stand of oaks. Since they were headed downwind there was no warning but the cry of a crossbill, which the men ignored. Only the Lycanthrope looked uneasy, padding silently along, ears cocked forward, claws extended.

Suddenly the werewolf froze, hairs quivering. She braced herself. This was it. The next seconds would decide if she lived or died. The Lycanthrope spun about and vanished into the undergrowth. An archer called out, "What scared the wolfman? Why has he run off?"

As if to answer him, the troll-bear burst from his hidden lair, bellowing defiance at the intruders. Twice the size of a normal bear, with steelhard hide and razor claws, the beast roared into the column, scattering men and horses. Rolling out of her saddle, Katya dropped to a crouch and whispered her spell. Instantly she vanished.

From her invisible crouch she got a close-up view of the swift horrific conflict. The troll-bear's forepaws flailed about, mace-headed battering rams slashing through plate armor like parchment. The Master-at-arms seized a lance from a squire, slapped down his visor, and charged the monster full tilt. His lance shattered on the troll-bear's hornlike hide. The enraged beast backhanded him out of the saddle, crushed him with a hind foot, then bit his horse's head off.

None of the other heroes who captured her tried to stop the troll-bear. The whole column—six lances of Horse Guards, with their attendant squires, valets, and archers, along with Prince Sergey's entourage of pages, Ensign, steward, and butler—vanished in an eyeblink, as if they too knew an invisibility spell. The troll-bear went howling after them, snapping pine saplings and uprooting boulders.

Which was why sensible woods creatures avoided a troll-bear's lair. The carrion stink was like a viper's hiss, a warning to unwary neighbors. Silence settled on the forest. Clutching her straw doll, she surveyed the new made clearing out the corner of her eyes. The worst part of being invisible was the inability to turn her head. Absolutely maddening when you wanted to know if it was safe to be seen. She was frozen in place staring at the armored leg of the Master-at-arms, sticking out from beneath a headless horse. She saw no sign of the dwarf who had been riding behind him.

Finally she made herself close her eyes, trusting in her ears to see behind her. Nothing. No warning cries, no rustle of leaves. No smell but the stink of troll-bear from somewhere upwind. She was free.

And alive. From the moment the Witch had died, she counted herself dead as well. Her demise seemed certain. She had let herself be tracked, and had gotten the Witch killed. And she was in the hands of men who meant to dispose of her in some grotesque fashion once she did their bidding. Now her life had been saved by a troll-bear. Few indeed could make that claim.

So what to do with her newfound freedom? Her first thought was for her knight. He was at the heart of this. He and the Firebird's Egg. She did not believe Prince Sergey would risk the Iron Wood just to put an end to some foreign born Castellan of Byeli Zamak. Love did not make her that blind. Her knight was not nearly as important as the Egg he had carried.

Moving stealthily downwind, ears tuned to the slightest sound, she crept up on the rocks and spring. She did not think any of the men could have caught up with her, even if they escaped the troll-bear. But having gotten her life back, she did not mean to let down her guard. Hot afternoon air hung heavy and expectant. And unnaturally quiet. Beyond the bubbling spring, the forest seemed to be holding its breath.

Suddenly she heard the firebird's shrill cry. She froze against a big boulder speckled with bird lime, whispering her spell. This was the second time today she had heard the bird's warning. It was as if the jay were watching over her. This cry was different than any she had heard before, the man-call mixed with an unfamiliar trill.

As she strained to survey the rocks without moving her head, a heavy form dropped on her from atop the boulder. Hairy arms seized her waist, and vice-hard thighs gripped her hips. Her struggles broke the invisibility spell, which had been no match for the Lycanthrope's supernatural senses. She was merely an unarmed young woman, fighting immensely strong arms, while the man-beast's fanged hairy face leered into hers.

Horrified, she struggled harder. Keeping her arms pinned, the Lycanthrope dragged her back away from the spring—but did nothing else to harm her. No clawing. No fangs in the neck. Not reassuring in the least, with his steel-like erection digging into the small of her back.

Then she felt the Lycanthrope relax. Looking up, she saw horsemen staring down at her. Prince Sergey sat bareheaded on his charger, having lost his gold-crowned helmet. His Ensign was beside him, along with a single horse archer, several frightened squires, and a bedraggled looking butler—all that was left of the proud cavalcade that had ridden boldly into the Iron Wood. The Lycanthrope must have been stalking ahead of them. Coming on her scent trail, he had gone up the backside of the boulder and dropped down onto her.

Prince Sergey trotted over to where she stood, glaring down at her. "Did you know we were riding into a troll-bear's lair?"

Her immediate impulse to lie died on her lips, when she spotted the dwarf riding behind the butler. She shook her head instead. "I will not tell you anything unless you let me go."

"Be cooperative," Prince Sergey warned. "I have only to say the word, and the beast holding you will savage you on the spot."

"You will not learn a lot from that," she pointed out.

"Yes," Sergey admitted, "but I might very much enjoy it." Nonetheless he waved to the wolfman. "Let her go."

The Lycanthrope let go of her, a little victory, and likely to be her last. Katya took a deep breath, wishing she could just disappear right here. What had she done to deserve all this? Not a thing so far as she could see. Prince Sergey leaned forward in the saddle. "Now, tell us what we want to know."

"If I do, will you let me go?" She stared past the prince at the dwarf seated behind his butler.

"Just tell the truth, and you have nothing to fear."

The dwarf's nose wrinkled, as if he whiffed something foul. So much for honesty. Prince Sergey had no intention of freeing her. She closed her eyes, taking another slow breath, prolonging the inevitable. "What do you wish to know?"

"Tell where the Castellan is," Prince Sergey demanded, royally impatient.

"Right here," came the cheerful reply. Her eyes flew open. There was her knight, standing tall and nonchalant, sword in hand, a wry smile on his handsome face. Seeing him appear out of nowhere was like suddenly getting her life back. He made a mocking bow to Prince Sergey. "Baron Roy d'Roye, Chevalier de l'Étoile, and until late Castellan of Byeli Zamak. At your service."

Sergey sat up in the saddle. "My God! You! Why did you not open Byeli Zamak to me?"

Her knight shrugged armored shoulders. "You did not say *s'il vous plait*. King Demitri gave me Byeli Zamak to hold for his heir."

"I am Prince Ivan's uncle. Byeli Zamak should have come to me."

"And it has," D'Roye reminded him, smiling at his latest defeat.

Prince Sergey leaned forward again. "But not the Firebird's Egg."

"That is what brings us here." Her knight looked smug.

"So you have the Egg?"

"Not on me. But I know where it is."

"Where?" Sergey demanded.

"What will you pay to know?"

"Half my kingdom?" Sergey suggested sarcastically.

"I will give it up cheaper than that. Set this wood sprite free. Her and me, alive and ahorsed—that is all I ask."

Katya fought back tears. Her knight had given up his hiding place, and the Egg he protected, all to save her. A foolish impetuous gesture that would probably get them both killed. Still, she was touched.

"Almost too cheap," Sergey mused. "Generosity from an enemy is always suspect—but perhaps you are merely a fool."

"Obviously. Pray indulge me nonetheless."

"You, the girl, and two horses—easy enough." Sergey lifted a steel-gloved finger. "After I have the Egg."

"As you wish." Keeping his big two-handed sword drawn, her knight turned to her. "*Mademoiselle*, I must go with these men—hopefully I will be coming back with a pair of horses."

"She comes with us," Sergey insisted.

D'Roye rolled his eyes apologetically. "Alas, *Mademoiselle*, I fear this Grand Duke means it. Fortunately, it is but a short way into the forest. . . ."

"By a stand of big oaks," she reminded him.

His eyes lit up. "I see you know the place."

She nodded excitedly. She knew better than he did. And the deeper they got into her woods, the safer they would be. Get far enough into the forest, and she and her knight were more than a match for any number of killers on horseback. But she did not say that aloud, for fear the killers would hear. She had to rely on him reading it in her smile.

He did seem to understand, setting out happily, not the least worried by the armed men around them, laughing, and making light of things. She wanted to tell him about the Bone Witch, but that too must wait. This time they approached the troll-bear's lair from downwind—by far the safest direction. So long as you stayed out of the beast's hearing you had little to fear. But as soon as they whiffed the carrion scent, Prince Sergey's men revolted, none of them wanting a rematch with the monster. Their horses too refused to go any farther, shying and whinnying at the fearful stench.

Sergey immediately demanded that the dwarf sniff her knight for a lie. D'Roye submitted with good grace, for once having nothing to hide. But the dwarf went right up to him, sniffing vigorously. Katya could guess why. The little man desperately hoped to smell a lie. If her knight was telling the truth, they would have to march straight back toward the troll-bear's lair.

Finally, the dwarf admitted D'Roye smelled sincere. Sergey was forced to leave the horses and squires behind, but he bullied the Ensign, horse archer, and butler into accompanying him on foot. Katya did not fear any of these men half so much as she feared the Lycanthrope.

The dwarf did not get a choice. Like her, he was too valuable to leave behind, and would come whether he willed it or not. She went out of her way to comfort the little man, whose only concern was for the truth. He and the Witch were the only ones she had never been able to lie to, which she very much respected. "Stay close to me," she told him, "and I will try to see you are safe."

He looked warily up at her, "Is that so?"

"I thought you would know." He was the one with the supremely educated nose. As they set out walking, she slid her hand inside her dress, stroking the straw doll hidden next to her breast, just for luck.

When they got to the oak grove, the butler had to go down on his beribboned knees and dig for the Egg with his bare hands. Prince Sergey would not let him use so much as a toothpick, for fear of harming the Egg. Her knight stood watching calmly, leaning on his big two-handed sword. She motioned for the dwarf to get behind her. Which he immediately did, backing away toward the bushes. A bad sign—the little man who knew his master best was expecting the worst.

Reaching his hands into the hole, the butler drew forth the Firebird's Egg. As he unwrapped the dirty tapestry, everyone stared in awe at Markovy's greatest wonder. Except for the Lycanthrope, who kept his hungry eyes fixed on her. What had he been promised when Prince Sergey had the Egg?

Her knight spoke first. "*Excusez-moi*, this may be exceptionally foolish of me, but I beg you to listen to the advice of your late king."

"What advice?" Sergey looked suspiciously at her knight, as if he was an insect with an especially annoying hum.

"King Demitri sent a deathbed message to me, ordering that this Egg be returned safely to its Nest. Not an easy task, but one I heartily endorse. There is a terrible curse on this Egg. How many lives has that damned Egg cost in the last two days alone?" Her knight was right, Byeli Zamak had been burned. And so had the Bone Hut. Prince Sergey's proud company had been reduced to a scared handful, standing around the magical Egg.

Prince Sergey gave a snort of contempt. "We need no lessons from the loser."

"There are worse things than losing," her knight pointed out. "My own fortunes have improved mightily since I put that ill-fated Egg in the ground."

"Really?" Prince Sergey arched an eyebrow.

"Absolutely." Her knight smiled at her. "I was beaten and bleeding, fleeing yet another defeat. But as soon as I parted from that Egg, there came this delightful forest nymph, stitching my wounds and serving me caviar."

"How lucky for you," Sergey laughed. "My own ambitions are a bit higher."

Her knight shrugged, "To each their own. Hopefully, King Demitri will know I tried. Now if I may depart with my own prize." He reached a steel-gloved hand out to her.

"You may inform Demitri in person." Prince Sergey nodded to the Lycanthrope. "Kill him and the girl is yours."

Faster than thought, the Lycanthrope leaped at D'Roye's throat, claws extended. But her knight had expected treachery. His blade came up in a terrific backhand swipe. Only the wolfman's supernatural agility saved him from being cut in two. Twisting in midair, the beast managed to evade the blade, landing on all fours.

All eyes were on her knight, so Katya stepped back against a tree, whispering her spell. The dwarf had already vanished into the under-growth. Holding her breath, she stood rigid, smelling sap sweating from the pine behind her, watching the fight and wanting to help, but not knowing how.

D'Roye kept his sword between himself and the werewolf, feinting and slashing. Despite his speed and cunning, the Lycanthrope could not get past the flashing blade. Twice he tried to duck under the sword, and got nicked in the shoulder and the ear. But the wolfman moved too fast for D'Roye to land a killing blow. Stalking sideways, he searched for an opening.

"Help the beast," Prince Sergey commanded. "Take him from behind."

His butler just stood there, stupidly holding the Egg—but the Ensign and horse archer obeyed, drawing their swords and trying to slide around behind D'Roye. So long as the Lycanthrope kept him busy in front, it would only be a matter of time before one of the others got at his back.

Being the bolder of the two, the Ensign was first to get in position. As D'Roye aimed a slash at the werewolf, the Ensign raised his own sword, stepping in to strike.

Seeing the Ensign lunge past her, Katya leaped forward, seizing the man's sword arm. Coming out of nowhere, she took the Ensign by surprise. As he struggled to shake her off, D'Roye spun about, hitting him a wicked two-handed blow just beneath the breastplate. Groaning, the Ensign went down, rattling like a pile of dropped pans.

Instantly the Lycanthrope bounded at D'Roye. But her knight seemed to know what was coming. Ignoring the downed Ensign, he let his momentum spin him completely about. This time his backhand caught the Lycanthrope between the neck and collarbone, severing the beast's jugular in a hideous spray of blood. The werewolf landed in a gory heap at his feet.

Strong arms grabbed her from behind. The horse archer had not dared to take on D'Roye, but he seized her to use as a living shield. Prince Sergey whipped his sword out, and she felt the sharp point at her throat. "Stop," the Grand Duke commanded. "Drop your sword or I will kill her."

Her knight let his point drop, saying, "Come now, Your Highness, that is hardly sporting. All we want is to be on our way."

"Drop your sword," Prince Sergey demanded. "Or I swear by God Almighty I shall slit her throat."

With a sigh, D'Roye jammed his sword point first into the ground beside the dead Lycanthrope. Then he stepped back, away from the blade, folding his arms. "I warn you, this will bring nothing but grief."

"Perhaps," Sergey admitted with a grin. "But you will not be there to see it." Katya's heart sank. Her knight would die—merely for showing mercy—and she would have to watch. Sergey stepped toward D'Roye, hefting his sword.

As he did, a black and amber body dropped on him from the branches above. Prince Sergey gasped as the leopard sank her fangs into his neck. Staggering beneath the weight of the leopard the Grand Duke dropped to his knees, then pitched forward onto his face. Katya watched in astonishment as the big cat continued to bite down on the Grand Duke, making sure he never got up.

D'Roye jerked his sword out of the ground, saying to the horse archer holding her, "Let the girl go, if you want to live." The arms holding her vanished, and she heard footfalls behind her as the horse archer took off into the forest. Her knight turned to Prince Sergey's butler, who still held the Firebird's Egg, a sick look on his horrified face. "Carefully set down that Egg, and you too may go."

Placing the Egg gently on the ground, the butler backed slowly through the bracken, bumped into a tree, then turned and ran for his life. All that remained of Prince Sergey's expedition into the Iron Wood was a trio of bodies, lying around the Firebird's Egg. "*Mon Dieu*," D'Roye muttered, "that went far better than I could ever have imagined."

Slowly the leopard rose up, changing as she did, becoming a withered naked old woman with wrinkled skin and bone white hair. And not a single arrow mark on her. The Bone Witch smiled at Katya. "I told you I would be here if you needed me."

Her knight lowered his point and looked over at her. "This I suppose is your witch?"

She hastened to introduce the Bone Witch to her knight, proud of the way he went down on one knee before the withered old woman, saying, "*Madame* Witch, Baron Roy d'Roye, at your service."

"Is that just a gallantry," asked the Witch, "or are you really at my service?"

"Absolutely. *Madame* has saved my life, and I owe her anything that honor allows."

"Good," the Bone Witch declared, "I have need of your honor." Then the Witch turned to her. "Come here, my daughter."

She walked happily over, grateful to be free of Prince Sergey's killers and glad to see the Witch alive—but utterly ecstatic to have someone finally call her "daughter."

Giving her a wrinkled kiss, the Witch took the slave collar from around her neck. "Now I have one last chore for you."

"Whatever you wish." For once she truly meant it.

"Return the Firebird's Egg to its proper nest, so it may hatch and the curse on Markovy can be lifted."

"But how will I get there?" She felt surprised the Witch would give her a task so important, and so seemingly impossible.

"These will take you there." The Witch snapped her bony fingers and a trio of horses ambled into the clearing—the knight's war horse, a black mare with a horse archer's bow and quiver hanging from her saddle, and a big bay palfrey laden with supplies. D'Roye's eyes lit up, seeing the gray charger he had clearly given up for lost.

"I mean, how will I find the Nest?" All Katya knew of the Firebird's Nest was that it lay deep in the Iron Wood.

The Witch gave a low call, holding out her finger, and the flame jay flew down to land on it. Stroking the bird's breast, the crone cooed, "You can take them there, can you not?" Throwing back his head, the jay gave a confident raucous reply, flying over to land on the black mare's saddle. "See," the Witch told her, "he is more than ready. Are you?"

Katya nodded solemnly, seeing that this is what the Witch had been training her for—how she would finally be "useful."

When she had the Egg safely tucked into the palfrey's pack saddle, Katya kissed the Bone Witch good-bye, and climbed onto the black mare. She watched her knight bow good-bye to the Witch, then mount his gray charger, grinning merrily. Her whole life led her to this point. As an orphan growing up, she invented royal parents and a magical future for herself. Just when puberty and poverty were about to lay waste her fantasies, she was given to the Bone Witch, making the magical part real. Now the rest was coming to pass—she had a horse beneath her, a charming knight at her side, and a quest ahead with the kingdom's future at stake. She took her straw doll out of her dress, putting it in the black mare's saddle bag.

Only one thing made her uneasy: her knight was a foreigner, not required to care if there was a curse on Markovy. And he was a real baron to boot, who did not need her royal dreams and extravagant lies. She asked softly and sincerely, "Are you sure you want to do this? You are free to go your own way if you wish."

"Heavens no, *Mademoiselle*." He grinned happily. "Not when my lady has at long last landed me on the winning side."

My Case for Retributive Action

Thomas Ligotti

Thomas Ligotti (longshadows.com/ligotti) lives near Tampa, Florida. He is one of the most important living writers of supernatural horror fiction, and a master of the short story. In an interview he listed the writers who have most influenced him: Edgar Allan Poe, H.P. Lovecraft, Vladimir Nabokov, and Bruno Shulz—"masters of depicting warped realities or warping the usual picture of the world that realistic fiction provides. The challenge for such writers is to make tangible their distorted, or merely intensified, experience. A morbid hyperattentiveness to the most inward imaginings and feelings is evident in this type of writer. And once feeling becomes the principal determinant of expression, all kinds of warping, or what appears to be warping, will occur in the structure, style, and content of a narrative." Ligotti's stories have been collected in Songs of a Dead Dreamer, Grimscribe, Noctuary, The Nightmare Factory, *and others, including many small press volumes.*

"My Case for Retributive Action" appeared in Weird Tales, *and is a fine example of Ligotti: One reviewer called it "Kafka meets Lovecraft." It is one of several recent Ligotti stories involving the sinister Quine Corporation, and its malign effects on its workers.* Weird Tales, *along with* Interzone, *comprised the top rank of small press magazines publishing fantasy in 2001. Ligotti's work has appeared often in* Weird Tales, *and other small press magazines.*

It was my first day working as a processor of forms in a storefront office. As soon as I entered the place—before I had a chance to close the door behind me or take a single step inside—this rachitic individual wearing mismatched clothes and eyeglasses with frames far too small for his balding head came hopping around his desk to greet me. He spoke excitedly, his words tumbling over themselves, saying, "Welcome, welcome. I'm Ribello. Allow me, if you will, to help you get your bearings around here. Sorry there's no coat rack or anything. You can just use that empty desk."

Now, I think you've known me long enough, my friend, to realize that I'm anything but a snob or someone who by temperament carries around a superior attitude toward others, if for no other reason than I simply lack the surplus energy required for that sort of behavior. So I smiled and tried to introduce myself. But Ribello continued to inundate me with his patter. "Did you bring what they told you?" he asked, glancing down at the briefcase hanging from my right hand. "We have to provide our own supplies around here, I'm sure you were told that much," he continued before I could get a word in. Then he turned his head slightly to sneak a glance around the storefront office, which consisted of eight desks, only half of them occupied, surrounded by towering rows of filing cabinets that came within a few feet of the ceiling. "And don't make any plans for lunch," he said. "I'm going to take you someplace. There are some things you might want to know. Information, anecdotes. There's one particular anecdote . . . but we'll let that wait. You'll need to get your bearings around here."

Ribello then made sure I knew what desk I'd been assigned, pointing out the one closest to the window of the storefront office. "That used to be my desk. Now that you're with us I can move to one of the desks farther back." Anticipating Ribello's next query, I told him that I had already received instructions regarding my tasks, which consisted entirely of processing various forms for the Quine Organization, a company whose interests and activities penetrate into every enterprise, both public and private, on this side of the border. Its headquarters are located far from the town where I secured a job working for them, a remote town that's even quite distant from any of the company's regional centers of operation. In such a place, and many others like it, the Quine Organization also maintains offices, even if they are just dingy storefront affairs permeated by a sour, briny odor. This smell could not be ignored and led me to speculate that before this building had been taken over as a facility for processing various forms relating to the monopolist Q. Org, as it is often called for shorthand, it had long been occupied by a pickle shop. You might be interested to know that this speculation was later confirmed by Ribello, who had taken it upon himself to help me get my bearings in my new job, which was also my first job since arriving in this little two-street town.

As I sat down at my desk, where a lofty stack of forms stood waiting to be processed, I tried to put my encounter with Ribello out of my head. I was very much on edge for reasons that you well know (my nervous condition and so forth), but in addition I was suffering from a lack of proper rest. A large part of the blame for my deprivation of sleep could be attributed to the woman who ran the apartment house where I lived in a single room on the top floor. For weeks I'd been pleading with her to do something about the noises that came from the space underneath the roof of the building, which was directly above the ceiling of my room. This was a quite small room made that much smaller because one side of it was steeply slanted in parallel to the slanted roof above. I didn't want to come out and say to the woman that there were mice or some other kind of vermin living under the roof of the building which she ran, but that was my implication when I told her about the "noises." In fact, these noises suggested something far more sizable, and somehow less identifiable, than a pack of run-of-the-mill vermin. She kept telling me that the problem would be seen to, although it never was. Finally, on the morning which was supposed to be the first day of my new job—after several weeks of struggling with inadequate sleep in addition to the agitations deriving from my nervous condition—I thought I would just make an end of it right there in that one-room apartment on the top floor of a building in a two-street town on the opposite side of the border from the place where I had lived my whole life and to where it seemed I would never be able to return. For the longest time I sat on the edge of my bed holding a bottle of nerve medicine, shifting it from one hand to the other and thinking, "When I stop shifting this bottle back and forth (an action that seemed to be occurring without the intervention or control of my mind), if I find myself holding it in my left hand I'll swallow the entire contents and make an end of it, and if I find myself holding it in my right hand I'll go and start working in a storefront office for the Quine Organization."

I don't actually recall in which hand the bottle ended up, or whether I dropped it on the floor in passing it from hand to hand, or what in the world happened. All I know is that I turned up at that storefront office, and, as soon as I stepped inside, Ribello was all over me with his nonsense about how he would help me get my bearings. And now, while I was processing forms one after another like a machine, I also had to anticipate going to lunch with this individual. None of the other three persons in the office—two middle-aged men and an elderly woman who sat in the far corner—had exercised the least presumption toward me, as had Ribello, whom I already regarded as an unendurable person. I credited the others for their consideration and sensitivity, but of course there might have been any number of reasons why they left me alone that morning. I remember that the doctor who was treating us both, and whom I take it you are still seeing, was fond of saying, as if in wise counsel, "However much you may believe otherwise, nothing in this world is unendurable—nothing." If he hadn't gotten me to believe that, I might have been more circumspect about him and wouldn't be in the position I am today, exiled on this side of the border where fogs configure themselves with an astonishing regularity. These fogs are thick and gray; they crawl down my throat and all but cut off my breathing.

Throughout that morning I tried to process as many forms as possible, if only to keep my mind off the whole state of affairs that made up my existence, added to which was having to go to lunch with Ribello. I had brought along something to eat, something that would keep in my briefcase without going rotten too soon. And for some hours the need to consume these few items I had stored in my briefcase was acutely affecting me, yet Ribello gave no sign that he was ready to take me to this eating place he had in mind. I didn't know exactly what time it was, since there wasn't a clock in the office and none of the others seemed to have taken a break for lunch, or anything else for that matter.

But I was beginning to feel light-headed and anxious. Even more than food, I needed the medication that I left behind in my one-room apartment.

Outside the front window I couldn't see what was going on in the street due to an especially dense fog that formed sometime around mid morning and hung about the town for the rest of the day. I had almost finished processing all the forms that were on my desk, which was far more work than I initially calculated I would be able to accomplish in a single day. When there were only a few forms left, the elderly woman who sat in the corner shuffled over to me with a new stack that was twice the size of the first, letting them fall on my desk with a thump. I watched her limp back to her place in the corner, her breath now audibly labored from the effort of carrying such a weighty pile of forms. While I was turned in my seat, I saw Ribello smiling and nodding at me as he pointed at his wristwatch. Then he pulled out a coat from underneath his desk. It seemed that it was finally time for us to go to lunch, although none of the others budged or blinked as we walked past them and left the office through a back door that Ribello pointed me toward.

Outside was a narrow alley which ran behind the storefront office and adjacent structures. As soon as we were out of the building I asked Ribello the time, but his only reply was, "We'll have to hurry if we want to get there before closing." Eventually I found that it was almost the end of the working day, or what I would have considered to be such. "The hours are irregular," Ribello informed me as we rushed down the alley where the back walls of various structures stood on one side and high wooden fences on the other, the fog hugging close to both of them.

"What do you mean, irregular?" I said.

"Did I say irregular? I meant to say *indefinite*," he replied. "There's always a great deal of work to be done. I'm sure the others were as glad to see you arrive this morning as I was, even if they didn't show it. We're perpetually shorthanded. All right, here we are," said Ribello as he guided me toward an alley door with a light dimly glowing above it.

It was a small place, not much larger than my apartment, with only a few tables. There were no customers other than ourselves, and most of the lights had been turned off. "You're still open, aren't you?" said Ribello to a man in a dirty apron who looked as if he hadn't shaved for several days.

"Soon we close," the man said. "You sit there."

We sat where we were told to sit, and soon afterward a woman brought two cups of coffee, slamming them in front of us on the table. I looked at Ribello and saw him pulling a sandwich wrapped in wax paper out of his coat pocket. "Didn't you bring your lunch?" he said. I told him that I thought we were going to a place that served food. "No, it's just a coffeehouse," Ribello said as he bit into his sandwich. "But that's all right. The coffee here is very strong. After drinking a cup you won't have any appetite at all. And you'll be ready to face all those forms that Erma hauled over to your desk. I thought she was going to drop dead for sure."

"I don't drink coffee," I said. "It makes me—" I didn't want to say that coffee made me terribly nervous, you understand. So I just said that it didn't agree with me.

Ribello set down his sandwich for a moment and stared at me. "Oh dear," he said, running a hand over his balding head.

"What's wrong?"

"Hatcher didn't drink coffee."

"Who is Hatcher?"

Taking up his sandwich once again, Ribello continued eating while he spoke. "Hatcher was the employee you were hired to replace. That's the anecdote I wanted to relate to you in private. About him. Now it seems I might be doing more harm than good. I really did want to help you get your bearings."

"Nevertheless," I said as I watched Ribello finish off his sandwich.

Ribello wiped his hands together to shake free the crumbs clinging to them. He adjusted the undersized eyeglasses which seemed as if they might slip off his face at any moment. Then he took out a pack of cigarettes. Although he didn't offer me any of his sandwich, he did offer me a cigarette.

"I don't smoke," I told him.

"You should, especially if you don't drink coffee. Hatcher smoked, but his brand of cigarettes was very mild. I don't suppose it really matters, your not being a smoker, since they don't allow us to smoke in the office anymore. We received a memo from headquarters. They said that the smoke got into the forms. I don't know why that should make any difference."

"What about the pickle smell?" I said.

"For some reason they don't mind that."

"Why don't you just go out into the alley to smoke?"

"Too much work to do. Every minute counts. We're shorthanded as it is. We've always been shorthanded, but the work still has to get done. They never explained to you about the working hours?"

I was hesitant to reveal that I had gotten my position not by applying to the company, but through the influence of my doctor, who is the only doctor in this two-street town. He wrote down the address of the storefront office for me on his prescription pad, as if the job with Q. Org were another type of medication he was using to treat me. I was suspicious, especially after what happened with the doctor who treated us both for so long. His therapy, as you know from my previous correspondence, was to put me on a train that traveled clear across the country and over the border. This was supposed to help me overcome my dread of straying too far from my own home, and perhaps effect a breakthrough with all the other fears accompanying my nervous condition. I told him that I couldn't possibly endure such a venture, but he only repeated his ridiculous maxim that nothing in the world is unendurable. To make things worse, he wouldn't allow me to bring along any medication, although of course I did. But this didn't help me in the least, not when I was traveling through the mountains with only bottomless gorges on either side of the train tracks and an infinite sky above. In those moments, which were eternal I assure you, I had no location in the universe, nothing to grasp for that minimum of security which every creature needs merely to exist without suffering from the sensation that everything is spinning ever faster on a cosmic carousel with only endless blackness at the edge of that wheeling ride. I know that your condition differs from mine, and therefore you have no means by which to fully comprehend my ordeals, just as I cannot fully comprehend yours. But I do acknowledge that both our conditions are unendurable, despite the doctor's secondhand platitude that nothing in this world is unendurable. I've even come to believe that the world itself, by its very nature, is unendurable. It's only our responses to this fact that deviate: mine being a predominantly response of passive terror approaching absolute panic; yours being predominantly a response of gruesome obsessions that you fear you might act upon. When the train that the doctor put me on finally made its first stop outside of this two street town across the border, I swore that I would kill myself rather than make the return trip. Fortunately, or so it seemed at the time, I soon found a doctor who treated my state of severe disorientation and acute panic. He also assisted me in attaining a visa and working papers. Thus, after considering the matter, I ultimately told Ribello that my reference for the position in the storefront office had in fact come from my doctor.

"That explains it, then," he said.

"Explains what?"

"All doctors work for the Quine Organization. Sooner or later he would have brought you in. That's how Hatcher was brought in. But he couldn't persevere. He couldn't take the fact that we were shorthanded and that we would always be shorthanded. And when he found out about the indefinite hours . . . well, he exploded right in the office."

"He had a breakdown?" I said.

"I suppose you could call it that. One day he just jumped up from his desk and started ranting about how we were always shorthanded . . . and the indefinite hours. Then he became violent, turning over several of the empty desks in the office and shouting, 'We won't be needing these.' He also pulled out some file drawers, throwing their contents all over the place. Finally he started tearing up the forms, ones that hadn't yet been processed. That's when Pilsen intervened."

"Which one is he?"

"The large man with the mustache who sits at the back of the office. Pilsen grabbed Hatcher and tossed him into the street. That was it for Hatcher. Within a few days he was officially dismissed from the company. I processed the form myself. There was no going back for him. He was completely ruined," said Ribello as he took a sip of coffee and then lit another cigarette.

"I don't understand. How was he ruined?" I said.

"It didn't happen all at once," explained Ribello. "These things never do. I told you that Hatcher was a cigarette smoker. Very mild cigarettes that he special ordered. Well, one day he went to the store where he purchased his cigarettes and was told that the particular brand he used, which was the only brand he could tolerate, was no longer available."

"Not exactly the end of the world," I said.

"No, not in itself," said Ribello. "But that was just the beginning. The same thing that happened with his cigarettes was repeated when he tried to acquire certain foods he needed for his special diet. Those were also no longer available. Worst of all, none of his medications were in stock anywhere in town, or so he was told. Hatcher required a whole shelf of pharmaceuticals to keep him going, far more than anyone else I've ever known. Most important to him were the medications he took to control his phobias. He especially suffered from a severe case of arachnophobia. I remember one day in the office when he noticed a spider making its way across the ceiling. He was always on the lookout for even the tiniest of spiders. He practically became hysterical, insisting that one of us exterminate the spider or he would stop processing forms. He had us crawling around on top of the filing cabinets trying to get at the little creature. After Pilsen finally caught the thing and killed it, Hatcher demanded to see its dead body and to have it thrown out into the street. We even had to call in exterminators, at the company's expense, before Hatcher would return to work. But after he was dismissed from the company, Hatcher was unable to procure any of his old medications that allowed him to keep his phobias relatively in check. Of course the doctor was no help to him, since all doctors are also employees of Q. Org."

"What about doctors on the other side of the border," I said. "Do they also work for the company?"

"I'm not sure," said Ribello. "It could be. In any case, I saw Hatcher while I was on my way to the office one day. I asked him how he was getting along, even though he obviously was a complete wreck, almost totally ruined. He did say that he was receiving some kind of treatment for his phobias from an old woman who lived at the edge of town. He didn't specify the nature of this treatment, and since I was in a hurry to get to the office I didn't inquire about it. Later I heard that the old woman, who was known to make concoctions out of various herbs and plants, was treating Hatcher's arachnophobia with a medicine which she distilled from spider venom."

"A homeopathic remedy of sorts," I said.

"Perhaps," said Ribello in a distant tone of voice.

At this point the unshaven man came over to the table and told us that he was closing for the day. Since Ribello had invited me to lunch, such as it was, I assumed that he would pay for the coffee, especially since I hadn't taken a sip of mine. But I noted that he put down on the table only enough money for himself, and so I was forced to do the same. Then, just before we turned to leave, he reached for my untouched cup and quickly gulped down its contents. "No sense in it going to waste," he said.

Walking back to the office through the narrow, fog-strewn alley, I prompted Ribello for whatever else he could tell me about the man whose position in the storefront office I was hired to fill. His response, however, was less than enlightening and seemed to wander into realms of hearsay and rumor. Ribello himself never again saw Hatcher after their meeting in the street. In fact, it was around this time that Hatcher seemed to disappear entirely—the culmination, in Ribello's view, of the man's ruin. Afterward a number of stories circulated around town that seemed relevant to Hatcher's case, however bizarre they may have been. No doubt others aside from Ribello were aware of the treatments Hatcher had been taking from the old woman living on the edge of town. This seemed to provide the basis for the strange anecdotes which were being spread about, most of them originating among children and given little credence by the average citizen. Most prevalent among these anecdotes were sightings of a "spider thing" about the size of a cat. This fabulous creature was purportedly seen by numerous children as they played in the streets and back alleys of the town. They called it the "nobby monster," the source of this childish phrase being that, added to the creature's resemblance to a monstrous spider, it also displayed a knob-like protrusion from its body that looked very much like a human head. This aspect of the story was confirmed by a few older persons whose testimony was invariably dismissed as the product of the medications that had been prescribed for them, even though practically everyone in town could be discredited for the same reason, since they are all—that is, we are all—taking one kind of drug or another in order to keep functioning in a normal manner. There came a time, however, when sightings of the so-called nobby monster ceased altogether, both among children and older, heavily medicated persons. Nor was Hatcher ever again seen around town.

"He just abandoned his apartment, taking nothing with him," said Ribello just as we reached the alley door of the office. "I believe he lived somewhere near you, perhaps even in the same building. I hear that the woman who ran the apartment house wasn't put out at all by Hatcher's disappearance, since he was always demanding that she accommodate his phobias by bringing in exterminators at least once a week."

I held open the door for Ribello but he didn't take a step toward the building. "Oh no," he said. "My work's done for the day. I'm going home to get some sleep. We have to rest sometime if we're to process the company's forms at an efficient pace. But I'll be seeing you soon."

After a few moments Ribello could no longer be seen at all through the fog. I went back inside the office, my mind fixed on only one thing: the items of food stashed within my briefcase. But I wasn't two steps inside when I was cornered by Pilsen near the lavatories. "What did Ribello say to you?" he said. "It was about the Hatcher business, wasn't it?"

"We just went out for a cup of coffee," I said, for some reason concerned to keep Ribello's confidence.

"But you didn't bring your lunch. You've been working all day, and you haven't had anything to eat. It's practically dark now, your first day on the job. And Ribello doesn't make sure you take your lunch."

"How do you know we didn't go somewhere to eat?"

"Ribello only goes to that one place," Pilsen said. "And it doesn't serve food."

"Well, I admit it. We went to the place that doesn't serve food, and now I'm famished. So if I could just return to my desk . . ."

But Pilsen, a large man with a large mustache, grabbed the collar of my coat and pulled me back toward the lavatories.

"What did Ribello say about the Hatcher business?"

"Why don't you ask him?"

"Because he's a congenital liar. It's a sickness with him—one of many. You see how he dresses, how he looks. He's a lunatic, even if he is a very good worker. But whatever he told you about Hatcher is completely false."

"Some of it did sound far-fetched," I said, now caught between the confidences of Ribello, who may have been no more than a congenital liar, and Pilsen, who was a large man and probably someone I didn't want to offend.

"Far-fetched is right," said Pilsen. "The fact is that Hatcher was promoted to work in one of the company's regional centers. He may even have moved on to company headquarters by now. He was very ambitious."

"Then there's nothing to say. I appreciate your straightening me out concerning this Hatcher business. Now, if you don't mind, I'd like to go back to my desk. I'm really very hungry."

Pilsen didn't say another word, but he watched me as I walked to my desk. And I felt that he continued to watch me from his place at the back of the office. As I ate the few items of food I kept in my briefcase, I also made it quite conspicuous that I was processing forms at the same time, not lagging behind in my work. Nevertheless, I wasn't sure that this ferocious display of form processing was even necessary, as Ribello had implied was the case, due to the monumental quantity of work we needed to accomplish with a perpetually shorthanded staff. I wondered if Pilsen wasn't right about Ribello. Specifically, I wondered if Ribello's assertion that our working schedule was "indefinite" had any truth to it. Yet several more hours passed and still no one, except Ribello, had gone home since I arrived at the office early that morning. Finally I heard one of the three persons sitting behind me stand up from his, or possibly her, desk. Moments later, Pilsen walked passed me wearing his coat. He was also carrying his large briefcase, so I surmised that he was leaving for the day, which was now evening, when he exited the office through the front door. After waiting a short while, I did the same.

I had walked only a block or so from the storefront office when I saw Ribello heading toward me. He was now wearing a different set of mismatched clothes. "You're leaving already?" he said when he stopped in front of me on the sidewalk.

"I thought you were going home to get some sleep," I said.

"I did go home, and I did get some sleep. Now I'm going back to work."

"I talked to Pilsen, or rather he talked to me."

"I see," said Ribello. "I see very well. And I suppose he asked what I might have said about Hatcher."

"In fact he did," I said.

"He told you that everything I said was just nonsense, that I was some kind of confirmed malcontent who made up stories that showed the company in a bad light."

"Something along those lines," I said.

"That's just what he would say."

"Why is that?"

"Because he's a company spy. He doesn't want you hearing what's what on your first day. Most of all he doesn't want you to hear about Hatcher. He was the one who informed on Hatcher and started the whole thing. He was the one who ruined Hatcher. That old woman I told you about who lives on the edge of town. She works for the company's chemical division, and Pilsen keeps an eye on her too. I heard from someone who works at one of the regional centers that the old woman was assigned to one of the company's biggest projects—a line of drugs that would treat very specific disorders, such as Hatcher's arachnophobia. It would have made Q. Org twice the company it is today, and on both sides of the border. But there was a problem."

"I don't think I want to hear anymore."

"You should hear this. The old woman was almost taken off the company payroll because she was using more than just her esoteric knowledge of herbs and plants. The chemical engineers at company headquarters gave her detailed instructions to come up with variations on their basic formula. But she was moving in another direction entirely and following completely unsanctioned practices, primarily those of an occult nature."

"You said she was *almost* taken off the company payroll."

"That's right. They blamed her for Hatcher's disappearance. Hatcher was very important to them as an experimental subject. Everything was set up to make him a guinea pig—denying him his usual brand of cigarettes, taking him off his special diet and his medications. They went through a great deal of trouble. Hatcher was being cleansed for what the old woman, along with the company's chemical engineers, intended to put into him. The spider venom made some kind of sense. But, as I said, the old woman was also following practices that weren't sanctioned by the company. And they needed someone to blame for Hatcher's disappearance. That's why she was almost taken off the payroll."

"So Hatcher was an experiment," I said.

"That's what happens when you explode the way he did, ranting about the unending workload we were expected to handle and how the company always left us shorthanded. The question remains, however. Was the Hatcher experiment a success or a failure?"

Ribello then looked at his wristwatch and said that we would talk further about Hatcher, the Quine Organization, and a host of other matters he wanted to share with me. "I was so glad to see you walk into the office this morning. We have so many forms to process. So I'll be seeing you in, what, a few hours or so?" Without waiting for my response, Ribello rushed down the sidewalk toward the storefront office.

When I reached the door to my one-room apartment, everything within me was screaming out for sleep and medication. But I paused when I heard footsteps moving toward me from the end of the dim hallway. It was the woman who operated the apartment house, and she was carrying in her arms what looked like a bundle of dirty linen.

"Cobwebs," she said without my asking her. She turned and pointed her head back toward a set of stairs down the hallway, the kind of pull-down steps that lead up to an attic. "We do keep our houses clean here, no matter what some people from across the border may think. It's quite a job, but at least I've made a start."

I couldn't help but stare in silence at the incredible wadding of cob-webs the woman bore in her arms as she began to make her way down-stairs. Some vague thoughts occurred to me, and I called to the woman. "If you're finished for the time being I can put up those stairs to the attic."

"That's good of you, thanks," she shouted up the stairwell. "I'll bring in the exterminator soon, just as you asked. I don't know exactly what's up there but I'm sure it's more than I can deal with myself."

I understood what she meant only after I ascended into the attic and saw for myself what she had seen. At the top of the stairs there was only a single lightbulb which didn't begin to illuminate those vast and shad-owed spaces. What I did see were the dead bodies, or parts of bodies, of more than a few rats. Some of these creatures looked as if they had escaped from just the sort of thick, heaping cobwebs which I had seen the woman who ran the apartment house carrying in her arms. It clung to the bodies of the rodents just as the dense, gray fog clung to everything in this town. Furthermore, all of these bodies seemed to be in a state of deformity . . . or perhaps transition. When I looked closely at them I could see that, in addition to the four legs normally allowed them by nature, there were also four other legs that had begun sprouting from their undersides. Whatever had killed these vermin had also begun to change them.

But not all of the affected rodents had died or been partially eaten. Later investigations I made into the attic, once I had persuaded the woman who ran the apartment house to defer calling in the extermina-tor, revealed rats and other vermin with physical changes even more advanced. These changes explained the indefinable noises I had heard since moving into my one-room apartment just beneath the roof of the building, with the attic between.

Some of the things I saw had eight legs of equal length and were able to negotiate the walls of the attic and crawl across the slanted ceiling just under the roof. Others had even begun making webs of their own. I think you would have recognized much of this, my friend, as something out of your own gruesome obsessions. Fortunately my own fears did not include arachnophobia, as was the case with Hatcher. (Nonetheless, I did ingest heavy doses of my medication before proceeding into the attic.) When I finally located him in the most remote corner of the attic I saw the knob-like head of a human being protruding from the pale, puffy body of a giant spider, or spider-thing. He was in the act of injecting his own venom into another verminous citizen of the attic. As soon as his pinpoint eyes noticed mine he released the creature, which squeaked away to begin its own transformation.

I couldn't imagine that Hatcher desired to continue his existence in that state. As I approached him he made no move of either aggression or flight. And when I took out the carving knife I had brought with me it seemed that he lifted his head and showed me his tiny throat. He had made his decision, just as I had made mine: I never returned to the storefront office to process forms for the Quine Organization, in whose employ are all the doctors on this side of the border . . . and perhaps also on your side. It is now my conviction that our own doctor has long been working for this company. At the very least I blame him for my exile to this remote, two-street town of fog and nightmares. At worst, I think it was his intention to deliver me across the border to become another slave or experimental subject for the company he serves.

I prepared two vials of the venom I extracted from Hatcher's body. The first I've already used on the doctor who has been treating me on this side of the border, even if the culmination of that treatment was to be imprisoned in a storefront office processing folders for an indefinite number of hours lasting the remainder of my indefinite existence. I'm still watching him suffer his painful mutations while I help myself to all the medications I please from the cabinets in his office. Before morning comes I'll put him out of his misery, and his medications will put me out of mine.

The second vial I offer to you, my friend. For so long you have suffered from such gruesome obsessions which our doctor did not, or would not, alleviate. Do with this medicine what you must. Do with it what your obsessions dictate. You might even consider, at just the right moment, giving the doctor my greetings . . . and reminding him that nothing in this world is unendurable—nothing.

The Shadow

Thomas M. Disch

*Thomas M. Disch (www.michaelscycles.freeserve.co.uk/tmd. htm) lives
in New York City and in rural Pennsylvania. He is a prominent science
fiction writer who occasionally writes fantasy and horror. Though his
early reputation was based on the excellence of his SF novels—*The
Genocides *(1965),* The Puppies of Terra *(1966), and* Camp Concentration *(1968)—he has a broad range and has had success outside the SF &
fantasy field as a poet, critic, and novelist.* On Wings of Song *(1979) was
his last published SF novel. He published two horror novels,* The Busi-
nessman: A Tale of Terror *(1984) and* The M. D.: A Horror Story
*(1991). His most notable contributions to American pop culture are his
children's books,* The Brave Little Toaster *(1981) and* The Brave Little
Toaster Goes to Mars, *(1988), both of which have been made into Dis-
ney films. Though the Toaster books have the earnestness appropriate to
their audience, usually Disch has a wicked sense of humor.*

"The Shadow," which appeared in F&SF, *shows Disch in his dark
satirical mode. It is one of several good stories we've seen recently dealing with Alzheimer's. Here Disch gives this sensitive subject a treatment
reminiscent of the dark fantastic tales of E.T.A. Hoffmann, something
that shouldn't work, but does!*

Her neighbors said of Angie Sweetwater that she was afraid of her own shadow, and in a way they were right, though not in the way they meant and not in any way that Angie—or her neighbors, for that matter—could have understood. The thing is, Angie had a nasty shadow, always thinking dark thoughts and itching to have a life of its own away from Angie and the little brick house on Wythe Lane where she lived all by herself. She'd lived there alone like that for eighteen years ever since her husband Roy's freak accident on I-95. He'd taken the exit ramp too fast, there was ice, and the car went over the shoulder. Roy, who never used his safety belt, was catapulted forty feet and had his head laid open by the sign that set the speed limit on the ramp at 30. The Buick wasn't scratched.

Angie had never learned to drive a car, so after the accident she was pretty much at a loss for how to do all those ordinary things like shopping that she'd depended on Roy for. There wasn't a grocery or convenience store anywhere within walking distance. Not that Angie ever did that much walking or would have. She got the exercise she needed out in the garden—or she used to, before the accident. The neighbors joked that she was getting to be just as planted as the old Buick inside the garage. Mrs. Deaver, two houses down the street, offered to teach her to drive, but Angie's reply was a flat no thank you. She relied on her son Tom to chauffeur her anywhere she needed to go, or else a taxi. And the Shop-Rite manager, who lived at the very end of Wythe Lane, delivered her groceries to her door as a special favor, even though Shop-Rite as a general rule didn't do deliveries.

So that was how she'd got along for years, eating frozen dinners and getting out of the house less and less, especially after Tom and his family moved to Tacoma. His company was leaving the area, and it was either that, Tom said, or food stamps. Once he was settled, he promised to look for a city apartment for her nearby where he lived, but that was out of the question. Angie wasn't going to start living in any city at this point in her life. Tom swore Tacoma wasn't dangerous, but how would he know? That was ten years ago, since when Tom had managed to get back for a visit almost every year, and twice, for Christmas, he'd brought his family along.

She never complained. She didn't even have complaining thoughts. But her shadow did. Her shadow got to be one big knot of gloom and hungers, like a pot-bound houseplant with its roots all sickly and tangled together. Shadows are like plants. They need sunlight simply to exist. They need to feel the air stir around them. They need to feel something physical—a bug will do—light down from time to time and rub against them. Plants like a nice squirt of birdshit that'll leach down into their dirt, and our shadows have equivalent needs. They have hungers and daydreams and vague longings for what they think would be freedom. Usually, those daydreams come to nothing, like most people's, but that doesn't matter, so long as there is some kind of input. They can get along on next to nothing. TV will serve their purpose most of the time, just like for people. Shadows may not have much of a life of their own, but what they can see on TV supplies that basic lack. But Angie didn't watch much TV. Wythe Lane wasn't wired for cable, and the channels she could receive didn't show anything but foul language and violence. That would have suited her shadow fine, of course, but it was Angie who was in control of on and off. Shadows are usually helpless in that regard.

It finally reached the point where the only time Angie or her shadow ever stirred from the house was on Sunday mornings and, sometimes, on Wednesday evenings, when Angie's friend Lucille would pick her up and take her to the United Baptist Church in Chambersville. Lucille had been a beautician before she was married, so she also did Angie's hair and nails every two or three weeks, at Angie's home, after the Wednesday prayer meeting.

Angie's shadow was always keenly attentive to everything that Lucille said or did during the beauty treatments. Those Wednesdays were the high points of the shadow's limited life, and probably of Angie's as well. So when Lucille brought up the subject of *The Throne of Darkness* Angie's shadow was transfixed. It began to vibrate like a tuning fork that's heard the vibration it's been designed to pick up.

The Throne of Darkness was a paperback book by Cassandra Knye that Lucille had checked out, with four other paperbacks, from the Chambersville Municipal Library. Lucille had had a long-standing grievance with the library's book selection process and with the chief librarian, Edward Holme, but *The Throne of Darkness* represented something worse than anything up to now, an assault against the moral well-being of the entire community, especially the children. It was a threat that had to be met head on, and so Lucille was circulating a petition to have the book, and a number of others just like it, taken off the library shelves. Everyone at the prayer meeting had signed Lucille's petition, even Pastor Raines, though he'd refused to let Lucille read aloud the most offensive passages from the book, since they were there in the church basement.

But Lucille insisted on reading one of those passages now, while they waited for the tint to take. "Listen to this part, just listen. 'Locking herself away from the curious stares and whispers of the others, Sister Rosemond began to fear herself. She couldn't sleep, and when she did the figure of Ariston would appear before her robed in white with golden sandals on his feet. The sands of the desert eddied about him, as though obedient to his will. She, too, was obedient to his will. Nude and wet, she walked toward him across the burning sand. His arms embraced her, his lips parted in an obscene invitation. He drew away his white robe to reveal his grotesque nakedness and threw her down across—' "

"Please," said Angie. "Please don't read anymore. It's just too. . . . I wish you wouldn't."

"It gets worse," Lucille promised.

"I'm sure it does."

"But you can see, just from that much, that it's Satanism pure and simple. And any child can walk into that library and check out the book." There was no getting her off it, and Angie had to sit there while Lucille finished with her hair and listen to it all, how children were playing a game called Dungeons and Dragons and then committing suicide, and how there were books in the library along the same lines. How there were crimes that the police couldn't explain. Children who were missing. Pets dying mysteriously. On and on. Finally Angie had to claim a headache and ask Lucille to leave without doing her nails.

When Lucille was gone, Angie went on sitting in the middle of the kitchen with the queerest feeling inside her. She looked down at her hands, where they were resting on her knees, and they looked wrong, all wrinkled and knobby and discolored. Roy used to joke that her name was really Angina at times like that when she'd sit off by herself, not saying anything, claiming a headache. Which wasn't true, the name on her birth certificate was Angelica, but no one had ever called her by that name in her entire adult life. Roy said it made her sound like a Catholic.

While she sat there, with the peculiar feeling, her shadow was breaking loose. Shadows usually can't do that. Most of them always stay fastened to the people they're born with. Only if the person gets very weak and the shadow gets strong at the same time can the shadow break loose, and then the person usually dies soon after. You can see them like that in hospitals sometimes, though it mostly goes unnoticed, or misunderstood. People sitting by the bed may think a light comes into the person's eyes just before they die, but it's actually the reverse. Their shadows have left them, so their eyes look brighter for a little while before they finally go cloudy and dull at the very end.

Angie's shadow had been gaining strength all the while Lucille had been reading from *The Throne of Darkness*. When Lucille had taken her leave, she'd left the book behind, thinking Angie might look at it while she was by herself. Angie hadn't even noticed the book sitting there on the kitchen counter, but her shadow had.

Her shadow wanted to know more about Rosamond and Ariston, but from where Angie was sitting only the spine was visible, not the picture on the cover. So there was a kind of tug of war between Angie's feeling of queerness and her shadow's feeling, which was simpler and stronger, and finally it was her shadow who won. It broke loose, and now it was Angie who was helpless and her shadow who could move around and do things.

The shadow went over to the kitchen counter and looked at the cover of *The Throne of Darkness*. There was Ariston, his face all red but with deep shadows, as though he were standing above a bonfire, and there was Rosamond in a red silk gown that matched Ariston's face. Yes, the shadow thought. I'm so hungry. I want. . . .

But that was as far as it could get. It couldn't think what it was it wanted. It opened the book and turned some pages, but that didn't help. Shadows can't read. Once they tear loose from people, shadows can get pretty stupid. They are like cockroaches, hungry and restless.

The shadow remembered the Buick sitting in the garage. Tom had tried to get his mother to sell the car to a dealer he knew, but when she'd proved stubborn about that, Tom didn't insist. He respected her feelings, and besides he figured the car would be his soon enough—a vintage 1976 Buick with low mileage and not a flake of rust. So each time he'd come back to Wythe Lane, he'd futzed with the car, keeping it tuned and polished. An investment.

Angie's shadow got the keys from the kitchen drawer and went out to the garage and started up the Buick and backed it straight into the garage door. Each of the four little panes of glass in the door was cracked, but they didn't shatter. The shadow didn't know quite what to do. It tried to raise the garage door, but it had got stuck to the Buick's bumper. It got back into the car and put it into Drive and managed to tear the back bumper off the car. And that was it for the Buick. Its battery was dead. The shadow wasn't too stupid to understand that.

At that point Angie's shadow gave up on any idea of having a night on the town and went for a walk in the night air, which was freedom enough after all the time it had sat beside Angie in the house, doing nothing and wishing Angie were dead. It walked through the nearest backyards, setting a few dogs to barking, and then along a drainage ditch, where it finally fell asleep beside a cyclone fence designed to keep the neighborhood children from wandering onto the highway. Shadows need their sleep the same as people.

The shadow was awake and back in charge at the first glimmer of direct sunlight. For someone who had spent the night in a drainage ditch Angie looked in pretty good shape. Her metabolism had risen to the occasion, and though she was stiff in all her limbs, once her shadow had got her on her feet and brushed off the dead leaves, she looked like any other old lady standing in a drainage ditch at five A.M. on a May morning. Ordinarily just that would have been unusual and embarrassing enough to have incapacitated Angie, but the shadow had no compunctions about the neighbors and what they might have thought. It was aware of them, but only as a cockroach might be aware of the jars and boxes in the cupboard it inhabits, as potential sources of what it needed.

One of the neighbors in question appeared before the shadow now, Natalie, Mrs. Deaver's teenage daughter. She said, "Mrs. Sweetwater— you're up early."

The shadow smiled, and extended Angie's hand to be shaken. It said, "Could I have a cigarette." When there was no immediate response, it remembered to add, "Please."

"A cigarette? I'm afraid I don't smoke. I didn't think *you* did either, Mrs. Sweetwater."

"I used to. Then I didn't for a while. Now I'm a smoker again." The shadow smiled its most plausible smile, but it resolved, even as Natalie politely disengaged and started jogging again, not to risk another such encounter. The strain of pretending to be even such a simple creature as Angie Sweetwater was too taxing.

The shadow returned along Wythe Lane to Angie's little brick house, drawn there by its memory of something on the kitchen counter. And it was there still, unemptied, the ashtray in which Lucille had stubbed out her three cigarettes last night. One of the things that Angie, and her shadow, had enjoyed about Lucille's Wednesday visits was that Lucille was a smoker. Roy had been a smoker, too, and Angie had been as addicted to his secondhand smoke as Roy had been to it at firsthand. "I like how it smells," she would tell people when they asked her if they could smoke when they visited.

She even liked the smell of these old butts in the ashtray, or her shadow did. It bent low over the little square of stippled amber glass and took a deep, luxuriating whiff. Shadows have a special affinity for the *other* side of anything, its inverse, or obverse, or opposite. Not just whatever lies in darkness, but the dregs and refuse and wreckage that is left behind by floods or fires, the ashes in the grate, the fumes that linger in a garage or a basement. They take to such things by the same simple tropism that makes plants strain toward the sun or attracts bees to bright colors.

While certain complex tasks would have been beyond the shadow's limited competence (it could not have done the laundry, for instance, or made the bed), the shadow did understand that to smoke one of the butts from the ashtray it would have to be able to light it. But it could not think where Angie kept the matches, since she so infrequently had need of them that using them was not an ingrained habit, an automatism that came with the vehicle. It stood there stymied and peevish until it realized (it would probably have taken Angie as long to do so) that the stove could be used as a cigarette lighter.

It turned on the right front burner, and then, positioning the cigarette in Angie's pouted lips, stooped to get a light. It took care not to let anything but the splayed tip of the butt get close to the flame. At the first sting of smoke it drew back and savored the vaporized poisons of Lucille's Salem.

The very qualities that made tobacco lethal to human health made it dear to the shadow, but even so the tissues of Angie's throat, unused to the tickle of the smoke, reacted badly. The shadow could not stop coughing, but neither could it resist another drag of mentholated smoke, nor a third, though by then the coughing had become violent, a convulsion. It flicked the cigarette across the kitchen, a bull's-eye into the plastic garbage can beside the sink. Angie herself would not have been so accurate. In many ways her shadow was more comfortable in her skin than she.

While Angie's lungs recovered from their coughing fit in the platform rocker in the living room, the cigarette smoldered inside the garbage can, as it was engineered to do. A single wadded Kleenex caught fire, and flared, and, as it died, relayed its flame to the dry corner of an otherwise damp paper towel. Those flames in turn reached the crumpled cellophane that had been a cookie wrapper, after which, the entire contents of the can became a torch, the flames of which rose high enough to ignite the roll of towels in the dispenser and then the kitchen curtains and the flounce above.

From where it sat in the living room the shadow could not see the fire in the kitchen until it had spread beyond the area around the sink. Even when it became aware of what was happening it did not bestir itself to phone for help. Indeed, its impulse was rather to feed the flames than to damp them, from a sense that they were its own. Anyone who has built a great leaf-fire and seen the flames leap high has felt a similar vanity. It is our own shadow's rapture we share at such a moment, its sense of itself as something immense and unbounded, the shadow in mad-emperor mode.

As the flames spread through the house, flitting among those things most flammable, they also kindled scraps of psychic tinder in Angie's own sere soul. For it was she, not the shadow, who began to hum "Some Enchanted Evening," which long ago, at a bar in Orlando, Florida, a pianist had sung to her at Roy's particular request on their fourth anniversary. Somehow this May morning, as she sat in her burning house, the dear old tune seemed the key to her whole life. The melody seemed endless, with no point along the way she could stop at, so that finally it was the shadow and not Angie who had to take the initiative and stagger up from the rocker and out the front door, almost invisible by then behind the billowing black smoke.

While the neighbors gathered to watch the arrival of the firemen and their losing battle, Angie sat on the other side of Wythe Lane, sprawled in an Adirondack chair, a spectator at her own disaster, yet as little distressed as if it had been a crisis on the evening news, a war in West Africa or riots at the Mexican border.

The shadow, meanwhile, gorging on the fire's triumph was in a state of comatose surfeit, like a tick swollen with blood. When the emergency medical team showed up, it was determined, after Angie didn't answer their questions and they had filled out the appropriate forms, that she was in a state of shock. To spare everyone the discomfort of her inappropriate and weird lack of affect, Angie was sedated and taken off in the EMT ambulance.

When the sedative had worn off, Angie continued to pose a problem for the staff at Mercy Hospital, for she would not remain in her bed in the recovery ward (a temporary assignment) but would go wandering through the halls and lobby, confused and querulous. She couldn't understand why her clothes had been taken from her and she had nothing to wear but a paper examination gown that left her backside bare.

Anger was not an emotion in Angie's usual repertory. She could do nothing but weep and ask to talk with her son in Tacoma. But Angie could not remember his number, which was unlisted. The shadow, still gorged, did nothing to help, nor could it have. It let her dither about in the public areas of the hospital and make a fuss like an ill-tempered pet locked in a parked car.

By the time Tom was contacted and had got to the hospital, Angie had calmed down, and the shadow had again assumed control. It lay in the hospital bed and glowered dully at Tom and the various strangers who had questions about the fire. Once or twice it had asked for a cigarette, but this produced no response except, from Tom, a suspicious string of questions.

The hospital's diagnosis, which Tom did not think to question, was advanced Alzheimer's. Tom did not want to complicate his life by bringing his mother back to Tacoma with him. To what purpose? She couldn't be trusted under his family's roof, even if his wife would have accepted that idea, since Angie had probably been responsible for the fire that had destroyed her own house. A neighbor's daughter had seen Angie wandering about in a dazed manner on the morning of the fire, and at the hospital they had had to use restraints to keep her in her own bed. It was a sad situation, but not really that unusual.

For Alzheimer's the standard solution was a nursing home and then an averted gaze. Living at a great distance might actually be an advantage—out of sight, out of mind. And so, before Tom returned to Tacoma, Angie was taken to live at Raines Adult Home outside of Chambersville. The home was operated by Amos Raines, a cousin of the pastor of United Baptist, which made it seem not quite as heartless as leaving Mrs. Sweetwater with complete strangers. She would have her own room, and Tom was introduced to two of the other female residents, who were sufficiently self-possessed to shake his mother's hand and, with prompting, to say hello to her.

However, those two ladies, Mrs. Filbin and Mrs. Lynch, were about all the establishment could show for itself in terms of good P.R. The other residents, six males and three females, had been placed there by Chambersville Psychiatric Center under an adult care contract with the state. Basically, the Psychiatric Center used Raines Adult Home as a storage facility for its most hopeless geriatric cases, those with diagnoses, like Angie, of advanced Alzheimer's. Most of them were also like Angie in being under the control of their shadows, a not uncommon condition among those in nursing homes. Indeed, just as certain insects and the orchids that imitate them have co-evolved over the centuries so that their resemblance becomes ever more congruent, so shadows have co-evolved with those genuine behavioral disorders which offer them an alibi and a disguise—Alzheimer's commonly, but also autism, bipolar disorders, and some forms of schizophrenia.

It was not only Angie and other residents of the Raines Adult Home who were ruled by their shadows; so were two of the employees, the twin brothers Wilbur and Orville Halfacre. The Halfacres had spent almost their entire lives in institutional care, first, when abandoned in infancy, as recipients, now as dispersers. They were neither of them very bright, but they had both earned high school equivalency diplomas and gone on to receive training as medical technicians, and, in Wilbur's case, as a cosmetologist. Thus, they were qualified to minister to the needs of the home's residents, and the residents, in turn, met theirs.

Angie became the Halfacres' particular favorite, chiefly because there was something unusually docile in the way she submitted to male sexual demands. That had been so with Roy, who had tried to encourage her to play a more active and responsive role in their conjugal relations. It was even more the case with the Halfacres, who had spent some time in custody in their teenage years for practicing necrophilia. Because of their age there had been no permanent record of that unfortunate episode, but during the time they spent in a supervised environment their shadows had become ascendant in their lives. That they should become employees in such a place as Raines Adult Home had been almost inevitable, shadows being drawn to other shadows in the way that insects swarm about light bulbs. If it had not been the home, it would have been one of the local prisons, or a school of Special Education.

Such were the Halfacres. For we may as well speak of their shadows as though they *were* the Halfacres, and of Angie's shadow as though she and it were the same entity, for when a shadow has long been in command, the conventional boundaries between self and shadow blur and become unimportant. Who shall say that a particular crime was the work of someone's shadow or her own? More than once in her years at the home Angie's shadow committed an opportunistic act of malice (accidents are so common among the elderly), and the other resident shadows did the same, or tried to. Had her role ever been discovered, Angie could have protested that she was innocent, that she could not remember having released the switch or pulled the plug, and she might have passed a polygraph test when she testified to that effect. But increasingly Angie remembered nothing that she did, as her mind continued its long slow fade to gray. In such cases innocence becomes a semantic quibble, as it is so often in courts of law.

When shadows dominate those who are young and virile, like the Halfacres, their control has a different character than with someone like Angie. The shadows of the robust must give their hosts a freer rein, so that they can play an active role in the everyday world—at a job or a gym, on the highway, in a bar—and still be on call, as it were, for the shadow to command. These are the shadows who become momentarily notorious for some impulsive and seemingly motiveless crime, pushing a stranger in front of a train or shooting another driver in a fit of "road rage." Working at the home, the shadows of the Halfacre boys had achieved a modus vivendi that made such extreme outbursts unnecessary. Like children taking ritalin or diabetics protected by insulin, the Half-acres got along from day to day with the calming assistance of their own private harem, among whom Angie, as the most recent arrival and sturdiest, figured as odalisque-in-chief, a golden-age and mute Scheherazade.

Even for a genuine Alzheimer's victim, someone too out of it to resent having no other wardrobe than a blanket and adult diapers, the Adult Home might have seemed a sorry fate. Angie did have moments unattended by her shadow when she became conscious of the horror of her circumstances. Orville or Wilbur would be spooning cubes of Jell-O into her mouth (to their credit, they kept their charges clean and well-nourished), and she would be overwhelmed by a sense of abasement that made it impossible to swallow the food. Tears would run down her heavily rouged cheeks (Wilbur used his cosmetology training to keep his old ladies looking nice), and Wilbur would pause in his duties until the fit had passed and her feeding could resume. Surely, the oblivion of complete submission to her own shadow would have been preferred to such nightmare flickers of self-awareness.

As well to wish for death, however. Oblivion is never one of our options. Half of all Adult Homes would stand empty if one could just wish away unremitting misery and pain. Africa would be depopulated, along with all the prisons in Texas.

But who is to say there is no joy in Africa or in the prisons of Texas? Or none in the life of Angie Sweetwater, at least in her life as a shadow? She enjoyed good physical health, the attentions of two devoted admirers, and an uncommonly long life. When she was dressed for public display and it was her turn to be taken to a Sunday morning service at United Baptist, everyone agreed that Angie Sweetwater was the most presentable and best behaved of any of the visitors from the home. Sometimes just this mite of respect was all the comfort she required. At other times she would remember what churches were for and she would fold her hands and pray for her deliverance.

And you must pray along with her, good people, and hope to die before the same thing happens to you. For it makes no difference whether you are rich or poor, a homeless beggar or an ex-president, like Ronald Reagan. Like Angie, we all have shadows. Stand in the light and you will see your own.

Stitchery

~~~~~~~~~~

Devon Monk

Devon Monk (www.sff.net/campbell-awards/98auth.htm#Monk) lives in Salem, Oregon, with her husband and two sons, in what she describes as "a fourth-generation home, where the walls are reputed to be elastic and the back door is never closed." Her stories have appeared in Altair, Marion Zimmer Bradley's Fantasy Magazine, Odyssey, Pulp Eternity, *and* MZB's Sword and Sorceress Anthology. *She also writes a column and essays for a national fishing and hunting magazine. She is a member of the Next Wave Writers' Collective, along with fellow writers Charlene Brusso, Lynn Flewelling, James Hartley, and Jason Tanner.*

"Stichery" appeared in Black Gate, *the ambitious new genre fantasy magazine (subtitled* Adventures in Fantasy Literature) *in its second year of publication. This surreal tale is a really fantastic fantasy story, wild and outside, and worth comparing to the work of R.A. Lafferty. It's in the SF & fantasy tradition of stories about rural families with special talents, exploited by everyone from Ray Bradbury to Zenna Henderson in the last half-century or so. It's about families, love, and caring for others, about everyday heroism.*

Tilly shaded her eyes with her hand and peered over at the house. The grandma was sitting on the second-story window ledge, one bare foot rocking in the wind. Tilly had told her spring was a time of pastels and pinks, of fresh new things, but the grandma never paid her any mind. An endless trail of knitting spilled from her needles to the porch roof below, red as Christmas berries and as cheerfully out of season as the old girl herself.

Tilly sighed. Ever since she'd found the grandma at the DMV, knitting up all the wasted time folks left behind, she'd wondered what to do with her. The DMV people had wanted to send her to an old folks home, but Tilly had stepped in and taken the grandma home instead. Anyone who had the patience to catch up loose seconds and save them for later deserved to be looked after, as far as Tilly was concerned, even if the old girl wasn't in her right mind most of the time.

But then, most of Tilly's good intentions made for bad decisions. She shook her head and caught sight of her own hand held up to the sun. Patchwork scars deep in her flesh showed like a crazy-work of seams beneath her skin. Ned never liked to look at her hand when she put a light behind it, and Tilly didn't blame him. Normal folks stayed away from stitchery like her. As long as she didn't talk to Ned about stitching, they got along fine. She liked having him around, enough that she was pretty sure she'd fallen in love with the man, even if she'd never come out and told him so.

The beast beside her shifted and groaned, golden hooves sinking into the soft soil. Tilly looked down and tightened her grip on its halter.

"Ned!" she hollered. "I need your help with the beast." She stroked the poor thing's neck and squinted at Ned's boots, which stuck out from under the old gray Chevy in front of the house. The grandma, two stories up, hummed and knitted.

The beast lowered its head. Tilly stepped back. She'd secured half a tennis ball over its forehead nub with duct tape that wrapped around its jaw, but she wasn't stupid enough to get in the way of the beast's head. She'd seen it root up anthills and such with that nub. Didn't matter it was broke, it still worked.

Clouds stretched across the sky, fizzled away and still Ned didn't come out from under the truck. "Damn," she whispered. She patted the beast's neck a couple times and wondered what its coat really felt like. Ned had described it to her once, his hands being the ones he was born with and still full of feeling. He'd said the beast's coat was as soft and silky as her copper-brown hair. Tilly smiled at the memory. That man had a way with words.

"Ned! Now, ya hear?"

"Yes dear," the grandma called back.

"Not you, Granny. Ned."

"Really? I'm not sleepy. But if you say so."

Tilly caught sight of her easing back in through the window, then watched as she pulled the knitted scarf up and up like a red tongue. Tilly figured the grandma was making to come down to her.

"No. You stay there!"

And of course, that's when Ned decided to scoot himself out from under the truck and show his heads.

"Make up your mind," Right Ned called out to her. Left Ned just grinned that hard grin of his around a strand of grass in his teeth.

These were the kind of moments when she wished she'd never stopped work on that heat-seeking dung thrower.

Tilly took a nice deep lungful of pollen-laden air, sneezed and let go of the beast's halter while she wiped oil from her eyes. She hated her tears. Unlike Ned's, or the grandma's, hers were oily and smelled like hot sulfur. If she didn't scrub them off right away, they left streaks down her freckled cheeks.

Once Tilly could see straight again, she noticed the poor beast was even lower to the ground.

She cleared her throat and put some volume in her voice. "Ned, get over here, both of you! And Granny, you stay right where you are. Just keep knitting. You're doing fine."

The grandma poked her head out the window. A teasing wind lifted the white tendrils of her hair like dandelion down riding a child's wish. She waved one hand, bracelets clinking. "I'll be right there."

Tilly sighed. Best intentions and all that.

Ned walked over to where she and the beast stood under the apple tree. He was wearing his clean overalls today, which meant he wasn't thinking to get any real work done. Time to put another thought in those heads of his, she thought.

"Ned, you know you're my boyfriend, and I like you plenty, right?"

Right Ned nodded. "I reckon, Tilly," he said in that shy soft way that made her wish she'd rubbed off the stains beneath her eyes.

"Then you know that sometimes I need help with things around the property."

Left Ned must have known where she was going, 'cause he made that here-we-go-again look.

Tilly ignored him.

"The beast is looking pretty poor and I'm not sure what it needs. My hands don't work much for this, but yours should. Would you try and figure out what it wants?"

"Tilly," Right Ned said, "you know I gave up mingling with creatures when I gave up chew last winter."

"I know. And I know what it is, me asking this of you. But touching a mind isn't as addicting as chew, is it? And you kicked that habit, right? I mean, I wouldn't ask you to do it, but I just don't have any ideas left."

As if she'd told it to do so, the beast dropped and lay on its side. It stretched its neck out and rolled its eyes, each breath an effort.

Right Ned sighed, but Left Ned said, "You know I hate this, Til. You know I can't ever do it just once."

She looked down at the beast to avoid Left Ned's gaze. "If you have to, you could always mingle with me, Ned." She waited a moment, but there wasn't nothing but the sound of the beast's labored breathing. Tilly felt heat pulse out from the center of her cheeks and she swore inwardly. No matter how hard she tried, she just never seemed to handle things right. Ned and she were lovers, but he never touched her mind, not even when he was in the fever grip of passion. She hadn't asked him why, but figured it was her patchwork nature he took a dislike to. She swallowed once and tried again. "I mean if you'd want that."

"Tilly," Right Ned said, his voice soft.

"For the beast," Tilly cut in. Mingling was his business, and if he preferred animal minds, then that's the way it'd be. But there was no reason he should refuse to help the beast. "Please, Ned?"

Right Ned looked down at the beast with something like sympathy in his eyes. Left Ned just glared at Tilly hard and long.

Sometimes, Tilly thought, that man was a real pain.

"Just to see what it wants," Right Ned said.

Tilly nodded and Ned kneeled down. He held his hands above the beast's dirty white flanks.

Tilly watched, like she used to way back in his circus days, while Ned finally got his heads together, closed both sets of eyes and placed his palms on the once snowy-white side of the beast. Ned stiffened. He lifted up off of his heels a bit, then his whole body slumped.

Tilly bit her lip and waited. She knew it'd been a long time since he'd done this, and she hoped she was right about him not getting stuck mind-to-mind cozy with the ailing beast.

That's what had ended his days in the circus. He'd mingled with the ringmaster's daughter, and made her scream. The girl accused him of being dirty, illegal, patchwork, but Tilly knew none of that was true. When Ned was born, his mama didn't let doctors change the way he looked. Ned, all both of him, was more natural than most folks, certainly more than Tilly.

Ned still didn't move. His heads were bent so low, if she caught him from a side-view, she'd think he only had one head. His shoulders were hunched, soul-sensing fingers spread wide and palm-tight against the beast.

"Too hard," both Neds said, and Tilly shivered despite the warm air. When those boys worked in unison, it gave her the creeps.

The beast grunted, but it seemed each breath took just a little longer getting to.

"Warm, sunlit fields and soft, untouched laps. Home." Right Ned looked up at her, tears caught on his girl-pretty lashes. "Tilly, the beast wants to die."

"No," she said shaking her head. This had been the first beast she'd taken in, back when Mother and Father had left her to tend the property and all the souls within. It couldn't be old enough to die. "You're wrong, Ned," she said.

But Right Ned had closed his eyes again, bent toward the beast like his ears were in his palms.

Left Ned stared at her. She knew that look. It was the same one he used when the Sheriff had tried to take him to the medical research center back when he was just a little boy.

"You check again," she said. "Tell it we fenced the back field and the grass is plenty sweet, sweeter than those crazy dreams it's having. Tell it there's no reason to die."

"There's no time left for it, Til," Left Ned said. "Belly-wailing isn't gonna change anything."

She scowled, torn between trying to decide if she should take the beast to a doctor in town, or try to fix it herself. Then she heard the steady click, click of knitting needles coming closer. The grandma shuffled up to them, wearing a pale yellow nightgown and a pair of Tilly's black panties underneath. She knitted and looped, her huge black bag hanging from the crook of her arm. The yarn coming out of the bag was white now, instead of red.

Tilly gave Left Ned a look to let him know this wasn't done yet then turned to the grandma.

"Granny, why you coming down here? I told you it was okay to keep knitting back at the house."

"Yes, dear. But there's no time left, so I thought I'd come down. It's going to rain, you know."

Tilly glanced up at the sky. The sun was so hot, it'd practically burned a hole in the blue. Weren't a chance clouds could gather on a day like this.

"Sure thing, Granny," Tilly said gently. "You go on back to the house now. Don't want you to get wet."

She nodded. "So sweet," she said.

The beast groaned and Tilly spun on Ned.

"What did you do? You better not tell it to die, Ned, or so help me I'll give you headaches you'll never forget."

"Oh," the grandma said. "Maybe a little more time then?" She stopped knitting and began unraveling the string on the scarf, starting on the red side, farthest away from the loops of white thread on the needles. As she pulled, the yarn disappeared, melting before it even hit the ground. The beast took a couple nice, clear breaths, and moved its head a bit.

"Tilly, let it go," Right Ned said. "This fellow is old. It's his time to die."

"You're just being pigheaded, Til," Left Ned said.

Right Ned cleared his throat and Tilly knew he'd been thinking the same thing, just hadn't had the guts to say it.

The grandma hummed and pulled thread.

"It's not going to die," Tilly said.

"Tilly," said Right Ned, "it doesn't want to live anymore."

"I don't care what it wants," Tilly said, trying to keep the sound of tears out of her voice. "I'm going to take it into town to the doctor. You tell it to hold on. Spring isn't no time for dying."

"No time," the grandma agreed.

Granny stopped pulling on her yarn and right that second, the beast stopped breathing.

Under the apple tree got real quiet all of a sudden. Tilly glanced at the beast, lying still, its eyes fogged over and rolled up at that hard hot sun. Then she glanced at Ned. He looked white too, deathly white. That's when she remembered he still had his hands and probably his mind on the beast.

Damn. She took a couple big steps forward and pushed Ned hard. He tipped over onto the back of his nice clean overalls. He was stiff, his arms stuck up in the air, hands flat against the wind.

"Breathe, Ned," she said, as she moved around to touch his face with her fingers. "Both of you."

Ned breathed. He shuddered once and Left Ned moaned softly, then clamped his mouth hard.

Right Ned wiped tears from his eyes. "Holy, Tilly, that hurts, you know."

"Well you should have taken your hands off the beast before," and right there she just couldn't say anymore. The beast was dead, poor thing, and it was her fault. If she would have made up her mind faster, if she would have just taken it down to the doctor the moment she knew it was ill, it would still be alive. Tilly looked down at the pitiful collection of hide and bone and a hard hand of grief closed her throat.

Tears slipped down her face. She should have done something, anything, to save it.

The grandma tottered over to her, her huge knitting bag swinging on her elbow. She shushed Tilly and patted her arm with a paper-dry hand. "There, now, sweetness," she crooned. "There just wasn't any time left for it."

"Sure, Granny," Tilly whispered, eyeing the seven feet of red knitting that trailed from her bag. Seemed like there was plenty of time if the grandma had wanted to give it up. But Tilly didn't say anymore. That time was the grandma's to keep or give.

The grandma brightened. "Who wants some hot cocoa?" She took up the needles and pulled a handful of white thread from the bag. Loop, tuck, remove, she knitted her way slowly back to the house.

Tilly leaned against the trunk of the apple tree.

"I'm real sorry, Tilly," Right Ned said.

"It was my fault," Tilly said. "I didn't do the right thing. I didn't do anything. I killed it."

Left Ned said, "Shee-it," and spat.

"Tilly, you know better," Right Ned said gently. "Everything dies."

Ned came over and stood close by her, his arm wrapped over her shoulders. He was warm and strong and it felt real good to be comforted by him right then, though Tilly wouldn't have asked him to do it. She supposed that was one of the things she liked about him. He always seemed to know the right thing to do.

The wind picked up and a flock of starlings threw shadows against the ground. Tilly knew she had to fix what she'd done wrong. She pulled away from Ned and shivered as wind cooled the sweat down her back.

"I need you to go into town and get some pigs for the lizard. Would you do that for me, Ned?"

"Sure, Tilly, but . . ."

"But nothing," she said, maybe a little too fast. She smiled. "I'm fine, really. I've just got some burying to do."

Ned stood, and for a moment, both heads stared at her hard. She stared back at him.

"You did all you could, Tilly," Right Ned said.

Tilly nodded.

Ned turned and walked to the house. Tilly watched him swing into the battered Chevy. It wasn't until he had wrestled the truck down the road and around the bend that she looked at the beast again.

"But this mistake I can fix," she said.

The beast didn't reply, which was good considering the state it was in.

Tilly rolled up the sleeves of her cotton shirt. She picked up the beast and carried it to Father's workshop.

The workshop was away from the house a bit—down on the creek bank and so covered in brambles, not a brick or window showed through. Tilly was sweating pretty hard by the time she reached the door. She shifted the beast's weight, leaned back and stuck her fingers through bramble runners to catch and lift the wooden latch. Thorns scratched her hands, deep enough to be painful. She pushed the door open and stepped in.

It was cool and damp here, and smelled like earth, and river and sharp antiseptics. The shop was about the size of a double-wide horse stall, but instead of hay on the ground, there was concrete. A tall wide table took up most of the middle of the room and drawers lined the walls.

Tilly laid the beast on the table, then flipped the switch by the door. Lights powered by the water wheel up-creek snapped, clicked, then flickered on. Father told her it wasn't right to run the workshop on the house's electricity. He said all the power needed to do stitchery was in the river itself.

Tilly rubbed her hands on her jeans and saw the long scratches on her fingers. Blood seeped out, just enough to make sure the cuts were clean. Then hot pain flashed across her fingers. She breathed out real hard a couple times and tipped her palms to the light. The cuts were gone.

She was glad Ned wasn't here to see that.

"Awfully dark in here, dear."

Tilly spun. The grandma stood in the doorway and was practically naked, her thin nightgown translucent from the sunlight at her back. The knitting bag swung at her elbow, needles sticking out of the top of the bag like giant insect feelers.

"Granny, what are you doing down here?"

"I thought there'd be a little time before it rains." She shuffled into the room, her hands clasped in front of her. "Oh, now. Here's the poor thing. Is there anything we can do for it?" she asked.

Tilly shut the door and stood next to the table. "I think so. But I might need a little time."

"Oh my, yes." The grandma smiled and rummaged for her knitting.

Tilly opened drawers, and shivered at the cold air they expelled. One drawer was filled with thin spools of crystal thread—thread that held new parts to old parts and melted into whatever kind of flesh or muscle or bone needed so the new and old accepted each other as a complete whole. Tilly figured it was those crystal stitches in her hands that heated up so bad whenever she healed. She took a spool of the thread and opened another drawer.

Needles, wires, jars of liquid, delicate saws, tubes with rainbow colored labels, and every once in awhile, the leftover bits of something Father hadn't managed to put back together, filled the drawers. In one of the bigger drawers, Tilly found the body of a small pony. Its legs were missing, and its coat was brown, but other than that, it was nearly perfect.

"Granny," Tilly said as she put on a pair of heavy gloves, "I could use a little time now."

The grandma hummed and pulled stitches.

Tilly lifted the cold-preserved pony out of the drawer, and set it on the table next to the beast.

The room temperature had dropped to near-freezing. Tilly's breath came out in clouds, and her skin was cold with old sweat. She took off the gloves and used one of the saws on the beast's legs. She used tiny hot crystal stitches to attach the legs to the pony. Next, she removed and attached the forehead nub. Crystal thread and needle slid through bone and flesh equally and sent a thin line of steam into the cold air.

"My, you do this well," the grandma said.

"I just hope I do it right." Tilly opened the beast's chest and searched for its heart.

"Right as rain," the grandma said, "don't you worry, dear."

Right as rain, Tilly thought. No matter how hard she tried, she'd never done anything right in her life. She pushed that thought out of her mind and paid attention instead, to the beast.

* * *

Long after dark, she heard the grumble of the Chevy. Ned must have bartered with Mr. Campbell for the pigs, which was fine. Tilly liked a man who could stick to a budget.

The truck growled past the house and straight out to the lizard's corral.

Tilly got up from the chair she'd been dozing in and stretched stiffness out of her arms and back. She pulled her coat from the corner closet and listened a minute for the grandma. All was quiet from her upstairs room.

Tilly slipped out the front door, the screen snicking shut behind her. The night air was clear and cold. Stars chipped holes in the otherwise soft, black sky. Way off in the west, the moon hung, distant and oblivious to anything earthly. Tilly crossed her arms over her chest, and headed out to see if Ned needed any help with the pigs.

The track to the lizard's corral was rutted and hard to follow, but Tilly's feet knew it as well as every other inch of ground on the run-down ranch. She'd been down this path with Mother and Father the day she was born, and later, when she'd lost a year to the hot healing. Father said he'd carried her in his arms back and forth on the road, letting her body cool in the living air. That was a long time ago, before they left for better things in the big city.

The wind slipped down from the stars, carrying a breath of ice with it. Tilly shivered. She wondered if Ned would understand what she'd done. Wondered if he'd leave when he found out. Ned believed that stitchery was wrong. He never had himself re-made, though he'd had a chance to when he was a boy, before the laws against such things were passed.

Tilly took the curve in the track and walked into the grass. She could smell the lizard, musty and dry, like mold found in old closets, but ten or a hundred times stronger than that.

She expected to hear the pigs, but only heard the lizard shifting inside the fence—his claws sheathing in and out of the ground, like shovel blades cutting dirt.

There was a boat-sail snap and Tilly felt heat as the lizard pulled its wings away from its body, but no charred smell of pig-ka-bob, no flame in the air.

Something was wrong.

Tilly picked up the pace and climbed the fence. She ducked the electric line at the top, sidled through the bars and dropped down inside the corral.

The lizard, a good four-feet taller than her, swung his big triangle head her way, eyes shining with ambient moonlight. It didn't see too good anymore, so Tilly held still and let it smell her. Then she walked across the corral toward the silent pigs in the fenced-off feeding chute.

As she drew closer, she saw a bigger shadow in with the pigs. Ned was on his knees in the middle of them all, hands spread wide and pushed tight against dirty hides.

Freak, Tilly thought fondly. You'll mingle with pig brains, but won't touch your willing girlfriend.

"Ned," she said. She unlatched the electric wire at the gate to the chute and stepped in. "Now who's being pig-headed?"

Left Ned looked up and scowled. Right Ned looked up too, but his pretty eyes were glazed, his face slack.

"Ned. Let the pigs go," she said, her words soft and sure, and for Right Ned only.

He looked down at his hands and after a minute seemed to realize they were on the pigs. He drew back, embarrassed.

Left Ned chuckled.

"Sorry," Right Ned said. "I'm sorry, Tilly. It was just after today. Getting caught in the dying, I guess, I needed to feel living again. I told you once I do it, I want it more." He stepped away from the pigs and rubbed his palms on his overalls. "I'm sorry." The pigs began grunting and rooting around.

"That's okay," Tilly said because he didn't know what she'd done either. "Let's go on back to the house and get some sleep, okay?"

The night was interrupted by a whinny. It was a far off, spooky sound, but any fool could tell what it was. The beast.

Ned was no fool. "Tilly," he said, "what did you do?"

"I fixed it up a bit, that's all."

"Did you bring the beast back from death?" Real honest horror carried his words up an octave.

"Granny and I, we used a little time so I could get the fix-up bits out of Father's workshop and apply them to the beast. I didn't really stitch it, Ned, I took parts of the old beast and made a new beast just like it."

"Holy, Tilly," Ned said. "That's plain wrong. You don't fix up dead things and you don't make copies of them. Don't you know how illegal that is? For Holy sake, it's why your Daddy left you."

"You're talking crazy," Tilly said, trying to be calm, even though he was starting to scare her. "Father and Mother went to the big city for better things."

"For jail time, Tilly. They went to jail. Because they made things, like the beast, the lizard and worse, they re-made their own. . . ." He stopped a second, then looked down at his feet. When he looked back up at her, she knew he was dead serious.

"Now you promise me," both Neds said in chilling unison, "right now, right this second, that you will never stitch nothing or nobody back together again."

"But, Ned," she said, feeling shaky inside and wanting more than anything for him to stop acting crazy.

"But nothing," he said. "Promise me."

She took a deep breath. It was a scary thing giving the power of a promise away, but Ned was real upset and she figured they'd have time to talk this over later.

"I promise," she said.

Just then, the lizard opened its wings and lunged whip-quick for the pigs. In the same instant, Tilly realized she had forgotten to close the electric line behind her.

The lizard aimed for the pigs but instead of pigs, it got Ned.

It felt like a cold fist punched Tilly and her mind tried hard to make sense of things. She hollered at the lizard until it dropped Ned in a bloody heap. She picked him up, stumbled out to the truck and managed to get him into the front seat, though he wasn't conscious.

"You keep living," she said, her words rough with panic. She ground gears and the truck sped down the rutted road. "Keep living."

Both Neds were silent, their eyes cinched with pain.

Once she made the house, she lifted Ned out of the truck careful as she could. She took him into the front room and laid him on the couch. Blood the color of the grandma's knitting covered him, darkest over his stomach. She peeked under his shirt and swore. The bites were deep, and Ned's life pumped out with every breath. He was going to bleed out before she could get the crystal thread from the workshop.

She needed more time.

The grandma.

She ran across the wood floor, then up the stairs, up and up, and the stairs kept on going and she wasn't getting any closer to the end of them, until finally, she reached the landing.

She ran to the right, to the grandma's room, but her feet took twice as long as they should to get her there, and on the way she noticed the hall was in need of new paint, and a layer of dust had grown along the edge of the floor, and then finally, finally, she got to the grandma's room and opened the door.

The grandma was sitting in her bed, pulling red yarn out stitch by stitch, just wasting time.

"Granny, you got to help me. Ned's hurt bad."

The length of red knitting that had been at least seven feet long this morning was down to its last foot, and shrinking ever closer to white.

The grandma looked up and smiled. "Hello, Tilly. It's going to rain, you know."

Tilly ran across the room, grabbed the grandma by the wrist and took her, bag and all, down the stairs.

The only thing different about Ned since she'd left him, was the pool of blood on the floor had grown.

"Granny, you stay here and pull out a little time for him while I go get the stitchery from the workshop." Then Tilly stopped. She'd promised Ned she'd never stitch nothing or nobody again.

Holy. . . .

Thip, thip, thip, the grandma sat herself down in the old rocker and unwove another row of red.

Tilly stepped over to Ned and looked at his wounds again. The blood flow wasn't stopping.

Thip, thip, thip, stitch after stitch of time pulled out.

"Ned," Tilly said, hoping he could hear her. "I have to fix you up. Just some stitching, but nothing fancy. You'll still be you—not like what I did to the beast, okay?"

Tilly couldn't believe her eyes when she saw Right Ned shake his head.

She looked at the grandma, saw how she was trying to pull the yarn real slow so it would last.

"Ned," Tilly said, "you can't die."

Thip, thip, thip.

There were only a few rows of red left, and then the grandma would be into the white. As soon as the white was gone, there'd be no time left. She had to do something now.

She knelt down and put her hands above Ned's stomach, her unnatural, patchwork hands. She closed her eyes, just the way she'd seen Ned do it. Then she tried to find his spirit, the living thing that made him what he was. Somehow, she had to convince him to stay living until she could stitch him.

She sensed his heartbeat and the sluggish push of blood under her fingers. Briefly, something else flashed past her closed eyes, something sweet as honey and fresh as lemons. Ned's soul.

She held on to the idea of that, hoping it wasn't just her imagination. Her feet and face and hands tingled as she wrapped her mental self gently as she could around that warm sweet core of him.

"Please keep living, Ned. I love you."

The words seeped down, running through her skin to his skin.

Words filled his veins where there wasn't enough blood. His heartbeat stuttered and fell into beat with the rhythm of time unstitching.

"Spring's supposed to be a time of life, not death. You and I have a lot of living left." Tilly poured her soul into those words, and felt the brush of his mind against hers. Then she felt his breath as if it were her own—his pain shooting through her body, his fear sharp within her mind. She kept her thoughts calm, sending snatches of happy memories to him, until his pain and fear eased. "Live, Ned." She whispered, and then she opened her eyes.

Thip, thip, thip. The grandma pulled yarn. Tilly looked over her shoulder. The white yarn was almost gone.

"No," she said.

Thip. The last loop.

She felt the world shudder and pause.

Beneath her hands, Ned's heart stopped.

Tilly took a deep breath and watched Ned's chest rise. His heart stumbled and began beating on its own again.

"Keep breathing," Tilly said while she got to her feet. She was dizzy, but somehow managed to find the trauma-kit in the kitchen, filled with cotton thread, painkillers and antiseptics.

Tilly concentrated on breathing whenever Ned forgot, and tried to send him memories of warm summer days. She didn't know if the grandma helped her sew and dress Ned's wounds or not. But the tingling she'd felt in her hands and feet and face ever since she'd started touching Ned's mind all picked the same moment to rush inward. It was like the world had just taped her up and pulled that tape away, stripping her to the bone.

She didn't know she had passed out until she woke, down in the bed Ned and she shared. Ned was beside her, his breath no longer connected to hers, warm and real and alive all on its own, against her cheek.

Tilly stared up at the ceiling for awhile, blinking back tears. She'd made mistake after mistake—let the beast die, stitched, left the gate open, and had made Ned live too. She'd kept her promise, but keeping it had almost killed him. She hadn't stitched, but she'd done something else he'd never wanted. She mingled with his mind and touched his soul. She'd made him a part of her long enough to keep him alive, even though his body had been set on dying.

Now she knew why touching a mind once wasn't ever enough for him.

Ned shifted. He woke with a quiet moan and she propped up on her elbow to get a good look at the both of him.

Right Ned opened his eyes. "Did you . . . ?"

She shook her head. "No. You're healing on your own."

"How?" he asked.

"Shhh," she said, resisting the urge to reach out and touch his mind again. "I-we mingled. I'm sorry I touched you that way, but I couldn't bear the death of you." Guilt soured her stomach, and her tears dropped to the sheets.

"You mingled with me?" Right Ned asked. Then a faint smile touched his mouth. "With your hands?"

"I know it's wrong. . . ."

"It isn't wrong, Tilly."

Right Ned swallowed, so Left Ned said, "Wasn't that I hated the thought of being close to you . . ."

". . . I just wanted it so fierce," Right Ned said, "I knew I'd never let go once we touched that way. If you ever left me, or told me you didn't want me around, I knew I couldn't leave you."

Tilly couldn't believe what he was saying, but felt the truth in his words as if they were her own. All this time, he had wanted her too much, so he hadn't touched her at all.

"Now, that kind of thinking won't do us any good," she said. "I love you, Ned. Both of you."

Ned smiled, and though he didn't say it, Tilly felt his love spread tenderly across her mind.

This time, Tilly knew just what to do. She leaned down and very gently kissed first Right Ned, then Left Ned, then Right Ned again, touching him with her mind, her soul and her patchwork hands.

To Others We Know Not Of

Kate Riedel

Kate Riedel is originally from Minnesota but is now a card-carrying Canadian citizen living in Toronto. She has been published in On Spec, Realms of Fantasy, *and the anthology* Divine Realms *(Turnstone Press, Winnipeg, 1998), as well as in a quiltmaking magazine. Pressed for further information, she says, "I write fantasy because sometimes I believe that everyday life is, in its own way, magic. I cut my SF teeth on Heinlein's teen novels and my fantasy teeth on a little-known children's novel,* The Oldest Secret *by Patricia Gordon. For pleasure I re-read Rex Stout and P.G. Wodehouse. The writers who most influenced me and to whom I aspire are Robert Louis Stevenson, Shirley Jackson, and Tove Jannson. The novel I wish I had written is* True Grit."

"To Others We Know Not Of" is about a married woman and a sensitive guy she used to know in college, who has dropped back into her life. But this time something magical is explained, and also something meaningful that underpins her mainly successful life. It might have been published in an SF magazine in the 1950s. It reminds us of the stories of Theodore Sturgeon.

What do you say when the best lay you ever had in your life turns up on your doorstep at three in the morning, twenty-some years after he sent you the Dear Jane letter? "Hello, Graham," seemed inadequate. So did "You son of a bitch."

In the end I didn't say anything, but turned and walked back to the kitchen, leaving him to follow. The coffeemaker was already chugging away; I like to stay up after working night shift, until Will and the boys have had breakfast and gone their separate ways. I took down a second mug, set it on the counter next to mine, and sat down myself.

He hung his parka on the back of a chair, squatted in front of me, took off my slippers and began to massage my feet, thumb and fingers going unerringly to all the spots that ached the worst.

"Someone died here," Graham would say of a particular intersection. Ordinary pavement and stoplights, a vacant lot, a variety store kitty-corner, tipsy row houses with verandahs populated by battered wading pools, bicycles and bags of garbage. "A bicycle accident, I think."

He wouldn't walk down the alley behind the pancake house where I worked my way through school. "A hooker met a bad trick there."

"How do you know?"

"Pain soaks into the pavement like blood."

But the intersection lay gray and bland under the wheels of the traffic, and yellow dandelions shoved cheerfully through cracked asphalt under the graffiti decorating the back wall of the pancake house.

When he moved out of the shared house where I first met him, he turned down a nice, sunny, cheap bachelor flat in an old house, for an overpriced refurbished storeroom over one of those commercial blocks that seem to disintegrate even as they're built.

"Abuse," he said shortly, although the woman who showed us the flat was sunny and cheerful as her house, with none of the symptoms I'd learned to recognize during a work-study session at a shelter.

All that, of course, was after I'd known him long enough to do things like apartment hunting with him.

If I was the blaming sort, I suppose I could blame Alicia for my having met Graham at all.

The last thing I'd wanted to see, after getting off a double shift waiting tables at that pancake house, was Alicia sitting in her car out front. Not that I would have minded a ride home. But Alicia and I went back a long way—she the beauty queen, the lead in every high school play; me the plain, wholesome best friend—and I knew her too well for that.

"C'mon, Shirl," she said, "we're going to a party."

"My feet are killing me, Lish," I said. "I just want to go home and go to bed."

But I was still in the car when she pulled up in front of one of those big old houses that in their old age become havens for students, warrens of cheap rooms or flats, or, as in this case, a kind of communal habitat for whoever could be pulled in to share the rent.

Light spilled across the front yard; music drifted across the street with the fall leaves.

"Who is it this time, Lish?" I asked.

"Hamlet," she exhaled.

I'd seen him. Alicia was one of the court ladies in the current student production. Alicia's type; I didn't go for the sexy Jesus look. But he was a good Hamlet, the only one I've ever seen who didn't declaim, but spoke his lines as if thinking aloud.

Alicia disappeared into the noisy sardine tin of a room. I collapsed in an armchair in a dim alcove, closed my eyes and let the music, the rising and falling voices, the clink of glasses, go over my head like deep water.

I was halfway between waking and sleeping, the noise of the party advancing and receding like waves, when I felt someone tugging at my shoes.

"Leave 'em alone, Lish," I said without bothering to open my eyes. "Take 'em off now and I'll never get 'em on again to go home."

The shoes came off anyway. Someone began to massage my feet, firm grip increasing and relaxing on the ball, strong thumb rolling across the inside of the arch.

I had never felt anything so good in my life, not even sex.

Especially not sex. They say you always remember your first time, but I don't; just a haze of fumblings and insertions, and only dubious pleasure.

This was what sex was supposed to feel like.

I opened my eyes.

In the bright center of the room groups broke and reformed.

Alicia's Hamlet smiled up at me, rose to sit on the arm of the chair, took my face in his hands and kissed me, sweetly, carefully, lips and tongue delicately following every reaction like a train of thought.

A few minutes later he was locking a bedroom door against any other couples who might have the same idea.

The hands that had known exactly what my aching feet had wanted were as sure over the rest of my body.

This one I remembered.

"It's okay," he said, speaking for the first time. "It's my bed." I didn't bother to wonder how he knew that I wanted so badly to sleep. I just did it.

He introduced himself to me next morning. Graham Piper.

"Why the guilt?" he asked me over breakfast at a local greasy spoon.

"Alicia," I admitted. I hadn't thought it showed.

"I can't give her what she wants," he said. "How do you know Alicia? I didn't think you were in theater."

"From high school. And I'm not in theater, I'm in nursing." And then, somehow, for the first time since he'd died, I was talking about my dad, telling Graham how I'd looked after him, that long year he took to die of cancer.

"How could you?" Graham asked, more horrified than I'd thought my careful neutrality justified.

"I grant you, it was no fun." The neutrality was crumbling at the edges. *Think about the man who built you a treehouse, taught you to ride a bike . . .*

"You know how to deal with pain. That's unusual."

"It was better than leaving him to strangers. And I was good at it, so I decided to go into nursing."

"Why not a doctor? Easier on your feet."

"Oh, I can marry one of those," I said, raising the coffee cup to hide the blood I could feel rushing to my face.

"We could go back and do it again," he said, and I had to laugh.

"Do you do this sort of thing often?"

"Only once before you. Scared the hell out of me."

"So tell me about *your* father," I asked quickly.

"I hate him," he said.

"Ah . . . your mother?"

"She's an emotional mess."

I was about to apologize when he leaned over and kissed me.

We went back and did it again.

Now, two decades later, he replaced my slippers on my feet, rose, and kissed me.

"Great sex isn't the answer to everything," I said.

But that fall and winter, it had seemed to be.

Astonished, every time I looked in a mirror, that my face was plain as it had always been. Played like a violin, for heaven's sake; with Graham it really was like all the cliches you laugh at, but how else do you describe it?

Spring term, Alicia got the part of Clara Eynsford-Hill in "Pygmalion" and snagged herself Colonel Pickering. Graham played a particularly callous Henry Higgins. The audiences loved it, sometimes even hissed at the slippers scene and cheered for Eliza.

We went to the cast party. If you've ever encountered a group of would-be actors *en masse*, without being one yourself, you'll know how I felt.

"They're all so confident," I said.

"They're all terrified."

"Oh, come on!"

"So many actors, so few parts. Not to mention the people who become actors because they can't stand their real selves, . . ." He shrugged.

"They still make me feel . . . unglamorous," I said.

"I don't want glamor. I want you."

We didn't stay long at the party.

"You won't let me do anything," I protested later.

"You wouldn't enjoy it as much."

"That's not the point, dammit. You're supposed to enjoy it too."

"Oh, I do."

"What are you, some kind of voyeur?"

"Maybe."

"He's using you," was Alicia's diagnosis.

"How?"

"He never takes you anywhere. I never see you after school or work, anymore."

"I'm usually too tired to do anything then, anyway."

But the cast party had been the last social event we'd gone to. On the other hand, what I'd said to Alicia was true enough.

"Does he even take you to movies?"

"Of course. For acting technique."

But the last movie we'd seen that wasn't on TV, Graham had walked out in the middle. When I realized he wasn't coming back, I followed, and found him emerging from the men's room, wiping his forehead.

"Sorry," he mumbled. "Claustrophobia. Or maybe something I ate."

"It's okay," I said. "Let's go home."

By that time we were living together in his refurbished storeroom. My mother didn't like it, but she did like Graham, and trusted me. My only contact with Graham's parents was the monthly check from his mother.

"Mind if we walk?" he asked. "I don't think I could stand the bus. I know it's a long way . . ." He managed a smile. "I'll give you a foot rub when we get there."

He had to raise his voice to be heard over the sound of the motorcycle that roared past us, a young man driving, a girl behind him, her arms wrapped around his waist.

The driver slowed for the red light, then hit the gas as the light changed to green.

We were right at the corner when the big car ran the red light and sent the motorcycle spinning like a toy, the girl flung like a doll from the passenger seat. The young man clung to the motorcycle as it went end over end to come to rest against the curb, the wheels still spinning.

"Get the bastard's license number!" I yelled at Graham as the car straightened and took off down the road. "Stop the traffic!" as another car screeched around me.

The helmet saved the girl. Someone helped me lay her flat, loosened the helmet and shoved a jacket under her head; someone else put a coat over her. I thought it was Graham, but when I looked up I saw a stranger. Another stranger directed traffic.

Graham was already half a block away, walking quickly.

Someone was trying to move the driver onto the sidewalk.

"Leave him the hell alone," I yelled. "Call an ambulance!" I pulled off my jacket and shoved it over the gaping, sucking wound in his chest. And then I forgot all about Graham.

Because it all came together then. I was the right person in the right place; I'd chosen well for the rest of my life.

Something, maybe one of the gear shifts or something on the handlebars, had punctured a lung. Blood bubbled around my jacket; my own chest ached with his labored breathing. I pressed harder.

The breathing stopped. Started again. He opened his eyes, looked around, jerked one arm spasmodically, as if trying to reach for me.

"Lie still," I said. His hand closed, opened again.

From behind me, someone reached out and took his hand. The young man's lips moved, his face slackened, and he lay back quietly and closed his eyes. The broken chest stopped laboring.

"You did what you could," the ambulance attendant said. I'd been so absorbed I'd barely heard the approach of the siren. "It would have taken a miracle."

I stood, shaking now. Graham extricated his living hand from the dead grasp.

"Don't worry about it," I told Graham when we finally got home. "Lots of people go faint at the sight of blood. And you came back."

"How do you do it?" he asked.

"Everyone has to deal with it their own way."

He started to make love to me. I let him.

He stopped.

"It's all right," I said.

"You don't want to."

"You do. It works both ways, stupid."

"Not for me."

He lay back beside me, reached for my hand and held it tightly.

"He thought I was his mother," he said.

"You're right," Graham said, getting up to pour the coffee. "Sex isn't the answer to everything. That's why I left." He handed me a mug, honey, no milk, and sat opposite.

Now I saw that middle age sat only a little more lightly on him than on me. There were crows feet around his eyes, a gray hair here and there among the brown, and the curls were tangled more from neglect than artfulness.

"Where the hell did you go to?" I asked.

"To a cabin in the north woods, eventually. I do long-distance accounting by computer. Only good thing I ever got from my father was a head for numbers."

"What a waste. You were a good actor."

He shrugged. "It's a living, and it's low stress." He sipped at his coffee, looked over at me. "You're happy. You married your doctor."

"You're not here about my happiness. So what *do* you want?"

"A ride to the airport."

"There are taxis. They run all night."

"And the driver might remember me."

"Long distance embezzling to supplement the long distance accounting?"

"What do you know about Lucy Demers?"

"As little as possible."

Except what screamed from the newspaper boxes; *Where did Lucy spend her final hours?* Droned on the evening news: *The unnamed man assisting the police in the Lucy Demers case . . .*

"I was the man held for questioning."

Alicia was dumped by Colonel Pickering for Clare Zachenasian when he got a part in "The Visit" and she didn't. She shifted to a straight English major and by our senior year she was engaged to the son of her mother's best friend. A lawyer.

"Actors are poor marriage material," she said. "Too prone to go astray with actresses."

"Not Graham," I said.

"You'll end up supporting him."

"Just until he gets his foot up in the theater. We'll wait until then to have children."

Alicia gave me a pitying look. "He hasn't had a part in a play for a year."

"He didn't try out," I said. "He's concentrating on theory."

"Shirl, where have you been? I hear he hasn't even been to class in the past month."

"Crowds make him uncomfortable," I said. "He's studying at home."

"It doesn't occur to you that a guy who has trouble with crowds just may have trouble with crowded theaters?"

The last term before graduation, I gave up my job at the pancake house for a final work-study period at a local hospital. Graham gave up meeting me after work. "Pain soaks into . . ."

"It's a hospital, for God's sake!"

"Don't be mad at me," with that sweet, persuasive smile. "You're just tired. Let me make you feel good."

I let him.

But Alicia's words had raised doubts that I had, perhaps, been suppressing. When my advisor handed me an invitation to her housewarming party, I accepted for both of us without consulting Graham.

"If it makes you happy," Graham said.

We walked. He now got nauseous on buses, and we were still saving for our own car.

On the way we passed a playground where a young father played with his little girl on the swings. At the end of the arc, she let go and tumbled forward out of the swing.

I gasped. But her father caught her, swung her around and lowered her to the ground, both laughing.

"He'd never hurt her," said Graham.

"Of course not," I said. "He's her father."

"There's no 'of course' about it." He kicked over a piece of scrap lumber, detritus of winter snowbanks come to rest beside the road. Where it had lain, the grass was twisted, flattened and pale.

"Listen, Graham," I said. "You'll be like that father, not like yours."

"Do you think so?" he said, and took my hand as we walked on in the twilight.

Dr. Jones hung Graham's jacket in the hall closet. Graham leaned into the closet for a hanger for mine.

And dropped hanger and coat together, and clutched the rod for support, white-faced.

"The bathroom's at the end of the hall," Dr. Jones said, without waiting for him to ask.

"I'm sorry," he said when he emerged several minutes later. "I can't stay. But you should; I don't want to spoil things for you."

He would have left without his jacket if I hadn't run after him with it.

He wasn't home when I got there.

He didn't even have the courage to do it face-to-face. He left a letter, saying I'd be better off marrying a doctor because he couldn't have any children.

"So what else did he lie about?" Alicia said.

Graham's mother turned up at the door a week later, asking if I knew where he was. She didn't look like an emotional mess. But a few months later she slashed her wrists.

The police turned up at Dr. Jones' house with a search warrant.

They took apart the front coat closet, put bits of it under a microscope, and then dug up the back yard.

They found a body, tiny bones broken, partially healed, re-broken.

The child had died confined in the closet.

I watched Graham's hands around the coffee mug.

"For years . . ." he said. "I don't know, I don't think I realized for a long time just what hell I was living in. Maybe I thought if I ignored it, it would go away. But it didn't. Just got worse. Just to get on a bus and feel the anger from one, the hopelessness from another . . ." He shook his head. "Happiness is so rare. Thank God for computers. At least I can make a living."

"What a waste," I said again.

"What right have you to say that?"

"Do you know what Will or I would give for your ability?"

"What good is it? Remember that motorcyclist?"

"You stood in for his mother while he was dying."

"It wasn't *his* mother I saw. It was mine. My mother killed herself, you know."

"So why haven't you?"

" 'The undiscover'd country, from whose bourne no traveler returns—' " he quoted, clutching his shirt in a melodramatic gesture he'd never have used in the role. " 'Puzzles the will, and makes us rather bear those ills we have than fly to others we know not of . . . ' "

"I wish you'd told me."

"You wouldn't have believed me."

"Perhaps not. Then."

"I shouldn't have left you like that. I'm sorry."

"Where does Lucy Demers come into all this?"

"The detective in charge thought he knew where she'd been confined. But he didn't have any proof, didn't know how to get it. Until he remembered how, back when he was still in uniform, this wild-eyed guy came charging into the police station, demanding a cross-check of missing children against the former owners of a particular house. Some crazy kid who claimed that fear seeped into the woodwork like blood."

"Do they really follow up on that sort of thing?"

"They have to consider everything. But for Lucy, he came to me on his own time."

He paused and gazed into his mug.

"I've spent all my life living with other people's feelings," he said after a long minute. "When I finally found myself alone, up in that cabin, it was as if I'd gone deaf. I began to wonder if I *had* any feelings of my own. Or if they'd all died under the constant barrage of others'."

"And?"

"They were there. Like grass, after you've moved a board that's been covering it. I began to hope . . ." He stopped again.

"Was it where he thought?" I asked finally. "The detective. Where she'd . . ." I found I just couldn't say, "confined." "Where she'd been?"

"Yes. Now he wants me to help him find where she died."

"But you're not going to."

"You think I'm afraid of the pain," he said.

"Well, aren't you?"

"They had me talk to the police artist about the child in the closet," he said after another long minute. "The sketch was useless. It was a picture of my father."

He looked at me now. His eyes looked just as I remembered from when I'd run after him with his jacket, the last day I'd ever seen him.

"Do you know what it's like," he asked, "to enjoy hurting someone?"

"I've never hated anyone enough for that," I said. "Although I suppose I could, if one of my children—"

"I'm not talking about hating," he said. "I'm talking about *enjoying*. I know. *He* enjoyed it. Hurting Lucy."

"Then he'll do it again. You have to—"

"You don't understand. I *know*. I knew, all the while I lived in the same house as my father. Do you think that all I felt in that closet was pain?"

"*You* couldn't do that."

"Of course I couldn't," he said in a voice like quinine sulfate. "The pain of the victim would rather negate the pleasure, don't you think?"

Let me make you feel good . . . "Whatever you are, you're not a sadist. You aren't your father. You aren't the man from the closet."

"Dammit, Shirley, I can't. She's not suffering anymore; why should I? He'll just have to finish the job without me."

"All right, Graham," I said finally. "I'll see that you get to the airport. Just answer one question for me?"

He forced a smile. "If I can."

"What did you ever see in me?"

The smile softened. "Someone whose pain I could do something about."

"The garage is through that door," I said. "The car's unlocked. I just have to get dressed."

My oldest son met me on the stairs, the son who, as a baby, had cried every time I had a headache, until he realized that crying only made the pain worse. A difficult child to live with, in some ways.

He's in med school now. Pediatrics. They say it's uncanny, the way he knows where babies hurt.

"I'll talk to him," he said, even before I handed him the keys and told him, "Your father's waiting in the car."

The Lady of the Winds

Poul Anderson

Poul Anderson (tribute website: 128.174.194.59/vaughn/english120/ anderson.htm), one of the Grand Masters who lent particular honor to that title, died at the end of July 2001.

He was a professional writer of astonishing competence, varied talents and interests, and a thoughtful stylist. Distinguished as a fantasy writer—The Broken Sword (1954) was his first adult novel and is still an underappreciated fantasy classic—he was principally one of the heroic figures of hard science fiction, a John W. Campbell man whose stories appeared in Astounding/Analog for the five decades. Of his many excellent collections, All One Universe is perhaps the best, since it contains not only first-class stories but also several fine essays and extensive story notes by Anderson, who has been notably reticent in his other books. Anderson was an important and influential figure in fantasy.

"The Lady of the Winds" features bard, lover, and thief Cappen Varra. A Jack Vancean fantasy character of Anderson's introduced in "The Valor of Cappen Varra," in the 1950s, Varra later reappeared in the 1980s in the Thieves' World anthologies edited by Robert Asprin and Lynn Abbey. It is a lighthearted adventure about an encounter with a vain goddess. To get all the musical jokes here, it helps to know Gilbert & Sullivan, but the story is always clear and sharp.

Southward the mountains lifted to make a wall across a heaven still hard and blue. Snow whitened their peaks and dappled the slopes below. Even this far under the pass, patches of it lay on sere grass, among strewn boulders—too early in the season, fatally too early. Dry motes blew off in glittery streaks, borne on a wind that whittered and whirled. Its chill searched deep. Westward, clouds were piling up higher than the heights they shrouded, full of darkness and further storm.

A snow devil spun toward Cappen Varra, thickening as it went. Never had he known of the like. Well, he had gone forth to find whatever Power was here. He clutched the little harp with numbed fingers as if it were his courage. The gyre stopped before him and congealed. It became the form of a woman taller than himself. She poised utterly beautiful, but hueless as the snow, save for faint blue shadows along the curves of her and eyes like upland lakes. The long, tossing hair and a thin vortex of ice dust half clothed her nakedness. Somehow she seemed to quiver, a wind that could not ever come altogether to rest.

"My lady!" broke from him in the tongue of his homeland.

He could have tried to stammer on with words heard in this country, but she answered him likewise, singing more than speaking, maybe whistling more than singing: "What fate do you seek, who dared so to call on me?"

"I—I don't know," he got out, truly enough. "That lies with my lady. Yet it seemed right to bring her what poor gift was mine to offer."

He could not tell whether he heard scorn or a slight, wicked mirth. "A free gift, with nothing to ask in return?"

Cappen drew breath. The keen air seemed to whip up his wits. He had dealt with the mighty often before now—none such as her, no, but

307

whatever hope he had lay with supposing that power makes for a certain way of feeling, be it human or overhuman. He swept his headgear off, holding it against his breast while he bowed very deeply. "Who am I to petition my lady? I can merely join all other men in praising her largesse and mercy, exalting her name forever."

The faintest of smiles touched her lips. "Because of what you brought, I will hear you out." It ceased. Impatience edged her voice. The wind strengthened, the frosty tresses billowed more wildly. "I think I know your wish. I do not think I will grant it. However, speak."

He had meant to depart from Sanctuary, but not so hastily. After some three years in that famous, infamous city, he remembered how much more there was to the wide world. Besides, while he had made friends high in its life, as well as among the low and raffish—with whom he generally felt easier—he had also made enemies of either kind. Whether by arrest on some capital charge or, likelier, by a knife in some nighted alley, one of them might well eventually make an end of him. He had survived three attempts, but the need to stay ever alert grew wearisome when hardly anything remained here that was new to him.

For a time after an adventure into which he fell, rescuing a noble lady from captivity in another universe and, perhaps, this world from the sikkintairs, he indulged in pleasures he could now afford. Sanctuary provided them in rich variety. But his tastes did not run to every conceivable kind, and presently those he enjoyed took on a surprising sameness. "Could it be that the gods of vice, even the gods of luxury, have less imagination than the gods of virtue and wholesomeness?" he wondered. The thought appalled.

Yet it wakened a dream that surprised him when he recognized it for what it was. He had been supposing his inborn restlessness and curiosity would send him on toward fresh horizons. Instead, memories welled up, and longing sharpened until it felt like unrequited love. Westward his wish ran, across plains, over mountains, through great forests and tumultuous kingdoms, the whole way home to Caronne. He remembered not only gleaming walls, soaring spires, bustling marts and streets; not only broad estates, greensward and greenwood, flowerbeds ablaze, lively men and livelier women; he harked back to the common folk, his folk, their speech and songs and ways. A peasant girl or tavern wench could be as fair as any highborn maiden, and often more fun. He remembered seaports, odors of tar and fish and cargo bales, masts and spars raking the sky, and beyond them the water a-glitter beneath a Southern sun, vast and blue where it reached outward and became Ocean.

Enough remained of his share of Molin Torchholder's reward for the exploit. He need not return as a footloose, hand-to-mouth minstrel, showman, gambler, and whatever-else, the disinherited and rather disgraced younger son of a petty baron. No, if he could get shrewd advice about investments—he knew himself for a much better versifier than money manager—he would become a merchant prince in Croy or Seilles at the very least. Or so he trusted.

Summer was dying away into autumn. The last trader caravans of the year would soon be gone. One was bound as far as Arinberg. That was a goodly distance, well beyond the western border of this Empire, and the town said to be an enjoyable place to spend a winter. Cappen bought two horses, camp gear, and supplies from the master. The traders were still trading here, and did not plan to proceed for another week. Cappen had the interval idle on his hands.

And so it came about that he perforce left Sanctuary earlier than intended.

Candlelight glowed over velvet. Fragrances of incense, of Peridis's warmth and disheveled midnight locks, of lovemaking lately come to a pause, mingled with the sweet notes of a gold-and-diamond songbird crafted by some cunning artificer. No noise or chill or stench from the streets outside won through windows barred, glazed, and curtained. Nerigo, third priest of Ils, housed his newest leman well.

Perhaps if he visited her oftener she would not have heeded the blandishments of a young man who encountered her in the gaudy chaos of Midyear Fair and made occasions to pursue the acquaintance. At least, they might have lacked opportunity. But although Nerigo was not without vigor, much of it went in the pursuit of arcane knowledge, which included practices both spiritually and physically demanding. Today he had indicated to Peridis, as often before, that he would be engaged with dark and dangerous powers until dawn, and then must need sleep in his own house; thereafter, duties at the temple would keep him busy for an indefinite span.

So she sent a note to Cappen Varra at the inn where he lodged. It went by public messenger. As she had made usual, her few servants retired to a dormitory shed behind the house when she had supped. If she needed any, she could ring a bell. Besides, like servants generally in Sanctuary, these cultivated a selective blindness and deafness.

After all, she must shortly bid her lover farewell. It would probably take a while to find another. She might never find another so satisfactory.

"You have asked about some things here," she murmured. "I never dared show you them. Not that you would have betrayed me, but what you didn't know couldn't be gotten out of you, were he to become suspicious. Now, though, when, alas, you are leaving for aye—" She sighed, fluttered her eyelashes, and cast him a wistful smile. "It will take my mind off that, while we rest before our next hour of delight."

"The wait will not be long, since it's you I'm waiting for," he purred.

"Ah, but, my dear, I am less accustomed than I . . . was . . . before that man persuaded me hither." With gold, Cappen knew, and the luxury everywhere around, and, he gathered, occasional tales and glimpses of marvels. "Let me rest an hour, to be the readier for you. Meanwhile, there are other, more rare entertainments."

A long silken shift rippled and shimmered as she undulated over to a cabinet of ebony inlaid with ivory in enigmatic patterns. Her single, curious modesty was not to be unclad unless in bath or bed. Having nothing else along, Cappen gratified it by resuming blouse and breeks, even his soft shoes. When she opened the cabinet, he saw shelves filled with objects. Most he couldn't at once identify, but books were among them, scrolls and codices. She paused, considering, then smiled again and took out a small, slim volume bound in paper, one of perhaps a dozen. "These amuse me," she said. "Let me in turn beguile you. Come, sit beside me."

He was somewhat smugly aware of how her gaze followed him as he joined her on the sofa. Speech and manner counted most with women, but good looks helped. He was of medium size, slim, lithe and muscular because hitherto he had seldom been able to lead the indolent life he would have preferred. Black hair, banged over the brow and above the shoulders, framed straight-cut features and vividly blue eyes. It also helped to have quite a musical voice.

She handed him the book. He beheld letters totally unfamiliar, laid it on his lap, and opened it. She reached to turn the pages, one by one.

Plain text mingled with lines that must be verse—songs, because it seemed the opening parts were under staves of what he guessed was a musical notation equally strange. There were pictures too, showing people outlandishly clad, drawn with an antic humor that tickled his fancy. "What is this?" he wondered.

"The script for a rollicking comedic performance," she answered.

"When done? Where? How do you know?"

"Well, now, that is a story of its own," she said, savoring his attention. He knew she was not stupid, and wanted to be more to him than simply another female body. Indeed, that was among her attractions. "See you, Nerigo's wizardly questings go into different worlds from ours, alike in some ways, alien in more. Different universes, he says, coexistent with this one on many planes, as the leaves of this tome lie side by side. But I can't really understand his meaning there. Can you?"

Cappen frowned, abruptly uneasy. "Much too well," he muttered.

"What's wrong? I feel you go taut."

"Oh, nothing, really." Cappen made himself relax. He didn't care to speak of the business, if only because that would spoil the mood here. It was, after all, safely behind him, the gate destroyed, the sikkintairs confined to their own skies.

And yet, raced through his mind, that gate had been in the temple of Ils, where the high flamen made nefarious use of it. He had heard that, subsequently, the priests of the cult disavowed and severely discouraged such lore. They could have found themselves endangered. Yet search through the temple archives might well turn up further information. Yes, that would explain why Nerigo was secretive, and stored his gains in this house, where nobody would likely think to search.

"He only lusts for knowledge," Peridis reassured. Her tone implied she wished that were not his primary lust. "He does not venture into the Beyond. He simply opens windows for short whiles, observes, and, when he can, reaches through to snatch small things for later study. Is that so terrible? But the hierarchy would make trouble for him if they knew, and . . . it might strike at me as well."

She brightened. "He shares with me, a little. I have looked with him into his mirror that is not a mirror, at things of glamour or mirth. I have seen this very work performed on a stage far elsewhere, and a few more akin to it. True, the language was foreign to both of us, but he could discern that the story, for instance, concerns a love intrigue. It was partly at my wish that he hunted about until he found a shop where the books are sold, and cast spells to draw copies into his arcanum. Since then I've often taken them out when I'm alone, to call back memories of the pleasure. Now let me explain and share it with you as well as I'm able." Heavy-lidded, her glance smoldered on him. "It does tell of lovers who at last come together."

He thrust his qualms aside. The thing was in fact fascinating. They began to go through it page by page, her finger tracing out each illustration while she tried to convey what understanding she had of it. His free arm slid behind her.

A thud sounded from the vestibule. Hinges whined. A chill gust bore smells of the street in. Peridis screamed. Cappen knew stabbingly that the bolt on the main door had flung back at the command of its master. The book fell from their hands and they read no more that night.

A lean, grizzle-bearded, squinting man, clad in a silvery robe, entered. At his back hulked another, red-skinned, seven feet tall, so broad and thick as to seem squat, armed with steel cap, leather cuirass, and unfairly large scimitar. Cappen did not need Peridis's gasp to inform him that they were Nerigo and a Makali bodyguard.

The woman sprang to her feet. As the bard did, the little volume slid off his lap. Almost without thinking, he snatched it and tucked it down his half-open blouse. A bargaining counter—?

For an endless instant, silence held them all.

When Nerigo then spoke, it was quite softly, even impersonally. "I somewhat hoped I would prove mistaken. But you realize, Peridis, I cannot afford blind trust in anyone. A sortilege indicated you were receiving a visitor in my absences."

She stepped back, lifting her hands, helpless and imploring. Nerigo shook his head. Did ruefulness tinge his words? "Oh, fear not, my cuddly. From the beginning, I knew you for what you are. It's not rational to wax angry when a cat steals cream or a monkey disarrays documents. One simply makes provision against further untowardness. Why should I deny myself the pleasure that is you? No, you will merely be careful in future, very careful. If you are, then when I want novelty you shall go your way freely, unharmed, with only a minor spell on you to lock your lips against ever letting slip anything about me or my doings."

Cappen heard how she caught her breath and broke into sobs. At the back of his mind, he felt a burden drop off himself. He would have hated being the instrument of harm to her. Not that she had been much more to him than frolic; yet a man wishes well-being for his friends. Besides, killing beautiful young women was a terrible waste.

Hope flickered up amidst his dismay. He bowed low. "My lord, most reverend sir," he began, "your magnanimity surpasses belief. No, say rather that it demonstrates, in actual incarnation, the divine benevolence of those gods in whose service you so distinguish yourself. Unworthy though I be, my own humble but overwhelming gratitude—"

Nerigo cut him off. "You need not exercise that flattering tongue which has become notorious throughout Sanctuary," the sorcerer-priest said, now coldly impersonal. "You are no wayward pet of mine, you are a brazen intruder. I cannot possibly let you go unpunished; my demons would lose all respect for me. Furthermore, this is an opportunity first to extract from you everything you know. I think especially about the eminent Molin Torchholder and his temple of Savankala, but doubtless other bits of information can prove useful too. Take him, Yaman."

"No, no, I beg you!" Peridis shrieked, but scrambled aside as the giant advanced.

If he was hustled off to a crypt, Cappen knew, he would welcome death when at last it came. He retreated, drawing the knife at his belt. Yaman grinned. The scimitar hissed forth. "Take him alive," Nerigo called, "but I've ways to stanch wounds once he's disabled."

Cappen was no bravo or brawler. Wits were always his weapon of choice. However, sometimes he had not been granted the choice. Thus he went prepared. His knife was not just the article of clothing and minor tool commonly carried by men. It was razor-honed, as balanced as a hawk on the wing. When in his wanderings he earned some coins by a show of prestidigitation, it had often figured in the act.

He poised, took aim, and threw.

A hoarse, gurgling bellow broke from Yaman. He lurched, dropped his weapon, and went to his knees. Blood spurted. The blade had gone into his throat below the chin. If Nerigo wanted to keep his henchman, he'd be busy for a while. Mainly, Cappen's way out was clear. He blew Peridis a kiss and darted off.

A yell pursued him. "You'll not escape, Varra! I'll have you hounded to the ends of the Empire. If they're Imperial troopers who find you, they'll have orders to cut you down on sight. But first demons will be on your trail—"

By then he was in the vestibule, retrieving his rapier and cloak, whence he slipped forth into the street. Walls and roofs loomed black along its narrowness. A strip of stars between barely gave light to grope by. Oh, lovely gloom! He kept to one side, where the dark was thickest and there was less muck to step in, and fled as deftly as a thief.

What to do? tumbled through his head. The inconspicuous silver amulet hanging on his breast ought to baffle Nerigo's afreets or whatever they were. It protected him against any supernatural forces of less than divine status. At least, so the wizard who gave it to him years ago had said, and so it had seemed to work on two or three occasions since. Of course, that might have been happenstance and the wizard a liar, but he had plenty of worries without adding hypothetical ones.

Equally of course, if such a being did come upon him, it could seize him or tear him apart. Physical strength was a physical quality. Likewise for human hunters.

Yes, Nerigo would have those out after him, while messengers sped north, south, east, and west bearing his description to castles, cantonments, garrisons, and watchposts. Once he had aroused the indignation of his colleagues, Nerigo would have ample influence to get such an order issued. Cappen's connections to Molin were too slight—how he wished now that he hadn't thought it best to play down his role in that rescue—for the high priest of Savankala to give him asylum and safe-guard across the border. Relations between the temples were strained enough already.

The westbound caravan wouldn't leave for days. Well before then, Nerigo would learn that Cappen had engaged a place in it. There were several others, readying to go in their various directions. He could find temporary refuge and get information in one of the disreputable inns he knew. With luck, he could slink to the master of whichever was depart-ing first, give him a false name and a plausible story, and be off with it—maybe even tomorrow.

That would cost, especially if a bit of a bribe proved advisable. Cap-pen had deposited his money with a reliable usurer, making withdrawals as desired. Suddenly it might as well be on the Moon. He was back to what lay in his pouch. It might barely stretch to getting him away.

He suppressed a groan and shrugged. If his most recent memories were dearly bought, still, they'd be something to enjoy on an otherwise dismal journey.

It was a long annual trek that Deghred im Dalagh and his followers made. Northward they fared from Temanhassa in Arechoum, laden with spices, aromatics, intoxicant herbs, pearls, rich fabrics, cunningly wrought metal things, and the like, the merchants and hucksters among them trading as they went. The route zigzagged through desert and sown, village and town, across dunes and rivers, by highroad and cairn-marked trail, over the Uryuk Ubur and thence the cultivated plains of the Empire, Sanctuary its terminus. That city produced little other than crime and politics, often indistinguishable, but goods of every kind flowed to its marts and profitable exchanges could be made. The return journey was faster, as direct as possible, to get beyond the mountains before their early winter closed the passes.

Well, Cappen consoled himself, this was not the destination he had had in mind, but needs must, he had never yet seen yonder exotic lands, and maybe he could improve his luck there.

It could stand improvement, his thoughts continued. Instead of the comforts he paid for and forfeited, he had a single scrawny mule, which he must frequently relieve by turning to shank's mare; a greasy third-hand bedroll; two similar changes of clothes and a towel; ill-fitting boots; a cheap knife, spoon, and tin bowl; and leave to eat with the choreboys, not the drovers.

However, he remained alive and at large. That was ample cause for cheerfulness, most of the time. Making friends came naturally to him.

Before long his tales, japes, and songs generated a liveliness that drew the attention of the merchants. Not long after that, they invited him into their mess. Deghred gave him a decent kaftan to wear while they ate, drank, and talked; everybody concerned was fluent in the Ilsig language, as well as others. "I think you have possibilities, lad," the caravan master said. "I'll lodge you for a while after we come to Temanhassa and introduce you to certain people." He waved his hand. "No, no, not alms. A modest venture, which in the course of time may bring me a modest profit."

Cappen knew he had better not seem a daydreamer or a fool. "The tongue of Arechoum is foreign to me, sir. Your men can scarcely teach me along the way."

"You're quick to pick things up, I've seen. Until you do, belike I can help."

Cappen understood from the drawl and the bearded smile that Deghred meant also to profit from that help, perhaps considerably. Not that he was ever unnecessarily unkind or hostile. Cappen rather liked him. But business was business. At the moment, nothing better was in sight.

Beasts and men plodded on. The land rose in bleakening hills. Now and then, when by himself, Cappen took from his meager baggage the book he had borne from Peridis's house and paged through it, puzzling over the text and staves, smiling at the pictures, mainly recalling her and their nights. Thence he harked back to earlier recollections and forward to speculations about the future. It bore him away from the trek.

At a lonely fortress on a stony ridge, the commander routinely let them cross the frontier. Cappen drew a long breath. Yet, he realized, that frontier was ill-defined, and Nerigo's agents might still find him. He would not feel altogether safe until he was on the far side of the Uryuk Ubur.

Those mountains reared like a horse. Mile by mile the trails grew more toilsome, the land more cold and stark. Unseasonably so, Deghred said, and burned some incense to his little private gods. Nevertheless the winds lashed, yelled, and bit, clouds raced ragged, snow flurried.

Thus they came to the hamlet Khangaii and heard that if they went ahead, they would almost surely die.

A storm roared about the huts. Sleet hissed on the blast. Moss-chinked stone walls and turf roof muffled the noise, a dung fire and crowded bodies kept the dwelling of headman Bulak odorously warm, but somehow that sharpened the feeling of being trapped.

"Aiala is angry," he said. "We have prayed, we have sacrificed a prime ewe—not in feast, but casting it into a crevasse of Numurga Glacier—yet she rages ever worse."

"Nor has she sent me a dream to tell why, though I ate well-nigh all the sacred *ulaku* left us and lay swooned through two sunrises." His elder wife, who was by way of being the tribal priestess, shuddered. "Instead, nightmares full of furious screams."

Flames flickered low on the hearth and guttered in clay lamps. Smoke dimmed what light they gave and blurred uneasy shadows. From the gloom beyond gleamed the frightened stares of Bulak's younger wife and children, huddled on the sheepskins that covered the sleeping dais. Three favored dogs gnawed mutton bones tossed them after the company had eaten. Several men and the senior woman sat cross-legged around the fire, drinking fermented milk from cow horns refilled out of a jug. They were as many as could well have been crowded in, Deghred and such of the merchants as he picked. The rest of the travelers were housed elsewhere. Even in this bad time, hospitality was sacred. Cappen had persuaded the caravan master that he, come from afar, might conceivably have some new insight to offer.

He was beginning to regret the mix of cockiness and curiosity that led him to do so. He had more or less gotten to ignoring the stench, but his eyes stung and he kept choking back the coughs that would have been impolite. Not that things were likely any better in any other hut. Well, maybe he could have slept. It was a strain trying to follow the talk. Bulak knew some Ilsig, and some of the guests had a smattering of his language. Between stumbling pidgin and awkward translations, conversation did not exactly flow.

At least, though, the slowness and the pauses gave him a chance to infer what he could not directly follow, correcting his mistakes when context revealed them to him. It became almost as if he listened to ordinary speech. He wasn't sure whether or not the drink helped, if only by dulling his discomfort. Foul stuff, but by now his palate was as stunned as his nose and he readily accepted recharges.

"Have you not gods to appeal to other than this—this Aiala?" asked the merchant Haran im Zeyin.

Deghred frowned at the brashness and shook his head. The wife caught her breath and drew a sign which smoke-swirls traced. Bulak took it stolidly. "She rules the air over the Uryuk Ubur," he answered. Light wavered across the broad, seamed face, almond eyes, and thin beard. "What shall they of the Fire, the Earth, and the Water do?"

"It may be she is even at odds with them, somehow, and this is what keeps her wrathful," whispered the woman. "There is a song among the olden songs that tells of such a time, long ago, when most of the High Folk died before she grew mild again—but I must not sing any of those songs here."

"So it could worsen things to call on them," said Deghred with careful gravity. "Yet—may she and you bear with an ignorant outsider who wishes only to understand—why should she make you suffer? Surely you are blameless."

Bulak half shrugged. "How else shall she vent her anger than in tempest and chill?"

Irreverence grinned within Cappen. He remembered infuriated women who threw things. The grin died. Men were apt to do worse when beside themselves, and be harder to bring to reason. More to the point, he happened to be on the receiving end.

The headman's stoicism gave way for a moment. "I have had my day. Our tribe will live through the winter—enough of us—I think—and may hope that then she has calmed—"

"For she is not cruel," the priestess said as if chanting. "Her snows melt beneath her springtime breezes and fill the streams, while the pastures turn green and starry with tiny flowers and lambs frisk in the sunshine. She brings the fullness of summer, the garnered riches of autumn, and when her snows have returned we have been snug and gladsome."

Isn't that the sort of thing a goddess or god is supposed to do? thought Cappen.

"—but how many of our young will freeze or starve, how many of our littlest ones?" croaked Bulak. He stiffened his lips. "We must wait and see."

And, Cappen reflected, *few gods are noted for tender solicitude. In fact, they often have nasty tempers.*

If this is even a goddess, properly speaking. Maybe she ranks only as a sylph or something, though with considerable local power. That could make matters even worse. Minor functionaries are notoriously touchy.

Supposing, of course, there is anything in what I've been hearing.

Deghred said it for him: "Again I pray pardon. No impertinence is meant. But is it not possible that what we have met is merely a freak, a flaw in the weather, nothing for the Lady Aiala to take heed of, and very soon, perhaps already tomorrow, it will go back to what it should be?"

Bulak shook his head. "Never in living memory have we suffered aught like this so early: as well you should know, who have passed through here, to and fro, for year after year. But there is the sacred song. . . . Push on if you will. The higher you go, the harder it will be. Unless we get respite within the next three or four days, I tell you that you will find the passes choked with snow and yourselves in a blizzard, unable even to go back. If afterward your bodies are found, we will make an offering for your souls." His smile held scant mirth. "Not that I'm at all sure 'we' means anyone here tonight."

"What, then, do you counsel we should do?"

"Why, retreat while still you are able. Tomorrow, I'd say. We cannot keep you through such a winter as is upon us. Barely will we be able to keep ourselves—some of ourselves. Go back north into the lowlands and wait. Could we High Folk do likewise, we might well, but if naught else, the Empire would seize on the chance to make us impoverished clients. We have had dealings with it erenow. Better that a remnant of us stay free. You, though, need but wait the evil out."

"At cutthroat cost," muttered Haran.

"Better to lose our gains than our lives," retorted Deghred. His tone gentled. "And yet, Bulak, we are old friends, you and I. A man should not turn his back on a friend. Might we, your guests, be able to do something? Maybe, even, as foreigners, give reverence and some unique sacrifice to the Lady, and thus please her—?" His voice trailed off.

"How shall we speak to her? In our broken Uryuk?" wondered another merchant. "Would that not be an insult?"

"She is of the winds," said Bulak. "She and her kind ken every tongue in the world, for the winds hear and carry the knowledge to each other." He turned to his elder wife. "Is that not so?" She nodded.

Deghred brightened. "Then she will understand us when we pray and make offerings."

The priestess pinched her lips together above the few teeth left her. "Why should she heed you, who are outlanders, lowlanders, have never before done her homage, and clearly are now appealing only to save—not even your lives, for you can still escape, but your mongers' profits?"

"Treasure? We have jewelry of gold, silver, and gemstones, we have garments fit for queens—"

"What are such things to Air?"

"To Earth, maybe," Bulak put in. "Aromatic woods might please Fire, spices and sweetmeats Water. Yet with them, too, I fear you would be unwise." Shrewdly: "For in no case will you offer your entire freight, when you can better withdraw and come back with most of it several months hence. It is . . . not well to try to bargain with the Powers."

That depended on which Powers, Cappen thought. He knew of some—but they were elsewhere, gods and tutelaries of lands less stark than this.

The drink was buzzing in his head. Dismay shocked through. *Why am I jesting? It's my life on the table tonight!*

Slowly, Deghred nodded. The one sensible thing for his caravan to do was retreat, wait out the winter, and cut its losses as much as might be. Wasn't it?

And absolute lunacy for Cappen Varra. Once he was back in the Empire, he himself would not bet a counterfeit lead bawbee on his chance of getting away again. The alert was out for him. If nobody else noticed first, one or another of his fellow travelers was bound soon to hear the description and betray him for the reward. Fleeing into the hinterlands or diving into some thieves' den would hardly buy enough time. Though his amulet might keep Nerigo's demons off his direct track, they could invisibly watch and listen to others, everywhere, and report everything suspicious to the sorcerer.

Stay here in Khangaii? Surely the villagers could feed one extra mouth. He'd pay them well, with arts and shows, entertainments such as they'd never enjoyed before, keeping heart in them through the grim time ahead.

Maybe they'd agree. Then maybe he'd starve or freeze to death along with so many of them. Or maybe Nerigo would get word of a vagabond who'd joined the men of Arechoum and stayed behind when they returned. He was not yet too far beyond the Imperial marches for a squad to come after him as soon as the ways became at all passable.

Deghred barked a harsh laugh. "Yes, most certainly not to dicker and quibble with a female already incensed," he said. "That would be to throw oil on a fire." He sighed. "Very well, we'll load up again tomorrow and betake ourselves hence. May we find it well with the High Folk when we come back."

The younger wife moaned softly in the shadows and clutched two of the children to her.

Let her live, Cappen thought wildly. *She's beautiful. Several of them that I've spied here are, in their way. Though I don't suppose I can beguile any—*

His heart leaped. His legs followed. The others stared as he sprang to his feet. "No, wait!" he cried. "Wait only a little span. A few days more at most. I've an idea to save us!"

"What, you?" demanded Deghred, while his traders gaped and Bulak scowled. "Has a *yawanna* taken your wits? Or have you not understood what we were saying, how easily we can give the Lady offense and bring her fury straight against us?"

"I have, I have," Cappen answered frantically. "My thought is nothing like that. Any risk will be wholly my own, I swear. Only hearken to me."

Risk indeed. A notion born out of half-drunken desperation, maybe. But maybe, also, sired by experience.

He called up coolness, to be a wellspring for a spate of eager, cozening words such as a bard and showman had better always be able to produce.

Day came bleak and bright. Washed clean, newly smooth-shaven, wearing the finest warm raiment to be found in the caravan's goods—plumed cap of purple satin, scarlet cloak, green tunic embroidered with gold and trimmed with sable, dark-blue hose, buskins of tooled leather—with a small harp in his hand from the same source, he left the village behind and made his way on up the path toward the heights. Wind whistled. Far overhead, a hawk rode it. The chill whipped his face. He hardly felt it, nor any weariness after sleepless hours. He was strung too taut.

But when he reached the cairn they had told him of, from which rose a pole and flew an often-renewed white banner, while a narrow trail wound off to the left, an abrupt sense of how alone he was hollowed him out. Though he seldom thought about it, his wish was to die, sometime in the distant future, with a comrade or two and a girl or three to appreciate his gallantry and his last quip.

He stiffened his sinews and summoned up his blood. He must not seem to be afraid, so best was to convince himself that he wasn't. Think rather of this as a unique challenge.

The trail went across the mountainside, near the edge of a cliff sheering down into dizzy depths. Elsewhere the land reached vast and tilted, here and there a meadow amidst the rock. A waterfall gleamed like a sword across the gorge. Its booming came faintly through the wind.

Before long he reached the altar where they prayed and sacrificed to Aiala, a great boulder squared off and graven with eroded symbols. Cappen saw few if any other traces of man. No sacred smoke, but thin gustborne streamers of dry snow blew past. Here, though, if anywhere, she should quickly discern any worshipper.

He took stance before the block and turned his gaze aloft. Give her a short time to see, perhaps to wonder, perhaps even to admire.

The air shrilled.

Cappen tucked gloves into belt and positioned the harp. His fingers evoked the first chord. He began to sing.

It was a song he had used more than once over the years, usually to good effect. Of course, it must be adapted to each occasion, even rendered into a different language, and he had lain awake working on it. However, if she really did know all human tongues, he could simplify the task by staying with the original Caronnais. If not, or if he was mistaken about her femaleness—he wouldn't weaken his delivery by fretting about that. He sang loud and clear:

> *Be merciful, I pray, and hear my cry*
> *Into the winds that you command. I know*
> *That I am overbold, but even so*
> *Adore the one whose queendom is the sky,*
> *In awe of whom the moonlit night-clouds fly,*
> *Who dances in the sunlight and the snow,*
> *Who brings the springtime, when the freshets flow*
> *And all the world goes green beneath her eye.*
> *Yet worship is not that which makes me call*
> *Upon you here, and offer up my heart.*
> *Although I, mortal, surely cannot woo*
> *As man to maiden, still, I have seen all—*
> *No, just a little, but at least a part—*
> *Of that alive enchantment which is you.*
> *And she came to him.*

"—However, speak," she said.

He suppressed a shiver. Now he must be as glib as ever in his life. "First, will my lady permit that I resume my cap and gloves and pull my cloak around me? It's mortal cold for a mortal."

Again something like amusement flickered briefly. She nodded. "Then say what is your name, your home, and your errand."

"May it please my lady, the caravaneers I travel with know me as Peor Sardan of Lorace." He was clearly from such parts. "But you of the high heavens surely recognize that this cannot be quite so." *Really? Well, anyhow, outright prevarication could be hazardous and should be unnecessary. She won't deign to give me away. If she chooses to destroy me, she'll do it herself. Battered to death by hailstones—?* "My motherland is farther west and south, the kingdom of Caronne, and I hight Cappen Varra, born to the noble house of Dordain. As for my errand, I have none fixed, being a wanderer—in spite of the birth I mentioned—who wishes to see something of the world and better his fortune before turning home. Rather, that was my only wish until this happy day."

"Yes, I've spied the pack train," said Aiala scornfully. "You hope I'll grant you better weather."

"Oh, my lady! Forgive me, but no. Who am I to petition you? Nor am I in their enterprise. I simply took what appeared to be an opportunity to visit their country, of which go many fabulous accounts. Now I see this for the velleity it was." He made his look upon her half shy, half aglow. "Here I find the fulfillment of my true and lifelong desire."

Was she taken a bit aback? At any rate, her manner grew less forbidding. "What do you mean?"

Cappen gestured from beneath his cloak. "Why, my lady, what else than the praise of Woman? She, the flower of earthly creation, in her thousandfold dear incarnations, no wine so sweet or heady as her presence, she is the meaning of my existence and my poor verses in her honor are its justification. Yes, I have found her and sung to her in many a land, from the soft vales of Caronne to the stern fjords of Norren, from a fisher hut on Ocean shore to a palace in Sanctuary, and my thought was to seek her anew in yonder realm, perhaps some innocent maiden, perhaps some wise enchantress, how can I know before she has kindled my heart?"

"You are . . . a flighty one, then." She did not sound disapproving— what constancy has the wind?—but as though intrigued, even puzzled.

"Also, my very love drives me onward. For see you, my lady, it is Woman herself for whom I quest. While often wondrous, no one woman is more than mortal. She has, at most, a few aspects of perfection, and they changeable as sun-sparkles on the river that is time. Otherwise, the flaws of flesh, the infirmities of insight, the narrowness of dailiness belong to being human. And I, all too human, lack strength and patience to endure such thwarting of the dream for long. The yearning overtakes me and I must be off again in search of that prize which common sense tells me is unattainable but the spirit will not ever quite let me despair of."

Not bad, Cappen thought. By now he half believed it.

"I told you to speak in few words." Aiala didn't say that quite firmly.

"Ah, would that I could give you obedience in this as I shall in all else whatsoever," Cappen sighed into the wind. "Dismiss me, and of course I will depart, grieving and yet gladsome over what has been vouchsafed me. But until then I can no more curb my tongue than I can quell my heart. For I have glimpsed the gates of my goal, loftier and more precious than any knight before me can have beheld, and I jubilate."

"And never before have I—" escaped from her. She recalled her savage dignity. "Clarify this. I'll not stand here the whole day."

"Certainly not. The heights and the heavens await your coming. But since you command me, I can relate quite plainly that, hitherbound, I heard tell of my lady. Beyond, perhaps over and above her majesty and mightiness, the tales were of visions, dazzlements, seen by an incredibly fortunate few through the centuries, beauty well-nigh too great to bear— and, more than that, a spirit lordly and loving, terrible and tender, mysterious and merry, life-bearing and life-nourishing—in short, Woman."

"You . . . had not seen me . . . earlier," Aiala murmured.

"But I had, fleetingly, fragmentarily, in dreams and longings. Here, I thought, must be Truth. For although there are doubtless other goddesses of whom something similar can be said, and I imply no least disrespect for any, still, Truth is One, is it not? Thus I strove to infer a little of the immortally living miracle I heard of. I wove these inferences into a humble tribute. I brought it to your halidom as my offering.

"To do worship is an end and a reward in itself. I dared hope for no more. Now—my lady, I have seen that, however inadequate, my verse was not altogether wide of the mark. What better can an artist win than such a knowledge, for an hour of his few years on Earth? My lady, I can die content, and I thank you."

"You—need not die. Not soon. Go back to the plains."

"So we had decided, the caravaneers and I, for never would we defy our lady's righteous wrath. Thence I will seek to regain my faraway birthland, that my countrymen too may be enriched by a hint of your glory. If I fall by the wayside—" Cappen shrugged. "Well, as I said, today my life has had overflowing measure."

She raised her brows. "Your road is dangerous?"

"It is long, my lady, and at the outset—I left certain difficulties behind me in the Empire—trivial, but some people overreact. My plan had been to circumvent them by going roundabout through Arechoum. No matter. If the cosmic cycle requires that my lady decree an early winter throughout her mountains, I shall nevertheless praise her while blood beats within me."

"It's not that." Aiala bridled. The wind snarled. "No! I am not bound to a wheel! This is my will."

"Your wisdom."

"My anger!" she yelled. The storm in the west mounted swiftly higher. "I'll show them! They'll be sorry!"

"They?" asked Cappen low.

"Aye, they'll mourn for that they mocked me, when the waters of Vanis lie frozen past the turning of the springtime, and the earth of Orun remains barren, and the fires of Lua smolder out because no dwellers are left alive to tend them." Under his cloak, Cappen suppressed a shudder. *Yes*, he thought, *human rulers don't take their subjects much into account either.* "Then they'll come to me begging my mercy, and I will grant it to them for a song."

I'm on the track. "But is it not my lady of the winds who sings to the world?" Cappen pursued, carefully, carefully.

"So they'll discover, when I laugh at their effort."

"I am bewildered. How could any being, divine or not, possibly quarrel with my lady?"

Aiala paced to and fro. The wind strengthened, the dark clouds drew closer. After a stark minute she halted, looked straight at him, and said, "The gods fall out with each other now and then." He forebore to mention that he well knew that. His need was for her to unburden herself. His notion that she was lonelier than she realized seemed the more likely when her tone calmed somewhat. "This—" She actually hesitated. "You may understand. You are a maker of songs."

"I am when inspired, my lady, as I was today." Or whenever called for, but that was beside the immediate point.

"You did well. Not that *they* could have appreciated it."

"A song was wanted among the gods?"

Locks streamed and tumbled the more wildly as she nodded. "For a wedding, a divine marriage. Your countrymen must perceive it otherwise, but in these uplands it is Khaiantai who wakens at the winter solstice from her sleep, a virgin, to welcome Hurultan the Lightbearer, her bridegroom; and great is the rejoicing in Heaven and on Earth."

On Earth in better years, Cappen thought. *Yes, the mythic event, forever new and forever recurrent.* A chill passed up his spine. He concealed it as best he was able. "But . . . the occasion is not always the same?"

"No. Is one day the same as the last? Time would come to a stop."

"So—the feast and—" his mind leaped—"gifts to the happy pair?"

"Just so. Of us Four, Orun may bring fruits or gold, Vanis a fountain or a rainbow, Lua an undying lamp or a victorious sword—such things as pertain to them—while I have given an eagle or a fragrance or—we go there together; for we are the Four."

"But now lately—?"

Her reasonableness began to break. "I had in mind a hymeneal song, like none heard before in those halls but often to be again. They agreed this would be a splendid gift. I created it. And then—" Elemental rage screamed through an icy blast.

"And they did not comprehend it," Cappen proposed.

"They scoffed! They said it was so unworthy they would not come to the feast in my company if I brought it. They *dare!*"

Cappen waited out the ensuing whirlwind. When Aiala had quieted down a grim trifle, he ventured, "My lady, this is often the fate of artists. I have learned how eloquence is meaningless to the word-blind, music and meter to the tone-deaf, subtlety to the blunt-brained, and profundity to the unlearned."

"Good names for these, Cappen Varra."

"I refer to no gods or other high Powers, my lady," he made haste to reply. One never knew who or what might be listening. "No irreverence. Absolutely never! I speak merely of my small human experience and of people whom I actually pity more than despise—except, to be sure, when they set themselves up as critics. Yet even persons of unimpeachable taste and discernment can have differences of opinion. This is an unfortunate fact of life, to which I have become resigned."

"I will not be. Moreover, word has gotten about. If I come lamely in with something else than a song—No!" Aiala yowled. "They'll learn respect when I avenge my pride with disasters like none since Chaos rebelled in the beginning."

"Ah—may that perhaps conceivably be just a minim extreme, my lady? Not that I can judge. Indeed, I am baffled to grasp how your colleagues could reject your epithalamium. The music of the wind pervades the world, lulling breeze, sough in forests, laughterful rainsquall, trumpeting gale, oh, infinite is its variety, and its very hushes are a part of the composition," said Cappen with another sweeping gesture.

She nearly thawed. "You, though, you understand me—" she breathed. "For the first time ever, someone —"

He intended to go on in this vein until he had softened her mood enough for her to stop punishing the land. But she paused, then exclaimed, "Hear what I have made, and judge."

"Oh, my lady, I cannot!" gasped Cappen, aghast. "I'm totally unworthy, unfit, disqualified."

She smiled. "Be not afraid," she said quite gently. "Only tell me what you think. I won't take offense."

Too many others had insisted on declaiming their verses to him. "But, my lady, I don't know, I cannot know the language of the gods, and surely your work would lose much in translation."

"Actually," she said, "it's in classical Xandran, as we're wont to use when elegance is the aim."

He remembered white temples and exquisite sculptures in the South and West, too often ruinous, yet still an ideal for all successor peoples. Evidently the local deities felt that, while their worshippers might be barbarians, they themselves ought to display refinement. "But I also fear—I regret—my lady, I was not very dedicated to my schooling. My knowledge of Xandran was slight at best, and has largely rusted out of me." True enough.

Impulsive as her winds, she smiled afresh. "You shall have it back, and more."

"That would, er, take a while."

"No. Hear me. All tongues spoken by men anywhere are open to me."

Yes, so Bulak had said. How remote and unreal the Uryuk hut felt.

"For the sake of your courteous words, Cappen Varra, and your doubtless keen judgment, I will bestow this on you."

He gaped. "How—how—And how can this weak little head of mine hold so overwhelmingly much?"

"It need not. Whenever you hear or read a language, you will be able to use it like a native. Afterward and until next time, there will be only whatever you choose to keep and can, as with ordinary memories."

"My lady, I repeat, I'm wholly unworthy—"

"Hold still." Imperious, she trod over to him, laid hands on his cheeks, and kissed him.

He lurched, half stunned. A forefinger slid into either ear. He noted vaguely amidst the tempest that this was a caress worth trying in future, if he had a future.

She released him and stepped back. His daze faded and he could pay close heed to what he said. "I, I never dreamed that Woman herself would—For that instant I was like unto a god."

Her hand chopped the air, impatient. "Now you are ready to hear me."

He braced for it.

Gaze expectant upon him, she cleared her throat and launched into her song. Fantastically, the Xandran lyrics rang Caronnais-clear. He wished they didn't. As for the melody, she possessed a marvelous voice, but these notes took a drunkard's walk from key to key.

> *The universe has looked forward with breath baited,*
> *Not only Earth but the underworld and the starry sky,*
> *For this day so well-known, even celebrated,*
> *When all of us assembled see eye to eye*
> *About the union of our shiny Hurultan, whose ability*
> *It is the daylight forward to bring,*
> *And dear Khaiantai, who will respond with agility,*
> *So that between them they become parents of the spring—*

Cappen thanked the years that had taught him acting, in this case the role of a gravely attentive listener.

Aiala finished: " '—And thus let us join together in chorusing my song.' There! What do you think of that?"

"It is remarkable, my lady," Cappen achieved.

"I didn't just dash it off, you know. I weighed and shaped every word. For instance, that line *'Birds also will warble as soon as they hatch from the egg.'* That did not come easily."

"An unusual concept, yes. In fact, I've never heard anything like it."

"Be frank. Tell me truly, could I make a few little improvements? Perhaps—I've considered—instead of *'as ardent as a prize bull,'* what about *'as vigorous as a stud horse'*?"

"Either simile is striking, my lady. I would be hard put to suggest any possible significant changes."

Aiala flared anew. "Then *why* do Orun, Vanis, and Lua sneer? How can they?"

"Sneering comes easily to some persons, my lady. It is not uncommonly an expression of envy. But to repeat myself, I do not propose that that applies in the present case. Tastes do differ. Far be it from me to imagine how your distinguished kindred might perceive a piece like this. Appropriateness to an occasion need have nothing to do with the quality of a work. It may merely happen to not quite fit in—like, say, a stately funeral dirge in a series of short-haul chanties. Or vice versa. Professionals like me," said Cappen forbearingly, "must needs learn to supply what may be demanded, and reserve our true art for connoisseurs."

He failed to mollify her. Instead, she stiffened and glared. "So! I'm unskilled, am I? I suppose you can do better?"

Cappen lifted his palms with a defensiveness not entirely feigned. "Oh, absolutely not. I simply meant—"

"I know. You make excuses for them on behalf of your own feelings."

"My lady, you urged me to be forthright. I hint at nothing but a conceivable, quite possibly hypothetical reconsideration of intent, in view of the context."

Indignation relieved him by yielding to haughtiness. "I told you how I would lose honor did I by now give anything but a song. Rather will I stay home and make them sorry."

Cappen's mind leaped like a hungry cat at a mouse. "Ah, but perhaps there is a third and better way out of this deplorable situation. Could you bring a different paean? I know many that have enjoyed great success at nuptial gatherings."

"And the gods will know, or in time they'll discover, that it is not new in the world. Shall I bring used goods to the sacred wedding—*I*?"

"Well, no, my lady, of course not."

Aiala sniffed. "I daresay you can provide something original that will be good enough."

"Not to compare with my lady's. Much, much less exalted. Thereby, however, more readily blending into revelry, where the climate is really not conducive to concentrated attention. Grant me time, for indeed the standard to be met is heaven-high—"

She reached a decision. "Very well. A day and a night."

"Already tomorrow?" protested Cappen, appalled.

"*They* shall not think I waver weakly between creativity and vengeance. Tomorrow. In classical Xandran. Fresh and joyous. It had better be."

"But—but—"

"Then I will give you my opinion, freely and frankly."

"My lady, this is too sudden for imperfect flesh and feeble intelligence. I beg you—"

"Silence. It's more than I think I would grant anyone else, for the sake of your respectful words and song. I begin to have my suspicions about it, but will overlook them if you bring me one that is acceptable and that my winds can tell me has never been heard before on this earth or in its skies. Fail me, and your caravan will not get back to the plains, nor you to anywhere. Go!"

In a whirl of white, she vanished. The wind shrieked louder and colder, the storm clouds drew nearer.

Villagers and Caravaneers spied him trudging back down the path and, except for those out forlornly herding the sheep, swarmed together to meet him. Their babble surfed around his ears. He gestured vainly for silence. Bulak roared for it. As it fell, mumble by mumble, he and Deghred trod forward. "What did you do yonder?" he asked, less impassively than became a headman.

Cappen had donned his sternest face. "These be mysteries not to be spoken of until their completion," he declared. "Tomorrow shall see my return to them."

He dared not spend hours relating and explaining, when he had so few. Nor did it seem wise to admit that thus far, in all likelihood, he had made matters worse, especially for the travelers.

Bulak stood foursquare. Deghred gave the bard a searching and skeptical look. The rest murmured, fingered prayer beads or josses, and otherwise registered an awe that was useful at the moment but, if disappointed, could well turn murderously vengeful.

Cappen went on headlong. "I must meditate, commune with high Powers, and work my special magianisms," he said. "For this I require to be alone, well sheltered, with writing materials and, uh, whatever else I may require."

Bulak stared. "Suddenly you speak as if born amidst us."

"Take that as a token of how deep and powerful the mysteries are."

Cappen forgot to keep his voice slowly tolling. "But, but does anybody here know Xandran?"

Wind whistled, clouds swallowed the sun, three ravens flew by like forerunners of darkness.

"I have some command of the tongue," said Deghred, almost as if he suspected a trap.

"Classical Xandran?" cried Cappen.

"No. Who does but a few scholars? I mean what they use in those parts nowadays—that is, the traders and sailors I've had to do with. And, yes, once a crew of pirates; but I think that was a different dialect."

The foolish, fire-on-ice hope died. Still—"I may want to call on what knowledge you have. That will depend on what my divinations reveal to me. Hold yourself prepared. Meanwhile, what of my immediate needs?"

"We have a place," Bulak said. "Lowly, but all we can offer."

"The spirits take small account of Earthly grandeur," his elder wife assured them, for whatever that was worth.

Thus Cappen found himself and his few possessions in the village storehouse. It was a single room, mainly underground, with just enough walls beneath the sod roof to allow an entryway. After the door was closed, a lamp gave the only light. While the space was fairly large, very little was available, for it was crammed with roots, dried meat, sheepskins, and other odorous goods. The air hung thick and dank. However, it was out of the wind, and private.

Too private, maybe. Cappen had nothing to take his mind off his thoughts.

He settled in, a pair of skins between him and the floor, one over his shoulders. Besides the lamp, he had been given food, a crock of wine, a goblet, a crock for somewhat different purposes, and his tools—a bottle of ink, several quill pens, and a sheaf of paper, articles such as merchants used in their own work. Now he began wondering, more and more frantically, what to do with them.

Ordinarily he could have dashed something off. But a canticle in classical Xandran, suitable for a marriage made in heaven? Especially when the cost of its proving unsatisfactory would be widespread death, including his? He did not feel inspired.

The language requirement was obstacle enough. His wits twisted to and fro, hunting for a way, any way, around it. Through Deghred, he could now get a doubtless very limited acquaintance with the present-day speech. He recalled hearing that it descended directly from the antique, so much of it must be similar. How would pronunciation have changed, though, and grammar, and even vocabulary? In his days at home he had read certain famous poems five or six hundred years old. It had been difficult; only a lexicon made it possible at all; and the archaic idiom of the Rojan hillmen suggested how alien the verses would have sounded.

He glugged a mouthful of wine. It hit an empty stomach and thence sent a faint glow to his head. He did have a bit more to go on. When he concentrated, he could drag scraps of the proper classical up from the forgetfulness in which they had lain. Maybe his newly acquired facility helped with that. But they were just scraps. He had yawned through a year of this as part of the education that even a bastard son of a minor nobleman was supposed to receive, but declensions, conjugations, moods, tenses, and the dismal rest set his attention adrift in the direction of girls, flowery forests, rowdy friends, composing a song of his own that might seduce a girl, or almost anything else. What stayed with him had done so randomly, like snatches of his aunt's moralizings when he was a child and couldn't escape.

And then he had Aiala's lyrics. That wasn't by design. Every word clung to him, like the memory of every bit of a certain meal years ago that he had had to eat and praise because the cook was a formidable witch. He feared he would never get rid of either. Still, the thing gave him a partial but presumably trustworthy model, a basis for comparison and thus for a guesswork sort of reconstruction.

He drank again. His blood started to buzz faintly, agreeably. Of course, he'd need his reason unimpaired when—if—he got to that task. But "if" was the doomful word. First he needed the poesy, the winged fancy, concepts evoking words that in turn made the concepts live. Anxiety, to give it a euphemistic name, held his imagination in a swamp of glue. And wasn't that metaphor a repulsive symptom of his condition? Anything he might force out of himself would belong in yonder crock.

So he must lift his heart, free his spirit. Then he could hope his genius would soar. After which he could perhaps render the Caronnais into Xandran without mutilating it beyond recognition. The basic difficulty was that to create under these circumstances he must get drunk, no good condition for a translator. He suspected the necessary degree of drunkenness was such that when he awoke he wouldn't care whether he lived or died—until much too late. The lady of the winds did not expect to be kept waiting.

Besides—he spat a string of expletives—she demanded not only words but music. The two must go together as naturally as breath and heartbeat, or the song was a botch and a mockery. This meant they must grow side by side, intertwining, shaping one another, as he worked. Oh, usually he could find an existing melody that fitted a poem he had in process, or vice versa. Neither was admissible in this case; both must never have been heard before in the world. He could attempt a double originality, but that, he knew, would only be possible with the Caronnais native to him. To force the subsequent translation into that mold—well, give him a week or two and maybe he might, but since he had only until tomorrow—

He glugged again. He would doubtless be wise to ballast the wine with food. It wasn't the worst imaginable food, caravaneers' rations, smoked meat and fish, butter, cheese, hardtack, rice cold but lately boiled with leeks and garlic, dried figs and apricots and—On the other hand, he lacked appetite. What use wisdom anyway? He glugged again.

If this was the end of his wanderings, he thought, it was not quite what he had visualized and certainly far too early. Not that he did well to pity himself. Think of his waymates, think of the poor innocent dwellers throughout these mountains. Surely he had enjoyed much more than them, much more colorful. It behooved a minstrel, a knight of the road, to hark back, as gladly as the wine enabled.

Most recently, yes, to Sanctuary. He had had his troubles there, but the same was true of every place, and the multifarious pleasures much outnumbered them. Ending with delicious Peridis—may she fare always well—and their last, so unfortunately interrupted moment—

He stirred on his sheepskins. By all the nymphs of joy, it happened he had brought away a souvenir of it! There he could for a while take refuge from his troubles, other than in drink. And perhaps, said practicality, this would liberate his genius.

Groping about, shivering in the chill, he found the book. Cross-legged, he opened it on his lap and peered through the dim, smoky, smelly lamplight.

The words leaped out at him. They were in no language he had ever heard of, nor was it anywhere named; but he read it as easily as he did his own, instantly understanding what everything he came upon referred to. Not that that brought full knowledge. The world he found was an abstraction, a bubble, floating cheerfully free in a space and a time beyond his ken. No matter. He guessed it was almost as airy there.

The musical notation stood equally clear to him, tunes lilting while he scanned them. Their scale was not too different from that common in the Westlands. He would need only a little practice before singing and strumming them in a way that everybody he met ought to like. What exoticism there was should lend piquancy. Yes, for his future career—

Future!

He sprang to his feet. His head banged against a rafter.

Hastily fetched through biting wind and gathering murk, Deghred in Dalagh hunkered down and peered at Cappen Varra. "Well, what do you crave of me?" he asked.

"In a minute, I pray you." Himself sitting tailor-fashion, the bard tried to arrange paper, inkpot, and open book for use. Bloody awkward. No help at all to the image of a knowing and confident rescuer.

"I've a feeling you're none too sure either," Deghred murmured.

"But I am! I simply need a bit of assistance. Who doesn't ever? The craftsman his apprentices, the priest his acolytes, and you a whole gang of underlings. I want no more than a brief . . . consultation."

"To what end?" Deghred paused. "They're growing dubious of you. What kind of Powers are you trying to deal with? What could come of it?"

"The good of everybody."

"Or the ruin?"

"I haven't time to argue." *If I did, I suspect you'd be utterly appalled and make me cease and desist. Then you'd offer an extravagant sacrifice to a being that no such thing will likely appease—for you haven't met her as I have.*

Deghred's voice harshened. "Be warned. If you don't do what you promised—"

"Well, I didn't exactly *promise*—"

"My men won't let you leave with us, and I suspect the villagers will cast you out. They fear you'll carry a curse."

Cappen was not much surprised. "Suppose, instead, I gain clemency, weather as it ought to be, and the passes open for you. Will they give me anything better than thanks? I'm taking a considerable personal risk, you know."

"Ah, should you succeed, that's different. Although these dwellers be poor folk, I don't doubt they'd heap skins and pelts at your feet. I'll show you how to sell the stuff at good prices in Temanhassa."

"You and your fellow traders are not poor men," said Cappen pointedly.

"Naturally, you'd find us, ah, not ungenerous."

"Shall we say a tenth share of the profit from your expedition?"

"A tenth? How can you jest like that in an hour like this?"

"Retreating to winter in the Empire would cost more. As you must well know, who've had to cope year after year with its taxes, bribes, and extortionate suppliers." Getting snowed in here would be still worse, but Cappen thought it imprudent to explain that that had become a distinct possibility.

"We are not misers or ingrates. Nor are we unreasonable. Three percent is, indeed, lavish."

"Let us not lose precious time in haggling. Seven and a half."

"Five, and my friendship, protection, and recommendations to influential persons in Temanhassa."

"Done!" said Cappen. He sensed the trader's surprise and a certain instinctive disappointment. But the need to get on with the work was very real, and the bargain not a bad one.

Meanwhile he had arranged his things just barely well enough that he could begin. Dipping pen in ink, he said, "This is a strange work I must do, and potent forces are afoot. As yet I cannot tell of it, save to pledge that there is nothing of evil. As I write, I want you to talk to me in Xandran. Naught else."

Deghred gaped, remembered his dignity, and replied, "May I wonder why? You do not know that tongue, and I have only some smatterings."

"You may wonder if you choose. What you must do is talk."

"But what about?"

"Anything. Merely keep the words flowing."

Deghred groped for a minute. Such an order is not as simple as one might think. Almost desperately, he began: "I have these fine seasonings. They were shipped to me from distant lands at great expense. To you and you alone will I offer them at ridiculously low wholesale prices, because I hold you in such high esteem. Behold, for an ounce of pungent peppercorn, a mere ten zirgats. I look on this not as a loss to me, although it is, but a gift of goodwill."

Cappen scribbled. While he listened, the meanings came clear to him. He even mentally made up for the stumblings, hesitations, and thick accent. The language was his to the extent that it was the other man's; and he could have replied with fluency. What slowed him was the search in his mind for words that weren't spoken. "Knot" and "insoluble," for instance. How would one say them? . . . Ah, yes. Assuming that what he pseudo-remembered was correct. Maybe the connotations were strictly of a rope and of minerals that didn't melt in water. He jotted them down provisionally, but he wanted more context.

Deghred stopped. "Go on," Cappen urged.

"Well, uh—O barefaced brazen robber! Ten zirgats? If this withered and moldy lot went for two in the bazaar, I would be astounded. Yet, since I too am prepared to take a loss for the sake of our relationship, I will offer three—"

"Uh, could you give me something else?" Cappen interrupted. "Speech not so, m-m, commercial?"

"What can it be? My dealings with Xandrans are all commercial."

"Oh, surely not all. Doing business in itself involves sociability, the cultivation of friendly feelings, does it not? Tell me what might be said at a shared meal over a cup of wine."

Deghred pondered before he tried: "How did your sea voyage go? I hope you're not troubled by the heat. It is seldom so hot here at this time of year."

"Nothing more—more intimate? Don't men like these ever talk of their families? Of love and marriage?"

"Not much. I can't converse with them easily, you know. Women, yes."

"Say on."

"Well, I remember telling one fellow, when he asked, that the best whorehouse in the city is the Purple Lotus. Especially if you can get Zerasa. By Kalat's cloven hoof, what a wench! Plump and sweet as a juicy plum, sizzling as a spitted rump roast, and the tricks she knows—" Deghred reminisced in considerable detail.

It wasn't quite what Cappen had meant. Still, association evoked words also amorous, ʋut apparently decorous. His pen flew, scrawling, scratching out, spattering the paper and his tunic. When Degredh ended with a gusty sigh, Cappen had enough.

"Good," he said. "My thanks—albeit this is toward the end of saving your own well-being and prosperity too. You may go now. Five percent, remember."

The merchant rose and stretched himself as well as the roof allowed. "If naught else, that was a small respite from reality. Ah, well. You do have hopes? Are you coming along?"

"No," said Cappen. "My labors are just beginning."

Day broke still and cloudless but cruelly cold. Breath smoked white, feet crunched ice. When he emerged at mid-morning, Cappen found very few folk outdoors. Those stared at him out of their own frozen silence. The rest were huddled inside, keeping warm while they waited to learn their fate. It was as if the whole gigantic land held its breath.

He felt no weariness, he could not. He seemed almost detached from himself, his head light but sky-clear. His left arm cradled the harp. Tucked into his belt was a folded sheet of paper, but he didn't expect any need to refer to it. The words thereon were graven into him, together with their music. They certainly should be. The gods of minstrelsy knew—or would have known, if they weren't so remote from this wild highland—how he had toiled over the lyrics, searching about, throwing away effort after effort, inch by inch finding his way to a translation that fitted the notes and was not grossly false to the original, and at last, not satisfied but with time on his heels, had rehearsed over and over and over for his audience of turnips and sheepskins.

Now he must see how well it played for a more critical listener.

If it succeeded, if he survived, the first part of the reward he'd claim was to be let to sleep undisturbed until next sunrise. How remotely that bliss glimmered!

He trudged onward, scarcely thinking about anything, until he came to the altar. There he took stance, gazed across the abyss to peaks sword-sharp against heaven, and said, "My lady, here I am in obedience to your command."

It sounded unnaturally loud. No echo responded, no wings soared overhead, he stood alone in the middle of aloneness.

After a while, he said, "I repeat, begging my lady's pardon, that here I am with that which I promised you."

The least of breezes stirred. It went like liquid across his face and into his nostrils. In so vast a silence, he heard it whisper.

"I humbly hope my offering will please you and all the gods," he said.

And there she was, awesome and beautiful before him. A phantom wind tossed her hair and whirled snow-sparkles around her whiteness. "Well?" she snapped.

Could she too, even she, have been under strain? He doffed his cap and bowed low. "If my lady will deign to heed, I've created an epithalamium such as she desires, and have the incomparable honor of rendering it unto her, to be known forever after as her unique gift at the turning of the winter."

"That was quick, after you protested you could not."

"The thought of you inspired me as never erenow have I been inspired."

"To make it out of nothing?"

"Oh, no, my lady. Out of experience, and whatever talent is mine, and, above all else, as I confessed, the shining vision of my lady. I swear, and take for granted you can immediately verify, that neither melody nor lyrics were ever heard in this world, Heaven or Earth or the Elsewhere, before I prepared them for you."

He doubted that she could in fact scan space and time at once, so thoroughly. But no matter. He did not doubt that Nerigo kept his half-illicit arcanum and whatever came to it through his mirror that was not a mirror well sealed against observation human and nonhuman. Whatever gods had the scope and power to spy on him must also have much better things to do.

Aiala's glance lingered more than it pierced. "I do not really wish to destroy you, Cappen Varra," she told him slowly. "You have a rather charming way about you. But—should you disappoint me—you will understand that one does have one's position to maintain."

"Oh, absolutely. And how better could a man perish than in striving to serve such a lady? Yet I dare suggest that you will find my ditty acceptable."

The glorious eyes widened. The slight mercurial shivers almost ceased. "Sing, then," she said low.

"Allow me first to lay forth what the purpose is. Unless I am grievously mistaken, it is to provide an ode to nuptial joy. Now, my thought was that this is best expressed in the voice of the bride. The groom is inevitably impatient for nightfall. She, though, however happy, may at the same time be a little fearful, certain of loving kindness yet, in her purity, unsure what to await and what she can do toward making the union rapturous. Khaiantai is otherwise. She is a goddess, and here is an annual renewal. My song expresses her rapture in tones of unbounded gladness."

Aiala nodded. "That's not a bad theme," she said, perhaps a trifle wistfully.

"Therefore, my lady, pray bear with my conceit, in the poetic sense, that she sings with restrained abandon, in colloquial terms of revelry, not always classically correct. For we have nothing to go on about that save the writings of the learned, do we? There must have been more familiar speech among lesser folk, commoners, farmers, herders, artisans, lowly but still the majority, the backbone of the nation and the salt of the earth. To them too, to the Life Force that is in them, should the paean appeal."

"You may be right," said Aiala with a tinge of exasperation. "Let me hear."

While he talked, Cappen Varra, in the presence of one who fully knew the language, mentally made revisions. Translating, he had chosen phrasings that lent themselves to it.

The moment was upon him. He took off his gloves, gripped the harp, strummed it, and cleared his throat.

"We begin with a chorus," he said. Therewith he launched into song.

Bridegroom and bride!
Knot that's insoluble,
Voices all voluble,

Hail it with pride.—
She hearkened. Her bosom rose and fell.
Now the bride herself sings.
When a merry maiden marries,
Sorrow goes and pleasure tarries;
Every sound becomes a song,
All is right, and nothing's wrong!—
He saw he had captured her, and continued to the bacchanalian
     end.
"Sullen night is laughing day—
All the year is merry May!

The chords rang into stillness. Cappen waited. But he knew. A huge,
warm easing rose in him like a tide.

"That is wonderful," Aiala breathed. "Nothing of the kind, ever
before—"

"It is my lady's," he said with another bow, while he resumed his cap
and gloves.

She straightened into majesty. "You have earned what you shall
have. Henceforward until the proper winter, the weather shall smile, the
dwellers shall prosper, and you and your comrades shall cross my mountains free of all hindrance."

"My lady overwhelms me," he thought it expedient to reply.

For a heartbeat, her grandeur gave way, ever so slightly. "I could
almost wish that you—But no. Farewell, funny mortal."

She leaned over. Her lips brushed his. He felt as if struck by soft
lightning. Then she was gone. It seemed to him that already the air grew
more mild.

For a short while before starting back with his news he stood silent
beneath the sky, suddenly dazed. His free hand strayed to the paper at his
belt. Doubtless he would never know more about this than he now did.
Yet he wished that someday, somehow, if only in another theatrical performance, he could see the gracefully gliding boats of the Venetian gon-
doliers.

His Own Back Yard

James P. Blaylock

James P. Blaylock (www.sybertooth.com/blaylock/) lives in Orange, California, and teaches at Chapman University. Along with his friends Tim Powers and K.W. Jeter, he was part of a circle of young writers associated with Philip K. Dick in the early 1970s. His first stories appeared in the late 1970s and only occasionally since. His first novel, The Elfin Ship, *appeared in 1982. Principally a writer of fantasy, he has published fourteen novels, the most recent of which is* The Rainy Season *(1999), and one collection,* Thirteen Phantasms and Other Stories *(2000).*

"His Own Back Yard" is a fantasy of time travel, in the manner of Jack Finney or Ray Bradbury. It was published online at SciFiction (www.scifi.com/scifiction) and is printed here for perhaps the first time. Blaylock said years ago in an interview, "I've written a short story set in downtown Orange where I live . . . in which I attempt once again to say in the backdrop what it is about the place that keeps me there and that will keep keeping me there."

This is sincere nostalgic fantasy about the power of place and setting.

The abandoned house was boarded up, its chimney fallen, the white paint on the clapboards weathered to the color of an old ghost. It was hidden from the street by two low-limbed sycamores in the front yard and by an overgrown oleander hedge covered in pink and white flowers. Alan stood by his car in the driveway, sheltered from the street in the empty and melancholy afternoon, half listening to the drone of an unseen airplane and to the staccato clamor of a jackhammer that stopped and started in a muted racket somewhere blocks away in the nearby neighborhood.

More than twenty years had passed since Alan had last driven out to his childhood home. A year or so after he had married Susan the two of them had stopped on the road, and he had climbed out of the car with no real idea what he hoped to find. A new family had moved in by then—his own parents having sold the house and moved north a year before—and the unrecognizable children's toys on the lawn were disconcerting to him, and so he had climbed back into the car and driven away.

His marriage to Susan was one of the few things in his life that he had done without hesitation, and that had turned out absolutely right. A few days ago she had gone back east for two weeks to visit her aunts in Michigan, taking along their son Tyler, who was starting college in two months in Ann Arbor. Alan had stayed home looking forward to the peace and quiet, a commodity that had grown scarce over the years. But somewhere along the line he had lost his talent for solitude, and the days of empty stillness had filled him with a sense of loss that was almost irrational, as if Susan and Tyler been gone months instead of days, or as if, like the old house in front of him now, he was coming to the end of something.

He walked into the back yard and tried the rear door, which of course was locked, and then tried without success to peer through a boarded-up kitchen window. He looked back up the driveway to make sure he was unseen, but just then a man came into view, walking along the shoulder of the road, heading uphill past the house. Alan moved back out of sight, waiting for an interminable couple of minutes before looking out once more. Hurrying now, he pried two of the boards off with his hands, wiggling the nails loose and setting the boards aside on the ground. He put his face to the dusty glass and peered through, letting his eyes adjust to the darkness within. There was a skylight overhead, which, like the oleander hedge out front, hadn't been part of the house twenty years ago. Filtered sunlight shone through its litter of leaves and dirt so that the interior of the kitchen slowly appeared out of the darkness like a photograph soaking in developer. He had been afraid that he would find the house depressingly vandalized, but it wasn't; and he stared nostalgically at the familiar chrome cabinet pulls and the white-painted woodwork and the scalloped moldings, remembering the breakfast nook and curio shelves, the dining room beyond, the knotty pine bookshelves topped with turned posts that screened the hallway leading to his bedroom.

He stepped away from the window and walked along the side of the property, between the house and the fence, toward where his bedroom stood—or what had been his bedroom all those years ago. There were no boards on the window, but the view was hidden by curtains. He rejected the idea of breaking the window, and instead retraced his steps, his hands in his pockets, careful not to look over the fence, beyond which lay the back yards of houses built a decade ago. In his day there had been a farm house on several acres, belonging to an old childless couple named Prentice who had the remnants of a grove of walnuts and a chicken coop and goats. There had been fruit trees on their property, peaches and Santa Rosa plums that he had eaten his share of.

He paused in the shade of a big silk oak tree near the garden shed in the back yard and stood listening to the breeze rustle the leaves, hearing again the distant clattering echo of the jack hammer. The heavy grapevines along the fence hadn't been pruned back in years, and the air was weighted with the smell of concord grapes, overripe and falling in among the vines to dry in the summer heat. The August afternoon was lonesome and empty, and the rich smell of the grapes filled him with the recollection of a time when he'd had no real knowledge that the hours and days were quietly slipping away, bartered for memories.

The shed at the back of the garage was ramshackle and empty except for scattered junk, its door long ago fallen off and only a single rusted hinge left as a reminder that it had once had a door at all. He remembered that there had been a brick pad in front of the door, but the bricks were gone, and there was nothing but compressed dirt. Inside, a short wooden shelf held a couple of broken clay pots, and on the wall below the shelf hung a single ancient aluminum lawn chair with a woven nylon seat. Alan was certain he remembered that very chair, in considerably better shape, hanging in this same place thirty years ago. On impulse he stepped into the shed, took the chair down, and unfolded it, wiping off dust and cobwebs before walking out under the tree, where he put the chair down in the shade and sat in it, letting his weight down carefully. The nylon webbing was frayed with age, and the aluminum was bent and weakened at the joints, but the seat held, and he relaxed and surveyed the back yard, feeling a sense of invitation, of growing familiarity. Now that the house was sold and abandoned, soon to be torn down, it was his as much as it was anyone's, and it seemed to him as if the years had passed in the blink of an eye, the house having waited patiently for his return.

The quarter acre yard was smaller than he remembered, although it was immense by southern California standards, and the untended Bermuda grass lawn, flanked by now-weedy flowerbeds, stretched away toward the back fence and garden as ever, with the same orange trees and the big avocado tree that had shaded it since as early as he could remember. On impulse he stood up and walked to the edge of the lawn, where he pushed aside the high brown grass with the toe of his shoe until he found the first of the brick stepping stones that led out to the back garden. He recalled the countless times he had clipped away the grass that had overgrown the bricks, like a gardener edging headstones in a cemetery—an idea that was almost funny, since he had in fact buried something beneath this very stepping stone, which had seemed to him as a child to be permanently set in the lawn, like a benchmark.

When he was a kid he had put together little treasures, collections of marbles and pieces of quartz crystal and small toys that he buried inside foil-wrapped coffee cans around the back yard. The first of his treasures he had buried right here. And now, within a matter of weeks, bulldozers would level the house and grade the yard, and that would be the end of any buried treasures.

He bent over and yanked at the Bermuda grass, pulling out tufts of it in order to expose the edges of the brick. The roots were heavy, a tangled mass that had grown between and around the bricks, packing them together so tightly that they might have been set in concrete. He walked back to the garden shed and looked at the remains of old tools that lay scattered inside: a broken spade, the blade of a hoe, a bamboo rake with most of the tines snapped off.

He picked up the spade, which had about a foot of splintered handle, and went back out to the stepping stone, where he slipped the blade in along the edge of the brick, leaning into it, pushing with his foot until he levered the brick out of its hole. The other bricks followed easily now, leaving a three-inch-deep square, walled and floored and criss-crossed with tangled white roots. Grasping the broken shovel handle he hacked through them, tearing clumps of roots and grass away with his hands, exposing the packed dirt underneath.

After scraping and hacking away an inch or so of soil he unearthed a rusty ring of metal—the top of a coffee can. A big shred of foil, stained gold, lay three-quarters buried in the orange-brown dirt, and he pulled it loose, the dirt collapsing into what must have been the vacancy left when the can had rusted away. Almost immediately he found a tiny porcelain dog—a basset hound that his mother had bought for him as a remembrance of their own basset, which had died when Alan was four or five years old. He tried to recall the dog's name, but it wouldn't come to him, and his losing the name filled him with sadness. It occurred to him that he couldn't actually recall the living dog at all, but had only a memory built up out of a few of his parents' stories, which had themselves been only memories.

He polished the dirt from the porcelain and set the figurine aside on the lawn. The wind rose just then, and the leaves overhead stirred with a sibilant whispering, and for a time the afternoon was utterly silent aside from the wind-animated noises. Fallen leaves rose from the lawn and tumbled toward the fence, and he heard a distant creaking noise, like a door opening, and the low muttering sound of animals from somewhere off to the east.

When he peered into the hole again he saw a tarnished silver coin, smashed flat, and instantly he recalled the morning that he and his parents had laid pennies and nickels and dimes on the train tracks near the beach in Santa Barbara, and how this dime had been flattened into a perfect oval, with the image still clear and clean, and had become his good luck coin. It reminded him now of the buffalo nickel that he carried for luck, one of his old childhood habits that he hadn't given up. He found three more objects: the lens from a magnifying glass, a carved wooden tiki with tiny ball bearings for eyes, brown with their own rust, and a pint-sized glass marble, a light, opaque blue with pink swirls.

He scraped the hole out a little deeper, getting well down beneath the rusty soil, but if there were other pieces of buried treasure lying around he couldn't find them. He pushed the soil and dug-up roots back in, rubbing the grass to disperse the leftover dirt, and then re-fit the bricks into their original positions as best he could, patting the edges back down before blowing the bricks clean. He sat down and polished the objects with the tail of his shirt, arranging them finally on the arms of the chair, remembering the day his father had come up with the idea of burying treasures and had helped him pick out these several trinkets from the scattered junk on the shelves of his bedroom. The two of them had made an elaborate map and burned the edges with a candle flame, but over the years he had lost track of the map, just as he had forgotten about the treasure itself.

He was vaguely aware again of the barnyard muttering from beyond the fence to the east. He closed his eyes, listening carefully, trying to puzzle out the eerily familiar noise, which faded now, seemingly as soon as he paid attention to it. He opened his eyes, looking toward the fence. A heat haze rippled across the old redwood boards and for one disconcerting moment it seemed to him that he saw right through the shingled rooftops of the tract homes beyond the fence. He blinked the illusion away and looked around uneasily, listening now to the ghostly whispering of the wind in the leaves. It seemed to him that something was pending, like the smell of ozone rising from concrete just before a summer rainfall.

He moved the treasure pieces around idly, letting each of them call up memories of his childhood. He recalled quite clearly his father's telling him that a buried treasure was better than a treasure that you held in your hand, that sometimes it was better that your birds stayed in the bushes, a constant and prevailing mystery.

In his reverie he heard a hissing noise, interrupted by a ratcheting clack, and in the very instant that he identified it as the sound of a Rainbird sprinkler, he felt a spray of drops on his arm. He looked up in surprise, at the empty dead lawn and the deserted house, but the sound had already faded, and his arm was dry. He turned his attention back to the objects, suddenly recalling the name of their basset hound, Hasbro; but no sooner had he formed the name in his mind, and recalled with it a memory of the dog itself, than a blast of wind shook the garden shed behind him, and the limbs of the silk oak flailed overhead so that a storm of leaves blew down. He half stood up in surprise, leaning heavily against the chair arm to steady himself, and the flimsy aluminum frame collapsed beneath him. He fell sideways, dumping the dug-up trinkets onto the lawn, and lay there for a moment, too dizzy to stand, listening to the wind, the tree and clouds spinning around him. There was a glittering before his eyes, like a swarm of fireflies rising from the lawn straight up into the sky, and his face and arms were stung by blowing dust as the wind gusted, its noise a deep basso profundo that seemed to shake his bones. He covered his face with his forearm and struggled to his knees, turning his back to the wind, which died now as suddenly as it had arisen. When he opened his eyes he saw that the aluminum chair had been lifted by the wind and tossed into the grape vines.

He stood staring at the chair and the vines, uncomprehending: the vines were carefully pruned now, stretched out along tight wires affixed to the fence. And he realized that the silk oak beside him was a sapling, maybe twelve feet high, its little bit of foliage sufficient to shade a cat. A car throttled past on the street, and he looked in that direction, feeling exposed, standing in plain sight, a trespasser. The oleander hedge was gone. The sycamores stood as ever, but where the hedge had been was the dirt shoulder of an irrigation ditch. Another car passed on the road, an old Ford truck.

He stepped back out of sight, hidden from the street by the garage and shed, dizzy and faint and hearing from beyond the fence the muttering sounds again: goats, the muttering of goats and chickens from the old Prentice farm. The smell of the sun-hot grapes was cloying, and he had the displaced confusion of waking up from a vivid dream. He heard the ratcheting noise and once more was swept with water droplets that felt as warm as blood against his skin. The lawn was green, and cut short. A hose stretched across from a spigot in the garden to where the Rainbird played water over the grass, the spray advancing toward him.

He saw then that the gate they shared with the Prentices—had shared with the Prentices—stood halfway open. The rooftops of the tract houses that had occupied the old Prentice property were gone, replaced by the dark canopy of a grove of walnut trees that stretched away east like billowing green clouds. The limbs of a plum tree, heavy with fruit, hung over the fence. The windows of his own house were no longer boarded up, the chimney no longer fallen. He remembered the treasure now, lying out on the lawn, and he looked around in a new panic, gripped by the idea that he would want those five objects, that unearthing the treasure was somehow connected to his being here. Getting down onto his hands and knees, he ran his fingers through the grass, but there was no sign of them; the trinkets had simply vanished.

He recalled the little firefly swarm that had lifted from the lawn and blown away in the wind, and he was filled with the certainty that his treasure had decomposed, metamorphosed into some sort of glittering dust. And blown away with it was his return ticket home. . . .

He stepped between the vines and the rear wall of the shed and sat down in the dirt, his mind roaring with the dark suspicion that he was alone in the world, that there was no place in it where he wasn't a stranger. With a surging hope he recalled the faces of old childhood friends; surely he could find his way to their houses. But what sort of greeting would he get, looming up out of the hazy afternoon, a forty-year-old man babbling about being displaced in time? He thought about Susan and Tyler, and his throat constricted. He swallowed hard, forcing himself to think, to concentrate.

An idea came to him with the force of an epiphany: the five objects, his small treasure, might still be buried in the ground. After all, he had dug them up twenty-odd years from now. He walked to the stepping stones, the grass around them now neatly clipped away, and without too much effort lifted one of the bricks out of its depression. He went back to the shed, opening the door and finding a trowel, returning to the hole and hacking into the soil underneath. The trowel sank nearly to its handle. There were fewer entangled roots, and the ground was wet from the recent watering. He wiggled out another brick and jammed the trowel into the dirt in a different place, but again the blade sank without contacting any resistance. He tried a third time, and a fourth and then simply hacked away at the soil until he forced himself to give up the futile search. There was no can, no treasure. Clearly it hadn't been buried yet. When would it be buried? A week from now? A year?

Methodically now, he tamped the soil flat and re-fitted the bricks, tossing the trowel onto the lawn near the base of the tree and stepping across to where the lawn was wet in order to wipe the mud off his hands. He heard a screen door slam, and, turning, he saw movement next door through the narrow gaps between the fence boards: someone—Mrs. Prentice?—walking toward the gate. He ran back toward the shed, and slipped inside, pulling the door shut after him, tripping over the junk on the shed floor and groping in the darkness for something to hold onto.

The objects roundabout him appeared out of the darkness as his eyes adjusted. He recognized them from when he was a kid, doing chores: the rakes and shovels and pruning saws, the old lawn mower, the edger that he used to push around the edges of the stepping stones. Hanging on a peg was the aluminum lawn chair.

He peered out through an open knothole in one of the redwood boards, seeing that old Mrs. Prentice had just come in through the gate. She crossed toward the back of the yard and turned off the sprinkler, then came straight down the stepping stones and passed out of sight. He heard her footsteps on the concrete walk adjacent to the shed, receding down past the garage toward the front of the house, and he pushed the shed door open far enough to step out. Wafering himself against the wall, he edged toward the corner until he could look carefully past it.

She was out on the driveway now, stooping over to pick up a newspaper. She straightened up, looked at the front of the house, and started up the walk in his direction, reading the newspaper headline. He ducked back, hurriedly re-entering the shed and pulling the door silently shut. Her footsteps drew near, then were silent as if she were standing there thinking.

The trowel! Of course she saw it tossed onto the lawn. He caught his breath. Don't open the door! he thought, and he grabbed a coat hook screwed into the top of the shed door and held onto it, bracing his other hand against the door jamb in order to stop her from looking in. A couple of seconds passed, and then she tugged on the door handle, managing to open the door a quarter of an inch before he reacted and jerked it back. Again she pulled on it, but he held it tight this time. His heart slammed in his chest, and the wild idea came into his head to throw the door open himself, and simply tell her who he was, that he was Alan, believe it or not. But he didn't let go of the hook. Finally, he heard her walk away. He peered out through the knothole, watching her retrace her steps across the lawn and through the gate, swinging it shut after her. When her screen door slammed, he stepped out into the sunlight. The trowel lay near the tree again, where she had returned it.

He hurried toward the house, keeping low. No one but a lunatic would assume that the shed door was latched from the inside. Along with the tossed-aside trowel it would add up to evidence. Would she call the police? Surely not now—not in the innocent middle of the century. He couldn't remember if Mr. Prentice had a day job: perhaps he was home, and she had gone to fetch him. He glanced at the driveway and the street and was struck with the latent realization that his car was gone. Of course it was gone, left behind, sitting in that other driveway thirty years in the future. There was no car at all in this driveway, his or the family's car. He looked around more attentively, forcing himself to slow down, to work things out. He saw that there were still puddles of water in the flowerbeds along the driveway, eighty feet from where the Rainbird had been chattering away before Mrs. Prentice had turned it off. The garden was wet, too. She had apparently watered the entire yard over the course of the day, which argued that maybe she wouldn't be back, that she was finished with her work.

And she had picked up the newspaper, too, which made it likely that the family—his family—was away, and must have been away for a while, long enough for it to have fallen to the Prentices to watch over the house and yard. Which meant what?—probably one of their two-week summer trips to Colorado or Iowa or Wisconsin.

Listening hard for the sound of the screen door slamming, he stepped to the back stoop, climbed the three stairs in a crouch in order to remain unseen, and tried the door knob. Again it was locked. Again—the idea of it baffled him, and he was once more swept with a dizzying confusion. This wasn't the second time today he had tried the knob; it was the first time. Although his own fingerprints might already be on it, they would be prints from a smaller hand. . . .

It dawned on him that the objects might be in the house right now, not yet buried. He had no real idea at what age he had buried them—ten, twelve? He heard the Prentice's screen door slam, and almost before he knew he had thought of it, he was heading up along the side of the house toward the front. There, right at the corner of the house, just where he remembered it, stood a big juniper, growing nearly up into the eaves. He felt around on its trunk, waist high, his hand closing on the hidden house key hanging on a nail. The cold metal sent a thrill of relief through him, and a few seconds later he was on the front porch, glancing back at the empty street and sliding the key into the lock. He opened the door and stepped into the dim interior of the living room, recalling the smell of the place, the furniture, the books in the bookcase.

He locked the door carefully behind him and pocketed the key, then moved through the house, into the kitchen, keeping low. Through the window in the door he saw that old Mr. Prentice was in the back yard now. Mrs. Prentice stood at the open gate, watching her husband. He walked to the shed, looking around him. Cautiously he tried the door, which swung open. He looked in, then picked up the trowel from the lawn and put it away. He closed the shed door, and then walked back toward the grapevines. There was nowhere in the yard for a person to hide, except perhaps out in the back corner, where the limbs of the avocado tree hung almost to the ground, creating an enclosed bower. He walked in that direction now, cocking his head, peering into the shadows. But apparently there was enough sunlight through the leaves for him to see that no one at all was hiding there, because he turned and walked back toward the open gate, saying something to his wife.

Then he stopped and looked straight at the house. Alan ducked out of sight, scuttling back across the kitchen floor and into the dining room, wondering wildly where he would hide if the man came in. He heard a step on the back stoop, and the back door rattled as Mr. Prentice tried the bolt. Alan glanced toward the dark hallway. Could he even fit under his bed now? But Mr. Prentice descended the wooden steps again, and by the time Alan crept back into the kitchen and looked out the window, the gate was already swinging shut. For another five minutes he stood there watching, relaxing a little more as time passed. Probably old man Prentice would simply think his wife was nuts, that it was just like a woman not to be able to open a shed door.

The several hours before night fell passed slowly. The newspaper beside the living room couch revealed that it was July of 1968. He was, in this other life, ten years old. Hesitantly he made his way up the hall and looked into his old bedroom. Although it seemed to him impossible, it was utterly familiar. He knew every single thing—the toys, the tossed pieces of clothing, the window curtains, the bedspread, the bubbling aquarium on the dresser—as if he had carried with him a thousand scattered and individualized memories all these years, like the trinkets in the coffee can. He picked up a small net and scooped a dead angel fish out of the aquarium, taking it into the bathroom, where he flushed it down the toilet. Then he returned to the room, possessed by the urge to lie down on the bed, draw the curtains across the windows, and stare at the lighted aquarium as he had done so many times so long ago. But he caught himself, feeling oddly like a trespasser despite his memories.

Still, he could be forgiven for borrowing a few things. He looked around, spotting the porcelain basset hound immediately, and then recalling in a rush of memory that the lens of the magnifying glass lay in the top drawer of his old oak desk. He opened the drawer and spotted it, right there in plain sight. The blue marble lay in the drawer too, rolled into the corner. It took him a little longer to find the tiki, which had fallen to the floor beside the dresser. He picked it up and cleaned the dust off it, noting that the ball bearing eyes were shiny silver. The train-flattened dime eluded him, though, until he spotted a small metal tray with a flamingo painted on it lying on the night stand, where, before bed, he used to put the odds and ends from his pockets. Seeing the tray reminded him that Alan would be carrying the dime in his pocket back in these days, just as he was carrying the buffalo nickel in his own pocket. So where would the dime be? Wisconsin? Colorado? Or homeward bound in the old Plymouth Fury, driving through the southwest desert? Maybe closer yet, coming down over the Cajon Pass, forty-five minutes away. . . .

He moved the four objects around on the desktop, arranging and rearranging them, waiting for the telltale rising of the wind, the sound of a door creaking open, signifying sounds. But nothing happened.

He thought about keeping the items with him, in his pocket, but in the end he set the tiki on the desktop, put the porcelain dog back on the shelf, and returned the lens and the marble to the drawer, where he could retrieve them all in an instant. He stepped to the window and unlatched it, pushing it open easily. There was no screen, so he could be out the window quickly. Their family had never traveled at night; they were motel travelers—five hundred miles a day and then a Travel Lodge with a pool and Coke machine and, later in the evening, gin rummy around the motel room table. By nine or ten o'clock tonight he could safely fall asleep and then take up his worries tomorrow.

He spent the rest of the afternoon and evening reading his mother's copy of Steinbeck's *The Long Valley*. The book was in his own library at home now—whatever now constituted. The heavy paper pages and brown cloth binding had the same dusty, reassuring smell that he remembered, both as a boy and later as a man, and the stories in the book, existing as they did outside of time, felt like a safe and stable haven to him, a good place to wait things out.

He became aware that it was quickly growing too dark to read, and at the same time he realized that he was ravenously hungry. He walked into the dim kitchen and opened the refrigerator. In the freezer he found a stack of Van de Camp TV dinners, and picked out the Mexican dinner—enchiladas, beans, and rice—and in a moment of stupidity looked around for a microwave oven. Smiling at his own foolishness, he turned on the oven in the O'Keefe and Merritt range, slid the foil-wrapped dinner onto the top rack, and then went back to the refrigerator, where he found a hunk of cheddar cheese to snack on. He opened a bottle of Coke to wash it down with and stood at the kitchen sink, watching the glow of sunset fade over the rooftops to the east.

The house was dark when he took his dinner out of the oven, removed the foil, and ate it at the kitchen table, thinking that the enchilada tasted better in his memory than it did now. Although this was something he had already come to expect over the years, it was still a disappointment. It occurred to him that he should look around for a flashlight: he couldn't turn on a brighter light to read by, not with the Prentices next door, probably still spooked over the garden shed mystery. And he wondered idly about the trash: the Coke bottle and the foil tray and wrapper. Who knew what-all he would accumulate if he had to wait out a week here? And what would his mother say when she discovered that the TV dinners in the freezer had vanished? If he was here for the long haul, he would work his way through the refrigerator and freezer and half the cupboard, too.

Thinking about it made him feel more desperately alone, and his shoulders sagged as the enormity of his problem dropped on him like a weight. The empty house around him was true to his memory, and yet it wasn't his anymore. He was reminded of the decades that had passed away, of the first happy years of his marriage when he and Susan had spent their money traveling, of Tyler's childhood, of his mother's death a few short years after she and his father had moved out of the house and retired up the coast in Cambria.

He breathed deeply and looked out the window, trying to focus on the night landscape. The lantern in the driveway illuminated part of the wall of the garage before it faded into darkness. A pair of headlights appeared out on the street, the car swinging around the uphill curve in the road, the noise of its engine dwindling with distance. At least, he thought, there was the happy coincidence of Susan and Tyler being away in Michigan. They might wonder why he wasn't answering the phone at home, but it would likely be days before they began to worry about his absence. Then his mind revolved treacherously back around to his dilemma, and he recalled that Susan and Tyler weren't away in the east at all, not now, not in this century. Tyler was a decade away from being born. Susan was a twelve-year-old girl, living in Anaheim, oblivious to his existence.

What if he couldn't get back? Simply never returned? He saw himself living as a transient, as a ghost, waiting for the years to drag by until he could catch up with them again, drifting on the edges of Susan's life and then of Susan and Tyler's life—of his own life—haunting the same restaurants, hanging around the Little League field, watching the three of them from a distance. But he could never insinuate himself into their lives. A strange interloper—particularly a copy of himself—would never be welcome, not by Susan and not by Tyler and most of all not by him, by Alan, who wasn't really the same him at all now that the years had passed, despite the blood that ran in his veins.

Of course on that far-off day when Susan and Tyler would travel back to Michigan, and Alan, feeling lonely and maudlin, would once again dig up the treasure, then a door would open and he could step in and fill his own shoes, literally, if he chose to. He could simply walk back into his old life, answer the long distance calls when they came, prepare himself to tell his phenomenal story to Tyler, whose father had now disappeared, and to Susan, whose husband had aged thirty years overnight, and might as well be her own grandfather.

This time he didn't hear the sound of the car engine or see the headlights, but he heard the car door slam, heard a boy's voice—his own voice!—shout something, his own father shouting back, telling him to carry his own suitcase. Without a second thought, Alan was on his feet, starting toward his bedroom. He stopped himself and turned back toward the kitchen table, picking up the TV tray and shoving it into the trash under the sink, cramming the empty Coke bottle in after it and wiping his hand across the table to clean up a smear of enchilada sauce. The back door, he thought, but even as he turned toward the service porch he heard his father coming up along the side of the house, headed for the back yard, and through the kitchen window he saw the shadowy figure carrying an ice chest. He ducked out of sight, hearing the clatter of a key in the front door lock, and slipped into the hallway, heading straight into his bedroom, sliding up the window. He stopped, hearing his mother's voice in the living room now, followed by his own voice complaining about something. But there was no time to listen. He grabbed the porcelain dog and the tiki and slipped them into his pocket, then opened the drawer and snatched up the lens and the marble, shoving the drawer shut even as he was pulling the window curtains aside. He swung his foot over the sill and simply rolled out sideways into the flowerbed, scrambled to his feet, and quietly shut the window. He crouched there catching his breath, and watched as the bedroom light blinked on and he heard the suitcase drop to the floor.

As silently as possible he walked up the side of the house, trying to stop himself from trembling. He was relatively safe right where he was as long as he made no noise: there was no reason on earth for his father to come out here to the side of the house. He heard a sound now the shed door closing, the ice chest no doubt returned to its place on the shelf— and he peered out past the corner of the service porch to see his father head back down the driveway toward the car. He looked at his watch. It was just eight o'clock, early yet, and he recalled the familiar nightly routine, the Sunday evening television, probably ice cream and cookies. But first Alan would have put on his pajamas so that he was ready for bed, which would mean either emptying his pockets into the tray if he was feeling organized, or, equally likely, simply throwing his pants onto the bedroom floor.

Impatient, he walked silently back down toward the bedroom, where the light still shone through the curtains. Whatever he was going to do, he had to do it tonight. It wouldn't get any easier. And what was the alternative? Spend his days and nights hiding in the garden shed, drinking water out of the hose, waiting for another chance? As soon as it was safe he would reenter the room, find the dime, and go back out the window. In the back yard he could take his time arranging the five items; he could take the rest of his life arranging and rearranging them until whatever had happened to him happened once more.

The moon had risen over the mountains to the east, and shone now on the wall of the house. He stood listening at the closed window, standing aside so that his moon shadow was cast on the wall and not on the curtains. The seconds passed in silence. It was impossible to tell whether Alan was still in the room or had gone out, leaving the light on. But then he heard the sound of the television in the living room, the channels changing. Had it been Alan who had turned it on? He held his breath, focusing on the silence, listening for movement.

Making up his mind, he put his hand softly against the top of the window sash and pushed on it gently and evenly. Just then the bedroom light blinked out, plunging the room into darkness. He ducked away from the window, his heart racing. Minutes passed and nothing happened, the night silent but for the sound of crickets and the muted chatter on the television. He stood up again, took a deep breath, and pushed the window open as far as it would go. After listening to the silence, he boosted himself up onto the sill, overbalancing and sliding into the room. He stood up, hearing voices—his mother and father, talking quietly but urgently.

He saw the smashed dime in the tray along with some other coins, and in an instant it was in his hand and he turned back toward the window, crawling through, his shoes bumping against the sill as he tumbled onto the ground. He clambered to his feet, grabbing the window to shut it. The bedroom light came on, and he froze in a crouch, the window not quite shut, the curtain hitched open an inch where it had caught on the latch. He hesitated, drawing his hand slowly away from the window frame, certain they knew someone had been in the house. And yet he couldn't bring himself to move: getting away—getting back—meant nothing to him.

"Don't say anything to him," his father said, close by now. "There's no use making him worry." Alan saw him briefly as he crossed the bedroom, disappearing beyond the edge of the curtain. "But the oven is still warm," his mother said, following him in. "And sauce on the tray in the trash isn't even dried out. I think he was here when we came home. What if he's still in the house?"

Alan bent toward the window until he could see her face. Somehow it hadn't occurred to him how young she would be, probably thirty-five or -six. He had known that she was pretty, but over the years he had lost track of how absolutely lovely she had been, and he found that his memory of her was shaped by her last years, when she was older and fighting with the cancer.

"He's not in the house," his father said. "I've been all through it, putting things away. If he's not in here, which he's obviously not, then he's gone. I'll check the garage and the shed just to make sure. For now, though, let's just keep this to ourselves."

"But what did he want? This is too weird. He was reading one of my books. Who would break into a house to read the books?"

"I don't know. I don't think anything's missing. There was money on the dresser in the bedroom, and it's still there. Your jewelry box hasn't been touched. . . ."

There was a sudden silence now, and Alan realized that the curtains were moving gently in the breeze through the open window. He ducked away down the side of the house as quickly and silently as he could, half expecting to hear the window slide open behind him or the sound of hurrying footsteps in the house. Without hesitating he set straight out across the back lawn toward the garden shed, looking back at the kitchen window and back door. The light was on in the kitchen, but there was still no one visible.

Should he get the chair out of the shed? Be sitting down for this? Reenact the whole thing exactly? He dug the five objects out of his pocket and held them in one hand, hopefully anticipating the disorienting shift, the rising of the wind, the rippling air. But nothing happened. He was simply alone in the moonlit night, the crickets chirping around him. His father appeared in the kitchen now, clearly heading toward the back door, and Alan moved back toward the grapevines, out of sight. He heard the door open as he sat down on the lawn, laying the objects on his knees, compelling himself to concentrate on them and not on the approaching footsteps, which stopped close by. He opened his eyes and looked up, feeling like an idiot. His father stood a few feet away, a golf club in his hands, staring down at him. Alan stared back in momentary confusion. He might have been looking at his own brother.

"Why don't you just stay there," his father said, "so I don't have to bean you with this driver."

"Sure."

"What were you doing in the house?"

For a time Alan couldn't answer. When he found his voice he said simply, "I'm Alan."

"Okay. I'm Phil. Pardon me if I don't shake your hand. What the hell were you doing in my house? What were you looking for?"

Alan smiled at the question, which was no easier to answer than the last one. "My past," he said. "I was looking for my past. You don't recognize me, do you? You can't."

"What do you mean, your past? Did you used to live here or something? This is some kind of nostalgia thing?"

"Yeah. I used to live here."

"So what are you doing with my son's stuff? That's from his room, isn't it? That dog and the tiki?"

"It's from his room. But I didn't steal it."

"You're just borrowing it?"

"Yes," Alan said softly. Then, "No, it's mine, too. I am Alan . . . Dad." He had to force himself to say it out loud, and he found that there were tears welling in his eyes. His father still stood staring at him, his own face like a mask.

Alan went on, pulling random bits from his memory: "You bought me the aquarium at that place in Garden Grove, off Magnolia Street. We got a bunch of fish, and they all ate each other, and we had to go back down there and buy more. And you know the cracked shade on the lamp in the living room? Me and Eddie Landers did that by accident after school on Halloween day when we were waiting for Mom to come home. That was probably last Halloween, or maybe two years ago at the most. I was the mummy, remember? Eddie was Count Dracula. He was staying here because his parents were out of town. Let me show you something," he said, carefully laying the five trinkets on the brick pad in front of the shed door and then shifting forward to get to his feet. His father took a step back, and the head of the golf club rose where it had been resting on the lawn. Alan stopped moving. "Can I get up?"

"Okay. Slowly, eh?"

"Sure. Just getting my wallet." Alan stood, reaching into his back pocket. He took his driver's license out of his wallet and held it out. "Look at the date." He pocketed the wallet, and his father took the card, turning it so that it was illuminated by moonlight. "Above the picture," Alan told him. He heard laughter from inside the house now, and realized that it was himself, probably watching television, still oblivious to everything going on outside here.

After glancing at it his father handed the license back. "I guess I don't get it," he said. But clearly he did get it; he simply couldn't believe it.

Alan put the license into his shirt pocket. "I came back from—from thirty years from now. In the future." He pointed at the objects lying on the bricks. "You and I buried this stuff in a coffee can, like a treasure, under the first stepping stone, right there."

"We did, eh? We buried them? When was that?"

Alan shrugged. "Any day now, I guess. Next month? I don't know, but we buried them. We will, anyway. I came back and dug them up."

There was the sound of the back door opening, and his mother came out onto the back stoop, looking in their direction. "What are you doing, dear?" she asked with feigned cheerfulness. "Is everything all right?" Probably she was ready to call the police.

"Yeah, it's fine," Alan's father said back to her. "Just . . . putting some stuff away." She stepped back into the house and shut the door, but then reappeared in the kitchen, where she stood at the window, watching. His father was still staring at him, but puzzled, less suspicious now.

"You remember the time we were up at Irvine Park," Alan asked, "and we found those old bottle caps with the cork on the back, and you got the corks out and put the bottle caps on my shirt, with the cork holding them on from the other side? And I picked up that cactus apple and got all the needles in my hand? And it started to rain, and we got under the tree, and you said that the pitcher of lemonade would get wet, and Mom ran back to the table to cover it?"

His father dropped the golf club to the lawn, letting it lie there. "That was thirty years ago," Alan said. "Can you imagine? It's still funny, though. And there was that time when Mom lost her purse, remember, and she looked all over for it, and you came home from work and found it in the refrigerator?"

"She put it away with the groceries," his father said. "That was last month."

Alan nodded. "I guess it could have been." He realized now that his father's silence was no longer disbelief, and he stepped forward, opening his arms. His father hugged him, and for a time they stood there, listening to the night, saying nothing. Alan stepped away finally, and his father squeezed him on the shoulder, smiling crookedly, looking hard at his face.

Alan reached into his pocket and took out the odds and ends that he carried, the buffalo nickel, his pocket knife. He showed his father the little antler-handled knife. "Recognize this? It's just like the one you gave me, except I lost that one. I found this one just like it at the hardware store and bought it about a year ago."

"I didn't give you a pocket knife like that."

"You know what? I guess maybe you haven't given it to me yet."

"Then I guess I don't need to bother, if you're just going to lose the damned thing."

Alan smiled at him. "But if you don't, then how am I going to know to buy this one at the hardware store?"

They listened in silence to the crickets for a moment. "How old would you be now?" his father asked him.

"Forty-two," Alan said. "How about you?"

"Forty. That's pretty funny. Married?"

"Yeah. Take a look at this." He dug in his wallet again, removing a picture of Tyler, his high school graduation picture. He looked at it fondly, but abruptly felt dizzy, disoriented. He nearly sat down to keep himself from falling. His father took the picture, and the dizziness passed. "That's Tyler," Alan said, taking a deep breath and focusing his thoughts. But he heard his own voice as an echo, as if through a tube. "Your grandson. Susan and I gave him Mom's maiden name."

Alan's father studied the picture. "He looks like your mother, doesn't he?"

"A lot. I didn't realize it until tonight, when she was standing in my bedroom. You must have seen that the window was open . . . ?"

"Your bedroom," his father said, as if wondering at the notion. "Here." Alan took his keys out of his other pocket. Among them was the loose house key that he had removed from the nail in the juniper. "That's how I got into the house."

Still holding Tyler's picture, his father took the key. He nodded at the other keys on Alan's key ring. "What's that one?"

Alan held out his car key. "Car key. One of the buttons is for the door locks and the other pops the trunk open from a distance. There's a little battery in it. It puts out an FM radio wave. Push the door button a couple of times, and an alarm goes off." Alan pushed it twice, recalling that his own car, in some distant space and time, was sitting just thirty feet away, and he found himself listening to hear a ghostly car alarm. But what he heard, aside from the crickets and the muted sound of the television, was a far-off clanking noise, like rocks cascading onto a steel plate. The night wind ruffled his hair. And from beyond the fence, just for a split second, the dark canopy of walnut leaves looked hard-edged and rectilinear to him, like rooftops. Then it was a dark, slowly moving mass again, and he heard laughter and the sound of the television.

"Thirty years?"

"It seems like a long time, but I swear it's not."

"No, I don't guess it is. What's the date back where you come from? Just out of curiosity."

Alan thought about it. "Eighth of July, 2001." He found himself thinking about his mother, doing the math in his head. What did she have? Twenty years or so? His father hadn't ever remarried. Alan glanced toward the house, where his mother still stood at the window, looking out at the night.

His father followed his gaze. "Tell me something," he said after a moment. "Were you happy? You know, growing up?"

"I was happy," Alan said truthfully. "It was a good time."

"You found your heart's desire?"

"Yeah, I married her."

"And how about your boy Tyler? You think he's happy?" He held the picture up.

"I think so. Sure. I know it."

"Uh huh. Look, I think maybe it's better if you go back now, before your Mom flips. Can you? It's getting late."

"Yeah," Alan said, realizing absolutely that the clanking noise he had heard was the sound of a jackhammer. He took the pocket knife and nickel out of his pocket again, and held them in his hand with his keys, then reached into his shirt pocket to retrieve his driver's license.

"I'd invite you in, you know, for ice cream and cookies, but your mother—I don't know what she'd do. I don't think it would . . ."

"I know. Alan too. . . ." He nodded at the house. "We might as well let him watch TV."

"Right. It would be like . . . a disturbance, or something. I guess we don't need that. We're doing pretty good on our own."

"And it's going to stay good," Alan said. "Is there anything . . . ?"

"That I want to know?" His father shook his head. "No. I'm happy with things like they are. I'm looking forward to meeting Tyler, though." He handed the picture back.

"If you can ever find some way to do it," Alan said, taking the picture, "let Mom know that . . ."

But he felt himself falling backward. And although it came to him later as only a dim memory, he recalled putting out his hand to stop his fall, dropping the stuff that he held. He found himself now in bright sunlight, lying on the dead Bermuda grass, the words of his half-finished sentence lost to him, the onrushing wind already dying away and the smell of grapes heavy on the sun-warmed air. The telltale glitter shimmered before his eyes, and he sat up dizzily, looking around, squinting in the brightness, hearing the clanging of the jackhammer, which cut off sharply, casting the afternoon into silence. He saw that the shed was dilapidated and doorless now, the house once again boarded up. His car, thank God, sat as ever in the driveway.

His keys! He stood up dizzily, looking down at his feet. With his keys gone he had no way of . . .

"Hey."

At the sound of the voice, Alan shouted in surprise and reeled away into the wall of the shed, turning around and putting out his hands. He saw that a man sat in the dilapidated aluminum lawn chair beneath the silk oak—his father, smiling at him. With the sun shining on his face, he might have been a young man. Alan lowered his hands and smiled back.

"Welcome home," his father said to him.

A Place to Begin
Richard Parks

Richard Parks is a Mississippi native, married, no children, three cats. He says, "Whether it's something in the environment or the local gene pool, Mississippi has always produced more than its share of scoundrels, myth-makers, and storytellers. I don't know why, but we can't help it." In his day job he's a computer network administrator. He sold his first story to Amazing SF back in 1980. After a hiatus, he sold his second to Asimov's SF in 1993. He was a frequent reviewer in the 1990s for SF Age. Since then he's placed stories in Science Fiction Age, Asimov's, Dragon, Realms of Fantasy, and Weird Tales, as well as in numerous anthologies. He published a number of fantasy stories this year, giving us several fine ones to choose from for this anthology.*

"A Place to Begin" is set in an oriental fantasy China, another of the traditional settings of fantasy. It appeared in Weird Tales, the oldest and still one of the best fantasy magazines. It is a transformed retelling of "The Sorcerer's Apprentice," with added depth and finely tuned prose.

Long ago, when the wind spoke with a voice you could understand, in a village by the sea there lived a poor girl of almost infinite potential. Her name was Umi, which meant "ocean." She had a sweet face, and hair long and glossy black, but so did most of her friends. Umi was hardly worth anyone's notice, to her own way of thinking.

So it was to Umi's great surprise that she returned from gathering wood late one evening to find her mother and father in intense but polite conversation with the most powerful sorceress on the island.

"Umi, this is Lady White Willow. She has come to take you into her service," her father said. "It is a great honor." Her mother said nothing, but merely looked sad.

The next morning Umi made a bundle of her few possessions, bowed to her mother and father, and followed the sorceress, leaving her family, her friends, and the village that had been her home. She never saw any of them again.

As they made their way out of the village, the folk there either bowed to White Willow as they would a priest or noble, or just avoided her gaze altogether, hurrying out of her path as decorously as possible. Umi couldn't decide if there was more respect or fear in their deference; there seemed to be a good measure of both.

Umi studied her companion as best she could while they walked. The sorceress's name fit her well. White Willow was tall and slim, and her hair was white as mountain snow. Umi tried to judge her age and failed. Despite the testament of her hair, White Willow did not look any older than Umi's own mother. Her robes were of fine silk, and silk wrappings cushioned the thongs of her sandals. She carried a stout stick, but so far had merely used it to help balance herself as the road turned into a mountain path as they traveled away from the sea.

"You're staring at me," White Willow said, finally. It was the first time she'd spoken to Umi directly.

"I'm sorry," Umi said, "but I've never met a sorceress before."

"Nor been bound in service to one, I suppose. Are you angry with your parents for selling you to a stranger?"

Umi shrugged. "It is often the lot of girls from poor families. Some fare worse, I hear. No doubt Father did what he thought best."

White Willow smiled then. "Strange how that seems to happen most often when gold and silver are involved. Well, then—are you afraid of me?" she asked. There was a pleasant tone in her voice that, for some reason, did not reassure Umi in the least.

"Yes, White Willow *sama*," Umi said. Indeed, she was even too afraid to lie about it.

The sorceress nodded in satisfaction. "That's as it should be, but don't worry—I will be fair to you. If you are obedient and work hard, I will not mistreat you. If you prove to be lazy or obstinate I promise you will regret it. Do you understand me?"

"Yes, Lady. I will try to please you."

"Well, then. Let us hope you succeed."

White Willow's home was on a small plateau on the side of a great mountain, a place so flat and green it was as if the forces of nature themselves had chosen to rest there before finishing the mountain they'd started. The plateau was high but not so high that trees would not grow; White Willow's home was a rambling collection of buildings nestled into birch, maple, and stone. It seemed part fortress, part temple, part woodland glade, and part cave and den all at once.

At first glance it was hard for Umi to tell where the house ended and the mountain began again. After a few weeks it was even more difficult, as spring had come to the land and new leaves were everywhere, hiding stone and timber.

Umi explored whenever her duties allowed, which was fairly often. White Willow required little of her except to sweep a certain stone path once a day, and fetch two pails of water from a nearby mountain stream at the end of that path, one in the morning and one at evening. An elderly woman name Kyuko did all the cooking, another slightly younger lady who may have been the cook's daughter served as White Willow's personal body servant. There were three thick-bodied men of indeterminate age who saw to the gardens and buildings and did most of the heavier work, including hauling water for the baths. This in itself seemed strange to Umi, since in her own village most of the women worked like don-keys, as hard as or harder than the men.

It was very light work, compared to what Umi was used to. She saw no reason to complain on that score, and didn't. Yet it was hard not to wonder why White Willow had brought her into service in the first place, to use her so little.

In time, Umi found it beyond her ability not to wonder about it. When the opportunity presented itself, she asked her mistress about it. White Willow had merely looked at her for a moment and said, with no trace of anger or any other emotion Umi could detect, "Starting tomor-row, sweep the maple grove path twice, morning and afternoon too." Not being a particularly foolish girl, Umi did not ask again. Yet still she wondered.

Spring turned into summer as Umi became more at ease in her new home. The questions in her mind were still present, but it was as if the warming days had lulled them to sleep, even as they soon coaxed a nap out of Umi on a particularly languid afternoon, when the sun was bright and fierce and the shadows of the maple grove were a welcome haven. She finished her sweeping and then rested against a tree. When she opened her eyes again it was nearly dark.

"Mistress will be wanting her water . . ."

Umi hurried to fetch the pail, then ran up the path to the place where the stream bubbled out of a fissure in the mountain slope and into a shal-low rock basin, a quiet place of ferns and shadow. Umi filled the pail, then hesitated. The run and her long nap had left her very thirsty, yet White Willow had warned her against drinking from that particular stream.

"Perhaps it's poison," she said to herself. The water certainly didn't seem tainted: there was no scent to it at all, and indeed it looked so cold and fresh Umi couldn't resist. Rather than disobeying White Willow directly, she took a drink from the pail itself. The water was as cool and sweet as it looked.

"That was reckless of you."

Umi couldn't see who had spoken. For a moment her vision had blurred; indeed she was afraid then that the water *had* been poisoned. Yet she felt no pain, and in a few moments she could see again.

In truth, she could see better than ever.

Suddenly, and even in the fading light, the leaves on the maples and the ferns growing by the basin looked extremely bright, as they might after a spring rain. Now Umi noticed that there were characters written on the stone basin, though she could not read them.

"Why didn't I notice this before?"

"Because this is the *Miru no Mizu*, the Water of Sight, and you drank it, silly girl. Or did you think White Willow uses it to bathe her feet?"

Now Umi followed the sound and saw something else she had never noticed before. There was a niche carved into the rock a scant few feet from the fissure, and in that sat a small bamboo cage, and in *that* sat a small bird. Its feathers were blue and red and gold; it was the prettiest thing Umi had ever seen. Yet when she looked at it closely the feathers and bright colors faded, and something very different sat on the perch. It was horned and taloned and it smiled at her with pointed teeth. Its skin was as red as fire.

Frightened, Umi stepped back. "You're not a bird!"

"Of course not, you ignorant child. Do birds commonly speak, even in this place of magic? I'm a *shikigami*. A creature summoned by White Willow to do her bidding."

"You look like a devil," Umi said.

"Is it so? I may resemble an *oni*, but who has heard of one as small as I? Perhaps we're a related folk, I do not know. That does not make me a devil. I looked like a bird a moment ago," the creature pointed out. "That does not mean I *was* a bird."

Umi could see the truth in that, but she was still careful to keep her distance. The cage looked strong, but the creature inside looked strong, too. "I must go," Umi said. "White Willow is waiting for me."

The creature smiled again. "Do what you must, but a word of caution, girl: until the water leaves your body many things will look quite different, perhaps startling, to you. Do not let White Willow catch you noticing any of it, or she will know you've disobeyed her."

Umi saw the sense in that. "Why are you helping me?"

The creature didn't look at her when it answered. "Because this time I choose to. Ask me again when the answer is different."

Umi didn't understand what it meant, but she had no time to ask. She took up her pail and hurried back down the path to White Willow's house.

"You are late, Umi."

The sorceress sat on a blue silk pillow while her servant unbraided and combed out her long white hair. Umi stood in the open doorway with her pail. There was movement at the edges of her vision, colors, devices, *things* that she had never noticed before. She tried not to pay attention to them now, but that was surprisingly easy. Umi used most of her concentration trying not to tremble.

It wasn't simple fear at White Willow's obvious displeasure that shook her so; it was the sight of White Willow herself. She didn't look so greatly different now. She was still a human woman, her hair still long and white as the snow on their mountain's top. No, what Umi saw now were things just below the surface of White Willow's face, things hidden to Umi before now.

The first was time, or more correctly, *age*. White Willow had the surface appearance of a fairly young woman, but Umi now understood this was not true—the sorceress was very, very old. Her unlined face now seemed as cold and lifeless to Umi as that of a painted porcelain doll.

That wasn't the worst part. Under White Willow's cold, distant stare, Umi felt herself constantly weighed as if on a merchant's scale, her value falling this way or that, constantly changing, constantly reconsidered.

How long before the scale turns the wrong way?

Umi bowed low. "*Gomen nasai*, White Willow *sama*. I foolishly let the warm sun lull me to sleep."

"Is it this, then? Nothing more?"

Umi felt White Willow's gaze on her as a bird might feel a cat's, but she kept her eyes averted and her head bowed! "I didn't wake until nearly dark, and thus am only now come to bring your water."

White Willow said nothing for very long moments, then sighed wearily. "I've had a long, tiring day. I may not even require the water. Still, failure must bring punishment. Is that just?"

"Yes, Mistress."

White Willow contented herself with a sharp blow of her fan across the back of Umi's hand, with dire warnings of what would happen if she proved tardy a second time. Umi left the water and scurried gratefully out of the room, the sting of her punishment already fading. She tried to put as much distance between White Willow's chambers and herself as she could, short of leaving the house. She had seen much to disturb her in White Willow's room, but she had seen more along the path from the spring, and was in no hurry to encounter them again in the present darkness.

Umi considered what to do for a moment, but only for a moment. She smelled something wonderful coming from the kitchen and remembered she hadn't had supper yet. Kyuko the cook was tending the coals under the grate, which was empty, but there was a bowl of rice and three pickles sitting on the windowsill. The old woman grunted. "About time. I was about to toss this to the foxes."

Umi doubted that; she had yet to see Kyuko express more than mild annoyance at anything, and certainly not to the point of wasting food. Still, she was careful to express her gratitude, and the old woman smiled. With her round face it made Kyuko look something like a melon with teeth.

Umi ate in comfortable silence as Kyuko went on with cleaning up the kitchen. The kitchen seemed safe from the disturbing visions Umi had discovered elsewhere, but Umi found herself studying the old woman now with an intensity that she didn't understand. It was as if Kyuko had been here all this time and Umi had only now noticed her. The way the glow from the embers traced a line of gold along the side of her face, damp with perspiration. The way all her movements seemed practiced and precise, almost unconsciously so. Umi found herself wondering how many times the old cook had done just this, in the very same kitchen, performing these very same duties with gentle good humor.

"If it is not impertinent to ask, how long have you been with Lady White Willow?"

Kyuko had been looking out at the woods, a distant expression on her face. The question apparently caught her by surprise. She hesitated for several long moments, clearly giving the matter some thought. "Well, I'm not sure one can really be said to be *with* our mistress, since she is mostly complete unto herself. I've been in her service since I was a little girl."

"Like me?" Umi asked.

Kyuko smiled. "Much like you. I remember the day she came to our village. She looked at many young girls, but she chose me. It was a fine day."

"Weren't you sad to leave your family?"

Kyuko raised an eyebrow. "Weren't you?"

Umi bowed her head. "Forgive me; it was a foolish question."

Kyuko dismissed that. "I hadn't thought of it in such a long time. The days here seem to flow together like currents in a river; there's no separating them."

Umi nodded. Until today, that had been true for her, too.

Umi's dreams were vivid and frightening. She woke early and visited the privy; afterwards she felt more than normal relief—the world seemed to have lost its strangeness. Now the leaves on the maple trees did not suggest disturbing patterns, hints of things unseen. They were just leaves, the stone wall that ran along one side of the grove path was simply a wall and did not, as it had seemed the evening before, have a section with eyes and small, stout legs. Umi swept the grove path carefully and then went to see Kyuko in the kitchen for her breakfast.

Now it was time to fetch the water.

Umi took her pail and trudged up the grove path. Not dragging her feet, exactly, but not hurrying either. When she came to the spring she filled her pail as usual and then stood there beside the water for several long moments, waiting for she didn't know what, looking for the same. She looked where the writing was, where the *shikigami* had been, and saw neither. She finally turned her back on the spring and hurried back to White Willow. Umi didn't want to be late a second time.

It was three days before Umi drank from the pail again. The little creature was in its cage as before, now regarding her thoughtfully. In fact Umi had taken a little more of the water this time, and she looked at the creature very long and intently when it appeared.

It ignored her scrutiny. "I wondered how long it would be before you took the water again," it said.

"How did you know I would?"

The creature smiled, showing very pointed teeth. "When a person is touched by magic it is hard to let the world go back to the way it was. Some people can do it with no problem at all, like old Kyuko. I did not think you would be like her."

"She's a fine woman and has been very kind to me," Umi said. "I would not have you speak ill of her."

It laughed. "And have I? No, Umi-chan. I merely spoke the fact; I made no judgment. I think that part came from you."

"I—" Umi blushed crimson. The *shikigami* was right. "What do you know of Kyuko?" she finally asked.

"Just that she came as a young girl to White Willow's service, as have you, and when her time came to drink the water she drank once and never again. Perhaps that was best for her, who can say? She is content enough with her life . . . or so one could suppose."

Umi frowned. "You make it sound as if drinking the water was expected!"

The creature showed its teeth again. "Isn't it? In my experience the one infallible way to make sure a certain thing will happen is to forbid it." Another smile. "She'd rather reduce her power than be insecure in the power she does possess. I think White Willow is very wise in that."

"I do not understand," Umi said.

"Of course not. Else you would not be standing here talking to me."

Umi took a deep breath. "Then what should I be doing, save hurrying with my pail to my mistress?" Umi asked. "And, come to that, what does White Willow really want of me? My duties are but few; such that I'm hardly worth even the small price I'm sure she paid my father."

The small creature was grinning from ear to ear, almost literally.

"You have little wisdom as yet, but you're a clever enough girl as your kind go. Yes, there is more to this matter as you have guessed. But what? That would be good for you to know."

"Do you know what White Willow really wants from me? Will you tell me?"

"Of course I know." The *shikigami* seemed to consider. "I might tell you. For a price."

"What do you want?"

"My freedom, of course. Release me."

"Why are you imprisoned?"

"That's my affair," it said, but Umi shook her head.

"If I were to release you then it would be my concern too. I want to know what I am doing by releasing you, if I choose to agree. There may well be more to *that* than one can guess, as well."

"Clever girl," the creature repeated, almost admiringly. "But there's no time now. Run along to White Willow or you'll be late. And remember what I said about letting her find you out; you'll be no good to me if she suspects. Come back when you are ready to bargain."

Umi was almost late again, because she came across a vision that was very startling. She thought about what she had seen as long as she could, then hurried on with the water.

It seemed that White Willow stared at her long and hard for a bit, but in the end she had dismissed Umi without saying anything. Umi was relieved, but also certain that, if she kept drinking the Seeing Water, she wouldn't be able to fool White Willow for much longer. Frankly, she was surprised she'd done it as long as this.

Soon Umi found herself once more in Kyuko's kitchen, where, as usual, her supper waited. Umi was nearly through with her meal before she finally worked up the courage to ask what was on her mind.

"Kyuko-san?"

The old woman didn't look up from her washing. "Hmm?"

"Did you ever wish your life had been different?"

Kyuko paused. "What possesses you to ask such a thing, child?"

"I just wondered . . . if you ever thought about it."

Now Kyuko did look at her, with an expression lost somewhere between a frown and a smile. "You are a strange child, Umi. What should my life have been, other than it is?"

Umi shook her head. "I think your life is a fine one as it is. Yet aren't there choices, or circumstances, that might make one choose or follow one path over another?"

Kyuko smiled. "A passing scholar once tried to seduce me, in my younger days. He spoke of different paths and life's potential, when what he really wanted was me under the maple grove. You sound a lot like he did, *Umi-chan*. Do you want something of me, too?"

Umi blushed, but did not waver. "I want to know."

Kyuko shrugged. "White Willow bought me from my parents, as she did you. I suppose I might have wound up a farmer's wife, and more likely dead now from overwork and too many children. Or perhaps a merchant's concubine, married off or comfortably and discreetly retired. You may not believe this, child, but I was more than a little fair in those days."

Umi, looking at Kyuko's sweet face, had no trouble at all imagining it and said as much, but Kyuko didn't seem to hear.

After a bit she went on, but Umi wasn't sure she was speaking to her at all. "What should I have been? I was not born to be a great lady, nor a sorceress like White Willow. Those paths were closed, what was left? White Willow treated me well, my duties were—and are—easy to bear. What should I have done . . . ?"

Umi bowed her head. "Pardon my foolish curiosity. My head is full of fancies these days."

Kyuko looked up. It was as if she had only now remembered that Umi was in the room. She leaned over and tousled Umi's black hair. "You are a strange girl, Umi-chan, but sweet. I don't know the answer to your question. I can't remember ever asking it myself. I-I guess at the time things seemed well enough as they were. Now run along and get your bath; it's late."

Umi had more questions, but she didn't think they were for Kyuko to answer. She finished her rice and hurried off to the bath house, where White Willow's menservants would have already prepared the tubs. This time she didn't avert her eyes from the bits of strangeness her new sight promised to reveal to her. She found herself actually eager for them now, and was a little disappointed when none appeared.

Umi drank from the pail the very next morning. "I don't suppose," she said, "that it would do any good for you to swear to tell me the truth?"

The *shikigami* grinned at her. "By what *kami* should I swear, that you would believe me?"

Umi considered. "I do not think there is any power that you respect enough to compel truth. Nor do I know that your nature will even allow for the truth."

"My warnings were true enough." The creature actually looked offended. "Consider, Umi—the *shikigami* are as much a part of the Divine as any venerated hero or goddess. We are family, in a way. What sibling really holds another more worthy than himself, proper forms of deference and respect not withstanding? There is no power by which I will swear, so Instead I suggest this: test me."

"How?"

"Ask me a question other than the one you really want to know. I'll answer, and you can test the truth of my answer. It's not as compelling as an oath, of course, but it will show that I am at least *capable* of speaking truth, and, perhaps, wise enough to know the answer you seek. After that, what you choose to believe from me is up to you. As it would be in any case."

Umi considered. "All right—why was Kyuko brought into White Willow's service?"

The creature sighed. "For the same reason you were, silly child; and therefore I won't tell you that. Ask another, and don't be so clever this time."

Umi blushed again. "Very well: Do you intend any harm to me or to Mistress White Willow?"

The *shikigami* frowned. "Why do you care what happens to White Willow?"

"She has been kind to me. You can well say that it only serves her purpose, but I am not certain of that, nor is that less reason to be grateful. I would not do anything to harm her."

"Such loyalty a dog might show its owner. You're welcome to it, Umi, but this question doesn't serve either of us. You will not know my true intentions until I act on them. Such is the way of things. Ask again, and be quick. Neither of us has much time here."

Umi put her hands on her hips. "Well then, tell me this: yesterday by the path I thought I saw a young woman, just for a moment. She was very beautiful, and wore robes of blue silk. I was distracted for a moment. When I turned back, she was gone. Do you know who she was?"

"She was and is a ghost. She often walks the path."

Umi felt a little chill. "Whose ghost?"

"Kyuko's."

Umi stared at the creature. "This is a lie on the face of it! Kyuko is very much alive."

"Kyuko as you see her now? Certainly. But . . ." the *shikigami* waved a clawed finger at her, "Kyuko as she *was*, now that is a different matter. What you saw was an echo, a memory. Something remained after the Kyuko you know moved on down time's river. Caught in an eddy along the shore, perhaps, or stubbornly clinging to a branch, who can say? Yet there it is. Those with eyes to see, will see."

"So how do I know you speak truly of what you understand?"

The creature smiled. "In the hour after breakfast, when Kyuko washes the bowls and her eyes seem to look at a place beyond here and now, then come to the maple grove path where the stream crosses it. Say nothing. Do nothing, save take careful note of what you see. Then come back here and tell me if my words are weeds or blossoms."

Umi waited for the right time, and had no trouble seeing it.

Kyuko grew distant, as indeed Umi remembered from many times before. She excused herself but doubted Kyuko heard her. She slipped out the back way to the maple grove path. She felt the need to relieve herself now, but she did not; the effect of the Water of Sight was already somewhat diminished and she did not want to lessen it further. At least not yet.

Mists were gathering in the forest, summoned by the waning sun. Umi thought that, perhaps, she could see more than mist in the grayish-white wisps if she tried, but she did not try. She walked very quickly to the place the *shikigami* had spoken of, and there she waited. It did not take long.

Umi watched the ghost approach. She wondered how she would perceive the spirit without the magic water coursing through her now. Perhaps a bit of mist, or the wind blowing leaves along the path; a flash of blue that might have been a bird, but not seen well enough to guess, or even wonder. Perhaps all those things, or none of them. What Umi saw now was a young woman in a blue silk robe, her glistening black hair carefully arranged. There was very little shadowy about her; Umi almost fancied that she could reach out and touch flesh. She remembered the *shikigami*'s instructions and kept her hands still. She waited, and she watched.

The grove seemed very quiet now. Umi heard the sound of her own heartbeat, not even masked by the tickly chatter of the stream flowing beneath the small stone bridge. Now and then she heard something from the water that sounded almost like a word, but she didn't turn her attention away from the vision in front of her.

Umi saw the pail.

She hadn't noticed it before; her attention was on the specter's face, and clothes. It was Kyuko, or was. Umi was certain of that now; it had taken her a while for that particular seed to sprout, but now it grew fast and strong. When Umi saw the eyes, she knew. They were Kyuko's eyes.

Younger, clearer, perhaps not yet so weary, but very familiar. It was only after that certainty had arrived that the pail was clear to her, too.

It's the same as mine . . .

Umi knew she should not have been surprised by that. The *shikigami* has said that Kyuko came into White Willow's service for the same reason Umi had; it wasn't unreasonable that she'd perform the same duties at first.

Until when? Another of her servants dies and everyone moves a step forward, as in a dance?

In her heart Umi did not believe matters were as simple as that, but she put the thought aside to consider later. She needed her attention for what was happening now. She watched *Kyukoghost* glide up the path in complete silence; not even the rustle of her silks carried on the faint breeze; it was as if Umi watched a moving reflection. The vision came to where the stream crossed the path under the small stone bridge. Umi looked directly into the ghostly eyes; there was barely an arm's reach between them, but Umi saw no recognition there. The spirit, like Kyuko herself, seemed to be looking at something beyond. In this case, something off the path, deep in the maple grove.

Someone, rather.

Where Kyuko's image was clear and bright, the man stood in shadow. Umi could not make out his face. His robes could have been those of a mountain monk or a scholar; she couldn't be sure. Umi could easily guess, though, after what Kyuko had told her before.

This isn't a memory at all. This is a regret.

Kyuko stood on the maple grove path. She didn't move, or speak. She only stared out into the woods at something she obviously saw much more clearly than Umi did. Perhaps because it was only the shadow of a shadow, but it was real for this echo of the Kyuko that had been. Still, even after a while Kyuko's younger image began to fade too. Umi almost let it go. She remembered the *shikigami's* warning. Yet Umi found that, at the end, she could not do nothing, or at least the "nothing" that the creature had asked of her.

"Why do you stop now?" Umi asked, aloud.

Silence. Umi walked forward, into the spirit's line of vision. Umi didn't know if it could see her, but she wanted to try. "Why do you stop now?" she repeated.

Umi knew the ghost didn't turn its head a fraction, or look directly at her, but she also knew that, somehow, it answered her.

I always stop. One cannot change the past.

"That is true," Umi said, "but this is not the past. Is he your regret?"

Now Kyuko did look at her. She seemed to peer at Umi as if *she* were the shadow, fading, hiding. The spirit smiled faintly. *There are two sorts of regrets, child: those things one does . . . and those things one does not do. The latter are the worst.*

"Then why hold on to it?"

The spirit smiled sadly. *Because it's all I have of him.*

"Then make something else, something better. Go to him. Change what is."

That is not possible. . . . She stopped.

"This is not the past," Umi repeated. "This is now, and all things are possible."

Umi spoke with a fierce conviction that surprised her. She spoke of things she could not possibly understand, and yet she did not see the mystery in them. She knew what she said was true, and she was certain that the ghostly Kyuko knew that too.

Child, this doesn't concern you.

"You are my friend," Umi said. "It does concern me."

The image was fading fast, but not before Umi saw it hesitate for the barest of moments, then walk slowly across the small stone bridge and take the side trail into the maple grove where the other shadow waited. Umi almost felt as if it were her will alone that forced the spirit in that direction; she wondered if that were possible.

More than that, she wondered if it was right.

Kyuko didn't speak to her that next morning, or to anyone as far as Umi could see; the cook seemed to be in a daze. Umi wanted to speak to her friend, but she couldn't think what she should say. In the end she had gone off to face the *shikigami* one last time.

Umi stood before the basin at the end of the trail, the taste of the Water of Sight still cool and sweet on her tongue. The *shikigami* sat in its cage. "Did I speak the truth?"

"As far as you did speak, yes," Umi said.

Another fierce grin appeared. "Don't start laying traps and puzzles, Umi. I am far better at it than you are. Are you saying that there is truth I have not spoken?"

"I'm saying that you lied without saying a word."

The creature frowned. "When did I not speak?"

"You always spoke. Of many things and nothing. I think that was part of the problem."

"That's no puzzle, girl. That's a contradiction."

Umi shook her head. "Sitting in that cage, appearing to be what you claimed to be. That was the lie." Umi leaned over and took up a handful of the magic water. With the first drink still working within her, Umi took another. The cage disappeared. Umi took another handful, another drink. The *shikigami* disappeared.

White Willow stood in its place in a cleft of the rock, her white hair flowing around her like the glory of an albino sun. She was beautiful and terrible all at once. Umi was afraid, but she did not run.

All choices operate in the "now," as I said to Kyuko. This one is mine.

Umi picked up another mouthful of the water.

White Willow raised her hands. "I can't stop you, Umi, but I would not advise it. Mortals were never meant to see the world with *that* much clarity."

Umi thought about it. She finally let the water drip between her fingers to fall back into the basin. "You knew all along, didn't you?"

White Willow opened her fan and considered. "Of course I did," she finally said. "The real question is: how long did you know there was no *shikigami*?"

"The second time I took a bit more of the water than at first. The edges of the creature were . . . shadowed, almost like a picture in a lantern. I knew he wasn't what he seemed. I also never really believed that my perception could alter so drastically and still escape your notice, however fervently I might wish to believe that."

White Willow looked grim. "You've disobeyed me, Umi."

Umi bowed, but she did not falter. "As you knew I would. He— you—said as much. If you merely wanted to punish me for that you could have done it the first day. I assume there was something you wanted to know about me. I must be impertinent enough to ask if you found your answer."

"Yes, Umi. I have. Or perhaps more importantly, you have."

"I don't understand."

"I dare say." White Willow smiled again. "You have a great deal to learn. But will I teach you? That is yet to be decided."

Umi bowed again. "You own me," Umi said frankly, "and may do as you will. Yet I think there is something besides obedience you require of me."

"And I would take it from you if I could," White Willow replied with equal frankness. "but that is not the way this particular sort of magic works."

"What magic?"

"Yours," White Willow says. "Or rather, your potential. All human beings have potential all their lives. To be something greater than they are, or something worse. To choose one path and not another. To hone one skill and let another go fallow. Yet, before one path is chosen, all paths have almost equal potential, and are just as real. There is power in that potential, Umi. Power that one such as I knows how to tap, and use. Everyone has it to some degree, as I said, but no one has potential without limit. Some, however, come very close."

"Kyuko," Umi said. "I thought she was my friend. Why didn't she warn me?"

White Willow laughed harshly. "Warn you, child? How could she do so, without steering you toward one path instead of another, even though only *you* would bear the responsibility if you chose wrong? Do you think her so cruel, to deny you the same choice that she had?"

As cruel as I might have been to her . . . "No," Umi said. "Kyuko and I are the same?"

White Willow seemed to consider. "In a way. You both have great capacity. As long as it exists, I can use it. In time it fades, since potential is a child of time and as mortal as we, but it never completely leaves so long as breath is in the body. As for us, so for it—there is a place to begin, and a place to end."

"So why say anything to me at all? Why test? Why tempt me to interfere, as I did with Kyuko? If I remained ignorant, couldn't you continue to use me all the days of my life?"

"Clever girl. Yes, I could," White Willow admitted. "And there are many of my sort who've chosen that path. Yet if you think of potential as a well, then thwarted potential is poison to that well. Sooner or later I would choke on it. No, Umi. Kyuko drank from the spring as you did, and she made her choice. You'll do the same because, in this one matter, there *is* no choice. In time you will stay or go, but which path you take will be up to you. Which will it be?"

Umi thought of the ghost of Kyuko's regret. *What you do not do is always the greater regret. Perhaps Kyuko did warn me, in the only way she could.* Umi looked at White Willow. She was still afraid, but there was something greater than her fear working now. A sort of hunger that Umi hadn't known before. "Will you teach me what you know?"

"Yes. You may not always like the methods I choose, nor what must be learned, but I will teach you. Learning those lessons is also up to you."

"Then I will stay," Umi said, "and I will learn. I have already begun, I think."

White Willow smiled. "I can feel the potentials weaving their tapestry even now."

Umi fancied she could as well, but perhaps that was her imagination. No matter; she would soon know. For the moment, however, she took leave of her mistress and sought out Kyuko. She thought she might have an apology to make and, perhaps, gratitude to show. Umi wasn't really sure, but that, too, seemed worth learning.

Nucleon
David D. Levine

David D. Levine (www.spiritone.com/~dlevine/) and his wife Kate Yule live in Seattle and publish the SF fanzine Bento. *His nonfiction writing includes "Why Usenet Is Like a Penis" and "Just Another Day on the Microsoft Barney Help Line." "Truly we are living in the End Times," he says. He attended the Clarion West SF Writing Workshop in 2000, and began to publish stories in 2001. He won a second prize in the Writer of the Future contest in the second quarter of that year, and this story won the 2001 James White Award (a short story competition open to non-professional writers and decided by an international panel of judges, for which the winner gets "a check and a trophy to keep and the winning story is also published in* Interzone, *Europe's leading magazine of speculative fiction"). He says, "Despite the science-fictional premise, the story turned out a gentle fantasy, a variation on the well-known "mystery shop" trope. I have often had my hard science fiction ideas turn into fantasy. . . ."*

"Nucleon" is a fantasy story in the Unknown Worlds tradition. That fine magazine introduced contemporary urban settings into fantasy fiction. The "mystery shop" tradition includes such classic stories as "What You Need" by Henry Kuttner. "Nucleon" is a worthy addition to this tradition.

"Tatyrczinski," he said, extending his hand. "Karel Tatyrczinski." His blue eyes sparkled under bushy white eyebrows, set in a round pink face. Wispy white hair tried, and failed, to cover a shiny pink scalp. That clean pink and white head emerged from the world's grimiest coverall. It was a fascinating contrast; I thought he'd make a great colored-pencil sketch. I liked him immediately.

I took the hand and shook it. "Pleased to meet you, Mr. Tat . . . um . . ."

"Tatter-zin-ski," he repeated. "Call me Carl. What are you looking for, Mr. . . . ?"

"James. Phil James. It's kind of difficult to explain. I'll know it when I see it."

"Well," he said, extending his hands to encompass the piles of objects all around him, "whatever it is, I've got it." I was inclined to believe him.

STUFF FOR SALE read the sign above the gate, matching the one-line listing in the Yellow Pages that had led me to this place. It was way, *way* off the beaten path; I was glad I'd called ahead for directions.

The name was apt. A stolid 1920s Craftsman-style house, with an unfortunate skin condition of yellow 1970s asphalt shingles, sat in the middle of piles and piles of . . . stuff. Heaps of sinks. Stacks of televisions. Three barrels of shoes. File cabinets labeled CHAINS, DOORKNOBS, ALTERNATORS. A haphazard-looking structure of pipes and blue plastic sheeting kept the rain off the more fragile pieces, but a row of toilets standing by the fence wore beards of moss. The piles went on and on . . . he must have had at least a couple of acres. Through a window I saw that the house was just as crowded inside.

"I'm a commercial artist," I explained. "I'm doing a series of illustrations I call 'junklets'—gadgets made of junk. It's for a new ad campaign. The company wants to show how innovative and inventive it is. So what I need is stuff that *looks* interesting, things I can put together with other things in my pictures. It doesn't matter what it is, or whether or not it works." I pulled my digital camera out of my coat pocket. "Actually, all I need is reference photos. But I can pay you for your time."

"No need. I'm always glad to help an artist." He rubbed his chin with a grime-encrusted hand. The work-hardened skin scratched against his beard stubble. "Lessee. I think I had some old dentist equipment . . ." Suddenly he burst into motion and I had to scramble to keep up.

Down an alley of refrigerators, right turn at an old monitor-top Frigidaire, hard left at an ancient glass-fronted Coke machine, and there we were at a barrel of dental drills from the early 1900s. All joints and cables and black crinkle-finish metal struts, it looked like a family reunion of daddy-longlegs. "This is great!" I said. I snapped a dozen pictures of the barrel just as it stood, then asked him to haul out a few choice pieces for closer examination. I wanted dozens of jointed arms for my Shoe-Tying Machine, and these would be perfect. "What else have you got that's like this? Mechanical. Early Twentieth-Century stuff."

"Hmm. Follow me." And he was off again, past racks of doors and windows, with me trailing in his wake. A moment later he was lifting a blue tarp from a huge shelving unit, revealing ranks of radios: streamlined Bakelite Emersons, shiny chrome Bendixes, squat, blocky Motorolas. A harvest of design from the '20s to the '50s.

"These are phenomenal! I love old radios!"

"Most of 'em don't work anymore, I'm afraid . . ."

"I don't care." I picked up a sleek Emerson from the '30s. The original ivory finish had yellowed, but it was in gorgeous shape. "They just don't design things like this anymore. How much do you want for it?"

"Twenty-five. Naah, make it twenty-two fifty."

"I'll take it." I tucked the radio under my arm. "But. These are too . . . unitary. For my junklets I need parts. Moving parts."

"I know just the thing." He zipped through a gap between two piles of tires. Juggling the radio and my camera, I followed as best I could.

The entire afternoon went like that. I filled the camera's memory— over 300 images—and wound up taking home two boxes of stuff as well. Not that I needed any of it, not that I had room for any of it, but it was all just fabulous. How could I leave this keen little eggbeater behind? I'd never seen another one like it. I put most of my finds on my knick-knack shelves as soon as I got home.

After dinner I transferred the pictures into my computer, then started sorting, organizing, and cogitating. The hydraulic cylinder from the old forklift could support the seat of that office chair, and I could pull in the control panel from the red generator as well. By the time I reluctantly shut down at 3 AM I had images for a dozen junklets sorted into folders.

Bright and early the next day—by which I mean noon—I booted up my computer again and put a big newsprint pad on my drawing board. All afternoon I sketched, popping up images on the monitor whenever I needed reference or inspiration. Most of my friends think I'm weird, using paper and pencil to draw images from a computer screen, but it works for me. I've never been comfortable drawing with a mouse or a stylus, but managing reference photos with a computer beats shuffling piles of prints.

Three days later I was back at STUFF FOR SALE again. "Carl, the pictures I got last time were great. I need some more. What have you got that's big and flat and heavy and goes around?"

"What, like an old record player?"

"Yeah, but bigger."

"I think I might have something for you." He took me to a huge rotating platform, must have weighed a ton, made of rusty waffle-patterned iron. Neither of us could figure out what it had originally been used for, but it would be a perfect base for my Plastering Machine. While we were clearing some mannequins out of the way so I could get far enough back for a good photo, the bell on the front gate rang. " 'Scuse me while I tend to a paying customer," Carl said.

"Take your time," I replied. "I can look around on my own." Carl vanished down a row of bookcases.

After I finished up with the platform, I wandered around. I needed a big, tubby body for the Automated Barber, some tubes and pipes for the Plant Waterer, and a whole lot of irons for the Ironing Machine. But everywhere I went, all I found was . . . junk. Boxy, boring washing machines. Cracked water bottles. Hundreds of olive-drab ammo cases. Rusty metal shelving. I took a picture of a row of vending machines because I thought it was a nice composition, but I didn't see anything remotely useful for my project. I was getting pretty frustrated when Carl returned.

"I haven't found anything. Where's the good stuff?"

"It's all good stuff, to the right person. What are you looking for?"

"Well, first off, something with a round, tubby body. Person-sized."

"I know just the thing." He jogged down the row of washing machines, took a left turn. "How's this?" he asked, gesturing to a bulbous chrome 1950s water cooler.

"It's perfect!" I started snapping pictures, but something nagged at me. "Wait a minute. I was just here a minute ago. I stood on this very spot and took a picture of those vending machines over there. See?" I paged back through my stored pictures, showed him the vending machines on the camera's screen. "This water cooler is just what I was looking for. Why didn't I see it before?"

"I dunno. It hasn't moved lately." Indeed, there was grass growing through the holes in its base. How could I have missed it? "Sometimes folks can't find what they're looking for even if it's right in front of them. Sometimes they need a little help. Speaking of which, can I help you find anything else?"

"Uh, yeah. Some irons. Clothes irons."

"Right over here." But as I followed, I couldn't help but look back over my shoulder at the water cooler. I would have sworn there was nothing interesting in this whole area.

I visited STUFF FOR SALE two more times in the next three weeks. Carl never failed to find just the gizmo, gew-gaw, or whatchamacallit I needed to complete my drawings, and I never failed to buy something. I spent over 200 dollars on old radios alone. But it was worth it. I had all the reference images I needed; I had inspiration; I was happy. I turned out more and better work in less time than I ever had since art school.

That was just the beginning. The agency loved my junklets. The client loved my junklets. The industry loved my junklets; I even got my name in *Advertising Age*. The client ordered a second series of junklets, then another. They used my Automated Barber as the background image on their corporate stationery.

With all that publicity, I was inundated with new clients. I soon found myself with more work than I could handle and more money than I'd ever imagined. But I knew I was just the flavor of the month; I'd seen other artists rise meteorically and then vanish just as quickly. So I got myself a financial adviser, kept my frugal lifestyle (well, mostly), and put the extra cash into mutual funds.

Everyone wanted junklets, or something like junklets. I was constantly in need of more mechanical images, more inspirations. I sometimes visited Carl three times in a week. We got to be pals.

One day we were sitting in Carl's kitchen, sharing a beer after a long hot afternoon tramping around the junkyard. "Tell me, Phil," he said, "how did you get into this crazy advertising business anyway?"

I thought about it for a moment. "I suppose you'd have to blame my dad. He was an automotive designer at Ford. When I was a kid I'd visit him at his office during the summer; he'd always let me play with his colored pencils. I guess that's where I caught the art bug."

"Ford, eh? Did your dad design anything I might have seen?"

"He was on the team that did the '66 Fairlane. But mostly he did conceptual designs. It was exciting for him to be out beyond the cutting edge like that, but he was always disappointed that none of his designs made it into actual production." I took a swig of my beer. "He worked on the Nucleon."

Carl put down his beer. "Nucleon?"

"It was a concept car for a World's Fair or something like that. A nuclear-powered car, can you believe it? Atoms for peace."

Carl got a strange look on his face then. "I have something out back that I think you ought to see."

The sun was low in the sky, casting neon-orange glints off the hoods of a row of old cars all the way at the back of the yard, where we'd seldom gone before. Bees buzzed in the shrubs that grew along the fence. Near one end of the row was a bulky shape shrouded in a moss-covered olive-drab tarp. "Help me haul this off, would you?"

We pulled off the tarp and revealed one of the strangest-looking cars you've ever seen. It looked like a cross between an old Caddy with big pointed fins and a pickup truck, and where the trunk, or pickup bed, should have been there was a big square hole that went all the way down to the ground. It looked like a car with a built-in swimming pool.

It was painted in that godawful turquoise color that was so popular in the '50s.

On the tailgate was a name in chrome script: *Nucleon.*

"Sonofabitch! You've got the mockup! I didn't even know they built one!"

"Take a closer look."

I looked. It was no fiberglass mockup. It was real steel, and a little rusty. The doors were scarred with parking lot dings. The tires were bald. The seats and the steering wheel were worn from use. The odometer showed 71,000 and some miles.

There was no gas gauge.

Suddenly I got a queasy feeling in the pit of my stomach. "Carl . . . do you, by any chance, have . . . a Geiger counter?"

"You know, I think I might. Hang on a sec."

I just stood and stared slack-jawed at the thing while Carl left and came back.

"Here it is."

"Check out the back first. The reactor was really heavy; it had its own wheels. It rode in that hole, kind of like a trailer, only surrounded by the car." Carl waved the Geiger counter's wand around inside the hole. There was a slight increase in the chattering noise it made, but only a little. "Any idea how much radiation is too much?"

"Not a clue."

"Still, it doesn't seem too bad."

"No."

"But it's not zero. That means this car once had a nuclear reactor. It was a fucking *nuclear car*!"

"Jesus."

We sat in the grass, leaning our backs against a nearby Camaro, and watched the air shimmer over the Nucleon's sun warmed roof. Crickets chirped. Carl plucked a long stalk of grass and chewed on it thoughtfully.

"Where did you get this thing, anyway?" I asked.

He stared off at the setting sun for a while, then shook his head. "Sorry, I don't remember. I know it wasn't here when I bought the place back in '48."

"How can you forget buying an atomic car? You remember everything else about this place."

"It's a funny thing." He looked down into his cupped hands "Usually it's pretty simple. Like, suppose you wanted a carburetor for a '52 Mercury. I'd know where to look, and I might find one or I might not. But sometimes, like with the Nucleon here"— he gestured at it with the stalk—"I remember exactly where it is, but I don't remember remembering it before, if you catch the distinction." He looked right at me then, his eyes hard. "I'm only telling you this because you're an artist. If I told my buddies at the VFW they'd have me locked up."

"My lips are sealed."

"I knew you'd understand."

The sun was setting behind the Nucleon, and the breeze was cooling. "What are we going to do with this thing?" I asked. "I sure don't have any place to park it."

"Cover it over with the tarp again, I guess. Maybe it'll be here tomorrow, maybe not. There's no telling."

We hauled the tarp back over that impossible car and walked back to the gate in silence. Then I turned to him and said, simply, "Thank you."

"You're welcome," he replied. He closed the gate behind me, and as I drove off I saw him sitting on the porch, staring off into the darkening sky.

* * *

After another year or so the blush was off the apple and I was no longer the hot new thing. Just as well, really; I was tired of junklets, tired of juggling assignments, tired of airports. I settled back into a career that was a lot like it had been before, only now I had a cushion of investments that meant I didn't have to hustle so hard between assignments. I was happy enough, I suppose, though sometimes I missed those crazy junklet days.

I was doing a lot of stuff based on natural forms and landscapes then, getting my reference photos on nature hikes, and I didn't see Carl very often. We always exchanged Christmas cards, though. Then one day I got a phone message from him: would I please come out to the yard, as soon as possible?

"Glad you could make it," he said as I walked up his porch steps the next day. He was sitting on a battered wire milk crate, looking like a broken gray umbrella. His health had been poor for months, though he rarely complained.

"No problem," I said. "How did you get my number?" He'd never called before.

"It was on your checks. Listen, I know this is going to seem strange, but I found this at the bottom of a coffee can full of bolts and somehow I just knew it belongs to you." He held out a small metallic object.

It was a key, a scarred brass thing, one of those ones that's the same on both sides. Smaller than a car key, bigger than a suitcase key. "I don't recognize it."

"You're sure? I don't get these feelings often, and when I do they're usually right."

"I'm pretty sure. Sorry."

"Well, keep it anyway. Memento of an old man's folly. Sorry I dragged you out here for nothing."

"That's OK, I was thinking of coming out for a visit anyway." We spent a pleasant hour on the porch, watching the leaves fall and talking about contact lenses, fast food, and the weather. Then I bought some flowerpots and went home.

Two weeks later I got a call from Laurel Hernandez, Carl's lawyer. Carl had died in his sleep, at the age of 78, and I was mentioned in his will. The funeral was Tuesday; the will would be read the next week.

I met dozens of people at the funeral, all of whom Carl had touched in some significant way. A woman for whom Carl had found a vibrating chair that was the only thing that made her bad back tolerable. A man who had kept a fleet of delivery trucks going with spare parts from Carl's yard. A family that had rebuilt a shoddy old house into a showplace, using materials and fixtures provided by Carl, and helped to revitalize their whole neighborhood. We spent the afternoon swapping Carl stories; it was a sad occasion, but not somber.

The will reading was a lot less crowded. There was me, and Ms. Hernandez, and a clerk, and a couple of cousins. The cousins got the investments, which were not trivial. I got the junkyard.

I told Ms. Hernandez I needed a couple of days to think about my options. But I was only halfway down the stairs from her office when I realized I already knew exactly what to do. I sat down right there on the steps and cried, overwhelmed by the generosity of Carl's final gift.

Ms. Hernandez drove me out to the yard after the transfer of title, a complicated ceremony involving the signing of more papers than I'd ever seen in my life. "Are you sure you don't want me to find a management company to run the business for you?" she asked as we got out of the car.

"I'm sure. I plan to keep on as a contract artist part-time, at least for a while, but this is what I want to do. Where I want to be. However, I'd appreciate the services of an experienced business lawyer."

"I would be happy to help."

The gate was padlocked. I'd never seen it padlocked before.

I stood there for a moment, not knowing what to do, and then I put my hands in my jacket pockets and felt something hard. It was the key Carl had given me the last time I saw him, which was also the last time I'd worn that jacket.

On impulse, I tried it in the padlock.

It worked.

We got inside and wandered around the yard. Ms. Hernandez didn't seem to think it was odd that I had a key to the gate, and I decided not to mention the circumstances under which I'd acquired it.

We paused before a rank of vacuum cleaners, a faded rainbow of aqua and pink and beige plastic. "Mr Tatyrczinski was one of my favorite clients," Ms. Hernandez said. "He gave me a bust of Kennedy for my birthday one year. Kennedy was my hero, but I don't think I ever mentioned that to him. Somehow he always knew just the right thing to do."

"Maybe he didn't know. Maybe the junkyard knew."

"What?"

"Never mind. Wait a minute, I just remembered something." I walked down to the end of the row of appliances, paused a moment, turned left. There, on a battered chrome dinette table, was a jar of buttons. I opened it, dug around for a moment. "Here. I think Carl would have liked you to have this."

It was a campaign pin in red, white, and blue. It was a little faded, but still plainly readable: RE-ELECT JFK IN '64.

"This must have been some kind of joke," Ms. Hernandez said.

"Maybe. Or maybe it's a little memento from a time that never was. A time that was better than this one."

"What a . . . a lovely thought. In any case, if I were your business lawyer I would caution you against giving away merchandise to friends and relatives. It's a common problem for new business owners."

"OK, I'll take three bucks for it. Naah, make it two-fifty."

"It's a deal."

We stood side by side and watched the sun set over the junkyard.

My Stolen Sabre
Uncle River

Uncle River describes himself as a writer of cultural science fiction: "Trained in Jungian Analysis and holding what he believes to be the world's only earned Ph.D. in Psychology of the Unconscious (Union Institute, 1974), Uncle River has lived as a hermit/writer in the mountain Southwest for the past twenty years. In 1972–73, while studying Jungian analysis in Zurich, I sent some writings to friends in Oklahoma that I whimsically signed Uncle River. When I next visited Oklahoma in 1975, I found myself known as Uncle River, the writer." You can find out a great deal more about him in a fascinating interview with him by Don Webb (cyberpsychos.netonecom.net/cpaod6/6river.html), who says Uncle River "has written and directed plays with magical remanifestations both light and dark. He has spoken with men who ballast their boats with gold. He has seen Carl Jung's pants and worked on building a pyramid." And "he writes about the most basic problems of social justice in his own magazine Xizquil and in columns elsewhere, yet the magazine (as well as his own writings) is full of surrealism and speculative fiction." He has published one novel, Thunder Mountain, *much poetry, and some short fiction.*

"My Stolen Sabre," a fantasy story about a sword, appeared in Asimov's, the sort of unusual fantasy one sometimes finds in that SF magazine, and is a tale of ancient and mythic powers. It is told with wit and style.

My sabre . . . well, I thought of it as that for over thirty years . . . was asleep at the time that it was stolen.

My sabre acquired its particular personality as a Power Being, early in its corporeal existence, during the most-violent (so far) trauma of the United States of America as a Nation. At the time, the sabre was the prize possession of Cavalry Lieutenant Jereboam Starr, a dirt farmer, who happened to own the Devil's own stallion, and who had relatives in both the Cherokee National Jail in Tahlequah, Indian Nation Territory, and the English House of Lords. The latter, and the fact that Lieutenant Starr was literate (in both English and Cherokee) was why he received an officer's commission. Well, the horse didn't hurt. It *was* wartime.

Jereboam Starr's fancy British relatives did not know he existed. He could have proved the lineage, but had neither reason nor means to make any point of it to people he didn't know and didn't expect to. Locally, well—the regiment's colonel, who recruited Jereboam, was a relative too . . . and knew about the horse.

The sabre came to initial awareness in the realization that the Nation which had killed Jereboam's maternal grandmother on the Trail of Tears and pretty well broke Grandpa's heart, was *having* a big-time trauma. This wasn't just a *fight*. This was a crack in the Nation's soul! Flat-out weird, from Jereboam's view, when you considered *what* Nation. Now, the sabre, becoming self-aware, did not think of itself as Cherokee, nor Southern, nor American, nor human at all. But being in circumstances to acquire an identity . . . well, you know who you know to know yourself by.

Jereboam and the sabre and the horse cracked skulls, smashed shoulders, and generally kicked ass off and on for four years. They got knocked down a time or three too. Jereboam, the sabre . . . and the stallion . . . survived the war. Eventually, the side they were fighting for lost. Jereboam went back to the farm. The stallion went back to causing runaway wagons and related mayhem all over Tahlequah *every* time Jereboam rode that Devil-spawn to town for *twenty-three* years.

The horse also hated skunks and snakes. That stallion was *fast*. The snakes ended up red-wolf-bait. But the horse was also stupid. He never caught on to the skunks' range. They usually got away before he stopped sneezing. They nearly always got him first even when he *did* get them too. You'd think a horse that had been around that much gunfire would catch on to the concept of range. But, oh no!

Jereboam never would name the horse . . . unless "Damn You!" counts, as in, "Whoa, Damn You!" Probably not. The horse certainly didn't pay any heed. Jereboam never named the sabre either. The sabre woke up anyhow, *in* the aroma of blood, sweat, and powder, but *to* the poignant flavor of cracked souls.

Jereboam never married, and never lived with any of his children, though he acknowledged all he knew about, including a couple of maybes. He out-lived the God-damned horse and settled to a tranquil old age with a tranquil mule that worked hard and willing a good six or seven hours a week, and with a still. He lived long enough to buy an automobile. But he didn't like it. It was kind of fun to drive, and he was smarter than that sneaky arm-breaking crank every sumbitchin' time even if he was a slow old geezer by then. But the fumes ruined the flavor of the whiskey. His customers agreed. "Hell with it," Jereboam said. "When I get too old to tend the mule, the customers can come to me. If they're too old, they can send a grandkid."

It was a warm spring afternoon in 1927 when Jereboam fell asleep on the porch in his ratty easy chair while watching the chickens eat ticks and the hawks eat chickens, and didn't wake up. Jereboam's grandson, Benson Catron, found the sabre, hung it in his tool shed, and gave it to his boy, Ben, Jr., for a tenth birthday present, three years later.

Ben, Jr., didn't remember his Great-Grandpa Starr very well, but he did pull out the sabre and wave it around every now and again, sometimes even from horseback. He also brought it with him when he married Emalee Salt and they moved into a room they weathered in on the side of Emalee's grandma's barn, the last of November, 1941.

It never even occurred to Ben, Jr., not to enlist so soon after marrying on hearing of the Declaration of War, following Pearl Harbor. He was somewhat embarrassed to learn, though, that his and Emalee's two months in the snug, hay-aromatic room on the side of Emalee's grandma's barn had not sufficed to seed a son to come home to. He promised Emalee (in English, letters in Cherokee never getting past wartime censors, who didn't know what the language was) to remedy this failing as soon as he got home . . . from wherever he was, which the letters didn't say, another wartime precaution. The letters stopped coming in late '43. Out of respect (and a lack of suitable prospects), Emalee waited till after the war ended to remarry. By then, no one quite remembered what the sabre was all about. But it obviously deserved some sort of respect. Emalee gave it to the Aximanda Fire-Baptized Holiness Church rummage sale.

Rev. Pice spotted the sabre while encouraging the ladies setting up goods (including many freshly home-baked) for the rummage sale. Among the church ladies that day was Myrna Gouldin, who told the preacher that her boy, Jimmy, was heading up to Chicago for a factory job. A preacher looks out for his flock. Rev. Pice figured that sabre would help Jimmy keep his Spirit up among so many Damnyankees. (Rev. Pice grew up in Georgia. When he accepted the Call at the Aximanda Fire-Baptized Holiness Church, one of his new congregation, Leonard Dalton, asked him, "How old were you when you learned 'Damn Yankee' is two words?" Rev. Pice replied, "*Is* it?" He knew he'd feel right at home.)

Rev. Pice bought the sabre himself for three dollars and a quarter, and presented it to Jimmy Gouldin with a fervent prayer for protection among the Heathen . . . a somewhat mixed metaphor, Jimmy having Cherokee, Dutch, Creek, and English in his ancestry, in about equal measure. But so it goes.

The sabre never made it to Chicago. Jimmy's car broke down in Springfield (Illinois, not Missouri). Jimmy sold the sabre to a tourist in front of Abe Lincoln's house—along with an assortment of suitable instructional narrative incantations. Jimmy didn't really give a damn which side the tourist was on, but did regard proper handling of a Power Being as a duty.

Jimmy went on to Chicago, where he made enough money to bring his family up a year later, and they all lived well-fed and miserable ever after.

The tourist didn't get it. He didn't know that the incantations were *for* anything. He thought Jimmy was just embellishing his sales price with folk tales. Charming, but insignificant. He kind of admired the artistry of Jimmy's pitch though. Parted with a whole seven and a half bucks for the sabre.

The tourist may not have noticed the sabre as a Power Being, but the sabre noticed. . . . Cracked souls. No soul! The sabre found the tourist (who from the sabre's point of view had no name) weird.

The tourist eventually hung the sabre on the wall of a room with a miscellany of other souvenirs, in his house in suburban Philadelphia, where he lived with a wife, 3.7 baby booming rug rats, and a psychotic live-in Negro (to use the term of the times) maid who muttered to herself in fluent Greek and Latin. (Well, if you were fluent in Greek and Latin and could only find a job as a maid, mightn't *you* go nuts too?) The tourist was rich enough to have a house with more rooms than he needed . . . with central heat on in all of them. People used the souvenir room erratically, and more to store stuff in than to do anything in.

The sabre contemplated how its current condition differed from Ben Catron, Sr.'s tool shed. It concluded that old Jereboam had done a more thorough job braining Yankees than he realized.

Later, the sabre changed this opinion.

The tourist acquired miscellaneous stuff for several more years, until sheer quantity of acquisition turned treasures to clutter. Among those items disposed of was the sabre. At least *someone* would pay five bucks for the damn thing at the Saint Robert the Munificent parish rummage sale, which, unlike the Aximanda Fire-Baptized Holiness rummage sale, was not conducted to raise money for the church, but for the local suburban Philadelphia chapter of the Busy Bee Do-Good Philanthropic Society.

The sabre felt like it had come home. Turned out you didn't have to be Cherokee or Southern to have a cracked soul. What possessed Jim and Jeannie Parkins to settle in Cambridge, Massachusetts, was a quirk of the Commonwealth's liquor laws. They were, anyhow, both Yankees. Jim was twenty-nine at the time. Jeannie was fifteen. They carried a copy of their wedding certificate with them, as well as a copy of the Massachusetts statute that permitted an underage wife to be served alcoholic beverages in public establishments in company of her husband. Jim bought the sabre because he *had* five bucks, and figured he could get ten for it.

He was right. That's how much I paid him, in his crafts and whatever shop in the basement of the Pacifist Store, in Harvard Square in 1965. It was my friend, Mark, who I'd met at Herbert Marcuse's home when we were in high school (when Kennedy was president, and before Marcuse moved to California or the New Left was invented for him to be elder philosopher to), who spotted the sabre and recognized it as Civil War vintage. ("War Between the States" was terminology not then current in Harvard Square. When, during the presidential campaign of 1976, I asked people if they noticed that Jimmy Carter used that phrase rather than "Civil War" every Southerner I asked had noticed; not a single Northerner had.) Neither Mark nor I thought, in 1965, that there was any incongruity in finding such an implement as a Civil War cavalry sabre in the Pacifist Store.

Though it assisted me in occasional protective ceremonies over the years (and no, I will *not* tell you what incantations I used), I only actually employed the sabre as a physical weapon once. I was a senior in the most-experimental accredited college in the United States, in the scenic hills of 1969-psychedelic Vermont, settling into November and the customary months of frozen Hell to come. I had a nine A.M. class three days a week and taught a class (on C.G. Jung's work on alchemy) at ten on a fourth day.

This was 1969, an era when American economic genius had produced college dormitories with really thin, flimsy walls just at the time when really loud stereo systems became mass-affordable . . . not to mention the *rest* of what went on in 1969. Academic policy at this college effectively allowed students to do any damn thing they pleased, or nothing at all, for about two years; but you didn't get to *be* a senior unless you credibly studied *something*. The college actually had about an equal reputation for capable, creative graduates and for loony-tune students, but dormitory demographics did not make life easy for a studious senior who kept early hours. Not only that, but the campus coffee shop *jukebox* was directly below me. The coffee shop was open whatever hours someone was willing to tend it.

One night, at three A.M., I had *had it*! They *wouldn't* shut the jukebox off. They wouldn't even keep it down. After my third or fourth increasingly raving descent to ask for some *QUIET*, I charged down and pulled the plug. The coffee shop patrons plugged the jukebox back in. Several grinned. I suppose I *was* a pretty good show.

I didn't see it that way. After another few minutes in bed, an attempt more due to confusion as to what else to do than any hope of sleep, I got up yet once more, long hair a-fly. Wild-eyed, not to mention a bit blurry-eyed without my customary glasses, wearing just a knee-length blue-checked robe belted on (I slept naked), I grabbed the sabre, and stormed down the flight of stairs to the basement where the coffee shop was, yet once more.

. . . And realized that if I drew the sabre, nearly four feet long including its hilt, in that relatively small space with twenty or so 1969-experimental college-three-A.M. spaced people all around, someone was liable to get hurt.

So I hefted the sabre, sheath and all, and smashed the jukebox's thick glass top with the hilt. This did not stop the music. But after that, someone did shut it off.

A day or so later, I ran into the man who was in charge of supplies and equipment for the campus kitchen and coffee shop. He asked me why I'd smashed the jukebox. I told him.

Twenty-seven years later, I finally got up my nerve to ask my father if the college had sent him a bill for the jukebox. When I brought up the incident, he knew instantly what I was talking about. The college had not sent him a bill.

Less than another year later, on returning home from my father's eightieth birthday bash to my hermitage in a remote canyon on the old Outlaw Trail on the Arizona-New Mexico line. I found the sabre gone.

The sabre woke up. It did this every so often. It recognized a discontinuity. Not only was I not around (as sometimes happened for months at a time in the thirty-two years I had had the sabre), but someone else *was*. Was this like when old Jereboam croaked with his chickens? Or when Ben C., Jr., went off to the war and didn't come back? Or when Jimmy G.'s car broke down in that sleepy little Yankee political hotbed?

Well, no. I wasn't dead, and I didn't sell the sabre or give it to any church's rummage sale. Though it could have understood the concept: to steal, theft as means of transfer was only incidentally significant to its current position. *I* might wonder if it had somehow failed to protect me that it *could be* stolen. But *it* didn't see things that way. My opinion on the subject regardless, it was not *my* Power Being. It was a Power Being that lived with me for a period, whose essential quality intermingled with a certain part of my life.

Now. . . . Cracked souls (not to mention skulls). No soul. The sabre had experienced these in the span of its corporeal existence, as well as a measure of tranquillity, or at least placidity. (It wasn't around the Aximanda Fire-Baptized Holiness Church long enough to encounter some doings that might have added to its repertoire, but that's another story.)

Cracked soul. No soul. Cherokee. Southerner. Yankee. What now? . . . Perhaps, lost soul? What *would* you call the proprietor of the Antiques and Collectibles Mall Emporium of suburban Phoenix?

The sabre looked around. Junk. Kitsch. Household miscellany that would have been familiar to old Jereboam. . . . And several other Power Beings: A two-hundred-year-old squash-blossom silver and turquoise necklace. A similarly venerable samovar (also silver) that a rabbi's widow had carried from Odessa (Russia, not Texas) about the time Jereboam finally burned the three-days-gone and already maggoty carcass of that damned horse of his. A pair of gold-rimmed goblets whose original owner was a seventeenth-century French alchemist, who employed the goblets to share wine with his partner in the philosophical quest, before they retired to their laboratory-bedchamber. From the sabre's point of view, the presence of others of its own kind was far more noteworthy than my absence, or what other human might have replaced me.

It was the goblets that helped the sabre readjust.

The goblets had been seized by the Crown at the time of the alchemist's conviction (in absentia) for heresy and sodomy, and his abrupt departure for the colonies, where he eventually learned distillation techniques for seven different perfectly hideous deadly poisons at that time unknown in France, but died himself of gangrene due to tissue necrosis following an apparently minor scorpion sting, before achieving vengeance.

Being delicate, a significant portion of the goblets' identity as Power Beings derived from their having survived the vicissitudes of corporeal existence so long at all, including being stolen twice, and surviving through the chaotic time of the French Revolution.

When you get several Power Beings newly together in one place, they are liable to get talking to each other. After all, most of us will introduce ourselves to new acquaintances. All the more, being as old Jereboam Starr's sabre, the alchemist's goblets, the rabbi's widow's samovar, and the squash blossom necklace didn't none of them feel comfortable with the situation a'*tall*. Here they were ready and primed to dispense thunderbolts and philosophical elixirs, and no one around them knew how to tell a Power Being from a mouse turd. Well, they'd all been around the soul-dead before. But this present situation was even more irritating because there was *another* Power Being on the premises, utterly unrecognized as such though called on continually . . . which Power Being itself had about as much coherent consciousness as, say, your average two-year-old Devil-stallion.

"Cheezus Q. Rastaman!" exclaimed Antiques and Collectibles Mall Emporium proprietor Corman Wiegland, grey sideburns slick, his silk Western-style shirt sweat-stained at the armpits and stretched tight over his beer gut, "this [inarticulate growl] computer! Sumbitch done crashed the whole frumbuggerin inventory *again*!"

"Hey, you twit!," snarled the sabre.

"Wazzat?!" Corman jumped around in his osteopathically designed computer chair. How did a customer get in the store without the door bleeper bleeping? But no customer was there! Corman turned back around, shivering with what he thought was mere rage, though several present could have told him, had he been mentally disposed to take note, that it was the resonance of proximity to wakeful Power Beings. "You got me *hearing* things, Damn You!" he shouted, shaking his fist at the computer.

Jereboam's stallion, equally unimpressed by such imprecations, at least had behaved in such a manner as to keep Jereboam in shape. The computer merely beeped and flashed the repeated message: ERROR. FILE OR DIRECTORY NOT FOUND.

"Wake *up*, you twit!" the sabre hissed.

"Who, *me?*" the computer answered.

Antiques and Collectibles Mall Emporium proprietor Corman Wiegland leaped back, spun around. He was *losing* it! Well, he knew how to fix *that*. Mr. Daniels and Mr. Busch had just the cure. Corman rummaged purposefully. As it happened, the medicine he found first was a bottle of mescal. He downed what was in it on the spot, about a pint, worm and all. Saw God and the Devil in six shades of day-glo technicolor.

While our intrepid Mall Emporium proprietor was occupied with what he might have thought of as maintenance of his mental stability, if he had thought to think at all, the goblets gave the sabre a bit of elder-comradely advice: "Go easy. We didn't survive the French Revolution (not to mention the heresy trial) pushing lost souls over the edge."

"But that nitwit needs to wake up!" The sabre nodded (or *would* have, if it had been equipped with relevant anatomy; the goblets understood the implicit gesture) at the computer.

"No such luck, sweetheart," the goblets purred (they found the sabre's militant demeanor delicious, if dangerous). "What the nit's got to do is *grow* up."

The samovar and the necklace got a chuckle out of that. Both had been around enough to recognize the goblets' reference to nits as baby lice.

The sabre understood the goblets' somewhat archaic word play too, but the sabre did not so readily recognize what the goblets referred to in modern context. The sabre had been so isolated for so long.

You see, though I did have a computer, I didn't have a phone in my canyon hermitage on the old Outlaw Trail. No phone. No modem. No Net. No e-mail. You get the picture. (No lice either, thank God, only squirrels, skunks, flies and an occasional bear for company.)

The sabre, stimulated in its new, big city environment, excited, after a century and a half, to encounter even one, let alone so many, other Beings of its own kind, had not yet noticed the way in which the Mall Emporium proprietor's computer being hooked in with a lot of *others* played so significant a part in the computer *being* a Power Being at all.

Now the sabre looked, past the mercifully somnolent, reeking body of Corman Wiegland, to the obliviously flashing computer screen.

The sabre actually relished the prospect of pushing such souls as

Corman Wiegland over any edge handy. The more the merrier. But it did have an interest in the continued well-being of its new-found companions of its own kind.

What to make of the goblets' dual personality, with nuances ambiguous and unfamiliar to the sabre? Seriously risky or delectably risqué? The goblets seemed to mean both. What the hell?

"*Wake up*, you nitwit!" the sabre hollered.

"Huh?" the computer replied—not stupid, mind you, but distracted.

"It already has," the goblets smiled (as it were). "A little patience, darling." (The goblets knew a good deal more of personalities like the sabre than vice versa.) "The nit *will* grow up, and *then* these bald-assed monkeys are going to have one whale of a case of brain lice!"

"Huh!" said the sabre, comprehension crystallizing to the analogue of a smile in the general direction of the all-but-comatose Corman Wiegland. A smile to thrill the goblets as much as to terrify. "Maybe old Jereboam was doing those Yankees a favor."

Cavalry Lieutenant Jereboam Starr had known a trick or two that often worked on distracted troops (if rarely with his horse). The sabre turned to the computer once more and roared: "Look alive!"

Apologue

James Morrow

James Morrow (www.sff.net/people/Jim.Morrow) lives in State College, Pennsylvania, according to his website "with his wife, Kathryn, his twelve-year-old son, Christopher, and two enigmatic dogs: Pooka, a Border collie, and Amtrak, a stray Doberman that Jim and Kathy rescued from a train station in Orlando, Florida. He devotes his leisure hours to his family, his Lionel toy electric trains, and his video collection of vulgar Biblical spectacles." Morrow's novels include This Is the Way the World Ends *(1986),* Only Begotten Daughter *(1990, winner of the World Fantasy Award), and* Towing Jehovah *(1994, the first of a trilogy about the death of God). Much of his short fiction is collected in* Bible Stories for Adults *(1996), including the Nebula Award-winning fable, "The Deluge." His next book is an historical novel,* The Witchfinder General, *due out in 2002.*

This story somehow reminds one of the best fantasy fiction of Ray Bradbury. The year 2001 was one of great excitement, great tragedy in the real world, and great change. The world is in an economic recession, now officially dating from March 2001, which we hope will be in recovery by the time you read this in mid-2002, and there is a war going on. James Morrow reminds us that our contemporary fantasies, even our monsters, while they cannot solve our problems, can uplift us spiritually and give us solace in such times.

The instant they heard the news, the three of them knew they had to do something, and so, joints complaining, ligaments protesting, they limped out of the retirement home, went down to the river, swam across, and climbed onto the wounded island.

They'd always looked out for each other in times gone by, and this day was no different. The ape placed a gentle paw on the rhedosaur's neck, keeping the half-blind prehistoric beast from stepping on cars and bumping into skyscrapers. The mutant lizard helped the incontinent ape remove his disposable undergarments and replace them with a dry pair. The rhedosaur reminded the mutant lizard to take her Prozac.

Before them lay the maimed and smoking city. It was a nightmare, a war zone, a surrealistic obscenity. It was Hiroshima and Nagasaki.

"Maybe they won't understand," said the rhedosaur. "They'll look at me, and all they'll see is the berserk reptile munching on the Coney Island roller coaster." He fixed his clouded gaze on the ape. "And you'll always be the one who shimmied up the Empire State Building and swatted at the biplanes."

"And then, of course, there was the time I rampaged through the Fulton Fish Market and laid my eggs in Madison Square Garden," said the mutant lizard.

"People are smarter than that," said the ape. "They know the difference between fantasy and reality."

"Some people do, yes," said the rhedosaur. "Some do."

The Italian mayor approached them at full stride, exhausted but resolute, his body swathed in an epidermis of ash. At his side walked a dazed Latino firefighter and a bewildered police officer of African descent.

"We've been expecting you," said the mayor, giving the mutant lizard an affectionate pat on the shin.

"You have every right to feel ambivalent toward us," said the rhedosaur.

"The past is not important," said the mayor.

"You came in good faith," said the police officer, attempting without success to smile.

"Actions speak louder than special effects," said the firefighter, staring upward at the gargantuan visitors.

Tears of remorse rolled from the ape's immense brown eyes. The stench filling his nostrils was irreducible, but he knew that it included many varieties of plastic and also human flesh. "Still, we can't help feeling ashamed."

"Today there is neither furred nor smooth in New York," said the mayor. "There is neither scaled nor pored, black nor white, Asian nor Occidental, Jew nor Muslim. Today there are only victims and helpers."

"Amen," said the police officer.

"I think it's clear what needs doing," said the firefighter.

"Perfectly clear." The mutant lizard sucked a mass of rubble into her lantern-jawed mouth.

"Clear as glass." Despite his failing vision, the rhedosaur could see that the East River Savings Bank was in trouble. He set his back against the structure, shoring it up with his mighty spine.

The ape said nothing but instead rested his paw in the middle of Cortlandt Street, allowing a crowd of the bereaved to climb onto his palm. Their shoes and boots tickled his skin. He curled his fingers into a protective matrix then shuffled south, soon entering Battery Park. He sat on the grass, stared toward Liberty Island, raised his arm, and, drawing the humans to his chest, held them against the warmth of his massive heart.

Story Copyrights